THE WOMAN FROM
Dover

Betty Annand

Amberjack Publishing
New York, New York

Amberjack Publishing
228 Park Avenue S #89611
New York, NY 10003-1502
http://amberjackpublishing.com

Publisher's Cataloging-in-Publication data
Names: Annand, Betty, author.
Title: The Woman from Dover / by Betty Annand.
Description: New York, NY; Eagle, ID: Amberjack Publishing, 2017.
Identifiers: ISBN 978-1-944995-40-9 (pbk.) | 978-1-944995-41-6 (ebook) | LCCN 2017948561
Subjects: LCSH Marriage--Fiction. | Adultery--Fiction. | Homosexuality--Fiction. | Motherhood--Fiction. | Great Britain--History--Fiction. | Women--England--Fiction. | Historical fiction. | Love stories. | BISAC FICTION / Historical.
Classification: LCC PS3601.N5551 W66 2017 | DDC 813.6--dc23

Cover Design: Red Couch Creative, Inc.

Printed in the United States of America

Dedicated to my oldest friends, Irene and John Glowasky
and Lyle Fraser

Oh, look not at the face,

Young maid, look at the heart

—*The Hunchback of Notre Dame*

Victor Hugo

Part One

Chapter One

February 8, 1852

Gladys and Dolly were waiting at the gate when the carriage arrived. The driver, a tall thin man dressed in black, wore a very high top hat; Gladys thought it gave him the appearance of a giant exclamation mark. He looked down at them, doffed his hat, and jumped down to greet them warmly before assisting them into the carriage, which wasn't much larger than Gladys's own little shay even though it was drawn by two horses.

Gladys knew she could have saved some much needed money if she had taken her own horse and buggy, but she was afraid that the return trip from Dover to Sandwich would prove too much for her little gelding.

The morning air was quite damp and cold, so she was glad she had brought along a quilt to throw over their legs. She had also brought a pillow in case Dolly fell asleep.

For the first hour, Dolly kept her busy answering questions.

"Do you think the man shall give us a place to live, Mama?

When do you think we shall arrive? Do you suppose the man has children, like Lord and Lady Sorenson?"

"If the man hires me, yes, we shall have a place to live. I do not have any idea when we shall arrive, but I fear it is going to be a long day, my dear. Lady Sorenson did not say if Mr Hornsby has children or not, but if he has, I trust they will have a nanny to look after them," Gladys answered.

"I don't fancy having to tend to children along with my other duties, which would be plenty, according to what I have heard. I doubt anyone has children as unique as the Sorenson's three." They both smiled at the thought.

"When we arrive at Mr Hornsby's home, Dolly, you shall have to wait in the buggy for me. I do not think I shall be long. I've put one of your books in the bag and an apple for you. Do you think you can manage, my love?"

"Of course, Mother. I am seven years old. I am not a child anymore. You may rely on me from now on."

"Oh, Dolly, I've lost everyone else I ever loved, and I don't think I could bear living if I didn't have you."

They hugged each other for a long time, then, after a while, Dolly fell asleep. Gladys laid her down with her head on the pillow. Then she rested her own head back against the seat and closed her eyes.

The past two weeks had been so distressful that Gladys felt she was living in a nightmare. The jogging of the carriage seemed to relax her a little, and she did her best to enjoy the trip, but memories of recent events kept creeping into her thoughts.

The last happy thing she could recall was sitting on the divan wrapping a favourite ornament that she and Tom had received as a wedding gift to take to Oaken Arms, the estate her father-in-law had had built for the three of them to live in. The ornament was two beautiful china doves sitting on a branch, and she was trying to imagine what it would look like on the mantle in the sitting room of her suite in the lovely new mansion. Then she heard someone knock at her door.

She wished she could block the next scene from her memory, but she remembered opening the door and seeing Peter Pickwick standing there. She could still picture his sickly white, puffy cheeks as he took her hand in his and turned it over. When he saw the scar on her palm, he stared at her with an evil and smug look and said, "Aha! Gladys Tunner, I believe."

As soon as she heard her old name, she knew that her past had been discovered at last, but she had no idea how devastating that information would be for her and her daughter's future.

The carriage stopped, interrupting her thoughts, and the driver opened the door. "We're 'ere at Forbes junction, Mrs Pickwick, mum. Would yer likes ter use the facilities? They makes a good cuppa tea 'ere too, mum."

Dolly woke when she heard the driver and sleepily asked, "Are we there, Mama?"

"No, dear, but we can get out for a stretch and have a cup of tea and maybe a biscuit, if you like."

They only stopped long enough to partake of some refreshments and to use the outdoor facilities before returning to the carriage. Dolly went back to sleep a few minutes after resuming their journey.

Gladys's thoughts returned to that fateful day once more. She hadn't heard the name Tunner since she had left the slum neighbourhood of London known as Old Nichol some eleven years ago, and now it sounded foreign to her.

She had taken the name Tweedhope the day she ran away because it was the name of a dear lady in Old Nichol who had taught her how to read and write. Now, as the carriage rocked back and forth, she recalled how lost and frightened she had been back then, travelling incognito in a coach, to an unknown place called Dover with three strangers. There was something about the ride this day that was causing her to have the same feeling of trepidation.

She was not certain how much Peter's detective had found out about her past, but she could not afford to challenge him when he ordered her to take Dolly and leave town for good. She might have had a chance if her father-in-law had been alive, but Peter had been only too happy to deliver the painful news that Andrew had been murdered during his trip to Ireland.

She was sure that Peter had enough damning information to blackmail her, and there was nothing she could do about it. Now, instead of becoming the mistress of one of the most prestigious mansions in Dover, Gladys and Dolly were homeless.

She vowed she would do anything, no matter how degrading, to prevent being sent to the poorhouse, where it was said that they separated mothers from their children. Fortunately, Lady Sorenson, an old friend of her late father-in-law, had told her of a widower named James Hornsby who was looking for a housekeeper for his estate near the town of Sandwich.

Although she knew she should be thankful, Gladys wasn't looking forward to working as a mere servant again, but it seemed she had no choice. For a while she thought there may be an alternate solution.

Only two days ago, she had decided she would pay Hugh Mason, the minister's son, a visit and ask him if he still desired her hand in marriage.

Hugh had been smitten with Gladys ever since he returned to Dover. Having been away at Divinity College, Hugh was newly ordained and planned on spending a year working with his father at St Mary's Church in Dover before he sailed to North America to begin his life as a missionary. He also had hopes of finding a wife who would agree to accompany him.

Hugh was a handsome man, and Gladys hadn't enjoyed the company of a young man since her husband was killed in India six years earlier. She was flattered by his attentions, and for six months she had enjoyed his company and the socials they attended, but when he surprised her with a proposal on Christmas night, she had to tell him that although she was fond of him, she did not love him, therefore could not accept his offer of marriage. Hugh hadn't taken the refusal well, and he accused her of dallying with his affections. He had not spoken to her since.

Gladys was a member of St Mary's Church and enjoyed singing in the church choir and playing the organ, but she received such a cold reception the Sunday after she rejected Hugh's proposal that she hadn't returned. Now, she reasoned that being married to Hugh, even though she didn't love him, might be better than returning to the life of servitude. She knew Hugh would be a faithful husband and a good father. It would be a chance for her to leave England and her past behind—a past that had haunted her ever since she was forced to kill a lecherous landlord, steal his purse, and run away from Old Nichol, leaving behind the boy she had loved since she was four.

The next morning, she and Dolly were dressed in their best and about to leave to visit Hugh when his father, the Reverend Mason, and the superintendent of the cemetery, Mr Grimsby, arrived with their wives. They had come to express their sympathies over the death of Gladys's father-in-law, Andrew Pickwick, and to tell her of their concerns over his funeral arrangements. The undertaker had informed them that Andrew's service was not to be in St Mary's, nor were his remains to be interred in St Mary's cemetery.

"I cannot believe you would allow such a thing, Gladys," Reverend Mason exclaimed in an accusing tone of voice. "I know we were upset with you for not accepting Hugh's proposal, but that is no reason to deny Andrew his final resting place beside his wife and son."

"I have no say where my father-in-law will be buried. If I did, you may be assured that I would not have him buried anywhere else."

"But surely, you can have your say in the matter. We know how much Andrew thought of you and his granddaughter."

"According to the last will Andrew signed, his adopted son, Peter, inherits all of his property. I am sorry, Reverend, but you will have to approach him about it."

Mrs Grimsby took hold of Gladys's hand and in a soft voice said, "But, Gladys dear, don't you think it would be better if you were to ask him?"

Gladys didn't know what to tell them, but then she had an idea. Years ago, Peter, his sister, and his mother had left the church in anger when Reverend Mason refused to ask Gladys to leave, so she said, "Peter has made it perfectly clear that he, his mother, and his sister want nothing to do with us, so anything I say will only make things worse. Perhaps if you were to promise them that I will not be coming back to church and will not attend the funeral, they might return to St Mary's and allow Andrew to be buried there."

"But that is not right," Mrs Mason protested.

"Perhaps not, but if it means my father-in-law will be buried be-

6

side his family, I shall agree to stay away. Sometime later, Dolly and I shall come back to Dover and have a little service of our own beside his grave."

"What does that mean, come back?" Mr Grimsby asked.

"Dolly and I shall be leaving Dover in a few days."

"If it is because of the way we have treated you, I can assure you that the entire congregation would be happy if you returned. We miss that lovely voice, and our organist would appreciate having you back as well."

Gladys couldn't tell him she was being blackmailed and had to leave, so she just said, "Thank you, Reverend Mason, but I think it is time we moved. There are too many sad memories here."

Mrs Grimsby took Gladys's hand and said with sincerity, "Oh, my dear, how I will miss you."

"And I shall not forget your kindness, Mrs Grimsby. I don't know how I could have managed when Tom was in India if it wasn't for your help." After they hugged each other, Mrs Grimsby went over to Dolly, who hadn't said a word during the visit, and she held the child tightly in her arms for a long time.

Gladys waited patiently until they were ready to leave before she asked Mrs Mason if Hugh was planning to leave soon.

"Oh, yes! As a matter of fact, they plan to leave right after the wedding."

"Wedding?"

"Oh my, hadn't you heard? Hugh and Pricilla Mulberry are being married on the twentieth of this month."

"Would you give them my congratulations? Pricilla will make him a wonderful wife," Gladys managed to say in spite of her disappointment. Now she had no choice but to apply for the position of housekeeper. At least it was a far more attractive job than that of an ordinary housemaid.

Lady Sorenson's letter of recommendation had arrived two days later, along with James Hornsby's address. Her Ladyship had also sent a note saying she had sent the widower a message stating that Gladys would arrive before noon of the following Wednesday for an interview.

Chapter Two

It was past one when they arrived at Mr Hornsby's gate, and Gladys was afraid she had arrived too late to be interviewed and that someone else might have already been hired.

The gateman, a pleasant looking fellow, gave them a welcome smile as he told the driver to stay to the right and pull up to the side entrance when he came to the manor. Gladys was still feeling depressed after spending most of the ride thinking about the events of the last few weeks. Knowing that she would be conducting interviews herself if her father-in-law were still alive, instead of being interviewed, didn't do anything to brighten her mood.

However, by a strange coincidence, the sign on top of the iron archway over the gate read "Four Oaks," and Gladys felt a little less glum. The name reminded her of better times because her father-in law, Andrew, had chosen the name Oaken Arms for the estate he had built for them. There were four big oak trees at the entrance to Oaken Arms, so when Gladys and Dolly saw the two on each side of Hornsby's gate, they were both pleasantly surprised, thinking it a good omen.

When they came in sight of the mansion, they were even more impressed. It was much larger than Oaken Arms and far grander than Gladys had expected. When their driver pulled up to the side entrance, Gladys told Dolly to stay in the coach and she ordered the coachman to wait for her. Trying to appear calm, she went to the door, but her hand shook as she took hold of the huge ornate lion-head knocker and brought it down on the metal, making a noise so loud it made her jump. The door immediately opened which startled her even more.

James Hornsby had interviewed two housekeepers earlier in the morning, but hadn't hired either of them. Lady Sorenson had given him such a glowing recommendation for Mrs Pickwick that he thought he had better wait and see her before making up his mind. When she failed to arrive on time, he had decided she wasn't coming and had his lunch. He was about to leave the house to take a stroll and had his hand on the doorknob when Gladys used the knocker. Not waiting for his butler, James opened it himself.

The look of surprise on her face caused him to offer an apology before inquiring if she had come to see about the housekeeper's position. When she admitted that she had, and apologized for being tardy, he invited her into the parlour.

Having taken note of the rich appearance of the exterior of the house, Gladys found the parlour disappointing. Although it was a bright sunny day, both of the large windows were obscured by heavy drapery. The room was not only dark but had a dusty odour. Nevertheless, she noted that the furnishings were of good quality and plentiful.

James sat her in one of four comfortable wingback chairs then pulled on a nearby bell cord before taking a seat.

He sat without speaking for a while, and she wondered if he was waiting for her to say something but decided it wasn't her place to begin the conversation.

The silence was becoming awkward when, to her relief, a pleasant and plump middle-aged lady entered carrying a tray with a pot of tea and a plate of biscuits. When he noticed the amazed look on Gladys's face, James explained, "I've had several ladies here today—for interviews, that is—and Freda is beginning to prepare tea as soon as she hears the knocker."

"How very thoughtful of you," Gladys said to the woman, who she surmised was Freda.

Freda beamed and answered, "Oh 'tis no trouble at all. Have a biscuit now. The jam is made of strawberries." With a nod to Mr Hornsby, she left the room.

Gladys prayed it was a nod of approval.

After they sugared and creamed their teas, James Hornsby began, "Now, if you do not mind, I should like to ask you a few questions."

Gladys nodded her assent and sipped her tea as James inquired about her previous employment. She told him that she was forced to apply for work due to the misfortune of becoming a widow. She told him that she had had servants of her own, and, therefore, was confident she had the skills to manage his household efficiently.

The interview seemed to be going well, and Gladys learned that James's wife had been sick for many years and had succumbed to her illness several years previously. They had one son, Horace, who was twenty and had recently moved to South Africa. She also learned that James was involved in shipbuilding.

He seemed to be a mild-mannered man, and Gladys found him easy to talk to. Taking in his appearance as they were talking, she thought he looked to be middle-aged. He had a lean build, his light brown hair had begun to recede, and he had fine features. Although he was almost six-feet-tall, he appeared shorter due to a slight stoop he had acquired—not by deformity but by habit.

James also found he enjoyed talking to Gladys. In fact, he was enjoying their conversation so much that, without intending to, he told her more about himself in ten minutes than he had divulged to anyone since the death of his wife. He also noted that she was clad in clean and tidy clothing and emitted a pleasant odour. Being fastidious himself, these things were important to him, and he was favourably impressed. However, their conversation was suddenly interrupted by a knock at the door.

This time the butler answered and, shortly after, ushered Dolly into the room. "This young lady has asked to see her mother," he announced.

Before Gladys could speak out, James said, "But I have no idea who, or where, your mother is."

Dolly pointed to Gladys and replied, "That is my mother, sir, and my name is Dolly."

James's attitude toward Gladys suddenly changed. He was not fond of children.

Gladys sensed his displeasure, and all her hopes for the position died.

Dolly apologized, "I am sorry, Mama, but the coachman sent me in. He wants to know if he should wait any longer."

"You may tell him I will not be long now, Dolly."

Then before Dolly could leave, James said, "I think we are done, Mrs Pickwick. You may leave now. I am sorry, but you see, I would prefer someone without children. I did enjoy our visit though and feel assured you will find another position, especially with such a glowing report from Lady Sorenson."

As he was talking, Dolly's eyes, like most children's in a strange room, darted this way and that before they came to rest on a painting of a group of young soldiers. Without thinking, she blurted out, "That looks just like the picture we have of my father!" Then she turned and addressed James, "Father was a very brave soldier, and he was killed in a war."

Without looking at the picture, Gladys scolded, "That's enough, Dolly. I am sorry, sir, she didn't mean to be rude."

"Oh, it is quite all right," James answered then bent down to Dolly. "One of those soldiers was my young brother, and he was killed in a war too." James turned to Gladys. "What outfit was your husband with, Mrs Pickwick?"

"He served with the HM 62nd Foot and was just about to receive a commission when he was killed. If he had been commissioned earlier, we would have gone to India with him."

"Forgive me for asking, but on what date was he killed?"

"He was killed on the twenty-first of December, seven years ago," Gladys said, then, suddenly feeling tired, took hold of Dolly's hand and started to leave. "I am sorry, Mr Hornsby; I know that I would have enjoyed working here. Come along, Dolly."

James never replied or saw them to the door. He remained where he was standing as though in a trance. They were just getting into the coach when he came running out.

"Mrs Pickwick, wait!" he called as he hurried down the walkway and took hold of her arm.

"I was so stunned by your news that I was speechless. It seems that my brother, who was very dear to me, was killed alongside your husband. Please, Mrs Pickwick, you and your daughter must come back into the house."

"But the coach, I cannot afford to have him wait any longer."

"Do not worry about it. You and your daughter may return to the parlour and leave it to me. I shall send you home in my own coach presently."

Gladys's face lit up, "You mean that—"

James interrupted, "Yes, yes, Mrs Pickwick, you shall have the job; now please do go in. We have quite a few things to discuss." Gladys practically ran into the house, pulling Dolly along with her.

When James returned, he explained, "In view of the information you have given me, Mrs Pickwick, er, ah, it is Gladys, if my memory serves me correctly, is it not?"

"Why yes, but how did you know that?"

"I believe you knew my brother, or I should say my half-brother, Keith Corkish. He and your husband were the best of friends."

"Oh, my heavens, you are the brother Keith used to talk about, but he never mentioned that you were half-brothers and had different last names. He was very fond you, I do know that."

She recalled Keith saying his brother was a bit of fuddy duddy, but a jolly good sport as well. She, Tom, and Keith had spent a lot of time together when she worked at Watt's Inn. For a time, both men had courted her, and although Tom had won her heart, Keith had remained a steadfast friend.

As she thought back to Keith's courtship, she remembered him saying he would like to take her to meet his brother in Sandwich, but she had no idea that brother was James Hornsby. If Tom hadn't proposed the following week, she might have been here this day visiting James as a sister-in-law, instead of applying for a position.

Suddenly Gladys realized that she hadn't heard what James was saying. "I am sorry, sir, I didn't hear you."

"I said that I was very fond of him too. Now, Mrs Pickwick, you may be assured that the job is yours. Keith would haunt me if I were to turn you away. However, there is just one stipulation I must insist upon. It has to do with your daughter."

"Then perhaps you should address her."

"As you wish," James answered. However, when he looked into Dolly's eyes, he could tell she was not as imperceptive as most children, and what he had to say came out more as a friendly request than an order, "Ahem, Dolly, is it?"

"Yes, Your Lordship?"

"Firstly, I am not a lord, so you may refer to me as 'Sir' or 'Mr Hornsby'. Now that you will be residing in my home, there is one rule that I would like you to remember. You see, I am accustomed to my privacy and, in the past, I have found children to be rather noisy and invasive creatures. Running in the hallway and up and down the stairs is not acceptable, along with squealing and shouting. When I have a few leisure hours, I prefer to spend them in quietude—er, ah, that means undisturbed. Do you understand what I am saying?"

"Oh, yes, sir! I like to have my quiet, ah, quiet, ah—"

"Quietude," James coached.

"Yes, sir, I like my quietude too!"

James couldn't suppress a chuckle. Then he turned to Gladys. "Well, now that we have that settled, let me show you your apartment and the rest of the house. I trust your accommodations will be satisfactory. Since my wife passed away, I have been on my own, so I thought it rather absurd to keep up so many unused rooms; therefore, we do not use the west wing except for the basement and the back rooms. I am sure you shall find it less work that way. I know my last housekeeper did." He said the last sentence with a shrug, and Gladys could not decide if it was a positive gesture or a negative one.

"When do you think you can start, Mrs Pickwick?" he asked as he led them up the stairs.

"Just as soon as I can pack and arrange for a wagon to move us. I have my own horse and shay. Is there any place nearby that I can keep them?"

"There is plenty of room in my stable, and I have an excellent stableman who is most reliable."

The part of the manor that was being used included the basement kitchen, where most of the baking and cooking took place, a storage room, and several small rooms for the scullery maids and extra help, when needed.

The first floor contained a second kitchen, which had a stove to keep the food warm after it was sent up on the dumbwaiter; a dining area that seated all the servants and was big enough for them to use for their holiday celebrations; and the parlour where James had interviewed Gladys.

The first floor also contained a hallway that led to the front entrance and a great, ornate oaken stairway that flowed down and graciously spread out at the bottom. James said the big doors beside the stairway led to the ballroom and the formal dining room, but he didn't offer to show them to her, nor did he show her his library, which was on the opposite side of the stairway. James informed her that she could use those stairs to get to the other floors or she could use the narrow servant's stairs at the back of the mansion.

The rooms in use on the second floor were James's apartment, which consisted of a sitting room and bedroom, and another apartment that had been Mrs Hornsby's. That room had a small balcony. A hallway led to the west wing of the mansion and more vacant rooms.

The third floor had two apartments similar to those on the second floor. These apartments would normally be too grand to accommodate a servant, but since James's previous housekeeper had

served his wife's family faithfully for many years, he saw no reason she shouldn't spend her last years in comfort and with privacy. Now that she had left, Gladys and Dolly were fortunate in being allotted the same apartment. The other apartment on the third floor was kept in readiness for Horace, James Hornsby's son, who was working in South Africa.

The rooms on the fourth floor were not as spacious and grand as those on the other floors; nevertheless, they were nicely furnished and had good-sized windows. These rooms housed the cook, her kitchen maids, the butler, and the footmen. The stableman, the gardener, and their families lived in little cottages on the estate, and the stable boys had lodgings in the barn.

Gladys and Dolly were quite pleased with their future home. Their apartment, although not as clean as they would have preferred, was very roomy and had large windows that would let in a lot of light once the heavy drapes were replaced with lace curtains. There was plenty of room in the bedroom for another bed, and the sitting room had a comfortable settee and plenty of room for Gladys's sewing machine and Dolly's dollhouse and books.

On the way home in James's buggy, Dolly said, "Mama, I think Gamby would be happy if he saw where we are going to live, don't you?"

"I suppose so," Gladys answered rather sadly, still trying to process the change in their circumstances. James Hornsby's house was far pleasanter than she had hoped for, and she found her new employer a likable man, but it seemed a bittersweet dispensation for all she had lost. She was, once again, nothing more than a servant.

Chapter Three

Now that she was going to be a housekeeper, Gladys wished she had listened to Andrew and moved into a house big enough to have servants so that she would have learned what a housekeeper's duties were. She decided to visit Sorenson Hall and ask Lady Madeline for advice. If Lady Madeline refused to help her, she was afraid it wouldn't take long for James Hornsby to realize she hadn't told the truth when she said she knew how to run a household.

Lady Madeline's greeting was somewhat aloof, and instead of providing the information herself, she made it clear that Gladys was now a servant by sending her to the kitchen to talk to Annie, her housekeeper. Gladys wondered if, perhaps, the reason for her Ladyship's cool manner might have something to do with Lord Sorenson.

When Gladys had found out that her father-in-law had been murdered, and hadn't changed his will, she was at her wit's end and had broken down and confessed to Lady Madeline that she was being blackmailed and could not contest the will. Lady Madeline then told Gladys that her father-in-law, Andrew, had confessed to

Lord Cedric that he was trying to obtain a divorce so he could marry Gladys. Unfortunately, Lord Cedric blamed Gladys.

Gladys was shocked and she informed Lady Madeline that she had no knowledge of Andrew's plans, and that if he had asked her to marry him she would not have accepted his proposal. She surmised that Lady Madeline would tell this to his Lordship, and perhaps he would no longer blame her for Andrew's actions, but it seemed she was mistaken.

Before Gladys took her leave, Lady Madeline did offer an apology, "I am sorry, my dear; life can be so cruel! I wish you and your darling little girl all the best in your new surroundings."

There was both warmth and sadness in her eyes as she made a point of not including her husband in the offer, making it obvious that he still considered Gladys a wanton woman.

Although no longer a member of high society, Gladys had foolishly expected to remain friends with her Ladyship, so her indifferent attitude was both disappointing and hurtful.

Lady Sorenson, unlike many of the socialites Gladys had met since marrying Tom, didn't put on airs, and Gladys had always felt comfortable in her company. A few years ago, Gladys had told her Ladyship about a group of Romani that were planning to put on a show at their camp on the outskirts of Dover. Lady Madeline had offered to accompany her and Dolly when they went to see it.

But, now that she thought about it, Gladys realized that at that time she was married to one of Dover's richest young men. Unlike her situation today, they had both been members of the upper levels of society.

Gladys smiled and thanked her Ladyship as she bid her goodbye, knowing that she might have been obliged to act in the same manner, if their roles had been reversed.

Four days after their visit to the Hornsby residence, Gladys and Dolly, with the aid of Bob Hennessy and his horse and wagon, left Dover to take up residence at Four Oaks.

Gladys was relieved to find that Peter Pickwick had visited the blacksmith's shop and taken Andrew's horses and wagons without mentioning Tig or the shay.

"Sure and he must have thought they were yours all along," Bob reported as he hitched the gelding to the buggy.

Bob's wagon was big enough to take all their belongings, given that all Gladys could lay claim to were Millie's two trunks, the sewing machine, Dolly's dollhouse, Tom's collection of books, along with Gladys's treasured copy of *The Hunchback of Notre-Dame,* a few ornaments and other small wedding presents, and three dozen daffodil bulbs that Mr Grimsby had given her to plant along the driveway at Oaken Arms. She had tried to return them, but he insisted she take them with her as a remembrance of him and his wife. Because Peter Pickwick knew nothing of the three velocipedes Andrew had bought at the fair, Gladys took them along as well.

Before she and Dolly climbed into the shay, they stood and looked back at the cottage. "I don't want to go, Mama," Dolly said tearfully.

"No, darling, neither do I. Your daddy and I were so very happy here. I feel like I'm losing him all over again."

"I don't want to lose my Gamby again!"

"You can never do that, Dolly; he will be in your heart forever, I promise. We shall never forget them. Now let's get in the buggy and not look back."

Gladys was thankful that Dolly was young enough to make the adjustment to a life of a commoner without realizing what she had lost. As for herself, she felt fate could not have dealt a worse blow. Just two weeks earlier, everything she had ever dreamed of was coming true, and she was about to be the owner of one of the most prestigious estates in the country. Now she was one step away from being a pauper. Even Tom's death had, in some ways, been easier to bear.

She failed to consider how poor she had been when she first arrived in Dover and only thought about how unfair it was to have come so far, only to lose it all because Andrew had neglected to sign a paper. The thought that she might have suffered the same fate, even if Andrew had signed the new will, because Peter Pickwick had discovered her true identity, never crossed her mind.

Ever since Andrew had been killed, the sorrow of losing him had suppressed any resentment she felt toward him, but now as they drew nearer and nearer to the Hornsby estate, she couldn't help but silently curse the man who had been kinder to her than anyone she had ever known.

As before, they used the road leading to the side entrance, but this time they carried on to the servants' entrance at the back of the home. James was thoughtful enough to have his second footman lend Bob a hand with the unloading. As James watched the men unload, he noticed how few furnishings the young widow possessed, although he was very taken with the three velocipedes. Having been to the fair in London and seen Willard's invention, he had always regretted not purchasing one.

The fellow had different models to choose from. Although it seemed they were all driven by foot pedals, James was most taken with the two wheeled models like the three that Gladys had. He couldn't imagine how one would manage to stay upright on one though.

He also knew how expensive they were and was surprised that Gladys owned three of them. She noticed him admiring them and explained that Andrew had bought them each one, and she told him he was welcome to use Andrew's anytime.

Knowing that Keith's friend, Tom Pickwick, came from a wealthy family, James found it puzzling that his widow would be forced to seek employment. But no matter what the reason for her unfortunate circumstance, James felt obliged to help her any way he could because he knew that was what his brother would have wanted.

Besides, unlike his former housekeeper, who always wore drab greys and blacks that blended in with the gloom of the house so well that she appeared invisible, Gladys's clothes gave off an aura of colour and brightness. When she came to apply for the job, she was dressed in black, but now she wore a pretty blue blouse, a dark grey skirt, and a blue and green plaid shawl tied around her narrow waist like a gypsy. James could easily understand why his brother had found her attractive.

He had often wondered what had happened to Gladys. Kieth had written to him saying how beautiful she was and how he planned to propose to her. Then, he never mentioned her again. James thought how odd it was that that same girl was now going to be working for him. He could tell by the way she talked about Keith that she had been very fond of him, and, because of that, James worried that he might not ever be able to think of her as a mere servant.

"Put everything in my sitting room for now, if you don't mind. It will be far easier to clean the bedroom if it isn't cluttered," Gladys told the men.

Luckily, the previous housekeeper's family had come and collected her belongings, leaving the suite empty except for a bed, a chiffonier, a wardrobe, and a settee.

When she noticed that James was still watching the movers, Gladys approached him and asked, "Sir, I wonder if I may have the rest of the day to clean my rooms and settle in before I begin my work?"

"Most assuredly, perhaps you would like another day as well?" he replied.

At first, she thought his tone hinted of sarcasm, but she could only read kindness on his face. "Thank you, sir, that is very generous, but I shall be ready to start in the morning. Now I wonder if I could have a bucket of hot water, a scrub brush, and some soap."

"Of course, just go to the kitchen and the cook will supply you with whatever you require; I shall see that one of the housemaids assists you, if you would like."

"Yes, it just may do her good to see what I shall be expecting in the way of cleanliness when I am in charge. Oh, dear, I hope that didn't sound too overbearing. I do not intend to be too strict."

"I think you may be just what we need around here. I should have been more stringent with my rules as of late, but poor Mrs Cosgrave, my previous housekeeper, was very elderly and hadn't the strength or the eyesight to find fault with the help. I shall send one of the girls up to help you right away. And perhaps you will let me know when you are free."

Gladys thanked him again, then went out to say goodbye to Bob.

He and the footman had uncrated the sewing machine, and as they carried it up to Gladys's apartment they were watched by most of the household staff, all curious to know what the strange looking contraption could be. Bob laughed and said, "They didn't know what to make o' it, so I thought I'd keep them guessing until you told them. But you oughta seen their faces when I told them you were the only lady in all of England what has one."

"I'm sure there are many more women that have one by now, Bob. I only wish dear Millie had one in her dressmaking shop when she was alive. You know she took me under her wing when I first came to Dover. She taught me how to sew and so much more. I would have tried to open a dressmaker's shop myself instead of coming here to work, if I had a place of my own."

"I told them ladies that you could make any sort o' fancy gowns there was on that machine, Gladdy."

Gladys laughed and teased him for exaggerating. She knew how he liked to make the most out of a story, but then, he did profess to have been held by his heels, not once but twice, in order to kiss the Blarney Stone when he was a young lad in Ireland. She had always enjoyed his Irish humour. She would have looked forward to visiting him, but she didn't intend to return to Dover after she fulfilled her promise to Dolly to visit Andrew's grave.

After he left, she and Dolly went to find the stableman to make sure he was taking good care of Tig. She needn't have worried—the man had the horse all settled into a clean stall and had put the shay away with Mr Hornsby's buggies.

The coachman was the biggest man Gladys had ever seen. He had a huge moustache and deep creases in his cheeks, but none on his forehead—a good indication that he laughed more than he frowned. He reminded Gladys of her father before the liquor claimed him. After she thanked him, she asked him his name and had to suppress a giggle when he said it was "Horseman," since it so aptly suited his profession and his size.

"But I goes by Ruby, missus; hit's short for Ruben, you see," he added. Gladys had learned from Annie that a housekeeper was always referred to as missus by the other servants, except for the butler, even if she happened to be a spinster. The butler, whose position in the household was equal to hers, would address her as "Mrs Pickwick," and she should address him in the same formal way. Gladys made an instant friend when she told Ruby that she looked forward to talking to him again when she had more time.

Even Dolly was put to work cleaning, which, fortunately, kept her too busy to be homesick. The drapes and the rugs were taken outside and beaten, the floor scrubbed, and the wallpaper, bed, and other furniture wiped down with a damp cloth. The room was finally aired and ready to move into at nine that evening. They had only stopped cleaning for a half hour to have dinner. The chambermaid who James sent to help was a large, fair-haired, bonny girl of nineteen named Rita, who, after seeing how meticulous the new missus was, couldn't wait to rush off and warn the rest of the staff. But after Gladys thanked her and told her that she would only be expected to work half the following day, she left with a smile on her face and delivered a far more favourable account.

Although their new apartment wasn't as luxurious as the one that had awaited them at Oaken Arms, it was far more elaborate than their former dwelling. With their own bits and pieces about the room, it felt much more familiar.

After a cup of hot chocolate thoughtfully sent up by the cook, Dolly crawled into bed and fell asleep as soon as her head hit the pillow. Gladys would have done the same, but she still had to pay her employer a visit.

She found Jenkins, the butler, and asked him where she could find the master. Jenkins, thinking Gladys far too comely to be a proper housekeeper, told her rather sharply that she would find him in the library. The door of the library was open, but she knocked to let James know she was there.

"Gladys? Please come inside."

Chapter Four

As she entered the room, the first thing she noticed was the rich and pleasant smell of leather, a favourite scent of hers since she was a child in Old Nichol, spending time with Mr O's old horse Knickers. There weren't many pleasant odours in the slums. In fact, the smell of old Knickers' harness was the only one Gladys could remember.

Old Knickers belonged to Mr O'Brian or, as Gladys called him, Mr O. The O'Brians had a large family and they lived above their barn where the warmth of the animals—one horse, one sow, varying numbers of piglets, one boar, and a dog—all helped add heat in the winter. Mr O used old Knickers to pull a wagon loaded with horse and pig manure to gardens on the outskirts of Old Nichol. The horse had been in his twilight years, and his back had developed such a sway that two little O'Brians and Gladys could all fit nicely and Knickers never objected.

Gladys took a deep breath, smiled, and looked around. Three of the walls in the library, except for one good-sized window, were completely lined with books, most bound in leather. A ladder, which was attached to a track that hung from the high ceiling and ran around the walls, allowed access to the books on even the highest shelves. Facing the fourth wall, which contained a huge fireplace, there were three brown leather, high-backed chairs that reminded Gladys of the one in Andrew's office.

A writing desk and an oak armchair with a leather-padded seat and back were to one side of the fireplace, and a huge globe of the world was on the other. There were several paintings on the wall, but the one over the fireplace was so unusual it captured Gladys's attention. For a moment, she forgot where she was.

"It is interesting, isn't it?" James said.

Gladys hadn't seen him sitting in one of the chairs facing the fireplace, but now she turned to him and answered, "It is lovely—different from anything I have ever seen."

"A good friend of mine purchased it for me when he was visiting Paris last year. The artist was a Japanese man named Katsushika Hokusai, although, like most Japanese artists, he went by many other names—upwards of thirty, I believe. The title of this painting is 'Furoshiki-rekisi.'"

"It has such an interesting mixture of scenery: a lake, a waterfall, some exotic looking trees and mountains, and some oddly dressed men. It all looks a bit . . ."

"Mystical?"

"Yes, that's it! Is that what Japan really looks like?"

James, impressed with the woman's curiosity over his latest painting, replied, "I have never been there, but I have heard that Mr Hokusai enjoyed painting images of the daily lives of his countrymen, so I imagine it is."

"I enjoyed the Japanese exhibits last year when we went to London, and I would love to visit the country someday."

"Yes, so would I," he answered, nodding his head.

A little worried that her ignorance might be apparent if she pursued the subject, Gladys said, "You have a wonderful library, Mr Hornsby. Dolly's grandfather gave her all of Tom's books, and she loves reading. I would like to show her your library sometime, if I may."

"Yes, but I must tell you that I do not allow children in here on their own."

"I understand perfectly, sir."

For the first time since she entered the room, James realized that she had remained standing and said, "Forgive me for being so thoughtless. You must be worn out after all that work. Do sit down, Mrs Pickwick. Keith talked about you so much that in a way I almost feel as though I have known you for a long time."

"But I thought that Keith lived in Wales?"

"Yes, he did. You see, my father passed away when I was fifteen, and my mother remarried a Welshman by the name of Corkish. Keith was born a year later. After a few years, my step-father decided to move back to Wales, and because I was being trained to take over my father's business, I remained in Dover. I was very fond of Keith. We had some jolly good times whenever we had a chance to be together."

"Keith was very fond of you too. The three of us were planning on visiting you, but then Tom had his accident. He was riding one evening at dusk and didn't see a tree that had fallen across the road. Tom's horse had to be put down, and Tom was badly injured. His face was quite disfigured, and he refused to leave the house until not long before he and Keith left for India, so we weren't able to come to see you."

"Keith told me a little of what happened . . . But now, here we are. I am certain he would be pleased to know that we have met at last."

"And I am very pleased to finally meet you, even under these circumstances."

"Good, good! Now, I suppose we should talk about your job. As you already know, my wife passed away a few years ago, and our son, Horace, lives abroad, so being alone here, I've not felt the need to employ many servants. However, if at any time you feel you need more help, please do not hesitate to let me know."

Gladys nodded and he continued, "I pray you will not find what I am about to say offensive, but I must admit that my curiosity has taken precedence over good manners. You see, I had known Thomas and his father, Andrew, for many years. Andrew and I were both involved in the shipping business—mine being in the building of the vessels. Now, I would venture to guess that although you may have employed servants before, you have never had to be one. Am I correct?"

"Not entirely, sir. You see, my father was lost at sea when I was a child, and my mother, who was a governess, was left to bring me up the best she could. When she died, I was forced to find employment in order to live. Having a certain musical talent, I found a job as a barmaid and entertainer. It was there I met Tom and Keith. So you might say I was a servant. However, I can assure you that I am familiar with the duties of a housekeeper and that you won't be disappointed in my work."

"I am certain I shan't be. Now that you mention it, I do recall Keith saying you had a beautiful voice. Who was your teacher?"

Gladys hesitated for a moment, then she decided to tell the truth—up to a point. "My mother, but she could sing far better than I. She often sang solos in church and at many other social events."

"Do you resemble your mother too?"

"No, I look more like my father. Mother's hair was red and she was a very petite woman." What Gladys was saying wasn't all prefabricated; her mother did have an enviable voice, red hair, and small stature. However, her solos were performed in the pubs and streets of the slums, not in a church.

As she spoke, Gladys could picture her mother's red hair. She recalled how it sometimes looked like it was on fire. Curls would fly about her head like tentacles of flames as she twirled round and round dancing and singing while lifting her skirt up almost to her knees. James interrupted her thoughts.

"Perhaps you would sing for me sometime? I am not an accomplished pianist, but I do play a little."

"You have a piano?"

"Actually, I have two: one in the servants' hall and one in the parlour. Do you play?"

"Yes, I do!"

"Wonderful! I shall look forward to hearing you play and sing."

James took a few seconds thinking how he should phrase his next question without embarrassing her. "Please do not answer if you do not want to, Mrs Pickwick, but, knowing how well off Andrew was, I cannot help but wonder why you, his daughter-in-law, would be forced to seek employment."

"I don't know if you knew Andrew very well."

"No, but he and my father were good friends."

"Well, when Tom's mother passed away, Andrew was so grief-stricken and vulnerable that a scheming woman named Rose had no trouble convincing him that he needed a wife and a mother for Tom, who was only about ten at the time."

"Yes, I do remember my father saying that Andrew had married again and that the marriage didn't last." James remarked.

"That's right. She refused to stay on his estate in the country, so he moved her into a house in town. He and Tom stayed on the farm. She had also talked him into adopting her two children with the excuse that they would be good company for Tom, but they were both very naughty and Tom was happy when they moved out. The boy's name is Peter and the girl's name is Mildred.

"Andrew made sure they had a good allowance, but he had nothing to do with them from that time on. When Tom grew up and joined the army, his father really missed him so he decided to accept a government position in Dover and he moved into a flat near his office on the quay. He took the job intending to help the poor people in Ireland who were starving."

Gladys was suddenly afraid she was talking too much and said, "Forgive me, Mr Hornsby, I didn't mean to go on so, but it is rather hard to explain unless you know the whole story."

"There's no need to apologize, I understand. Please continue."

"Well, as you know, Tom was killed before he had a chance to come home and see his new little girl, Dolly, so Andrew was there for us both when we needed him the most. He absolutely adored Dolly, and she loved him just as much. He was determined to build us a grand home on an estate he purchased. I even helped design the mansion and picked out all the furnishings. We named the estate Oaken Arms.

"It was ready to move into when Andrew decided to make a quick trip to Ireland to bring back some relatives of Bob's—the man who brought my belongings here. Dolly and I were getting ready to move. We were packing when Peter came to the door and told me that Andrew had been murdered. Not only was I shocked to hear of his demise, but later Andrew's lawyer told me that he had him draw up a new will leaving Oaken Arms to Dolly and me, but he neglected to sign it before leaving for Ireland.

"As his only son, Peter inherited his entire estate and he ordered us out of the house we were living in. That is why I was forced to seek employment."

"You mean to say that this fellow, Peter, didn't even see to it that you and your daughter had an allowance decent enough to maintain the lifestyle you were accustomed to?"

"No. He gave us two weeks to vacate the home we were in. If not for Lady Madeline's assistance, we would now be homeless."

"Well, I am happy that she recommended you. Now, my dear, you have had a very busy day and I think a glass of sherry is in order." James poured two glasses as he talked, and when he offered one to Gladys, she finally relaxed and smiled.

They spent a pleasant half hour talking about the Great Exhibition, since they had both had the pleasure of attending it.

Gladys told him about receiving the sewing machine from Andrew after he had been murdered. James said he would appreciate a demonstration whenever she had the time.

Gladys was tired but found the big chair so comfortable, the warmth of the fire and the sherry so relaxing, that she was reluctant to leave. It had been a long and tiring day for her, but, as she sat talking to this soft-spoken man, she found herself wishing they were just good friends spending a nice evening together, not master and servant. However, she was determined to prove her worth, and her duties required an early rising. She refused a second drink, excused herself, and went up to bed.

After she left, James pondered over the unexpected feeling of friendship he felt toward her. He seldom felt at ease in the company of women and had married his wife, Ruth, not out of love but convenience.

Ruth, the only child of a wealthy merchant, had inherited Four Oaks and the rest of her father's fortune when he was killed. By an odd coincidence, the poor man, like Andrew Pickwick, had suffered an untimely end when he was stabbed to death and robbed while on a business trip.

He and James's father had been good friends as well as business associates. As a young boy, James had often visited Four Oaks with his parents. He and Ruth had one peculiarity in common. They both preferred reading to socializing and, therefore, got along tolerably well. Perhaps Ruth's lack of comely features and feminine contours had a lot to do with her mannerisms, but James was not unattractive in the least so his idiosyncrasies were thought to be caused by shyness.

Because of an extreme underbite, Ruth's lip-line slanted downward in the corners, giving her a dour countenance. This, and her shyness, did little to encourage fondness from family, friends, and relatives. Even her parents found her unresponsive to their show of affection. As she grew older, any efforts they made to engage her in conversation only received one word responses. Ruth enjoyed the company of a book more than people.

Although James, as a youngster, had tolerated his parents' fond embraces, he also preferred reading to socializing.

After his father passed away and his mother remarried and moved to Wales, James's visits to Four Oaks became more frequent. Since the death of her beloved husband, Ruth's mother had gradually become more interested in her daily intake of gin than the family's business affairs, and she began to rely on James's financial advice. James loved Four Oaks, and although his reasons for proposing to Ruth were partly honourable, the thought of becoming the master of such an imposing estate was irresistible.

The marriage was celebrated, in accordance with the wishes of both the groom and bride, with little pomp and very few guests. A week in London was planned as a honeymoon, but after two days of crowded streets and foul air, the newlyweds agreed that they preferred the tranquil surroundings of Four Oaks and the Sandwich countryside.

Although the marriage was consummated, the lack of ardour from both parties rendered the act dissatisfying; they readily agreed that respect for each other's privacy was all they required to enjoy a happy life together. Their brief honeymoon resulted in the birth of their son, Horace, or they would have remained childless.

James's marriage to Ruth made him the very wealthy master of Four Oaks. This allowed him to fulfil another of his aspirations and buy a shipyard in London. Not long after he bought the shipyard, one of his London lawyers told him about a flat for lease in the same neighbourhood as his own flat, close to James's office. The flat had three stories, with a sitting room on the first floor and two large bedrooms on the second. A middle-aged couple, who had worked for the former owner as caretaker and housekeeper, were living in the small apartment on the third.

Knowing that flats in London were seldom for sale, James purchased it sight unseen. Fortunately, it was very spacious, and he was so pleased with the cleanliness of the rooms that he hired the middle-aged couple, who were overjoyed.

Having his own place in London was quite a novelty, and whenever James stayed there, he experienced a heady feeling of sophistication. Thus, he began spending more time at the flat than he did at Four Oaks. As for Ruth, she seemed unaware of her husband's absence. Since the birth of her son, both she and her mother took little notice of anything but the baby's welfare.

Perhaps because of their liking for solitude, he and Ruth found the act of lovemaking awkward and embarrassing during their first and only time. Love had not blossomed between the couple, and their solitary natures had not allowed friendship to blossom either. Ruth had no idea what it was like to truly love someone until the first time she held their baby boy in her arms.

The joy she felt every time she kissed his fuzzy little head or touched his soft skin began to erase her cheerless expression. Even

James noticed the difference and was happy for her. But the bold and uncouth behaviour she had of breastfeeding the infant in front of him and the servants embarrassed him. Rather than make an issue out of it, he spent most of his time in his library or in London.

James's obvious revulsion toward breastfeeding either didn't bother Ruth, or she chose to ignore it, and she breastfed Horace until he was three. He was a bright little boy. By the time he was three, he had an extensive vocabulary, thanks to a very adroit mother, grandmother, and nanny. His precocious nature would have pleased James more if he hadn't witnessed the child jump up on his mother's knee every time he became thirsty, pull one of her breasts out of her dress and say, "Suck, suck, Mommy." James soon began taking his meals alone. Sadly, he never established a bond with his son.

Now, as he sat in his library, he wondered if he was making a mistake by hiring a woman with a child. He knew he could dismiss them if the arrangement proved unsatisfactory, but he had never fired a person before and didn't think he could. He decided that if Gladys was not up to the job, he would give her an excellent referral and have his butler Jenkins do it. Jenkins's frown when James told him he had hired Gladys as the new housekeeper was enough to signify his disapproval, and he would probably welcome the opportunity.

Chapter Five

The next morning, the entire female staff was lined up in the dining room waiting for Gladys's inspection: two housemaids, Rita, the girl who had helped Gladys clean her room the night before, and Betty, a short, chunky, dark-haired, pleasant-looking girl of fifteen; the scullery maid, Lorain, a pretty fourteen-year-old girl with curly dark hair and bright blue eyes; Little Ines, a petite, twenty-year-old parlour maid; Molly, a plain and sulky-looking fifteen-year-old kitchen maid; and Freda, the seemingly good-natured cook, whose plumpness portrayed her fondness for the excellent food she served.

Since there was no longer a Mrs Hornsby, Gladys, as housekeeper, was now in charge of these six servants. It was her duty to see that the female staff did their jobs well and were well spoken.

Although they were called servants, the title of slave would have been more fitting with the austere rules they were expected to follow. The maids were not permitted to speak to a lady or gentleman unless delivering a message or answering a question, and they were told to avert their eyes by turning away whenever they met a person of higher quality. There were so many demeaning regulations that Gladys realized she hadn't been treated as unfairly as she thought when she worked as a maid for Laura Watt at the inn.

It was up to the housekeeper to see that the maids kept the master and the staff supplied with fresh linens and bedding. She had to ensure that all the furniture was cleaned and polished and attend to the details of purchasing goods for the household, from the market and from tradesmen. One of her other duties was to keep an account of all expenses. And the accounts had to be in good order, because they were examined from time to time by the master of the house.

She had no idea what her wage would be until she looked at the ledger and was surprised to see that she was the highest paid employee on the staff at fifty-three pounds a year. Compared to the other servants, who only received ten to twenty pounds a year, it was a generous amount, but to Gladys, who had received a monthly allowance of fifty pounds from her father-in-law for the past seven years, it seemed like a pitiful amount. It depressed her to think of how many years it would take for her to save enough money to purchase a dress-making shop.

Gladys talked to each of the girls in order to find out how old they were and what their duties were. She was very disappointed in their appearance. Their pinafores and caps were soiled and their personal hygiene left much to be desired, but because she didn't want to begin her job with criticism, she made no comment.

She remembered Millie telling her that a cricket player would play all day in the sun without complaining just on the chance he might win a silly trophy. It only took a second for Gladys to think of what she could use for a trophy, but she decided to do nothing until she had a chance to make a list of all the changes she intended to make. She told the girls to carry on as usual and decided she would address them all again the following morning.

Gladys retired to her office, a small room under the staircase, and had begun sorting out papers when James knocked at the door. He asked if she found everything satisfactory, and she said she would know more in a few days.

"I suppose Jenkins has introduced you to his footmen?" he asked.

"No, but one of them was very helpful in assisting my friend when we arrived."

"Ah, that would be the second footman, Rex. However, I think you should have a proper introduction. I shall send Jenkins to see you in a few minutes, but before I leave, I wanted you to know that I am leaving for London today and shan't be back for a few days. I shall instruct Jenkins to be at your disposal if you need anything before I return."

Ten minutes later, Jenkins and his two footmen arrived.

Jenkins's posture was amazingly youthful considering he was in his late sixties. Gladys could tell by his demeanour that he was, in all respects, a proper gentleman. His features were decent enough, but they appeared to be chiselled in granite and lacked expression. From his restrained greeting when she had first met him, it was obvious that he had made up his mind she was far too young to run a decent household. Nevertheless, he had his orders and introduced the two footmen in a polite manner.

Since height and a pleasing appearance were the most important requirements regarding a footman's rank, John, a six-foot-two, blue-eyed, fair-haired man, was given the rank of first footman. Rex, the second footman and the one who had helped carry Gladys's belongings up to her room, was two inches shorter and had a darker complexion. Gladys found him to be far more attractive.

Jenkins's scepticism toward Gladys was disappointing, but since they ruled different realms of the household and servants, she thought it unlikely they would interfere with one another. A butler's duties were to supervise all the indoor male servants, arrange the dinner table, announce dinner, carve the meat, and serve the wine. He was expected to always be well dressed in the proper gentlemen's style of the day and was required to buy his own clothes. His wages amounted to forty-five pounds a year, quite a bit higher than all the other servants, and he was allowed to collect the ends of the candles and received one bottle of wine for every six opened.

The first footman was usually referred to as John or James, regardless of his real name. His duties were varied and included waiting on the mistress of the manor, accompanying her whenever she went out in her carriage, and brushing the mud off her boots, the hems of her dresses, riding habits, and cloaks. Because there was no longer a mistress at the Hornsby residence, the first footman waited on James, bringing him his breakfast in the mornings and looking after his personal needs. If there had been a mistress, these duties would have been allotted to the second footman, but, as it was, the second footman had the responsibility of cleaning mirrors, laying the table, bringing in coal and wood, and many other tasks. If there had been a third footman, he would be obliged to take over the most menial jobs.

Once Gladys had gathered all the girls and the cook together the following morning, she began by saying that the entire house needed a thorough cleaning. Even the cook couldn't mask her feelings of apprehension, so Gladys did her best to ease their fears by stating that she intended to ask the master to hire more help. They looked even more dismayed when she said she expected them to keep their clothes clean, until she added that, once a week, they would be given allotted times in which to bathe and wash their hair and their underpinnings—an unusual and pleasant surprise for everyone.

She knew from her own experience how difficult it was to work long hours and still find time to wash and dry one's clothing in time to wear the following day, so she also promised them a change of work clothes. She was rewarded for that with broader smiles. Then it was time for her to activate her plan.

"How many of you noticed the machine that the footman and my friend took up to my room?"

All the women except Freda nodded.

"Do you have any idea what it is?"

They all shook their heads.

"It's a wonderful invention called a sewing machine. All I have to

do is sit down and turn the wheel, and the machine does the sewing. A pinafore can be made in a few hours and a dress in two days. As it happens, I have some lovely pieces of material and I shall make a new dress for whomever I think deserves it by the end of this week." She had found her trophy.

After allowing them a few seconds to think about it, she added, "Now ladies, shall we get to work?"

The girls, delighted to be called ladies, were so excited about the prospect of having a new frock, that they began the chores she gave them with enthusiasm. By the end of the day, however, they began to wonder if a new frock was worth suffering with sore backs and calloused hands. They took down and carefully washed the drapes—exposing patterns not seen for years—washed windows clean of winter soot, beat carpets, scrubbed floors, polished brass to mirror brightness, and washed ornaments instead of dusting them.

By the end of the third day, they had only cleaned three rooms: the parlour, the dining room, and the library; but what an accomplishment it was. Instead of emitting odours of age-old grime, the three rooms now offered pleasant aromas of polish, soap, and freshly picked flowers. The clean drapes on all the large windows were pulled back and tied with braided cord, allowing the sun to enter, which gave the rooms a warm and cheery ambience.

James returned the evening of the third day, and when he entered the parlour, he was amazed. He sent a footman to fetch Gladys. "You have done wonders with this room," he exclaimed. "Tell me, how did you manage to buy new drapery without going to town?"

"I didn't, sir. Those are the same drapes."

"Nonsense; these are a different colour, and they are patterned."

"It is amazing what a little soap and water can do."

"I cannot believe what you have accomplished in only three days."

"Not I, sir. It's the girls who are responsible; they worked very hard. However, because of past neglect, they could only finish three

rooms. There is much to do in order to have your house in order, and I fear it shall require two or three more chambermaids to keep it this way."

"If the other two rooms are as immaculate as this one, it will be well worth the extra expense. I shall see to it tomorrow. There are always a number of young girls in Sandwich who are looking for employment, and I shall see that you have them before the week is out."

Feeling sorry for Rex, the second footman, inspired Gladys to make an additional request. Hoping she wasn't being too demanding, Gladys asked James if he could hire a boy to clean out the fireplaces, carry in fuel, and do other heavy and dirty jobs about the house. James's answer wasn't as hearty this time, but it was still affirmative.

Two days later, James brought three girls to Four Oaks for her to interview. There were twins, Pearl and Polly, and a girl named Mary. All three were fifteen and appeared to be strong and accustomed to hard work. They were pleased when Gladys hired them, and it didn't take long to prove she had made the right decision.

Pete, the young lad James hired to help with the heavy chores, was the son of one of James's tenants. He wasn't a very bright or lively boy, but once he learned his duties, he was dependable.

As the weeks went by, Gladys found her work much easier than she had anticipated, although it was time consuming. Her subordinates now took pride in their accomplishments and their appearance. Except for Molly, they all seemed happy with their new "missus."

Rita won the dress at the end of the first week, perhaps because she had previously worked with Gladys and understood what was expected of her. Rita had little time and almost nowhere to wear such a frock, but Gladys knew that every young girl liked having a pretty dress, so she made the skirt and sleeves out of a length of green and wine-striped sateen and the bodice of dark green velvet with a heart-shaped neckline trimmed with ruffles made of the same material as the skirt and sleeves. Rita had never owned such a treasure, and it was the envy of all the girls.

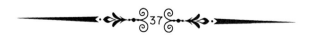

After seeing the look of longing on the cook's face, Gladys offered to make her a frock as well.

"Land's sake, missus, it'll take a good deal more'n a yard or two to go round my middle. And besides, I wouldn't know what to do with a fancy dress the likes o' Rita's. She's going to keep hers to get married in, but I don't think there's much chance of me getting a man now I'm near forty," Freda declared.

It was such fun sewing on her new machine that Gladys didn't stop until she had made each one of the girls a new frock, and she even surprised Freda with a coat that she had fashioned out of one of Millie's. It had fur trim on the collar and cuffs, and Freda cried tears of joy when she saw it. James also found the sewing machine a fascinating invention and came to her apartment twice to watch her sew.

Gladys was unlike any housekeeper the staff, or James, had ever known. She ran the household more efficiently than the previous housekeeper, and the rich life she had led for the past seven years showed in her bearing. Unaware she was doing it, she often burst out in song as she went about her duties, and the sound of her voice made everyone's chores seem less arduous.

Gladys had been certain she would never be happy again after losing Oaken Arms, but in a few short months, she was almost content. Having such an authoritative position had a lot to do with her recovery.

Dolly had made friends with Blossom, the eight-year-old daughter of Ruby the stableman, and seemed happy with her new surroundings. Ruby often allowed the two girls to ride on an elderly pony that had belonged to James's son Horace when he was a young lad. Although she rarely saw the master of the manor, Dolly never forgot his words from their first meeting, and whenever they did chance to meet, she would nod, smile politely and quietly, but swiftly pass him by.

Surprisingly, he felt more disappointed with her behaviour than pleased. There was an unusual maturity about the young girl that intrigued him. She was the only child he had ever had a sensible conversation with, and he thought it might be interesting to talk to her again.

Two months after they left Dover, Dolly asked her mother when they were going to have her grandfather's graveside service. Gladys was dreading going back to Dover, but she knew how disappointed Dolly would be if she broke her promise. She had told James that Peter had forbidden them to attend Andrew's funeral. He understood their need to have a service of their own and not only insisted she take a day off but offered to accompany them, having been a friend of Andrew's. Gladys sent off a letter to the Grimsbys and one to the Reverend and Mrs Mason, asking them to join her at the graveside at two in the afternoon on the twenty-second of April. She also asked the Reverend if he would say a few appropriate words.

She had no idea if the Masons would come, but not only were they there, but also the Grimsbys and over two dozen other parishioners. They were about to proceed with the service when, much to Gladys's surprise, Lord and Lady Sorenson arrived. It was a warm spring day, and a good showing of Mr Grimsby's spring flowers were in bloom. Reverend Mason gave a short but heart-warming talk, mostly to do with Andrew's benevolent accomplishments, and followed it with a prayer. Then Gladys led them in singing, "Amazing Grace." When the song ended, Mrs Mason announced that refreshments would be served in the church hall. Gladys couldn't refuse, but she was on edge worrying that Rose or Peter might come by and see what was happening.

They were making their way to the hall when she missed Dolly. She found her kneeling down digging in the dirt beside Andrew's headstone. "Dolly, what on earth are you doing? And where did you get that spoon?"

"I brought it with me, Mama. I want to bury Gamby's turtledove beside him so he will know I will love him forever." Dolly had given her grandfather an ornate stick pin with a little turtledove on it to put in his tie one Christmas and he always wore it. When he was murdered, the thieves took all his clothes, but he had the pin clenched in his fist and they didn't see it. Her grandfather's lawyer gave it to Dolly before she left Dover.

"But he wanted you to have it."

"No, Mama! He wanted to keep it forever, and that is why he had it in his hand. I know he wants it, Mama; I just know."

"Well, you will not be able to bury it deep enough with that little spoon. I think we should have a talk with Mr Grimsby; I am sure he will help you."

Mr Grimsby was very understanding, and he and Dolly slipped out while the others were enjoying their tea. With the help of a garden spade, they buried Andrew's pin deep and as close to his gravestone as they could.

Lady Sorenson was very pleased to see how happy Gladys and Dolly appeared, and on her way home, she told Lord Cedric that by the way James Hornsby and Gladys seemed to be getting along, she wouldn't be surprised if there was a new Mistress at Four Oaks before too long.

Although Cedric was convinced that Gladys had led Andrew on, he didn't think she deserved to be left penniless, and replied, "Let us hope so, my dear, for both her and her daughter's sake." Lady Madeline smiled up at him while patting his leg.

Before they left for home, Gladys learned that Hugh Mason and Priscilla had indeed been married and were in London arranging their passage to America. Surprisingly, she felt no envy and asked Mrs Mason to give them her best wishes. However, when she heard how Peter, his mother, Rose, his sister, Mildred, along with Rose's new husband, Richard the Duc de Artois, had moved into Oaken Arms, she almost cried out with jealousy. It seemed that Rose had sold the house in town and paid off Richard's debts after he agreed to marry her.

The thought of those dreadful people living in the house she had helped plan was so upsetting that she couldn't hide her tears. Fortunately, everyone thought her grief was over the loss of Andrew. Gladys thanked everyone then made her way to James's coach where the second footman, Rex, was waiting. He gave Gladys a friendly smile as he took her arm to assist her. If she had known the thoughts that were hidden behind his smile, she wouldn't have returned it.

Rex had been on the staff at Four Oaks for two years, and he doubted James Hornsby would recognize him if they met on the street. Then along came Gladys, and in no time at all, James was treating her like a guest rather than a servant. Even though she had James hire a boy to take over some of his duties, he was still jealous of her.

Rex's father had been a butler in a grand manor and had hopes his son would work his way up to the same position at Four Oaks. Rex was something of a narcissist, and since he thought he was far handsomer and more personable than John, he believed he deserved to be first footman. He was also a sly fellow and managed to hide his jealousy so well that Gladys was becoming very fond of him.

Molly's sullenness had always worried Gladys, but whenever she confronted the young girl and asked if she was ill, she was given the same answer, "No, missus, I aren't sick." Then, one day, Gladys paid an unexpected visit to the laundry room and passed Rex coming out the door as she was going in. He seemed to be in a hurry and went past her without a greeting. She found Molly in the room, and it was obvious by her red nose and eyes that she had been crying.

"What is the matter, Molly?" Gladys asked, although by the way Rex had avoided making eye contact with her as they passed each other, she had a good idea.

"Nothin', missus, I just got somethin' in me eye."

"Now, Molly, I know that isn't so. You do not need to be afraid to tell me. It is something to do with Rex, is it not?"

"I needs this job, missus. My da can't keep me anymore."

"You won't lose your job, Molly, I promise. Now tell me what he has been doing to you."

Molly broke down sobbing, and told Gladys that, "He don't really do it to me, missus, but he makes me do things to him. Oh, missus, don't tell, please. I can stand it long as he don't do it to me and gets me in the fam'ly ways. I'd have to go to the poor house then, and they says it's like goin' to hell."

Gladys assured the poor girl that everything would be taken care of and Rex would not bother her anymore. Molly found out that Gladys kept her promises, and from that time on, she truly believed that the new housekeeper was really an angel sent by God himself to save her.

Rex, on the other hand, believed it wasn't God who sent Gladys to Four Oaks but the devil himself. As soon as she left Molly in the laundry room, she tracked him down and confronted him. When he denied Molly's accusations, Gladys threatened to go directly to James and tell him what happened. Rex was aware of James's feelings toward her and knew that not only would he be sacked but turned over to the authorities as well. He had no choice but to confess and beg forgiveness.

Gladys threatened him, stating that if he gave Molly, or any of her subordinates, a reason for complaint, she would see that he was punished. After he left, she wondered if she had been too lenient and reproached herself for having a weakness for dark handsome men.

Chapter Six

Lady Madeline's housekeeper had said that she and the butler always took their meals apart from the rest of the staff, so Gladys asked Freda, James's cook, what the customary procedure was in the Hornsby residence. Freda said the entire staff ate together in the servants' dining room, just off the kitchen, and that James usually dined in the conservatory.

Gladys thought it might be a good idea to allow the rest of the staff a little privacy while they dined, but decided not to change the routine so soon. After the first week, she knew she had made the right decision. Jenkins's silent behaviour toward her was far less awkward and annoying when she had others to talk to. She was very pleased with Freda's cooking. As soon as the staff began to relax in her presence, they chatted away without concern, and mealtimes proved to be an enjoyable break in their busy day.

Dolly also seemed to enjoy the company and listened attentively to every little bit of gossip. Normally a quiet child, she even surprised Gladys when she began sharing some of her memories of her beloved grandfather.

One morning, not long after her conflict with Rex, Gladys was in her office when Jenkins dropped in to say that he had noticed an improvement in the appearance of the female staff. She was pleasantly surprised by his complimentary remark. From then on, their friendship grew, and, before long, they were sharing their various household concerns. Because of his many years of service, Gladys soon learned that she could always rely on Jenkins's advice.

One day, he mentioned that Rex seemed to have gone through a metamorphosis and his attitude toward his job appeared to be far more positive. Gladys had to bite her tongue to stop from replying that Rex's metamorphosis was nothing compared to Molly's. Now that Molly was no longer threatened by the second footman, her personality had changed amazingly. She was seldom seen without a smile on her face, and whenever she and Rex came in sight of each other, it was he who dropped his head.

Jenkins interrupted her thoughts and said, "You seem to have had an amazing effect on all the staff, Mrs Pickwick, and on my footman as well." Gladys had no idea if he had heard about their confrontation or not, so she just smiled and changed the subject.

James had been in the habit of spending most of his days at his club playing cricket or at one of his offices located in Sandwich, Dover, or London, even though he had plenty of competent employees to look after his interests. Although he had had a great deal of respect for his wife, he had found her company uninspiring and felt more relaxed amid the hustle and bustle of the shipyards.

Now that Gladys had made such remarkable improvements, both in the appearance and the atmosphere of the manor, he began to enjoy his home for the first time. He even took more interest in his grounds. One day he was walking in the garden and came across a bed of bright yellow daffodils he had never noticed before. When he remarked to Rahmir, the gardener, how pretty they were, he was told that Gladys had planted them shortly after her arrival.

He put his hand on Rahmir's shoulder and, laughing, said, "My word, she's even made a difference to the outside."

Rahmir, whose English was limited, had no idea what his employer was talking about, but thinking it must have been a joke, he politely and whole-heartedly joined in with a very comical mixture of loud "ho ho hos" and squeaky little "hee hees" which caused James to laugh even harder.

Ruby, the groom, happened to be passing by with James's mount, and he could scarcely believe his eyes when he saw the bearded and turbaned gardener dressed in his overalls and the master in his high collar and ascot laughing so hard that they had to lean against one another to keep from falling over. He had never seen the master laugh before and couldn't help but stare.

When James caught sight of him, he realized what a spectacle he was making of himself. He stopped laughing and said, "Don't worry, Ruby, we've not gone dotty." Then he gave Rahmir a friendly pat on the back, and, reminding himself never to laugh in the presence of the gardener again, he added, "Do not bother to walk him, Ruby; you may saddle him instead. It is high time I began riding the fat off him. I shall change my attire and be right with you, and perhaps I shall persuade Mrs Pickwick to join me on her mare. It is a mare, is it not?"

"No, sir. He's a gelding, sir. And a right fine horse he is, if I do say so. Shall I saddle him too, sir?"

"Well, perhaps I should ask her first. No, no, go ahead and saddle him. I shall insist she join me. It is about time she became familiar with her surroundings."

Gladys knew that what James admired most about her was her competence. However, he had no idea how much time it took her to run the house efficiently. When he came to her and asked her to go riding, she was busy going over the linen to ensure there was plenty of it ready for the housemaids to use the following day, so she thanked him for asking but said she couldn't possibly get away at the moment.

After James had left Ruby, he began planning where on his estate he and Gladys should ride first and was looking forward to showing her his grounds; therefore, he was most disappointed with her refusal.

He had been happy with everything she had done since she came to live at Four Oaks until now. Because she was one of the hired help, he felt she should feel honoured to receive the invitation, so in a tone of voice that left no doubt he was her master, he said, "I have told Ruby to saddle your horse, so I think you had better leave whatever you are doing and put on your riding habit. I shall meet you at the barn in twenty minutes." Then, without waiting for a reply, he abruptly turned and left.

Gladys had no choice but to obey, but she had plenty to say about it under her breath. At first, she thought about putting on the pair of men's riding britches that had shocked Tom, but she feared she might lose her job if she did. Ten minutes later, she arrived at the barn properly clad, except she wore a ribbon in her hair instead of a hat. Ruby had Tig saddled, and he helped her to mount, but the horse hadn't been ridden for quite a time and was so anxious to run that he had trouble standing still. Unfortunately, James arrived as he was prancing about and snorting.

"Are you certain you can handle him?" he said, not meaning the words to sound as sardonic as they did.

"I think so, sir." Gladys answered with a tone of false timidity.

"Well, we shall go at a slow pace, and if you have any trouble, I shall take hold of the reins and lead you."

"Thank you, sir," she replied again with a diffident tone. When Ruby brought James's horse out of the stable he was just as frisky as Tig, because he hadn't been ridden for a time either.

Gladys was delighted and couldn't resist saying, "Are you certain you can handle him, sir?"

At first James's emotions teetered on anger, but then he grasped the humour in her remark and took the jibe good-naturedly. "Touché!" he said with a grin. "Shall we give them their heads?"

It took more than a few hours for them to ride from one end of the estate to the other. They stopped to admire the scenery and watch a family of deer grazing in a field.

As they were about to leave a grove of trees and come out beside a small lake, they spotted a man sitting on the bank with a fishing rod. James motioned for Gladys to stop. Then he helped her down.

"That's old Lockhart," he whispered. "He has been fishing here for years and thinks I don't know. He professes to have a bad leg and walks about town with a limp, but watch this."

Stepping out from the cover of the trees he shouted, "You there, what do you think you are doing? This is private property!"

The "you there" was all it took. Lockhart didn't wait to hear more. He was up and running like a young boy, across the field and over the fence, before they could mount their horses. As they rode to where the old man had been fishing, James said, "Ah, we shall have a nice feast of trout for dinner tonight. Old Lockhart is the best fisherman around here, and he has left his catch behind."

"But why don't you stop him?"

"Oh, I could if I wanted to, but there's plenty of fish in the lake, and besides, I have heard tell he has made it known among the local poachers that I have granted him sole permission to fish here. He has even gone so far as to say that I have ordered him to report anyone else who drops a line in the water. By letting him think he is out-smarting me, I only have to contend with one thief."

As they were riding home, James mentioned how much he enjoyed her company and suggested they ride more often. Gladys decided there was nothing to do but tell the truth, so she explained that she would not be able to keep the house running efficiently and take so much time off. James merely nodded and they kept riding. Gladys had no idea whether he thought she was complaining or just being honest, and she was about to add an apology when he inquired, "Are the three girls I hired not adequate?"

"Oh yes, sir, very much so. And once I have them completely trained, I shall have much more time to myself. I am sorry if I sounded unappreciative. I had a wonderful time, and I would love to go again. I promise that I shall not say no the next time you ask me."

"And I shall be more considerate with my requests," he answered. Then he surprised her and added, "I suppose if you hadn't been such a good friend of Keith's, I would think of you only as a housekeeper and not a friend."

"It would be wonderful if I could be both, sir, but I suppose that wouldn't be proper."

"What is proper is not always what is right. Damned if I can see why we shan't be both. We do have a lot in common. We both enjoy music and riding, and since we live in the same house, why should we not enjoy them together?"

"I am looking forward to playing the piano again," she replied. "I am so thankful that I was Keith's friend, or you might not have hired me."

"That is probably true. I certainly had no intention of hiring a woman with a child. Speaking of your daughter, I think it is about time I showed her my library. Would you ask her to come and see me there, say around two o'clock tomorrow?"

Dolly was astonished when she saw the number of books James had. "I did not know anyone ever owned this many books. Have you read all of them, sir?" she asked.

"About three quarters of them. You see, many belonged to my father and some of the writers he admired are not to my liking. Do you have a favourite author or a favourite story?"

"When I was little, I liked Mother Goose stories the best."

"Ah yes, John Newbery's. I think Horace had a few of his books, including the alphabet book. But now that you are a little older, which one is your favourite?

"*The Rime of the Ancient Mariner* is my very, very most favourite."

"Do you know who the author is?"

"I do not remember his last name, but his first name is Samuel. I remembered that because Gamby's farrier had a big orange cat named Samuel."

"Well the last name of the Samuel who wrote *The Ancient Mariner* is Coleridge. I think it is important to remember the names of authors as well as the stories they write. Do you agree?"

Dolly nodded.

"But that is a very forbidding story for such a young girl. Why did you choose it?"

"It was one of my father's books and Gamby had read it to him

when he was little, so I thought it would be like he was there with us when Gamby read it to me. Does that sound silly?"

"No, Dolly. It sounds very profound. Did your grandfather read it to you?"

"Oh, yes. He read me ten verses every night. He was a very good reader. When he read about the sea, I thought I could taste the salt on my lips and feel the wind on my face. He could make everything sound so real." Dolly looked down at the floor and James could hardly hear her when she whispered, "He never came home to read the last ten verses."

James felt so sorry for her that he couldn't control his feelings, and he said, "Would you like me to read the last ten verses to you?"

Dolly looked up. She couldn't answer, but she nodded.

Before he began, he pulled the bell cord, and when Jenkins arrived, he ordered hot chocolate and cookies. Dolly sat across from him in one of the big, high-backed, leather armchairs. There was a fire going in the fireplace, and the wings on the chair captured the heat as it came off the flames, giving her a warm sense of comfort and wellbeing.

James read with such keen articulation that she enjoyed listening to his voice almost as much as Gamby's. When Jenkins returned with their refreshments, he stood holding the tray and listening to James read the last verse.

> "The Mariner, whose eye is bright,
> Whose beard with age is hoar,
> Is gone: and now the Wedding-Guest
> Turned from the bridegroom's door.
> He went like one that hath been stunned,
> And is of sense forlorn:
> A sadder and a wiser man,
> He rose the morrow morn."

Dolly felt as though a piece of her being had been replaced. When she thanked James enthusiastically, he was pleased, but also a little embarrassed at her show of gratitude.

Jenkins, pleasantly surprised over the atypical behaviour of his master, smiled as he set the tray down on a beautifully carved teak tea table between the two chairs and left.

James was enjoying the repast as much as Dolly. He was so taken with the girl's sensible manner that he told her about his favourite books when he was a young boy.

Then before she left, he said, "Dolly, you remember that I said you weren't allowed in here by yourself?"

"Yes, sir. I remember. I know how precious your books are and I would never disobey you."

"Well, I have changed my mind. Now that I see that you respect books as much as I do and will handle them carefully and put them back where they belong, I see no reason you can't enjoy them too."

"You mean I can come in here anytime I like?"

"Probably it would be best if I wasn't using the library at the time, but otherwise, you are welcome."

Dolly was overjoyed and thanked him before running to tell her mother.

James couldn't understand what there was about this rather plain-looking child that he found so trustworthy, but he instinctively knew that even his most treasured books would be safe in her care.

Before long, Gladys had the household running smoothly. She had plenty of help to keep the house clean and tidy, and, if she needed more, James had promised to hire them. Except for the time James had ordered her to go riding, she was allowed free rein and she found him to be a most obliging employer. She especially appreciated not having a mistress to answer to. James took no interest in her housekeeping methods, and she was free to run the household without interference. If James had a wife, she would never have approved of the way Gladys handled her subordinates.

Having been a housemaid herself, Gladys remembered how demeaning the job could be, and she had no intentions of treating any of the girls under her care like slaves. They, in turn, were so grateful for her show of kindness that they worked hard to please her. The news soon got around that a young girl was lucky if she found a job

at Four Oaks.

The few times Gladys tried to convince James to take a ride on Andrew's velocipede, he refused. However, unbeknownst to her, he often took the machine down into a pasture to practice where no one could see him.

One day when she and Dolly were going to go for a ride on their machines, he surprised them and offered to join them. Having no idea he had ridden before, they were amazed at his adeptness, and when Gladys remarked about how well he was doing, he couldn't resist adding a few tricky turns to show off.

From then on, whenever he visited his tenants, he used Andrew's velocipede as often as he used his horse. He insisted on paying Gladys for it, and although she tried to refuse, she appreciated having such a generous amount of money to add to her savings.

James had tenants living in four of his cottages. Having little interest in farming, he leased the cottages and portions of his property to the occupants for a fee, plus enough of their produce to satisfy his household. There were always plenty of vegetables, milk, butter, meat, and eggs at Freda's disposal, and she made good use of it all. She wasn't just an excellent cook, but an open-minded one as well and never took offense when Gladys offered her some of her own recipes.

Chapter Seven

Every month, James gave Gladys six pounds to purchase goods from the tradesmen who came by weekly, and she kept it inside an envelope in one of her dresser drawers. One day, when a tradesman was due, she went to the dresser to get the money, and was shocked to find it missing. James, having just finished his breakfast, was about to leave the house when she found him and reported what had happened.

"Have you any idea who the culprit is, Gladys?" he inquired. When she said she hadn't, he thought for a second before saying, "Then we shall have to have a search. I am afraid there is nothing else we can do."

"Oh dear, I suppose you are right, but I have gotten to know them all so well that I find it hard to believe any of them would do such a thing."

"I know how you feel, but we have no choice. You call your girls together, and I shall have Jenkins fetch his two footmen."

When Freda and the girls were all assembled in the kitchen,

along with the footmen, James explained the gravity of the situation and informed them they were to remain there until all the rooms were searched. Jenkins was to search the footmen's rooms, and Gladys and Freda were told to go through the girls' rooms.

"It's bad business, missus. To think anybody'd steal from someone as kind as yourself. It's right shameful," Freda declared.

The girls only had one small dresser each and a few pegs on which to hang their dresses, so it didn't take long to do a thorough search of each one's belongings.

Suddenly, Freda called out, "Oh, my Lord, missus. Here it is. Lord forgive her, it's our Molly." She had found the money under Molly's mattress.

"Oh, no, it can't be!" Gladys cried. "She must have needed the money very badly to have done such a thing, Freda, but we have to report her to the master."

When James heard about it, he insisted that they leave it in his hands.

"But she is my girl," Gladys said.

"Yes, she is your girl, Gladys, but it was my money that she has stolen. It is no longer a domestic concern, this is a criminal offense."

He then ordered them all back to work and told John, the first footman, to have Ruby rig his horse and buggy and bring it to the front of the house. Then he told Molly, who was crying so hard that her sobbing plea of innocence was incomprehensible, to gather her belongings.

"I never did it, missus," Molly said as they were on the way out to the buggy.

Gladys could do nothing but say how sorry she was. Tears were falling down her cheeks as well as Molly's when James helped the girl into the buggy, then climbed in and took the reins.

Gladys stood helplessly watching the buggy leave, but when she turned to go back into the house, she caught a glimpse of a face looking out of the parlour window. It was Rex, and he too was watching the buggy. There was a smug grin on his face—the same evil grin he wore when she first accused him of molesting Molly.

Suddenly, she knew what had happened. Hurrying into the

house, she told one of the girls to ask Ruby to saddle her horse as quickly as possible. Then she added, "With a man's saddle, not the side-saddle."

Once in her room, Gladys pulled the pair of men's trousers out of her trunk, knowing she would have to ride like a man in order to catch them before they arrived at the police station.

At first, Ruby thought the girl had heard wrong, but she kept insisting that the missus had said a man's saddle, so he finally gave in and had Tig ready to go by the time Gladys arrived at the stable. After a quick thank you, she jumped up on Tig without Ruby's help, and, leaving the shocked groom with his mouth hanging open, she took off at a full gallop. Before he could get his breath back, he had another shock when Gladys's mount jumped over the fence instead of waiting for someone to open the gate.

Tig was breathing hard and dripping lather when Gladys came galloping alongside James's buggy and motioned for him to stop. "Molly did not take the money, sir," she cried out as he was bringing his horse to a stop.

"I do not understand, and what in heaven's name are you wearing?"

"Oh, please, sir, never mind that; I shall explain later. I had to catch you before you reached the police station. Molly did not take the money, but I know who did."

"Are you quite sure about that?"

"I think so."

"Well then, I suppose we had better turn around."

Gladys arrived home before James and Molly and hurried to change her outfit. She was standing in the doorway when they arrived. Molly ran and threw her arms around her, crying "Oh, thank you, missus, I would never steal from you, or nobody else."

"I know, Molly, I know. Now go to your room and put your things away while I talk to the master."

James told Gladys to follow him into the library and demanded to know what it was all about.

"I am afraid I have made a terrible mistake," Gladys said, and then she told him what had happened in the laundry room. "I know

now that I had no right to handle the matter myself. I should have reported it to Jenkins, or come to you, but I thought I was being so clever in solving the problem without bothering anyone. Then, when you were driving off with Molly, I happened to see Rex looking out the parlour window. He was watching you leave with a self-satisfied grin on his face, and I suddenly remembered that was the look he wore when he first tried to deny what he had done to Molly.

"Sir, I am certain he took that money and put it under Molly's mattress to punish her for telling me about his indecent behaviour."

James was upset to learn about the footman and angry with Gladys for not reporting the incident, but under the circumstances, he had to agree that her suspicions made sense. He rang for Jenkins and asked him to find Rex and tell him he was wanted in the study. Rex passed by the kitchen on his way to the study and was shaken to hear the other girls welcoming Molly back. For a second he thought about running, but then he assured himself that there was no way anyone could prove he had anything to do with the theft.

When James said he knew what had happened in the laundry room, Rex said he was very sorry for what he had done.

"I thought Molly liked it, sir," he said. "But when the missus told me Molly was afraid of me, I never did it again. I've done my best to be a good footman ever since, sir. You can ask Mr Jenkins, and he will tell you."

"Well that is good to hear, but Molly said she didn't take the money, and we thought you may have taken it and put it in her room as an act of revenge."

"I have nothing against the girl, sir, and I would never take money from you, missus," Rex said, turning to Gladys. He lied with such proficiency that for a second she almost believed him, but it was only for a second.

"You are lying, Rex. You went into my room and stole that money and hid it in Molly's room. You might as well admit it because we know you did it."

Rex knew how fond James was of the housekeeper, and he realized he would have to put up a good defence. "I am sorry you feel that way, missus, but you have no reason, or evidence, to prove me guilty. Your money was found under Molly's mattress and not under mine."

He's right, Gladys thought, but then she realized the importance of what he just said, and she smiled. "Sir, could you have the rest of the staff come here for a minute?"

James looked puzzled, but sent for Jenkins then had him fetch the others.

When they were all in the room, Gladys said, "Freda, I would like you and Rex to leave the room, and don't come back until I call you."

After the pair had left and the door was closed, she said, "Now I want to ask the rest of you a question, and I want you to think about it very carefully before you answer. Where in Molly's room did Freda find the stolen money?"

Suddenly, James understood what she was getting at, and he couldn't repress a smile.

When it was clear that no one knew the answer, Gladys called Freda and Rex back into the room. "Freda, did you tell anyone except Mr Hornsby and I where Molly hid the money?"

"No, missus, I never told a soul!"

"And where was it?"

"It was under her mattress, missus."

Gladys had her proof. James wasted no time and delivered Rex to the authorities that afternoon. A few days later, Abdul, the gardener's eighteen-year-old nephew, was hired as the second footman.

For a while, Jenkins was short with Gladys for not confiding in him as soon as she found out his footman was molesting one of her chambermaids, but when she assured him she would never do such a thing again, he forgave her.

One evening after she had played and sung for James, Gladys mentioned that she enjoyed theatre, having been introduced to it by a very good friend she once knew. James was delighted to learn of something else they had in common. There were many socialites

who wouldn't enter a theatre because the Queen had let it be known that she thought thespians a sordid lot. James, on the other hand, enjoyed the plays the students put on in college and even took part in a few. Occasionally, a troupe of players or a single actor would come to Sandwich and perform in the local theatre, and, now knowing how Gladys felt, he began inviting her to accompany him whenever there was an evening performance.

At first, there was a great deal of speculation among the townspeople over the identity of James's beautiful companion, but when it became known she was his housekeeper, they were appalled. That a man of James's social standing would openly socialize with a mere servant was scandalous, and it managed to keep the tongues of the local gossips wagging for over a month.

Even the local peasants disapproved, and for a time, heads turned, faces scowled, and whispers hissed whenever they were seen together. James seemed oblivious to it all, but Gladys was aware that she was being labelled as a mistress, or worse, a whore. Nevertheless, she enjoyed going to the theatre so much that she finally decided to ignore the gossip, and like she had done when she became engaged to Tom, she held her head high wherever she went. It seemed to help, and after a time, some of the scowls were replaced with smiles.

James was fond of George Gordon Byron's poems, and one of his favourites was "The Prisoner of Chillon." When he heard that a young, local actor by the name of Lloyd Sylvester was doing a recitation of the poem, he invited Gladys to go with him. The only other person she had ever seen monopolize the stage was the popular writer Charles Dickens when he was staying in Dover, and she was certain that no one could compare with him. However, she was in for a pleasant surprise.

As they entered the theatre, they could see the stage was set with seven pillars evenly placed in a half circle where a man with long, grey, straggly hair and a beard was seated on the floor. He was leaning against one of the pillars with his back bent and his head down. A heavy chain attached to one of the pillars was shackled to his wrist. There were chains attached to two more pillars as well, but they lay open and empty.

As soon as the theatre seats were full, the candles were extinguished. Except for the dimly lit stage, there was total darkness. His chain rattled as the old man rose slowly. His back was so bent that his hands almost touched the floor. He leaned against the pillar for support. Then, with eyes almost hidden by grey, bushy brows, he looked out at the darkness and began:

> "My hair is grey, but not in years,
> Nor grew it white
> In a single night,
> As men's have grown from sudden fears:
> My limbs are bow'd, though not with toil,
> But rusted with a vile repose,
> For they have been a dungeon's spoil,
> And mine has been the fate of those
> To whom the goodly earth and air
> Are bann'd, and barr'd—forbidden fare;"

As he recited, his words transformed the stage into a dungeon for all those in the audience. Their imaginations supplied the dank smell of moist earth and mould. A small ray of light shone on the stage as he continued:

> "There are seven pillars of Gothic mould,
> In Chillon's dungeons deep and old,
> A sunbeam which hath lost its way,
> And through the crevice and the cleft
> Of the thick wall is fallen and left;
> Creeping o'er the floor so damp,
> Like a marsh's meteor lamp:
> And each pillar there is a ring,
> And each ring there is a chain."

Although the poem consisted of three hundred and ninety-two lines, the audience was sorry when he lifted up his arm and recited the last eighteen of them as the chain left his wrist and dropped noisily to the floor.

> "And thus when they appear'd at last,
> And all my bonds aside were cast,
> These heavy walls to me had grown

A hermitage—and all my own!
And half I felt as they were come
To tear me from a second home:
With spiders I had friendship made
And watch'd them in their sullen trade,
Had seen the mice by moonlight play,
And why should I feel less than they?
We were all inmates of one place,
And I, the monarch of each race,
Had power to kill—yet, strange to tell!
In quiet we had learn'd to dwell;
My very chains and I grew friends,
So much a long communion tends
To make us what we are:—even
Regain'd my freedom with a sigh."

Deservedly, the audience's applause was followed by a standing ovation. James insisted on waiting for the crowd to disperse before leading Gladys to meet the young actor. Surprised, Gladys noted that he looked nothing like the old man they had watched on the stage without his beard and long wig.

On their way home, James and Gladys talked about the poem.

"I think the last verse was the most poignant," Gladys said.

"Yes, from a romantic point of view, but realistically, I don't think one could live in such conditions without going mad."

"Oh, you are wrong there," Gladys blurted out.

"Now how would you know? I don't imagine you have spent much time in a dungeon!" he said, laughing.

"No, but I have met people who have lived in the ghettos where life can be just as horrible, and yet, like the poem, there is always something they miss when they leave."

Not wanting to continue on with the subject in fear of spoiling the evening, she added, "I cannot believe anyone could memorize all those lines, except Mr Dickens, of course. But it must be easier for him because he wrote the words himself."

James laughed and answered, "Yes, young Sylvester did very well, and I am sure no one else in the audience noticed that he left out two lines."

"He did?"

"I'm afraid so. He said 'There are seven pillars of Gothic mould, in Chillon's dungeons deep and old,' then he left out the next two lines, 'There are seven columns, massy and grey, dim with a dull imprison'd ray,' but his presentation was so brilliant, I forgave him."

"How on earth did you know those two lines were missing?"

"Well, you see, I happened to win an award at school for reciting the same poem. Of course, my recital was not as eloquent as young Sylvester's, and most of the class fell asleep before I finished, but I won an award and was quite proud of it."

"And so you should have been."

During the first two years Gladys lived at Four Oaks, James had never invited guests to the house. In some respects, this was disappointing. She recalled the wonderful times she'd had when she was a guest at Sorenson Manor. However, now that her status was that of a servant, she knew she wouldn't be allowed to join the guests anyway. Still, she reasoned, it might be fun to oversee such an occasion. She also wondered why James hadn't any friends, but was soon to find out.

James had had many business associates, but only one close friend other than his halfbrother, Keith. Sadly, that friend had died in London of a ruptured spleen the same year Keith was killed in India. Those two tragedies left him apprehensive about forming another close relationship until Percy Hudson, one of his corporate lawyers and the man who had told about him about the vacant flat in London, bought a flat in Sandwich.

Not long after moving into the small apartment he had purchased, Percy joined James's cricket team and club. The two men soon realized that they had a lot more in common than just the business. Both were well educated, spoke softly but precisely, were fastidious in their dress and their being, enjoyed playing cricket, and were avid readers.

James hadn't mentioned to Gladys that he had made a friend, so it came as a surprise to her and all the staff when he informed Freda that he had invited a guest for dinner the following evening. Jenkins, Freda, and Gladys spent the rest of that day guessing whether the guest would be a lady or a gentleman.

Just in case it happened to be a lady, Jenkins set the table with the finest china and cutlery, and Gladys made a beautiful arrangement of flowers for the centrepiece. Freda outdid herself, preparing a variety of meat and vegetable dishes along with a blackberry pie.

All were waiting anxiously for the mystery guest to arrive the next evening, and Jenkins, after one quick glance at the table to make sure he had it set just right, stationed himself by the door.

When Percy arrived, Jenkins took his overcoat and hat and showed him into the study where James was waiting to greet him. After pouring them both a drink, Jenkins hurried to the kitchen to report that the guest was a well-dressed gentleman who appeared to be in his mid-thirties.

After they had finished their dinner, Percy asked James to convey his compliments to the cook, since he had never eaten a more satisfying meal.

"You may tell her yourself," James responded. "Ask Freda to join us, Jenkins," he instructed.

Jenkins was just about to leave when James said to send Gladys in as well.

Freda blushed when Percy took her hand and kissed it before he complimented her.

Gladys felt awkward and embarrassed as she stood and waited to be introduced, but her discomfort didn't show. As soon as Percy saw her, he could see that James had not exaggerated when he said how pretty she was. Although she was dressed plainly, she didn't resemble any housekeepers he had ever seen. He also thought she had a lovely, warm smile, and it only took a few seconds to decide he liked her.

"James has told me about the difference you have made to his home, and by the look of this room, I should say he is a most fortunate man indeed. He also told me how beautifully you play and sing. Perhaps you will be so kind as to grace us with a tune before I take my leave?" he asked.

"I would be pleased to do so," Gladys said.

The two men retired to the library to talk about books and enjoy a sherry.

The rest of the staff was in the kitchen waiting for Freda and Gladys to tell them about the first guest any of them, except for Jenkins and Freda, had ever seen at Four Oaks.

Freda was the first to give her opinion, "He knows how to spread the honey, that one. But I can't say I minded! What do you think, missus?"

"Well, it is a bit soon to tell, but he does seem very nice. He is very good-looking and has nice thick hair and neatly trimmed mutton chops. I am not usually fond of mutton chops, but they suit his face. He also has a nice build, and, I would guess by the look of his clothes, he is a man of means."

Jenkins walked in and overheard her, and added, "I think you are right, Mrs Pickwick; he was wearing an expensive silk top hat and a fine, double-caped wool coat when he arrived. The coat is lined with red satin, and I must say that I would fancy a pair of boots like the ones he is wearing. They look to be made of the softest leather I have ever seen."

"What else was he wearin', missus?" said little Inis, her eyes wide with excitement.

"Well, he had on a fine linen shirt with ruffles at the neck, and sleeves with ruffled cuffs, and a beautifully embroidered silk vest under his tailcoat."

"Well, missus, if you're goin' to play and sing for such a dandy, you'd best get yourself up them stairs and put on a fancier frock," Freda said and gave Gladys a shove in the right direction.

Dolly followed her mother up the stairs, then sat on her bed and watched as she got dressed. "May I come and hear you play, Mother?"

"Not this time, darling, but perhaps if he comes again I shall ask James if you can join us."

Gladys had already begun to play when James and Percy came into the parlour. The difference in her appearance didn't go unnoticed. Percy leaned over and whispered in James's ear, "She is beautiful!"

Gladys sang a few solos before insisting they join her in singing the lively song, "Coming through the Rye." James had a pleasing
tenor voice, but Percy couldn't keep a tune. Fortunately, he didn't realize it and sang with such enthusiasm, it added a pleasant essence to
all the songs they sang during the remainder of the evening.

As he was leaving, Percy expressed how much he had enjoyed the
evening with the hopes of being invited back. James had also enjoyed
Percy's company and from that time on, Percy became a frequent
guest.

Gladys was delighted that they often invited her to join them.
Some evenings, Dolly got her wish and was also allowed to join in
with the singing for an hour before her bedtime.

As time went by, James was tempted to ask Gladys to join him
and Percy at the dinner table, but he knew such an arrangement
would be inappropriate. Nonetheless, she was invited to ride with
them whenever she had the time, and before long, they became such
good friends that Gladys couldn't help but compare their threesome
to the one she had shared with Tom and Keith. As flattering as the
thought was, she hoped it didn't end in having two men fighting over
her affections again.

Chapter Eight

The news that a handsome, middle-aged bachelor had moved into town soon spread, and Percy began receiving invitations from lonesome widows and hopeful spinsters. Since he enjoyed being a bachelor, he complained to James, who assured him that in due time, the invitations would subside, especially if he persistently declined. He also added that he had suffered with the same problem shortly after his wife passed away. His constant refusals soon convinced the ladies that he was determined to be faithful to his wife even after her demise, and from then on, he was looked upon with admiration and respect.

In fact, some of the ladies, especially the spinsters, romanticized over his reclusiveness, and he was often the topic of conversation whenever they were in the mood to share their most intimate thoughts. Some even boasted of having affairs with him in their dreams. They would have been disappointed had they known that James had always been a recluse and his aloofness toward them had nothing to do with a broken heart.

Percy took James's advice and, before long, the invitations became fewer and fewer, until they finally ceased. Although he was happy to be free of being toadied to by doting parents with hopes of acquiring a son-in-law, Percy had an outgoing nature and made friends easily. Two of his newfound friends were Bob and Tina Rudyard, who enjoyed card games. Because most of the games they enjoyed required four players, Tina often invited her widowed sister, Mary Baker, as a partner for Percy.

Mary, an intelligent woman in her late thirties, was tall and had the poise of a true aristocrat. She wore her ebony hair pulled back and fastened in a chignon instead of ringlets—a style too severe to suit most women, but, on her, it added elegance. She had flawless pale skin. In stark contrast, her red lips and striking black eyes were like magnets that drew the attention and admiration of both sexes.

The four often played whist or euchre, and, although Percy enjoyed the games, he still preferred to spend his evenings in the company of James and Gladys.

One day, he asked James if he could bring his three friends for a sing-along some evening. James would have refused, but, not wanting to jeopardize his friendship with Percy, he agreed. Unfortunately, he forgot to tell Gladys, and the evening the guests were expected, she had decided to take a stroll after dinner and didn't return until an hour after they had arrived. Freda was waiting for her when she came in the back door. "Oh, missus, he hasn't half tried to find you."

"Who, Freda?"

"Sir! He's been in my kitchen three times askin' for you."

"Well, I am here now. Where is he?"

"He's in the parlour, missus, and there's others there too."

"Others?" Gladys was beginning to be alarmed until Freda put her mind at ease.

"They're friends of Mr Percy's, missus."

Before Gladys could ask any more questions, James appeared, "Well it is about time you showed up," he said accusingly.

When Gladys tried to explain where she had been, he took hold of her arm and started leading her to the parlour.

"Can I at least take off my coat?" she asked as she pulled away from his grasp.

"Your coat? Oh yes, your coat. Yes, yes, take off your coat and your bonnet too, but do hurry. We have been waiting for you for an hour." Gladys hung her things on a clotheshorse before allowing him to usher her into the room.

"Ah, here is our girl now!" Percy announced as he jumped up from his chair. He then introduced her to the three guests without mentioning she was James's housekeeper, which did little to ease her discomfort due to the inequality between her attire and that of the other two women.

When James asked her to play and lead them in a sing-along, she felt obliged to comply, although she felt the request unfair.

They all joined her around the piano. After a few songs, she began to enjoy herself. They laughed and sang for almost two hours before Freda brought in a tray of hot chocolate and biscuits. As the rest sat down to their refreshments, Gladys slipped out the door and was on her way to her apartment when Percy ran after her and caught her by the hand.

"And just where do you think you are going?" he demanded. Gladys said she was going to retire, but he would have none of it and practically pushed her back into the parlour. "Now you seat yourself down here and drink your chocolate," he insisted as he sat her in a chair beside Mary.

Mary smiled at Gladys and said, "Yes, Gladys, you deserve this more than the rest of us." Gladys was impressed with Mary's appearance and felt dowdy in comparison. Although all three guests were exceedingly polite and offered flattering remarks about her musical talents, she was certain they were just being condescending.

After the guests had left, Gladys was obviously annoyed as she confronted James and said, "Sir, I realize I am a servant here, but I do not recall being informed that playing the piano would be one of my duties."

James was taken aback. This was a different side to Gladys than he had ever seen, and he felt both chastised and annoyed. His answer was as curt as her statement. "Yes, Mrs Pickwick, you are correct. I am sorry if I have infringed on your time and you may be assured it shall not happen again." Head high, he turned to leave, but Gladys grabbed his arm.

"Wait, sir, I have not finished what I wanted to say."

"Very well, say it and be done!"

"I only want to have a little notice if you wish me to entertain, sir. You see, I may be a servant, but I am also a woman. And, as a woman, I should like to have the chance to dress accordingly for special occasions. From now on, sir, if you would be kind enough to let me know when you are expecting guests and when you wish me to play the piano, I shall be pleased to do so."

Relieved, James laughed and said, "Forgive me, Gladys. I can see how thoughtless that was of me. It shan't happen again. And, Gladys, thank you for playing tonight. It was brilliant."

One day, James announced that his Aunt Jean, his father's youngest sister and James's only living aunt, was coming for a visit. He asked Gladys to see that one of the guest rooms would be ready for her. He also warned Gladys not to expect his aunt to be an agreeable visitor, adding that even though the woman was in her eighties, she could be quite formidable whenever things didn't meet her approval.

Gladys assured him that she and the rest of the staff would be on their best behaviour. She was looking forward to having a guest in the house until she told Freda.

Freda, who had met the woman before, moaned, then she exclaimed, "Oh, no!"

The day of Aunt Jean's arrival, Gladys had everything ready. Freda had spent the morning baking fresh bread, pies, and cakes. The tantalizing scents still lingered in the air, but the old lady didn't seem to notice, or, if she did, she never acknowledged it.

As soon as James brought her into the parlour, and before she took off her coat, she began her inspection. James stood silently by, waiting to hear her approval. Finally, after running a gloved finger over most of the furniture and not finding any dust, she demanded, "What happened to that old housekeeper of yours?"

"The poor old soul fell and broke her hip."

"Good!"

"Really, Aunt Jean!"

"I suppose that did sound a bit harsh, but if the old girl hadn't broken a hip, I think you would have had to call in an exterminator by now. The place was in such a state that I was thinking of finding lodging at the nearest inn. Your new housekeeper is obviously far more efficient at her job."

"Yes, she is, extremely so. I shall send for her, Auntie. I am sure she shall want to meet you and help you get settled in your room." After noticing the improvement in the cleanliness of the parlour, Jean envisioned the person responsible to have a stalwart build and a countenance that portrayed authority. Therefore, when Gladys entered smiling amiably and James introduced her as the housekeeper, Jean was shocked.

Gladys was about to reach out her hand, but something told her to wait and see if Jean offered hers first. When she didn't, Gladys said, "I am pleased to meet you, mum. I have your room ready. Perhaps you would like me to help you get settled now and bring you some tea. You must be ready for some refreshments after your journey. Or would you prefer to have it down here in the parlour?"

"I prefer to go up now, if you don't mind," Jean answered, then she wondered why on earth she had added the "if you don't mind." The girl was a mere servant, even if she didn't look like one.

Once they were in the guest room, Gladys rang for two of the girls, having left instructions that if the guest room bell rang they were to bring up a jug of hot water and a tray with tea and biscuits.

As she waited to take the aunt's coat and bonnet, Gladys had time to study the woman, who was busy assessing her accommodation. She was a petite lady but made use of what height she had by standing tall. She might have had nice facial features if she had a more pleasant personality. The suit she wore was clean but outdated and a little threadbare. She wore no jewellery, and her boots, although well-polished, were far from new. The longer Gladys studied her, the more she began to think the woman might feel more miserable than cranky and was surprised at the empathy she felt toward her. Then, when Jean finally took off her bonnet and handed it to Gladys to hang up, Gladys understood why.

The poor woman's hair was inundated with nits. Gladys didn't know what to do. She was afraid she might lose her job if she said anything, but if she didn't, the lice were liable to spread throughout the manor. She also felt so sorry for the poor old lady that she decided she had no choice but to do what she could for her.

She waited until the girls had delivered the hot water and tea and had departed before asking Jean, "Mum, do you have a lady's maid at home?"

Jean snapped back, "I do not know what concern that is of yours, but no, I do not require anyone to tend to my needs. I manage with very little staff, and I am proud of it. James shall never say that I squandered his inheritance on unnecessary frivolities. Although by the look of this home, he must employ a good many servants."

"He is fortunate to have a very capable staff, mum. They are all good workers."

"I can see that, but it must cost a pretty penny. Now, young lady, why did you want to know if I have a lady's maid? You are not looking for another position, are you?"

"Oh no, mum, I am quite content with my job here. It is just that, and please forgive me for what I am about to say, mum, but I could not help but notice that you suffer with head lice."

Jean gasped, then saying each word slowly and with added emphasis, she replied, "What did you say?"

"I am really sorry, mum, but I thought I might be of assistance."

"I have never heard such utter nonsense. How dare you! Get out of my room. Go!"

For a second Gladys felt like telling the woman that she was welcome to keep her nits and any other bugs she brought with her, but she knew the reason Jean was so upset was because of her pride. "Please, mum, just listen to me for one moment. Please."

When Jean didn't answer, Gladys took it as a good sign and continued, "You see, I have a very good friend, Lady Sorenson, whose estate is just outside of Dover, and she had the same problem. She thought they must have come from one of the wigs her hairdresser looked after. Lady Sorenson has a husband and three young children, and she was afraid they might get them too."

Impressed by the title "Lady," Jean swallowed her pride and asked, "What did the lady do?"

"Fortunately, there were some Romani camped nearby, and she had heard that they sold remedies for almost every ailment a person could have. Being a little too embarrassed to go to her doctor, she sent one of her maids to find out if they had something she could use. Luckily, they did, so she bought enough of the remedy for the whole family and even gave me some in case my daughter, Dolly, who often played with her children, got them. Dolly didn't, so I still have the remedy and would be more than happy to treat your hair with it. No one else need ever know. We shall say you are too tired to leave your room tonight except for a good wash in the bathtub off the downstairs kitchen, and then tomorrow you can say you never had time to wash your hair before you left home and wanted me to do it."

"How do I know you are telling the truth? Perhaps I do not have them at all."

"Has your head been very itchy lately?"

Jean knew Gladys was telling the truth. The constant itchiness had been driving her mad. "Very well, but if this remedy you have does any damage to my hair or scalp, I shall see to it that you are severely punished, as well as discharged."

After a week, Gladys assured Jean she was completely rid of the vermin, but instead of being grateful, Jean, who had never been so humiliated in her life, chose to forget it ever happened.

She had had a maid to look after her personal needs most of her life, but when that woman retired due to ill health, Jean had decided she could look after her own needs. Besides, age had begun to cause Jean a few bodily malfunctions, and she had no intention of allowing a stranger to witness her defects. She knew she owed Gladys a word of gratitude, but she couldn't bring herself to say thank you.

Gladys, aware of how embarrassed Jean felt every time they were in the same room, didn't resent her cool manner and managed to avoid her whenever possible. At first, James had been worried when his aunt kept to her room, but now that she was taking her meals with him, he did his best to make her feel at home. He told her about all the wonderful changes Gladys had made to the house since she began working for him. Jean, not wanting to hear any more about the housekeeper's virtues, tried to change the subject, but he kept on until she began to suspect that he was entirely too fond of the woman.

One afternoon, Gladys came into the parlour where James and his aunt were sitting to ask if she might go to town with Jenkins in the morning, as she needed some thread.

"Of course, Gladys," he replied. Then addressing his aunt, he added, "Gladys has a marvellous machine that sews for her. You must see it in action. Could you give Auntie a demonstration, Gladys?"

Before Gladys could reply, Jean offered a dismissive, "Another time, perhaps. I am sure she is far too busy."

"It will not take much time, Auntie, and I am sure Gladys can spare a moment for us," James insisted.

"Certainly, sir," Gladys answered.

Having no excuse, Jean had no choice but to follow Gladys to her suite. Gladys sat down at the sewing machine and sewed a hem on a pinafore she was making. Jean couldn't help but be impressed and, surprisingly, she smiled and said, "That is simply marvellous! How clever you are to be able to run such a contraption."

"Anyone can do it. You just turn this handle and guide the cloth through like this. Would you like to try it?"

Jean sat down and Gladys helped her until she was able to do it on her own. Her eyes were sparkling when she finished sewing the hem on a pretty little handkerchief. It was the first time she could remember doing something so practical, and the satisfying feeling it gave her was like a tonic.

"It is not nearly as tidy a job as you would have done," she said, smiling, "but perhaps if I were to practice a little longer, I could do better."

"I am sure you could. You know, mum, I had a dear aunt who was a seamstress, and I have often thought how wonderful it would have been if she had owned one of these machines. She made beautiful gowns and suits for some of the wealthiest women in Dover and did them all by hand. When she passed away, I inherited all the items she had in her shop. There was one dress amongst her things that she had made for someone, but since I had no idea for whom it was intended, I could not give it to the lady. I still have it and would like to show it to you—I think you will appreciate her work. It is far too small for me, but I think it would look lovely on you."

Before Jean could object, Gladys went into a trunk and brought out the dress. She had forgotten about the dress until she told Jean about Millie. It was made with a rich purple material and trimmed with black satin collar and cuffs.

"Do you like it, mum?"

"It is quite lovely! How much did your aunt charge for a nice frock like this?"

"I really don't know, but I think Auntie would be pleased if you were to have it—you have such a nice figure."

Jean hadn't received a compliment for such a long time that she had forgotten how to respond, and blushing, she tried her best to appear unruffled when she answered.

"I shall take it to my room and try it on, but I doubt if it will fit. However, if it does, I shall not accept it unless I pay for it."

Rather than argue, Gladys agreed, and Jean left.

That evening Percy, Mary, and the Rudyards came to call and when James told his aunt that Gladys would join them in the parlour, Jean didn't object. She wore Millie's dress, and when James remarked how lovely she looked, she glanced over at Gladys, smiled, and said, "You may thank Gladys for that, James."

The evening went very well. Jean was impressed with Gladys's piano playing and her singing, but it was Mary who captured her attention. Unused to late nights, Jean asked to be excused before the guests were ready to leave, and Gladys offered to go with her to see she was settled for the night. Jean never complained when Gladys helped her undress and put on her nightgown. She didn't even object when Gladys changed the cloth padding Jean wore pinned to her underpinnings. Then, as Gladys brushed and braided Jean's hair, the elderly lady realized how much she missed her old maid.

When she was settled in bed, Gladys said goodnight and turned to leave, but Jean asked her to stay and talk for a few minutes. "Gladys, I feel I should apologize for not thanking you for all you have done for me since I arrived." It had been the most enjoyable evening Jean had spent in years, and she knew it was because of James's housekeeper.

"I am glad to have been of service, mum," Gladys said and once again prepared to leave, but Jean reached out and took hold of her dress.

"I think James's friends are excellent company, and I was especially taken with that young widow, Mary. James has been a bachelor far too long, and I think she would make the perfect wife for him. She comes from a good family and I could tell that she is fond of him. What do you think?" Gladys had to agree, although for some reason she couldn't understand, she knew it would never happen.

"You must do all you can to see that the two of them are left alone now and again, Gladys," Jean insisted, fully intent on seeing Mary as mistress of Four Oaks.

By the time Gladys returned to the parlour, the guests had left.

Jean left the following week. She either forgot to pay for Millie's dress or she had never intended to. The caring attention she received from Gladys convinced her to hire another lady's maid as soon as she arrived home. Jean came to visit quite often after that, and when she did, she always brought her maid with her.

For quite some time, Jean did her best to talk James into marrying Mary, but when he became obviously annoyed with her prodding, she stopped bothering him.

Chapter Nine

Occasionally, Percy brought his best friend, Helmut Goldberg, to Four Oaks. Helmut was a London doctor who visited Percy once every two months, usually staying for a week. Percy had warned James and Gladys that Helmut was quite eccentric, despite being considered one of the most respected doctors in London. He also explained, with obvious pride, that Helmut was a close associate of Dr John Snow.

James was impressed, but it was clear by the blank look on Gladys's face that she had no idea who John Snow was, so Percy explained.

"Dr Snow is a very well-known British physician. He was one of the first to study and calculate dosages for the use of ether and chloroform as a surgical anaesthesia. In fact, Gladys, he administered chloroform to the Queen when she gave birth to her eighth child earlier this year."

What he didn't mention was that Helmut was suffering with a debilitating and incurable illness. His bimonthly visits with Percy in the clean salt air of Sandwich were all that was keeping him alive, as he worked mostly in London's slum districts.

When Gladys and James met the doctor, they could see that Percy hadn't exaggerated when he warned them of his eccentricities.

He was unkempt in his person and attire and had a sickly, sallow complexion. He spoke, or mumbled, with a German-Jewish accent that was, at times, incomprehensible.

In spite of Helmut's peculiarities, one couldn't help but feel honoured to be in his presence. Perhaps it had something to do with his shabbiness, a look often associated with genius, or it may have been because his eyes portrayed a great deal of intelligence and perception. Whatever it was, one felt compelled to treat him with respect.

It was difficult to understand how Helmut and Percy had become such good friends since Percy, like James, was meticulous in every respect. Helmut, on the other hand, dropped his coat, hat, and everything else he might shed on the handiest piece of furniture, and a morsel of his latest meal could usually be found on his vest, pants, or jacket. He seldom took note of the weather and would go out in a rainstorm without a hat or overcoat, or wear heavy-knit sweaters in the middle of summer.

Extremely absentminded, he had a habit of drifting off into a world of his own, which could be very annoying during a card game or in the middle of a lively debate.

However, each day he spent with Percy during his weekly visits resulted in a noticeable improvement in his appearance, and by the time he was ready to return to London, his hair would be neatly trimmed and his clothes cleaned and pressed. It was clear that Percy was extremely fond of the doctor and took it upon himself to tidy the poor man before allowing him to leave. If Helmut didn't come to Sandwich for his usual visit, Percy went to visit him. Sometimes James would join them in London for a night at the theatre.

James had as much enjoyment telling Gladys about the performances that he saw as he did attending them, and she loved listening to every little detail. He had also begun to relax more in the company of Percy and his friends when they came to Four Oaks. Gladys was flattered that both he and Percy insisted that she be included in most of their activities.

Percy, Bob, Tina, and Mary were so impressed with James and Gladys's velocipedes that they asked James to visit Willard's factory when he next went to Dover on business and order them each one. Willard's machines were a favourite with so many who had visited the exhibition that he was swamped with orders from all over the world, thus it took a few months before the ones James ordered were delivered.

Once they came, they were soon put to good use. Unfortunately, Helmut was only able to ride a short distance before tiring, so they only went riding when he was in London.

Once in a while, if they weren't going too far, Dolly was invited along, and when the seven of them all rode down the road behind one another, it made quite a spectacle. People came out of their houses and stores to call out and wave as they went by. Most had never seen or heard of such a machine. Each time they went for a ride, it caused as much excitement as a parade.

Because it was necessary to plan their activities around the work schedules of Percy and Gladys, they didn't have as much time together as they would have liked. When they did get together, they could always find something interesting to do such as riding their velocipedes, horseback riding, picnicking, playing croquet, cards, charades, board games, or singing songs.

Gladys enjoyed herself, except when Tina and Mary chatted away about the tea parties and shopping trips they had taken, unintentionally ignoring Gladys. Feelings of resentment and envy often overtook her, even though she realized she should be grateful that they considered her a friend instead of a servant. Being a housekeeper most of the time, and only a socialite whenever James decided to include her, made Gladys feel like one of James's possessions that he could use for whatever purpose he desired.

If it wasn't for the incident with old Gaylord, Gladys would have stood up to her father-in-law's adopted son, Peter, and taken her case to court. She had no doubt she would have won with such a clever man to plead her case as Andrew's friend and lawyer, Randolph Mansfield, but since she did not know how much Peter's detective had found out about her past, she was afraid to take the chance.

When she first arrived at Four Oaks, she was destitute and felt grateful to be given a job as well as a pleasant place for her and Dolly to live, but now that she was once more keeping company with aristocrats, the thought of what she had lost often plagued her.

She was also a little jealous of Mary, feeling certain that both James and Percy were enamoured with her. Not that she blamed them. Aunt Jean was right; the woman was not only beautiful but wealthy as well. She would be an asset to any man.

Gladys had many good traits to her character, but humbleness wasn't one of them, and it irked her that Mary and Tina were free to voice an opinion without having to worry about the consequences. Many times, she was tempted to use her father's words and say, "Yes, sir, no, sir, kiss me arse, sir!" Oddly enough, this thought usually cheered her up, perhaps because it brought back memories of Old Nichol and reminded her that things could be a lot worse.

Percy didn't have to tell James and Gladys that Helmut's health was failing; they could see his decline for themselves. During the next six months, he became gradually weaker until he became too sick to work or travel alone.

Percy knew the doctor hadn't long to live, so he went to London and insisted on bringing him back to spend his last days in Sandwich. Because he had such a small house and retained no live-in servants, Percy didn't object when James suggested Helmut move into Four Oaks where he would have someone to look after him while Percy was working.

When James told Gladys that Helmut would be moving in, he asked her if she would need extra help. Gladys suggested that it would be helpful if they could hire a woman experienced in looking after invalids so Helmut could have the best of care. James agreed, and he even allotted the woman a comfortable room in the west wing, so she would be close to her patient.

When he was having a good day, Helmut would spend it inquiring about everyone's health, and if they had an ailment, he offered

advice.

One day, Gladys went into his room and was shocked to find Dolly sitting by his bedside reading "Aladdin's Wonderful Lamp" aloud from the book *One Thousand and One Nights*. The doctor had become bedridden and unable to control his bowels, making it almost impossible to keep the room smelling fresh. His beautiful eyes were now hazy and sunken, and his cheek bones protruded, but if Dolly was appalled or sickened by his appearance or the stench of his room, she never showed it.

Thinking Dolly might be a nuisance, Gladys began to scold her, but Helmut frowned and waved his hand at her saying, "*Veschwenden sie!*" Gladys didn't understand his words but understood their meaning, and she left the room.

From then on, except for the times when his pain required double doses of laudanum, Dolly spent an hour every day visiting and reading to her friend. The sound of her young voice took the doctor back to his own childhood. When he closed his eyes and listened to her read, the terrible sights of the poor sick souls who lived in the slums slowly faded, along with the nagging urgency to return to do what little he could for them.

Dolly was also a good listener, and Helmut told her how he had been left at an orphanage when he was a baby in Germany and that he never knew his parents. There was a doctor who the proprietor of the orphanage summoned whenever an orphan became seriously ill. Because he was a compassionate man, the doctor often took the sick children home where his benign wife helped nurse them to recovery.

Helmut, a delicate child, was taken home with the doctor so often due to various ailments that finally the good man announced, "I don't think there's any sense taking you back to the orphanage, my little friend, since I will just be bringing you back again in a week or so. We may as well adopt you and be done with it."

He was then given the name of Helmut Goldberg—a name he was proud of for the rest of his life. He worshipped the doctor and his wife to such an extent that he made up his mind to study diligently and follow in his adoptive father's footsteps.

He studied in England, where his dedication to the profession soon earned him recognition among his peers. When he graduated with honours, he could have become a doctor to the rich and famous but chose instead to start a clinic in one of the slum districts of London.

"You know, my little *engel*," he told Dolly one day, "there are so many things we take for granted, things like our very names. I never had one until I was six years old and the Goldbergs adopted me. I remember how proud I was the first time someone asked me what my name was. I stood tall, stuck out my chest, and I said, 'I am Helmut Goldberg!' That was the happiest day of my life."

Dolly would remember his words for the rest of her life, and whenever someone asked for her name, she would stand a little taller as she answered, "My name is Dolly Pickwick."

Sadly, a few weeks before Christmas, Dolly's visits came to an end when Helmut's condition worsened and he was seldom conscious. Percy took time away from work and stayed at Four Oaks to be with his friend until the end. Although Percy insisted they continue with their holiday preparations, a poignant ambience hung over the manor.

The Rudyards and Mary often came to show their support, and their presence was always appreciated.

Now that the west wing of the mansion was opened, Gladys asked James if they could have a Christmas tree, and he said he would take care of it. His mother-in-law was Jewish, so after her Christian husband passed away, she reverted back to her original faith and refused to celebrate Christmas. Despite the old lady's addiction to gin, James was very fond of her, and out of respect, he hadn't celebrated the holiday either.

Now he was almost as excited about Christmas and the decorations as Gladys and Dolly. He had Ruby hitch a wagon to one of his horses, and they set off to find a suitable tree to put in the great room.

The tree they cut down was over eight feet tall, and James insisted that no one see it until it was in place and ready to decorate.

When it was ready, he invited Jean, Gladys, Dolly, Jenkins, and Percy in to see if it suited them. As they came in, he watched their faces carefully to see if they approved. He knew they liked it when Percy shouted, "Hooray!" and they all clapped their hands.

James had plenty of decorations, but Dolly asked him if they could use the ones they had brought with them from Dover as well. Gladys, afraid that Dolly was being too forward, suggested they put them on the tree in the servants' hall since they would be having their Christmas with the rest of the staff there.

"I think you should put them on this tree, Dolly, seeing as it was your mother who started all this," James said as he motioned toward the tree with his hand. "I will expect you both to join us here on Christmas Eve."

"Oh, yes, pray do! It shall make our Christmas far more festive," Jean exclaimed.

Helmut rallied before Christmas but was too weak to come down to the tree on Christmas Eve, so Gladys and Dolly took his presents up to him. Gladys had knit him a pair of long woollen stockings to keep his legs and feet warm, and Dolly had painted him a picture of the decorated Christmas tree. He could only manage a weak smile, but they could tell he was pleased.

Dolly had also painted a picture of daffodils for James because she had heard him say how much he liked them. She did a painting of one of Freda's apple pies for Percy—his favourite—and a picture of Ruby's cat for Jean. The pictures were all recognizable, if not perfect, and James, Percy, and Jean all declared it was the best work of art they had ever owned.

Gladys made a dress for Dolly and bought her some boots that were both stylish and warm. She knit stockings for James and Percy and bought bloomers—the latest style in ladies' undergarments—for Aunt Jean, who had come to spend Christmas with them. She even bought little gifts for all the girls and Freda.

James had given all the staff bonuses, but wanting to have a spe-

cial gift under the tree for Gladys and Dolly, he had asked Mary to buy them each a gold locket. Gladys and Dolly loved them, as well as the dainty little paintings in miniature frames that Percy gave them.

After all the presents had been opened, James said, "Now that is done, I think we should have some hot drinks and enjoy a carol or two before we go to bed."

Dolly had noticed that there was one little, shiny, black-lacquered box tied with a pretty red ribbon left under the tree so she gave her mother a nudge and pointed to it.

"Oh, look," Gladys said, "there is still one left."

James reached down and picked it up. "Now who do you suppose this is for? Look here, there is a tag tied to the ribbon, but all it says is, 'To *Meines Engel*.' Now I wonder who that could be?" he said, looking puzzled.

No one said anything until finally Dolly could keep quiet no longer and shyly spoke up, "Sir, I think it might be for me."

"For you? Now why on earth would you think that?"

"Because Dr Helmut always calls me *meines engel!* It means, 'my angel.'"

"Yes, but does he call anyone else here by that name as well?" His expression was very serious as he looked around the room. Then, when no one replied, a big smile spread across his face and he added, "Well then, young lady, I guess it must be yours." And he handed her the box.

"It is the most beautiful box I have ever seen," Dolly said with tears in her eyes, knowing it came from her dear friend.

"Why don't you have a look inside?" Percy suggested.

Dolly carefully untied the bow and lifted the lid, but it only contained a single piece of paper. "It is a letter," she said.

"Well, I think you had better read it out loud so we can all hear what it has to say," Gladys suggested. Dolly looked around the room to see if everyone agreed, and they all nodded. She began:

"To Dolly,

> Your company and your recitations have eased my pain and given me much happiness. You are truly an *Engel de Gnade!* Now I want to give you some-

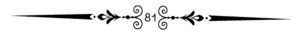

thing in return. You will find it out in the barn.

Your grateful friend,
Helmut

P.S. His name is Aladdin."

They all followed Dolly out to the barn where Ruby, forewarned of their visit, led a handsome black gelding with a white star on his forehead and a red ribbon tied to his halter out to greet them. The horse and Dolly took to each other immediately, and that night she went to bed happier than she had been since leaving Dover. When she said her prayers, she thanked Gamby for the gift as well as Helmut, certain that he had something to do with it.

Chapter Ten

During the next two weeks, Helmut was semi-conscious only a few times, and when he was, he would mumble, almost entirely in German. Then on the fourth of January, 1854, he looked up at Percy, who was sitting at his bedside, and smiled before taking his last breath, leaving Percy with the certainty that his friend was at peace.

Helmut left very little in the way of savings, since the biggest percent of his patients were paupers, but he had owned his home in London, and, according to his will, it was to be sold with the proceeds going to the clinic he had established in the slum district. His remains were laid to rest in London, and his funeral was attended by paupers, well-known philanthropists, clergymen, and physicians. His pallbearers were also an assortment of rich and poor. Helmut chose his friends not by the money in their pockets but the goodness in their hearts. Percy delivered the eulogy.

After Helmut died, Percy spent more time visiting James, and their friendship grew stronger and stronger. Although they still enjoyed the company of Gladys and the rest of their friends, they seemed to take the most pleasure in discussing together different books they had read.

Both men were impressed with Dolly's vocabulary and her love of books, and they suggested some volumes in James's library for her to read. Gladys had also developed a liking for literature, and they saw that she was supplied with books as well.

Each time Gladys finished a book, they would invite her into the library to discuss what she had read. One of the books they gave her to read was a collection of seven chapters about a parish and the characters associated with it, titled, *Sketches by Boz*, written by Charles Dickens. When she had finished the book, and the three of them were in the library enjoying their drinks, James inquired, "Now, Gladys, what do you think about this fellow, Dickens?"

"Well, I lived in Dover when he stayed there for a short time, and I even went to hear him recite. I shall never forget it! He was truly wonderful. So perhaps that is one of the reasons I enjoyed the book so much. I thought each of his character descriptions portrayed a clear enough picture to satisfy my imagination."

"Splendid. Now, which chapter did you like the most?" James asked.

"I think I liked chapter four, 'The Election for Beadle.'"

Percy jumped in, "Ah, yes, that would be my favourite as well. 'He is not one of those fortunate men who, if they were to dive under one side of a barge stark naked, would come up on the other side with a new set of clothes on.'"

Gladys laughed and said, "You didn't finish it. 'A new set of clothes on—and a ticket for soup in the waistcoat pocket.'"

James seemed very impressed and said, "You know, if you like Dickens so much, Percy has saved all his magazine stories from *Oliver Twist* to *The Haunted Man*."

"I shall bring them over the next time I come if you like," Percy offered.

"Please do; I think Dolly would enjoy them as well. You know, her grandfather taught her to read when she was only four."

"Having known the man, I can understand how he would appreciate her astuteness and want to spend time with her," James said.

Percy also shared James and Gladys's love of the theatre, and since both he and James kept flats in London, they were able to take Gladys with them to see the odd performance. James and Percy stayed in one flat and Gladys in the other. Whenever she went with them, she gave Dolly the keys to the pantry and the linens and left her in charge. Although she was only nine, she was tall for her age and seemed much older. She also showed no sign of pomposity, and the rest of the staff never resented her authority.

Not long after Helmut's demise, another outbreak of cholera broke out in the slum districts of London. Percy had to spend quite a bit of his time working in London and was afraid he might carry the disease, so he didn't visit Four Oaks for two months. They all missed his company, but no one as much as James.

By spring, Helmut's friend, Dr Snow, with the help of a Reverend Henry Whitehead, had persuaded the local counsel of a slum area of London that the water from the community pump might be the culprit, and the pump's handle was removed. It was later reported that this ended the outbreak, but it may have already been in decline.

Everyone welcomed Percy back to Sandwich, and life went back to normal.

One day, Percy mentioned that he had read in the paper that there was a troupe of talented actors who were performing Shakespeare's play, *The Tragedy of Othello, The Moor from Venice*, at one of the London theatres, so he had purchased three tickets for the performance. Gladys was thrilled when he said one of the tickets was for her. Then, when James said they might extend their stay in London for a few days, she looked forward to the trip even more. She wanted to buy more sewing material, and she had heard of a place in London where she could buy it for less than it cost in Sandwich.

Unfortunately, a few days before they were to leave, both Percy and James came down with nasty colds and were unable to travel. Percy suggested that Gladys go alone, and, because it wasn't considered proper for a lady to attend the theatre without an escort, he gave

her the name of a couple he knew who would be happy to accompany her as a favour to him. James, on the other hand, was a bit apprehensive because he had given his caretakers a month's leave to visit relatives in Scotland, and Gladys would be alone in the flat.

Nevertheless, he gave in, knowing how much she would enjoy the play. Promising to contact Percy's friends as soon as she arrived, Gladys left for London the day before the performance. The only time she had gone to London alone was to fetch girls from Old Nichol to work for the Watts, and it had left her with bad memories. This time, she knew she wouldn't have to go anywhere near her old home.

Dressed in her finest, Gladys kissed Dolly goodbye and left her standing on the station platform waving, along with Ruby and Blossom, as she boarded the train. Her face was flushed with excitement, and she felt an exhilarating sense of freedom. The glances she received from fellow passengers were unmistakably flattering and gave her a feeling of power. She knew she could be mistaken for the mistress of any mansion, a fact which she enjoyed but did not take advantage of.

When the conductor inquired, "Are you comfortable, milady?" she gave him a weak smile and answered, "Yes, quite," without offering as much as a thank you.

Not long after she arrived at James's flat, she left and took a cab to the address of Percy's friends where she received the news that they were holidaying in Scotland. Although she knew Percy and James would not approve, she decided she would go to the theatre alone. She spent the next day walking about the streets looking in shop windows, but she only bought an assortment of chocolates to take home to Dolly as a reward to show her appreciation for looking after her duties while she was gone.

That evening she dressed with the utmost care and was very pleased with the image she saw in her mirror.

Before entering the theatre, she waited until she saw a well-dressed elderly gentleman who appeared to be alone. Even though she knew she was being irresponsible and foolish, she approached him and asked if he would be so kind as to escort her into the theatre because her friends had fallen ill and she didn't want to waste the tickets. He was so impressed with her appearance that he smiled and said he would be flattered to have such a beautiful lady on his arm. When she handed him the tickets and he saw they were for the first row and far superior to the one he had, he also offered to sit beside her.

Gladys was enjoying the play, but whenever the actor who was portraying Cassio came on stage, she couldn't keep her eyes off him and was having trouble following the story. In the first scene of the fifth act Iago said to Roderigo, "He hath a daily beauty in his life that makes me ugly; and, besides, the Moor may unfold me to him; there stand I in much peril: No, he must die. But so: I hear him coming." Cassio entered and Roderigo continued, "I know his gait, tis he. Villain, thou diest!"

As he drew his sword to strike, Gladys had a sudden realization of who Cassio was. Without thinking, she jumped up and shouted, *"Toughie!"*

Her outburst brought an abrupt halt to the performance, and before she could apologize, two men hurried to her, took hold of her arms, and hastily escorted her from the theatre and into the vestibule. The elderly man who had accompanied her into the theatre sat for a few seconds deciding whether to remain seated and enjoy the rest of the play or to do the honourable thing and follow her to see if he could be of assistance.

His conscience won out and he hastened up the aisle and into the vestibule just in time to witness the men attempting to shove Gladys out the door while threatening to call a constable. Since he was carrying an umbrella, he made good use of it by poking one of the attendants and demanding, "Here, here, now, stop this harassment, do you hear? Surely you can allow the lady to explain."

"But, sir, we cannot allow such behaviour. This is an acclaimed show put on by renowned actors, and we cannot allow her to disrupt the enjoyment of the audience."

"Oh, I agree, my good man, but as you can see for yourself, this young lady doesn't appear to be the sort who would come to the theatre to cause trouble, now does she?" The men looked at Gladys and had to agree. "Now, my dear, perhaps you will explain your injudicious behaviour?"

"I am really very sorry," she replied, "but it is just that I recognized one of the actors. I have not seen him for many years, and I thought I should never see him again. He was like a brother to me, and I did not know it was him until Roderigo was going to hit him with his sword! It was such a shock that I forgot where I was and called out to him." She turned to the two men, "Please, I promise to be quiet if you will only let me go back in."

"We cannot allow that, madam, but if you leave now, we will say no more about it. However, you must leave immediately."

"But, don't you see, I cannot leave without seeing my friend."

"I'm sorry, madam, but that's impossible. Rules are rules, you understand."

"Perhaps I can be of assistance, my dear?" the elderly gentleman declared. "What if you were to leave now while I wait to see the young man as soon as the play is over? I can give him an address where he can get in touch with you. Would that do?"

"Oh, yes! Yes, that would be wonderful. I have the address here in my purse." She took it out and gave it to him.

"And whom shall I say it is from?"

"Tell him it's from Gladys."

The gentleman escorted her outside and since it had begun to rain, held his umbrella over her while he hailed a cab.

As Gladys was being escorted out of the theatre, the actors exited the stage. A few seconds later they came back on and began the fifth act once more. It was all Toughie could do to concentrate on his lines, and he was relieved when the play was over.

"Well, none of us will ever forget our last performance in London, will we, Angelo?" a heavyset, dark-skinned man, whose features were much like those of the young man he was talking to, said jokingly.

"I'm sorry, Uncle Vic, but if that was who I think it was, I had no idea she was still alive, let alone living here in London. I have to find her."

"Why on earth would you do that?" his uncle replied.

"She's not just any old friend, Uncle. She's the girl I told you about. I don't think we could have survived without each other."

"Having seen the hellhole you lived in, I can understand how you feel, but you know we are leaving in two days, so don't make any promises you can't keep."

Before Toughie could reply, there was a knock on the dressing room door. When Angelo opened it, the elderly gentleman handed him the piece of paper Gladys had given him containing the address of James's flat and said, "This is from a lovely young lady by the name of Gladys." Then, after explaining what had happened, he complimented them all on their performances and left.

"I'm going to see her!" Angelo said to his uncle while reaching for his jacket.

"But the hour is late. Tomorrow would be better, don't you think?"

"I can't wait, Uncle. I must go now."

"Beware how you behave, Angelo. You have to think of Rosa, you know."

"Don't worry. I just want to see her once more. I shall be back before morning."

Toughie had given up hope of ever seeing Gladys again, and if she hadn't called out his name he wouldn't have recognized her. She looked more like one of the high-society ladies who often came to see their plays than the Gladys he had known in Old Nichol. However, it had to be her; no one else knew him by that name. He wanted to run after her when she was being escorted out of the theatre, but he had been with the troupe long enough to know that no matter the circumstance, the play must go on.

Now his heart was racing as he flagged down a cab and gave the driver her address. Once seated in the coach, he closed his eyes and took a few deep breaths to calm himself. The thought of seeing Gladys again brought back memories of the days following her disappearance. She had come to his junkyard every day to see what progress he had made on his shed. When two days went by without a seeing her, he thought she might be ill, so he went to her house, but neither she nor her parents were there.

Toughie had a foreboding feeling of hopelessness as he went from one drinking establishment to another looking for Tonnie and Bert. When he finally found them, they told him that Gladys had run away from home two nights before, and they had no idea where she went.

Although they shed a few tears, Toughie knew they were lying; Gladys wouldn't have left Old Nichol without telling him first. He suspected foul play but had no proof. Tonnie and Bert had been drinking steadily for two days, and he was almost certain they had acquired the money to buy their booze by selling Gladys to one of the rich reprobates who often visited the slums looking for young girls.

He looked everywhere in Old Nichol for her to no avail. He knew if she had been kidnapped she could be anywhere—even in another country. Therefore, it would have been futile to begin searching outside the ghetto. Although he had worked hard trying to earn enough money to make his shed into a home for Gladys, he didn't have it ready in time to save her, and he blamed himself for her disappearance. He thought he had lost the love of his life forever.

"Here we be, sir," the driver called down from his seat, interrupting Toughie's thoughts. As he got out of the cab, he realized they were in one of the most prestigious neighbourhoods in London. He paid the man but forgot to ask him to wait. He hadn't realized how hard it was raining until the cab had left.

He checked the address Gladys had sent him to confirm he was at the right place. There was no light showing in the building, so he figured she thought he wasn't coming and had gone to bed. He was about to leave but changed his mind and, taking hold of the knocker, he banged it a few times.

When that didn't work, he banged it harder and harder while calling her name until a man wearing a nightcap stuck his head out a window in the building next door and hollered, "What's going on there? Stop that infernal racket." Toughie replied he was looking for a lady named Gladys and was informed in a loud voice that he had better bloody well look for her in the morning. Toughie reasoned that if someone from the next building could hear him, Gladys could too. He only had a quick glance at her in the theatre, but he could tell she was very well off, so he wouldn't blame her if she had changed her mind.

When Gladys arrived back at the flat, she was still in a state of shock. She thought she would never see Toughie again, but there he had been looking even more handsome than she had imagined. She made herself a cup of tea, but when she was carrying it over to the table, the cup slipped out of her hand, fell to the floor, and broke. Until then she hadn't realized she was shaking. After mopping up, she began to worry that the elderly man might not have delivered the note she gave him. She decided if Toughie didn't come, she would return to the theatre in the morning and attempt to find out where the actors stayed when they were in London.

By ten o'clock, she was certain he wasn't coming. Not only was it probably too late, but the weather had worsened and she doubted anyone would go out on such a stormy night if he didn't have to, so she went to bed.

Gladys woke with a start. At first, she thought she had dreamt that Toughie was calling her, but then she heard him again and realized he was outside her door. She jumped out of bed, but the knocking and the shouting had ceased by the time she reached the window overlooking the street. Unable to see directly below the window, she ran down the steps, unlocked the door and, heedless of her scanty attire, stepped out into the pouring rain.

Toughie was just about to turn the corner when he heard her call. He turned, and when he saw her standing there barefoot, dressed in nothing but her nightgown with her hair hanging loose and her face wet with the rain, he knew she hadn't changed. This was the Gladdy he remembered. They ran to each other, and when they met, he swept her up into his arms crying, "Oh my God, it is you, Gladdy. I can't believe it!"

Chapter Eleven

As soon as they were inside the flat and had a lamp going, Gladys realized that she was only wearing a nightdress—a very wet nightdress that clung to her body like a layer of skin. Blushing, she told Toughie to take off his wet coat and hat and put more coal on the fire while she ran upstairs to change. She had brought along another nightdress but not a robe, so she took one out of James's wardrobe. Fortunately, it was generous enough to render her decent.

When she came back downstairs, she had her hair wrapped in a towel and was carrying her wet nightgown. Toughie had a good fire going in the fireplace, and his coat was draped over the back of a chair drying. She pulled another chair up close to the fire and laid her nightdress over it.

For a few seconds, they stood staring at each other without a word. Then he reached out, took the towel from her head, and ordered, "Here, sit down and I'll dry your hair."

He was still looking after her. With Toughie standing beside her and the pungent smell of steam from their wet garments—an odour reminiscent of the ghetto—a sense of nostalgia came over her, and she felt like a girl again. Then Toughie interrupted her thoughts.

"What's this?" he exclaimed.

"What's what?"

"Ha! Methinks there's a little grey in here."

"Give me that!" Gladys said and grabbed the towel from him. "If there's grey there, it's you who's to blame! I've been worried about you for . . . for how many years now?"

"Twelve years, two months, six days, three hours, and let me see . . ." he said as he turned to look at a clock on the wall. "Eight minutes and twenty seconds."

"You just made that up."

He shook his head. "Maybe some of it, Gladdy, but not the years. It has been twelve long years since you left me. Why did you leave me, Gladdy? Why?"

"I had to. Oh, Toughie, there's so much to tell you."

He sat down on the divan and patted a place beside him. "Well then, I guess you better sit here beside me and get on with it."

"Please try not to hate me when you hear what happened, Toughie."

"I could never hate you, Gladdy."

"I know how hard you worked trying to make a place for us to stay so we could get married, but Ma and Da were so sick with drink they couldn't push the cart anymore, and we needed money to buy food and pay our rent. Ma said that there was a man who would pay us enough money to fix up two places for us all on your lot and you could have all our junk to go with yours. She said he only wanted to spend a few minutes with me alone and all our problems would be solved. God forgive me, Toughie, but I could not wait any longer for you to build us a home."

"Why didn't you come to me? I would have done something."

"It sounded so easy, so I agreed, but then, when she brought the man to the house, she let him in and left. The man was that horrid old Gaylord, the landlord, and I couldn't go through with it, Toughie. He was such a big man and he sat down and blocked both doors. There was no way out! Finally, I decided to trick him into thinking I liked him, and I got behind him and grabbed hold of Ma's old skillet from the stove. I used both my hands and swung that skillet as hard as I could, and I hit him right on his bald head. I killed him, Toughie, and I would do it again if I had the chance."

"My God! So that's what happened to him. A constable was around asking questions, but they never found him. What did you do with him?"

"Well, I guess Ma and Da found him when they came home. I wouldn't be surprised if they stripped him, sold his clothes, and dumped him in the river. I wasn't going to wait and see. I took a woman's cloak and bonnet from the junk yard, stole Gaylord's purse, and ran. I did leave some money for Ma and Da, but Ma didn't deserve any after what she did to me."

"You should have come and told me, Gladdy. I would have gone with you."

"I know you would, darling. That's why I didn't tell you. I didn't want you to hang too if we were caught. Mr O helped me escape and I made him promise not to tell anyone. He walked me to a coach station and I got a ride to Dover where I met a wonderful lady named Millie McIver. She was a dressmaker and helped me in so many ways. There is so much more to tell you, Toughie, but just for now, hold me close."

Toughie took her in his arms and kissed her. The kiss affected them both far more than he had intended. Afraid of what he might do if they stayed so close together, he got up and suggested they make a cup of tea before she continued.

As they sat drinking, Gladys told him how she had worked as a lowly chambermaid at the Watt's inn until she was promoted to their singing barmaid.

"I remembered all those songs Ma used to sing in the bars for money, so I guess she taught me something useful after all. It was while I was singing there that I met Tom Pickwick. He and his friend, Keith, were both soldiers in officer's training at the castle in Dover.

"Tom's father, Andrew, was a very rich man, and I was surprised when he didn't object to our marriage. Oh yes, I told everyone my surname was Tweedhope. I thought there was less chance of being caught if I changed my name, and the only one I could think of was Bob and Sally's."

"I wish I had known. I might have found you. I thought of trying to find Sally and Bob in London, but they wouldn't have known you were using their name either," Toughie said.

Gladys nodded before continuing, "But, to get back to my story. Tom and Keith were sent to India and were both killed before they received their commission. Sadly, Tom never saw our daughter, Dolly. Andrew was a very good father-in-law and grandfather, which helped ease my grief. There were some very happy years and some sad ones.

"Poor Millie had a bad stroke and it left her paralyzed. Before that, she had made me promise that if she ever became so hand-icapped that she couldn't tend to her toilette—vanity was her only fault—I would help end her life.

"Oh, Toughie, if you could have seen how she looked at me as she lay there suffering, you wouldn't blame me for what I did. I can still feel that pillow under my hands after all these years." Tears were running down Gladys's cheeks.

Toughie wiped her tears away, and, instead of criticizing, he said, "Millie was lucky to have a friend like you, Gladdy. Your story is like the story Sally read to us called Cinderella. And now, here you are, a proper lady."

"And I've found my handsome prince at last."

Instead of agreeing with her, he changed the subject and said, "Good heavens, do you know it's two in the morning? I really must go."

"I'm staying in London for another day. Please come back to-morrow and tell me where you have been and how you ended up a Shakespearean actor."

"I will try, Gladdy, but tonight was our last performance, and we are leaving for America in two days," he replied.

"America! Oh, Toughie, how wonderful. Dolly and I will come with you." Gladys was so excited she couldn't stop talking, and before he could interrupt, she added, "I've always wanted to visit America.

So has Dolly, ever since we came here to the fair when she was just a little girl. But I'm afraid it shall take at least a week or two to settle our affairs and pack. Can you put off going until then, my darling?"

Toughie frowned. "No. You can't come with me, Glad—now or ever."

The quick and abrupt way he replied left no doubt in Gladys's mind that he didn't want her or Dolly. She realized that she had spoken impulsively and felt ashamed and embarrassed. "I am sorry, Toughie. That was such a stupid and presumptuous thing for me to suggest. Please forget what I said."

"It wasn't stupid at all. I would like nothing better than to have you and your daughter with me, but it can never be. I've never stopped loving you, Gladys, but I didn't think I would ever see you again, so a year ago I married someone else. Her name is Rosa. I can't leave her, especially now that we are going to be parents soon. If only you had come to London two years ago. I'm so sorry."

The news was a shock to Gladys. She had thought that now that they had found each other again, they would spend the rest of their lives together. The realization of how vain she had been dawned on her, and she had to admit that it was a miracle that a man as handsome and talented as Toughie had remained single for as long as he had.

Trying to keep her voice from breaking, she said, "Of course you can't leave her. I understand perfectly." Her tears came in spite of her efforts, and she cried, "Oh, Toughie, I remember the day I first realized I was in love with you. It was the first time I saw you, when you weren't wearing that old overcoat and funny cap. You looked so handsome, and I swore that day that I would never love anyone else. I did love my husband, Tom, though, but not the same as I love you."

"I think the first time I knew how much I loved you was the time we were in Mr Scott's butcher shop and his son, Jude, dropped that big jar of pickles. We were so busy scooping those pickles off the floor that I didn't notice you had cut your hand until we had run up the road and stopped to eat them. When I saw the blood dripping off your hand with the pickle juice, I was afraid you were going to bleed to death and I would lose you," Toughie replied.

Past memories of their childhood came flowing back, and the pair sat quietly, drinking in the details of each other's face.

Before he left, Toughie kissed her on the cheek and promised, "I'll be back tomorrow evening."

The following day, Gladys couldn't relax. She could hardly wait to be with Toughie again. Finding him had been a miracle, but she knew that when they said goodbye this time, it was going to be forever. Shopping for sewing notions and yard goods helped occupy her thoughts for a short time, and she managed to find some very reasonably priced bolts of fabric and bought enough in different patterns and contrasting colours to last her for about a year, along with some pretty buttons and thread.

When the store clerk addressed her as "milady" and wanted to know if she was taking her purchases home with her in her carriage, she couldn't help but feel flattered. With her nose a little higher than usual, she answered that she didn't have her carriage with her because she had come to London by train but would leave her address so he could see that her purchases would be delivered as soon as possible. She had spent more of her savings than she had intended and was feeling rather guilty when she left the shop.

Arriving back at the flat, she was pleasantly surprised to find Toughie waiting for her. Wishing to spare Rosa's feelings, Toughie hadn't told her the truth about where he was going. Instead, he said that he wanted to spend the evening with some old chums because he might never see them again.

After Gladys freshened up, they decided to go out to dine. Unwilling to eat in a nearby restaurant in case she might be recognized, Gladys suggested they take a ride on the omnibus to another location. She remembered riding on one when she came to meet the girls from Old Nichol and how much she had enjoyed it.

Luckily, it wasn't raining and they could sit outside on the top deck. Toughie enjoyed it as much as Gladys. They laughed and waved at the people they passed, who usually waved back. Some even made a gesture as though holding up a glass of ale and shouted back, "'Ere's to you!"

They stayed on the bus for an hour and then found a pleasant little restaurant where the wine was as satisfying as the food. When they finished their meal, they ordered more wine, and Toughie began his story.

He started by telling her that his Uncle Victor had returned to Italy from Australia only to learn that Toughie's grandfather had passed away and his mother, Victor's sister—a promising young opera singer—had run off with Toughie's father, Hugh Matthews.

Hugh was English, a common labourer, and not a Catholic— three sound reasons for Maria's parents to refuse to accept him as a suitor for their daughter. Against their wishes, Maria left home and married Hugh in London. She wrote home often but never received a reply. Then, when she and Hugh fell upon hard times and were forced to move to Old Nichol, she was too ashamed to tell them and stopped writing.

Her mother had never opened any of the letters, but she couldn't bring herself to destroy them. When she gave them to Victor, he insisted she listen while he read them aloud. When she heard that Maria had a son whom she had named Angelo, after her father, his mother broke down and cried from both grief and guilt.

Victor held her until she stopped crying. He promised her he would find them and bring them home. Taking Maria's last letter with him, he left for England the next day.

"It took my uncle a year after he began searching to discover that we had moved to Old Nichol. Even though the filth and the stench sickened him, he continued his search, walking the streets day after day asking everyone he met if they knew us. He was just about to give up when he came to our street. Luckily, Mr Scott, the butcher, heard that there was a stranger looking for a Hugh and Maria Mathews and their son Angelo, and he remembered my father.

"I guess the reason he remembered Dad was because he had saved a little girl from burning to death. Of course, Mr Scott didn't know that my name was Angelo, but when he saw Uncle Victor, he knew we were related because we look so much alike.

"As soon as Uncle saw me, he knew I was his nephew. When I told him that Mother was dead, he was so heartbroken that I never told him how she died or how much she suffered. When he said he was taking me to Italy to meet my grandmother, I was happy to go with him. As Mr O told you, I gave the junkyard to his son, Rod. If it hadn't been for Mr O, I don't think I would have survived."

Gladys took hold of his hand and said, "And if it wasn't for you, I'm sure I wouldn't have either."

When they finished their wine, Toughie suggested they buy a bottle of sherry to take back to the flat where he would continue his story. Once they were back in the apartment, Gladys poured them each a drink, and Toughie said, "Now, where was I?"

"You had just left Old Nichol with your uncle. Did he take you to Italy?"

"He did, and I'll never forget how excited I was the day we left. Uncle said I behaved like a proper gawker. We boarded a boat, but it wasn't a very big one compared to the big ships that were beside it, but I didn't care. I had never seen a boat before and didn't mind what size it was. I stayed out on deck for the whole trip. I never knew anything could smell as wonderful as that salt air."

"I know what you mean!" Gladys exclaimed. "I had almost forgotten the day I left London and how wonderful it was to smell fresh air. It was even sweeter when we arrived in Dover. I remember asking a man what the smell was, and he said, 'Why that's good salt air, my dear.' But do go on, what happened after you went to Italy?"

"Well, we lived with my grandmother, who was so determined to put flesh on my bones with huge meals that I had to run up the hill behind her house every day so I wouldn't get too fat. She really is a clever woman. She can speak English and French almost as well as she speaks Italian. She was also a talented musician, so it was easy to understand how disappointed she was when Mother ran off and didn't continue with her singing career.

"Uncle and I only stayed in Italy for two months. You see, he had been with a troupe of Shakespearean actors for years in Australia and wanted to form a group of his own, so he decided go to England, find enough actors, and take them to America. He wanted me to join him, but I wanted to find a job and earn my own way. I came as far as here with him and found work on the docks. That way I sometimes found work on the boats going to Italy and could visit my grandmother from time to time.

"I courted a girl or two during the next five years, but I always compared them to you and couldn't settle down.

"Then, two years ago, Uncle Victor came back from America with his troupe of actors. One of them became sick and died, and he needed someone to take their place. When he asked me if I would do it, I felt I owed him so much that I couldn't refuse. I didn't think I would ever be able to memorize so many lines, but I was doing quite well until the night you called out."

"I am so sorry, Toughie," Gladys said softly.

"Well, I'm not. If you hadn't come and recognized me, we may never have met again. What did you think of my performance, by the way?"

"You were the most handsome and talented performer on the stage," Gladys smiled.

Toughie smiled back at Gladys before replying, "You, milady, are not only beautiful but you also have excellent taste."

"And you, sir, have developed a much larger head since you left Old Nichol. But tell me, when did you meet Rosa?"

"Rosa is the sister of my Uncle Victor's wife, Carlotta. Uncle met Carlotta in America, and now they have three-year-old twin boys. Rosa has never been very well, and Carlotta has looked after her ever since their parents died. Carlotta is a strong-minded woman, and she was so determined that I should marry Rosa that before I realized what was happening, she had announced our wedding. I know that sounds like an excuse, Gladdy, and maybe it is, but it made Rosa so happy that I couldn't break her heart and tell her I didn't love her, so I went along with it. Now she is going to have our child and she isn't very well, so I must stay with her. I have no choice."

Along with feeling jealous, Gladys couldn't help but feel betrayed, even though she knew that until yesterday he had no idea she was alive. "I know, Toughie, but to lose each other now after all these years is almost unbearable."

"I know, but I promise you I will never truly love anyone but you, even though we may never see each other again." Then he put his hand on his heart and vowed, "I shall go to my grave with your name on my lips."

"And I shall die with yours on mine," Gladys answered solemnly. The theatrical tone of their vows added a touch of drama and romance to their rendezvous, and they laughed in spite of their imminent separation.

They reminisced for hours, and the bond they had when they were growing up in Old Nichol grew stronger with each memory. Gladys wanted to know about their childhood friends, Billy and Mick, who were both orphans, and Toughie told her that Billy had died. "After you left, Gladdy, things in Old Nichol became even worse, and they couldn't both leave the coal bin they slept in at the same time or someone would chop it up and take it away for fire wood.

"Poor Billy wasn't very well, so Mick did most of the foraging for food, but one day Billy insisted that he do his share and he left Mick and went out to find something to eat. He begged all day and had no luck, so he stole a sack of nuts from outside Mr Goodrich's store and ran down the street. Mr Goodrich saw him and ran after him. Goodrich later told Mick that Billy would have gotten away, but his heart just gave out and he dropped dead right in the middle of the street."

"Oh no," Gladys cried. "Poor Billy. How did Mick find out?"

"Mr Goodrich picked Billy up, put him in his woodshed, and covered him with some sacks until he could give him to the cart when it came around to pick up the bodies the next day. When Billy didn't come home the following day, Mick left the bin and started looking for him. Mr Goodrich saw him and he took him in and showed him Billy's body.

"Mr Goodrich was a good man, and he felt responsible for Billy's death because he was chasing him, so he hired Mick and gave him a place to stay. You remember, Glad, how Mr Goodrich had lost all his family except for his daughter, Maud, the crippled one? Well, the last time I saw Mick, he looked like he was well and happy and he said that he and Maud were going to be married."

"I am glad at least Mick is doing alright, but I sure feel sad that poor Billy is dead," Gladys remarked. Talking about their childhood reminded Gladys of her mother, and she began singing one of Bert's favourite songs while dancing around the room. Toughie clapped his hands and wanted more. She said she would sing another one if he would dance with her. He had never danced before, but with Gladys's help, he managed to twirl around without falling down.

When they finished the dance, he kept his arm around her waist. "My God, Gladdy, you are beautiful," he moaned as he pulled her close and kissed her. It was a kiss that had waited twelve long years to happen, and one they both wished could last forever. "I have to go," he said as he broke away.

Gladys nodded her head but didn't speak as he picked up his coat and hat. He had his hand on the door knob when he heard her softly say, "Don't go, Toughie."

"Are you sure, Gladdy?"

"Yes, my darling. Quite sure."

Morning came too soon. They both knew their goodbye this time would be final, but their night together had surpassed their expectations and somehow made their parting a little easier to bear.

Gladys left for home early in the morning after she said goodbye to Toughie. James and Percy were still suffering with colds, but they were so anxious to hear what she thought of the play that Percy had come to Four Oaks around noon to wait for her return. James sent Jenkins to meet the afternoon train while he and Percy sat in the library together sipping brandy until Gladys arrived. They allowed her time to put her things away and to spend five minutes with Dolly before sending for her.

As soon as she entered the library, they began their inquiry without wasting time with salutations. They were disappointed when she lied and told them she hadn't gone to the theatre, but Percy promised they would take her to another one of Shakespeare's plays before too long. She managed to cheer them up by giving comical descriptions of some of the people she had seen on the train and describing the goods she had bought in London. When she was finished talking, she ordered a hot toddy for each of them and left to see to her duties.

For over a month after she returned from London, Gladys had a glow to her countenance that everyone noticed. James said the trip must have done her a lot of good and suggested that she should get away for a day or two once every few months.

Dolly had managed to keep up with the few duties Gladys had given her to do while she was away, but she wasn't sorry to see her mother return. Although she didn't spend a lot of time with Mother, she had missed her. Ever since her Gamby had been killed, Dolly felt an inkling of dread every time Gladys left home.

The memory of her night with Toughie was still vivid in Gladys's mind as the weeks went by. Even if they never saw each other again, she was thankful they had that one night to remember.

All rational thoughts flew from her mind though when she realized she was pregnant. For a moment, she was overjoyed and thought about how wonderful it was going to be to have Toughie's child. Now he would be a part of her life forever, even if he was married to another woman. She imagined the baby would be a little boy that looked just like Toughie and could picture how happy Dolly would be to have a baby brother or sister to fuss over. The three of them could take long walks. She still had Dolly's pram. She was trying to remember where she had stored it when the realization of her present situation hit her and shattered her dreams.

All romantic thoughts were replaced by fear, and she wished she had never gone to London. The realization of how foolish she had been plagued her. She knew what James would think of her when he found out. He would think she was a harlot, and she could hardly blame him. He was bound to tell her to pack her bags and leave. She and Dolly would be homeless, and she knew no one hired a pregnant woman with a child.

During the following weeks, she had trouble sleeping at night and was often cranky with Dolly and the servants. Even James had noticed the difference in her demeanour. She seemed reluctant to spend time with Percy and him and made up excuses to prevent taking part in any of their activities. She also appeared to be losing weight, but since they didn't dine together, he had no idea if she was eating her meals or not. He had begun to worry that she may be seriously ill when he happened upon her one afternoon as he was strolling around the garden.

She was sitting on one of the garden benches with her head buried in her hands and didn't see him approach. When he spoke, she tried to hide her tears but couldn't.

Sitting down beside her, James waited until she had control of her emotions before he asked if he could help in any way. He said it with such compassion that she decided to tell him what was happening. Besides, she knew he would have to know sooner or later.

With no doubt that she would be discharged no matter what she told him, she decided to make a complete confession and began by telling him that she had gone to the theatre that night in London and of her reunion with Toughie.

"I thought I would never see him again. You see, we were both born in a terrible place they called Old Nichol. When Toughie's parents died, he was only five and left to fend for himself. Luckily, a kind man named Mr O'Brian let him sleep in his barn, but he had to forage for his own food.

"I was lucky in that my parents had a junkyard and a shack to go with it so I had a roof over my head. But when I was born, the water in the neighbourhood was so vile that my parents drank ale and other kinds of liquor instead. By the time I was four, they were so addicted to alcohol that they seldom paid any attention to me. If it wasn't for Toughie, I don't think I would have survived. Toughie was like a leader among the orphans, and he did his best to help them all, but many died of starvation or sickness anyway.

"I guess I loved Toughie from the first day I met him and he gave me a piece of the bun he was eating. I cannot begin to tell you how utterly poor the people in the slums were. Most of us had been born in the slums, and we had no idea what the outside world was like, but there was one special lady, Sally Tweedhope. Sally taught me to read and write. She wasn't from the slums originally and she was well educated."

James had never met anyone who came from the slums before, and he could hardly believe Gladys's story. "My God," he exclaimed as he stared at her. "I cannot believe it! Why, you have impeccable manners and are as talented and gracious as any of the highborn ladies I know. I cannot comprehend how anyone born in a place so horrid could accomplish such a transition. From a guttersnipe to a beautiful lady. Tell me, how did you manage to leave there?"

"Well, you see, Sally's husband also had a junkyard, and when they had a chance to leave Old Nichol, they gave their business to Toughie and he planned on building a place for us to live. I think he would have done it in time, but my parents became so terribly sick with alcohol that they couldn't push the junk wagon anymore, and I could not push it alone. Soon we no longer made enough money to pay our rent. That's when my mother made a pact with the devil. That is exactly what our landlord was—a devil. He was a horrid, despicable person. He gave my mother money to have his way with me."

"How could any mother do a terrible thing like that?"

Gladys didn't know why, but suddenly she felt the need to defend her mother. She resented James's criticism, but how could she make someone like him, who never had to drink putrid water, understand what it was like? Sally had known enough to boil the water they got from the communal pump, but unfortunately, Gladys's mother hadn't and she had substituted it with alcohol. She knew he would never understand, so she just said, "She was too sick to know what she was doing."

James shook his head and waited for her to continue. Telling Toughie what happened had been easy because he knew how desperate things could be in Old Nichol. She did her best to find the appropriate words to describe how afraid she had been when she first realized she was about to be raped by a monster. She must have been successful because James was so shocked he couldn't speak.

When she had finished telling him of her escape, she said, "So you see, sir, that is how I managed to get to Dover where I eventually met Tom Pickwick and your brother Keith."

Finally, James found his voice, "But why on earth did you not go to your friend Toughie instead of running away?"

"I didn't tell Toughie because I knew he would run away with me, and if we were caught, he would be hung too. It broke my heart to leave him, but as far as I could see, I had no choice. You know the rest of my story, except I didn't tell you that Peter had hired a detective in London and found out that I married Tom under a fictitious name. I was afraid that he might have found out that I murdered our landlord too, and that is why I didn't protest when he insisted that Dolly and I leave Dover and never return.

"For a long time Toughie looked for me, but he couldn't find me. Toughie's mother was from Italy and when her brother, who had been away for years in Australia, returned home and learned that she had run away with an Englishman named Matthews, he began to hunt for her. Toughie's parents had died, but his uncle found him and took him out of the ghetto not long after I ran away. Toughie's real name is Angelo Matthews."

"But that still does not explain why you are crying. If you still love each other, I should think you would be happy to be together once more," James interjected.

Now Gladys had to confess, but before she talked to James, she looked up at the sky and silently talked to God, asking him to tell James to forgive her. "We were happy, James. Toughie came to the flat after the performance and it was like we had never been apart. It was so wonderful that we were both overtaken with passion, and I know it was wrong, but we spent the night together." James didn't look very forgiving but she made herself say, "Now I find I am with child." Then she began to cry again.

James was not only shocked but embarrassed. He had never discussed the subject of pregnancy with anyone, not even his own wife. He was tempted to excuse himself and run off, but he was a gentleman, and Gladys was obviously in a great deal of distress. He paced back and forth in front of her. Finally, he stopped and said, "Oh, dear. Well I suppose you should marry as soon as possible. I shall be sorry to see you leave—we all shall." He was quiet for a minute, then he smiled and in a cheerier voice said, "I say, why not have the wedding here at Four Oaks?"

"There won't be any wedding, sir. Toughie is already married and he has gone to America. He will never know about the baby."

James paced back and forth once again. The act of adultery was not something he could ever condone, and he felt somehow that Gladys had betrayed him. He had put her on a pedestal without knowing it.

Finally, he stopped in front of her and said, "Gladys, you realize that now you have gone and thrown everything you have accomplished away. Your behaviour was not the act of a lady. It was the act of an ignorant and selfish woman. You have a daughter to consider, and I cannot forgive you for putting your needs, or, I should say, your desires, before her welfare."

James sounded so angry that Gladys was certain he was going to toss her and Dolly out on the street, or worse still, report her to the police. She should never have told him about killing Gaylord. Not knowing what else to do, she began to plead, "Sir, please do try to underst—"

He stopped her, "No, Gladys, the only sinful act I can condone is what you had to do in order to escape from that hell you lived in. Although I admire your tenacity and your struggle to make something of yourself, I do not understand your irresponsible actions with that young man. What on earth do you intend to do now?"

Gladys hung her head and cried, "I really do not know, sir, but perhaps if you would allow me to work for you just until my condition is noticeable, I could save enough money to enable me to look for lodgings in town and perhaps earn enough with my sewing skills to pay rent and keep Dolly and the baby in food. If not, I am afraid it shall be the workhouse for us."

James paced back and forth again without speaking for what seemed to Gladys the longest minute she had ever known. Finally, he stopped and, looking down at her, said, "Give me a few days to think it over. It has been quite a shock, and I need time to digest it all." Then, without another word, he left.

Chapter Twelve

During the next week, both Gladys and James avoided making eye contact with each other. The stress of waiting for James to make up his mind was so nerve-wracking that Gladys almost asked him to stop torturing her with suspense. Finally, he sent for her to come to his library. When she entered the room, he appeared as nervous and uncomfortable as she was. He motioned for her to have a seat. The way he paced back and forth without saying anything convinced her that his decision wasn't going to be favourable.

When he finally broke the silence with a loud cough to clear his voice, she almost jumped off the chair.

James was having trouble finding words to convey what he wanted to say, but at last, he looked down at her and blurted it out in such a rush that each word ran into the other. She stared at him with a puzzled expression until he realized that his outburst was incoherent.

After a few deep breaths, he calmed down and began again, this time in a much quieter manner. "I have thought this over very carefully, and I have decided that the best thing for you, and for Dolly, would be for you and I to be married."

Gladys could hardly believe that she heard him correctly and was afraid to answer in case her ears had deceived her. James could see she was struggling with the idea, and he feared he had made a fool of himself. His face turned red with embarrassment, and he regretted his offer.

Then Gladys asked, "Did I hear you right, sir? Did you just ask me to marry you?"

It was too late for James to refute his words, so he just nodded his head.

"I am sorry, sir, but you have taken me so by surprise that I really do not know what to say."

Without looking at her, he answered, "You need not say anything right now. I have made you a proposal and shall leave you to think it over. But I would suggest the sooner, the better." Then he quickly left the room as he added, "Let me know when you decide."

James didn't have to tell Gladys that a swift answer was imperative, and she only took the rest of that day and that night to come to a decision. She realized that marrying James would not only solve her problem, but provide her with a life of luxury, and Dolly would benefit as well. However, she was not the least attracted to him physically. He was twenty years her senior and had none of the rugged features that she admired most in a man.

The knowledge that she could hurt him nagged at her like a festered sliver, but so did the thoughts of being sent to the workhouse. She spent most of the night imagining what her future would be like if she were to say yes to his proposal and then what it would be like if she said no. She had her answer ready when she came down to breakfast in the morning.

It was the most difficult decision she had ever made and the most magnanimous. She met him in the library again, and before she could change her mind, she told him that although she appreciated his thoughtfulness, she had decided to refuse his offer.

James was surprised. He was sure that she would jump at the chance to secure a future for herself and her two children. Her refusal also hurt his pride. He could have had his pick among the wealthy single women in the town, and here she was, practically penniless with a bleak future ahead of her, and she still had the audacity to say no to his proposal. His voice had an edge to it when he demanded to know why.

She stated candidly that, although she knew how generous his offer was, Toughie was the only man she could ever love. Then she tried to explain how she felt.

"When I left Old Nichol, it was as though I left my real self behind, and I have been living a lie ever since . . . that is, until Toughie took me into his arms. For the first time in years, I felt like I didn't have to pretend anymore. Can you possibly understand what I mean, sir?"

James had no idea why, but he did understand, and he replied, "Yes, I think I can. We all live a great deal of our lives in pretence." Then, as though addressing the carpet, he added in a melancholy tone, "Pretending to be happy when we're miserable is . . ." He didn't finish his statement, but instead shook his head slightly.

After a moment, he ran his hand over his face, as though to brush away unwanted memories, and said, "Anyway, Gladys, I want to thank you for being so honest. However, I think you may have misunderstood my intentions. You see, I have never known what it is to have good friends, except for my brother, Keith, and I suspect his feelings toward me were based on duty, or pity."

"No, sir, never. Keith had nothing but respect for you. The way he spoke, it was clear he looked up to you," Gladys insisted.

"Thank you for that, but what I was attempting to say is that I did not realize what a lonely and introverted soul I had become until you came to live here. Thanks to you, I now have friends, and this is a way I can repay you. Will you please reconsider?"

When she didn't reply right away, he continued, "And, as you know, I am very fond of Dolly. I would like to provide her with a secure future. The marriage would also legitimize your unborn child, and as to any worries you might have about our relationship becoming anything more than a friendship, you may count on my word when I promise that shall never happen."

His promise was all it took to change Gladys's mind. She

searched for words strong enough to express her gratitude but could only say, "I think that you are the kindest man I have ever known, James Hornsby, and I would deem it an honour to be your wife. I would be a fool to refuse. And, sir, you have my word that I shall make you a good wife, but what about Mary?"

"What has Mary to do with this?"

"I know your Aunt Jean was hoping you would marry her."

"Why would she think such a thing?"

"Perhaps because she comes from a well-to-do family, and she's beautiful; even I can see how you might be attracted to her."

"Perhaps Percy is, but she is nothing more than a friend to me. And as far as that goes, you are equally as attractive, and I am not in love with you."

Gladys clapped her hands together and without thinking said, "I'm so happy to hear that. I mean I . . . oh my, I don't really know what I mean. But we have had some good times together, haven't we?"

"That we have, and I shall look forward to many more. And, Gladys, you are wrong about who you are. You are no longer the poor little urchin you were when you were growing up in the ghetto. You have been through a metamorphosis and are now as gracious a woman as though you were born into aristocracy. From now on, I do not want to hear another word about that little waif, so forget the past and concentrate on being the mistress of Four Oaks."

But Gladys knew James was wrong. That poor little waif would always be hiding behind whatever disguise she wore. Nevertheless, she smiled and thanked him.

James was sincere in his desire to help Gladys when he proposed, but his reasons were not entirely unselfish. His lack of romantic passion toward the opposite sex often troubled him. He hoped that by appearing to be a happily married man, it would add normality to his life. Besides, Gladys was good company and would see that the household was run in an orderly and pleasant fashion.

They went to London the following week and were married by a justice of the peace. Gladys was astounded by James's generosity and thoughtfulness. Instead of taking her to his flat where she and Toughie had spent their last minutes together, James rented a large two-bedroom suite in an expensive hotel. The suite's furnishings were so grand and the service so pampering, that Gladys would have loved to stay a month, but because they were anxious to announce their marriage to everyone back home, they decided a few days would do.

James insisted Gladys order a wardrobe more suited to her new role as mistress of Four Oaks, but when she found out how costly it would be to have the outfits made, she suggested buying some bolts of material and making her own.

James refused in such a curt and firm manner that she knew it would be futile to argue. Although she knew she should be thrilled with the prospect of having so many elegant gowns, she couldn't help but be disappointed. Now that she owned a sewing machine, she would have preferred to create her own styles. On the other hand, she was delighted over the respect and high regard she and James received as they went from shop to shop.

It was apparent that James was enjoying it too, and he wasn't the least bit reticent in offering his advice on which styles and colours were the most becoming for her. Fortunately, he had good taste.

Gladys was amazed when she happened to glance into the back of one of the shops and saw how many girls the proprietors had working for them. It seemed to her that each girl had a certain job to do, allowing the gowns to be put together in a factory-like manner. The thought of how wonderful that would have been for Millie crossed her mind.

The patterns and materials in the shops were of the latest styles, and Gladys, being quite a seamstress herself, knew which ones to choose.

She had never seen anyone spend money so freely. The entire time they were in London, James spent money in such a blasé and, in her opinion, irresponsible manner that she was afraid they would return home penniless. When she had agreed to marry James, all she could think about was securing a decent future for her and her children, but now she was beginning to understand what it really meant to be the wife of a wealthy husband.

As they were riding from one store to another in a cab, Gladys wondered what sort of an allowance James was going to provide her with. She wouldn't be surprised if he gave enough to enable her to buy whatever took her fancy. Oddly, the thought didn't thrill her. Money could never provide her with what she most longed for.

James and Gladys spent four days in London: the first day getting married and signing all the necessary papers, the next two days shopping for Gladys's wardrobe, and on the last day she persuaded James to purchase two stylish outfits along with accessories to match because it had been a few years since he had bought new clothes for himself.

In one of the stores they visited, Gladys happened to notice a lovely silver case containing an extravagant looking dental set consisting of a toothbrush, a tooth powder box, and a tongue scraper, all crafted in sterling silver. She had never seen such a thing before and pointed it out to James.

When they were back in their suite that night, James presented her with it as a wedding gift. She knew it must have cost a great deal, and she appreciated his thoughtfulness, so she thanked him profusely, saying that he couldn't have bought her anything nicer. However, she knew she would never use it since she liked her old bone-handled toothbrush and brushed her tongue with it as well as her teeth. Nevertheless, she thought the silver set would look exquisite sitting on her washing stand.

When they left London, they left with boxes of hats, shoes, scarves, gloves, and other accessories to go with the outfits they were having made.

Dolly and Blossom had persuaded Ruby to take them along when he went to the train station to meet James and Gladys, and they were standing on the platform waiting as the train came in sight. Being at the station with the rest of the waiting crowd and seeing the big engine approaching was still a thrill and a novelty for not only the girls but many of the adults as well.

As soon as the train came into view, someone shouted, "Here she comes!" and Dolly and Blossom couldn't contain themselves. They began jumping up and down and clapping their hands. They kept it up until Dolly saw Gladys and James step down from the train.

When Dolly held out her hand to greet her mother, Gladys ignored the gesture and gave her a big hug instead. "How wonderful of you to come and meet us!" she said. Then she hugged Blossom and added, "Come on, you two, let's leave the luggage for the men to collect." She took the girls' hands in hers and swung them as they made their way to the buggy.

All the way home, Gladys chatted happily about the sights they had seen and the luxurious hotel where they stayed. When they arrived at Four Oaks, Jenkins hardly had time to welcome them home before James said, "Jenkins, please instruct all the staff to assemble in the parlour in thirty minutes. I, I mean we, have an announcement to make." He and Gladys then retired to their rooms to freshen up.

When her mother said they had stayed in a hotel instead of James's flat, it had given Dolly a hint of what the announcement would be, so she followed Gladys into her sitting room and, with a sly grin, asked, "What else did you do in London, Mama?"

"You will just have to wait until we are all together. Then I shall tell you, my dear."

Dolly felt let down. She didn't think it fair for her mother to treat her like one of the staff. If what she suspected was true, she should be the first to be told and not have to find out at the same time as the rest of the household.

"Run along now, dear, and please tell James I shall be right down."

When they were all together, James said, "I have asked you all here to make an announcement. As you know, Mrs Pickwick and I have just returned from London." He paused and cleared his throat before continuing. "I am happy to announce that we were married there two days ago."

At first, the servants were at a loss for words, but Freda broke the silence by clapping her hands, and the rest joined in.

As soon as they stopped, Jenkins bowed and said. "Congratulations, sir, mum."

They both thanked him. Then Gladys looked at Dolly and asked, "What do you say, darling?"

With a weak smile, Dolly offered a half-hearted congratulation, but the look of disappointment on her face was so apparent that Gladys knew she had made a mistake in not confiding in her before accepting James's offer.

Putting her arms around Dolly, she whispered, "I am so sorry; I should have told you." The sincerity showed in her eyes, and Dolly couldn't help but forgive her.

Before James dismissed everyone, he informed them that Gladys was now the mistress of the house and must be treated with due respect. He said a new housekeeper would be hired as soon as possible, along with a lady's maid for Gladys. Then, having no idea what else to say, he asked Gladys if she had anything to add.

Gladys looked at them for a second while collecting her thoughts. Then she said, "I have enjoyed working with each of you, and I hope you have felt the same about me." They all nodded enthusiastically.

"I shall endeavour to find a housekeeper who will have the same respect for those under her as I had. I expect all of you to maintain your high standards of work and loyalty to her as you did toward me. I shall still be here if any of you are in need of my help, and, until we find a good and honest housekeeper, I shall continue with the job myself. Now, are there any questions?"

Jenkins spoke up, "Mum, will you be taking your meals with sir?"

Gladys didn't get a chance to answer before James said, "Yes, Jenkins. Both Mrs Hornsby and Miss Dolly will take all their meals with me, either in the conservatory or the dining room, unless otherwise requested."

The first dinner they shared together as a family was in the large formal dining room. The table was long enough to seat thirty people, and they looked and felt so lost sitting down at one end that after Jenkins and the footman left the room they broke into laughter. That was the last time they ate there unless they had guests. The conservatory was closer to the kitchen, had a table large enough for three people, and was much brighter.

Dolly was very fond of James and approved of the marriage, although she was deeply hurt that her mother had neglected to confide in her before the wedding. She forgot her disappointment a few days later when James apologized for not asking her if he could marry her mother.

He explained that now that she was essentially his stepdaughter, she should have her own apartment and be treated with more respect by all the servants. It made Dolly feel very important and grown up, so she smiled and answered, "Well, sir, I would have said yes if you had asked me."

James laughed and then said, "You know, Dolly, I realize that you are too old to begin calling me 'father' but I rather think that 'sir' is a bit too formal, don't you?"

Dolly frowned and thought about it for a second before answering, "I rather like calling you 'sir.' That is, if you don't mind. You see, I believe that 'sir' is a title of respect, and I respect you almost as much as I did my grandfather."

"You never cease to amaze me. 'Sir' it shall be then, but, Dolly, if you ever do want to call me Uncle James or just James that will be fine with me as well."

It took a while for Gladys to become accustomed to having Jenkins and the rest of the staff refer to her as mum instead of missus. On the other hand, Dolly took to her new title of Miss Dolly with dignity and self-assurance.

Chapter Thirteen

There was no swifter mode of communication than servants' gossip, and all the help at Four Oaks were well aware of Gladys's previous place in society. They also knew about the sad circumstance that caused her to take a position as a housekeeper, so they had no trouble accepting her as their new mistress.

Gladys and James were anxious to announce their marriage to everyone, but they worried about breaking the news to his Aunt Jean. They knew that she would not approve.

Soon after their new outfits arrived from London, they invited Percy, the Rudyards, and Mary Baker for the evening. When Jenkins showed them into the parlour, James and Gladys were waiting for them. Their look of surprise and admiration gave James a pleasant feeling of importance, and he greeted them with an added air of self-esteem. Gladys was dressed in a gown as beautiful as any Mary and Tina had ever seen, and her hair was pinned up and adorned with her tortoiseshell and pearl comb. She looked so elegant that the ladies were awestruck.

Percy, on first noting the change in Gladys's attire and being aware of her past, came to the immediate conclusion that she had finally been awarded her inheritance. Taking her hands in his, he was the first to comment.

"Well now, what have we here? You look ready to be presented to the Queen herself! By Jove, Gladys, you make quite a picture, but who is this handsome and debonair chap you have beside you?"

Gladys laughed, reached up and brushed Percy's cheek with her lips, then replied, "That, sir, happens to be my husband." Percy dropped her hands as though they were hot coals and his mouth hung open. Mary appeared equally shocked, but Tina clapped her hands, and she and Bob offered their congratulations with such enthusiasm that no one noticed Percy and Mary's looks of disapproval.

Tina and Mary had always been sociable toward Gladys, but because she was just a servant, they didn't invite her to any of their society functions. Now that she was the mistress of one of the wealthiest estates in the neighbourhood, Tina looked forward to introducing her to some of Sandwich's elite. Mary, on the other hand, had secretly hoped to marry James herself, and it was all she could do to mask her resentment.

After their company departed, Gladys and James kicked off their shoes and retired to the library where James poured them each a generous drink of brandy.

"Did you see their faces when they came in?" Gladys asked.

"We've given them quite a shock."

"Tina and Bob seemed sincere with their congratulations, but Mary and Percy were rather cool, don't you think? Did Percy say anything to you, James?"

"No, now that you mention it, he didn't. I thought he must have said something to you."

"He hardly spoke to me. In fact, he was unusually quiet all evening."

"Hmm, I wonder if he had plans to marry you himself?"

"I think not. At least, he has never given me any reason to believe such a thing."

"Perhaps he was just feeling out of sorts. Well, it has been quite an evening, so I think I shall be off to bed. I am curious to know how you are coming along with your interviews, but it can wait until tomorrow. Good night, Gladys."

Although all the servants were pleased with the marriage, they would have preferred to have had the ceremony take place at Four Oaks. The ballroom had not been used since James's mother-in-law passed away, and only Freda and Rita remembered her using it, and only once. Freda said that if she remembered correctly, it was more work than fun. Even so, she suggested to Dolly that if she wanted to have a small surprise celebration for her mother and James, she would be happy to make a wedding cake.

Dolly thought it was a smashing idea, and said she would invite Percy, Mary, the Rudyards, and James's Aunt Jean. She then asked for Jenkins's help in sending off an invitation to Jean, who lived in Hastings. Unfortunately, the invitation Jenkins sent stated that her nephew had recently married and they were having a small surprise party for him and his wife, but it didn't mention his wife's name. Jean was delighted with the news, but felt a little put out over not being asked to the wedding.

Mary was determined to overcome her jealousy, so when she received her invitation, she said she would be happy to attend.

Percy wasn't able to hide his feelings nearly as well, and although he agreed to be there, he didn't appear to be happy about it. This surprised Dolly, and she mentioned it to Freda, who remarked that men seldom get excited over fancy dress up affairs, but she really suspected Percy's lack of enthusiasm was due to jealousy.

When Aunt Jean arrived unexpectedly a few days before the party, Gladys was taken by surprise. James had postponed telling his aunt about his marriage, and to make matters worse, he had gone to town on business that morning, so Gladys didn't know what to say. She decided to still play the part of a servant, at least until his return.

"Why hello, mum. This is a pleasant surprise! You look well," Gladys said and meant it. The woman's appearance had improved since her last visit, even though she was still wearing the dress Gladys had given her. Gladys thought that perhaps an absence of facial hair might be the reason for much of the improvement.

"Surprise? Oh yes, the surprise, that is right," Jean replied while giving Gladys, who had no idea what the woman was talking about, a collaborative nudge. Then she turned to a pleasant-looking, middle-aged woman who was standing a little behind her and said, "Gladys, this is my maid, Thora." She then informed the maid that Gladys was James's housekeeper and added, "She will take good care of you, my dear, but first you must come with me and unpack my case. Are the newlyweds at home, Gladys?"

Gladys had no idea how Jean learned that James was married, but her question left no doubt that she didn't know who he had wed. The only answer she could think of was, "James is not here. I shall take you up to your room and then see that you have tea in the parlour while you wait for him to return."

Leaving Jean and her maid to get settled, Gladys hurried down to the kitchen and called everyone together to tell them not to mention to Jean that she was the new Mrs Hornsby until James had a chance to break the news to her. She intended to leave him alone with his aunt, feeling certain the old lady was going to be quite upset.

As soon as Jean came down to the parlour, Gladys made the mistake of bringing her a cup of tea. The woman could hardly wait to ask Gladys how she liked working for her new mistress and insisted she sit down and join her. Gladys said she would love to, but there were chores she had to see to.

"Surely you can spare a few minutes," Jean said indignantly. "Do not tell me that Mary is working you so hard that you cannot sit for five minutes to talk to a guest."

Gladys almost blurted out the truth but hesitated as she sat down on the edge of her chair, praying James would come through the door before she was forced to answer. When he didn't, she tried to change the subject. "Did you have a pleasant journey here, mum?"

"Yes, it was fine, but tell me, Gladys, how are things now that James is married? You mustn't worry what you say, dear. I shan't repeat it!"

Fortunately, James saved the day. As he entered and made his way over to his aunt, he glanced at Gladys who shrugged her shoulders. "Well, I must say this is a surprise, Auntie," he said as he bent over and kissed the woman on the cheek. Gladys excused herself and made a quick exit before either of them could object. An hour later, Jenkins came to her apartment and said she was wanted in the parlour.

"Wish me luck, Jenkins!" His answer was an encouraging smile and a thumb's up gesture.

When Gladys entered the parlour, Jean was sitting in the same chair and James was standing over by the fireplace. For a few seconds, they just looked at her without speaking. She felt like a prisoner waiting to be sentenced. She even had a ridiculously funny thought that they may be planning to cut off her head and almost giggled.

Finally, Jean broke the silence. "I should not forgive you, Gladys, if James had not explained that you knew he wanted to be the one to tell me." Her tone wasn't nearly as reproachful as Gladys had feared, so she relaxed a little before apologizing and saying that she hoped Jean wasn't too disappointed.

"I shan't lie, Gladys. I had hoped James would choose that woman, Mary, as his wife." Then, with an accusing look, she added, "But you already knew that. Mary has a far more suitable background for a man of James's standing.

"Nevertheless, James insists that he is as much to blame as you in having to procure such a hasty marriage, and now that I know there will soon be a little one to consider, I shall not spend any more of my time wishing he had made a different choice. Instead, I shall look forward to becoming a great aunt once more." She rose from her chair and, holding her hand out, said, "Welcome to the family, Gladys."

The woman had a special candidness to her that Gladys couldn't resist, and she ignored her hand and hugged her. Jean enjoyed it much more than she thought she would.

Jean proved to be a good sport and managed to keep the party a secret along with the rest of the household, so, on the evening of the occasion, James and Gladys were completely taken off guard and didn't know quite how to behave. Stunned, they looked at each other helplessly. Fortunately, it was taken as a look of intimacy.

Just before they cut the cake, which Freda had taken such care in baking and decorating, Gladys insisted all the staff be invited to join them. James and his aunt managed to hide their displeasure, because they both felt she was being far too familiar with the servants. To make matters worse, Gladys seemed to be completely unaware of her erroneous behaviour and told Jenkins to see that they all had a full glass of spirits. Then she invited them all to stay and sing along while she played the piano.

James had never paid much attention to his household servants, and although he never treated them badly, he did ignore them, except for Jenkins. Now, the idea of spending a social evening with them was almost more than he could bear. His look of disapproval was obvious to everyone but Gladys, so at first the servants were hesitant to take part and sang very softly, but as the night wore on, they began to relax, and their voices filled the room with sounds of merriment.

James had tried to discuss Gladys's actions with Percy, but his friend didn't seem to want to listen. He was not only behaving in an unfriendly manner but also drinking more heartily than usual. Before the party was over, he became so inebriated that Jenkins had to help him into his carriage.

Gladys thought it was a lovely affair, and Freda and the rest of the servants were overjoyed, but the next day, James let her know how badly she had behaved.

"You are no longer one of them, Gladys, so you must not fraternize with them. Surely you did not behave that way when your father-in-law was alive?"

"Andrew did not believe in putting on airs, and I don't either!" Gladys said in her defence.

"That may be, but here we must act appropriately. As my wife, I expect you to behave accordingly. I could tell Aunt Jean disapproved, and I am certain that the Rudyards and Mary were shocked. It is a wonder they stayed as long as they did."

"But they said they had a wonderful time. At least the Rudyards did. As for Mary, I am not sure if she enjoyed herself or not. Sometimes I have a problem knowing what she is thinking. Anyway, I really cannot see why you are so upset, James. The girls all worked very hard to give us the party, and I only thought it fair to let them enjoy it too."

"Up until now, I have not objected to your unconventional methods of handling the help, but I must insist you obey my rules from now on. Is that clear?"

Gladys knew he was right. She hadn't behaved like any of the wealthy ladies she had met. She apologized and promised to do better, but she didn't look forward to it. She had made friends with all the girls and was going to miss hearing their good-natured chatter and spontaneous laughter. She would also have liked to voice her objections to the word "obey," but since James was going to provide her and the children with a secure future, she reasoned that he probably had a right to demand obedience.

James hadn't mentioned Gladys in his letters to his son Horace, but now that they were married, he felt obliged to let him know. However, he neglected to mention that Gladys had been his housekeeper. Instead, he wrote that she was the widow of Thomas Pickwick, a person that Horace knew came from a respectable family. Therefore, when Horace wrote back with his congratulations, he said he was looking forward to meeting her but couldn't see his way to returning home for at least another year.

Gladys and James soon became experts at playing the part of a happily married couple, which they were in their own way. Because she couldn't find anyone who would treat the maids with respect and kindness, Gladys gave Rita, the eldest housemaid, the job of housekeeper and hired another girl to take her place. With a little training, Rita soon learned to manage the finances, and Gladys began living the life of an aristocrat. At James's insistence, she even hired a lady's maid to care for her own personal needs.

The woman she hired was in her thirties. Her name was Rhoda Pitt, and she reminded Gladys a little of Millie, even though she was much younger. Although Rhoda was very efficient, Gladys couldn't get accustomed to having someone fussing over her, and, in order to keep the girl busy, she taught her how to use the sewing machine so she could do all the mending. She also had her look after some of Dolly's needs. Gladys had moved into James's first wife's apartment, across the hall from his apartment, and Dolly was left with the one they had shared.

Although Gladys still pined over Toughie, having part of him growing inside her helped ease her sorrow. She gradually began to take her new position seriously and became a little less uncomfortable with its code of behaviour. James gave her a generous allowance so she could afford to spend afternoons in Sandwich shopping with Tina, but Mary always had an excuse not to join them. When Tina invited her to go to Dover for a day's shopping, Gladys refused. The road from Sandwich to Dover went past Oaken Arms, and she still couldn't bear to see it again. Besides, she didn't want to take the chance of seeing Peter.

After James and Gladys were married, neither Percy nor Mary came to visit as often. On occasions when they did visit, their manner was not as genial as it had been. Their change of attitude hurt James more than it did Gladys, because he missed the hours he and Percy had spent together discussing books, politics, and sports.

Gladys had decided that the reason Mary was behaving so distant was because she was in love with James, but as for Percy, she couldn't think of any reason for his cool behaviour.

"It is almost as though he is upset over our marriage," Gladys said after Percy had refused to stay for dinner one evening.

"You might be right," James replied, looking up from the book he was reading. "Do you think I may have been right when I said he might be jealous? Perhaps he did intend to marry you himself."

Gladys laughed, "I really don't think so, but if he did, he certainly kept it a secret."

"I shall have a talk with him the next time I have the opportunity."

"Be careful not to embarrass him, James. I should feel terrible if it did anything to spoil your friendship."

The next time they were alone, James mentioned to Percy that he and Gladys had noticed the change in his attitude. When Percy tried to deny it, James decided to come right to the point, "Look here, old boy, if you had romantic feelings toward Gladys, you should have said so."

"Don't be ridiculous!"

"I fail to see what's ridiculous about that."

"Of course you don't, that's quite apparent, but you could have had the decency to tell me how you felt about her." Then, before James could answer, Percy realized how niggling his words had sounded. "I am sorry, James, I should not have said that. You certainly are not obliged to take me into your confidence. Perhaps I have, unintentionally, used your friendship to replace the one I had with Helmut. I had no right to assume you felt the same toward me."

"But I do, Percy, I bloody well do! I value your friendship more than you know. And I am sorry we did not have time to tell you we were getting married; you see, haste was of the utmost importance."

"I don't understand. Unless—I say, James, you have not gone and taken advantage of the poor girl, have you?"

"Most assuredly not. The blighter was not I. Look, Percy, I cannot explain it now, but it is quite an amazing story, and I feel I should have Gladys's approval before sharing it with you. How would it be if I meet you tomorrow at the club around two? We can talk about it then."

Percy agreed, and after he left, James told Gladys about their conversation and asked if she would mind if he told Percy her story.

At first, Gladys was angry. She also thought it would be foolish of James to admit that he wasn't the father of her unborn baby, but then she decided it might just help Percy to forgive her if he knew why she allowed Toughie to get her in the family way.

She needn't have worried. When Percy learned of the hardships she had endured and of her escape and accomplishments thereafter, he was as astounded as James had been. "It's all so unbelievably romantic! By Jove, James, it even makes some of Dickens's stories appear mundane. To think that such a talented and gracious creature as our Gladys could come from such a place is mindboggling. She is absolutely amazing. I can see why you are determined to help her, old boy, but marrying her when she is so in love with another chap. Wasn't that a bit rash?" Percy asked.

"I know it looks that way, but the marriage is merely one of convenience. I am not interested in any other kind, and neither is she. The thing is, I seldom hear from that boy of mine, not that I blame him. I was not a very attentive father. Too busy building up my business, I suppose. He's done very well for himself, you know, dealing in gems of all things. Anyway, as you must have surmised, Gladys has become a very dear friend to me, as has young Dolly, and because I enjoy their company, this arrangement will be beneficial to us all. But I must warn you, Percy. Gladys, you, and I, must be the only ones to know that the child is not mine. Do you understand?"

Percy was delighted to be part of their conspiracy and felt it would bring the three of them even closer. Gladys now seemed to have a certain intrigue and fascination that all the other women he had known lacked. After all, how many women did he know who would have the courage to commit murder if threatened? In spite of her pluck, there was also a sense of vulnerability to her character that he hadn't noticed before, and he began treating her with as much concern and dependability as did James.

Chapter Fourteen

James suggested to Gladys that their marriage would appear more indubitable if they began attending church every Sunday. The first Sunday they joined St Andrew's congregation, Lionel Buttershy, the choirmaster, heard Gladys singing and was determined to have her in his choir. Gladys missed singing with her fellow choristers in St Mary's church choir in Dover, so when Lionel asked her if she would join his choir, she said she would be pleased to. She soon became very fond of Lionel and admired his many musical talents. As well as being an excellent choir master, he was adept at playing the organ, the violin, and the harp.

When Gladys told Dolly she was going to have a baby sister or brother, Dolly was delighted and said, "I shall be able to read her all of father's books—the same stories that Gamby read to me."

"You sound very sure that it will be girl."

"Not really, Mama. I shall be happy with either, but if it is a girl, I know she will have a jolly good time as soon as she is old enough to play with my dollhouse."

Gladys suddenly realized how proper Dolly's diction had become, and she credited it to James's influence, but for some reason it seemed a little too proper to suit her.

James had no trouble being true to his word. Although Gladys was a beautiful woman, he never felt attracted to her in a sexual way. Except for Percy, all his friends at the men's club who had seen her were envious and often remarked about his good fortune. Some were even brazen enough to inquire what it was like to bed such a young beauty. Instead of resenting the remarks, James rather enjoyed them and would often add fuel to their imaginations with a sly grin and a wink.

Seven months after her marriage to James, Gladys gave birth to a five-pound, dark-haired, bright-eyed, little boy. Because of his size, it was easy to pass his birth date off as premature, but it wasn't so easy to convince some people that his dark complexion could be accredited to Gladys's maternal grandmother, who she declared was Italian.

Gossip and speculations were enjoyed by all who knew the Hornsbys, including their servants, in spite of their fondness for Gladys. Because neither parent showed the slightest sign of guilt or embarrassment, it soon took the flavour out of even the juiciest rumours, and they were soon forgotten.

Out of respect, Gladys named the boy Edward, because it was James's middle name. There was no doubt the baby resembled his father, but, fortunately, no one in Sandwich knew who that was. Gladys's heart burst with love and joy every time she looked at the small replica of her true love. She could hardly bear to be apart from him for any length of time, but since she had promised James she would be a good wife, she agreed to hire a nanny in order to spend more time socializing.

Soon after Edward was born, Mary and Tina came to visit bring-

ing lovely gifts for both the baby and Gladys. Gladys's face lit up with pride when they went on about how they had never seen a prettier baby, and, since she had no idea of what Mary was thinking, she was sorry to see them leave.

No sooner were they out the door and into their carriage when Mary burst out with accusations. "If that baby is James's, I am the Duchess of Kent. And if he was premature, I am the Duke!"

Tina, trying to deny that she was having similar thoughts, replied, "Oh, Mary, surely you do not believe Gladys could be guilty of such a thing. Do you?"

"I certainly do! I know I am right, and if you are honest, you have to admit that you think so too."

"But there are no other men around Gladys, except Percy, and the baby looks even less like him."

"Well, there has to be someone else." They had both come in Mary's chaise, and for a time, no one spoke. Then suddenly Mary pulled on the reins and stopped the horse.

She clapped her hands and said, "I have it. Do you remember that time last year when we sent a message to James asking him if we might borrow Gladys to play for our Christmas charity tea for St Andrew's orphanage?"

"That was last year and besides, Gladys was unable to be there, so I cannot see what that has to do with the baby."

"The reason she couldn't come was because she was in London. Now what month was that?"

"You know very well what month it was. It always takes place on the fifth of December."

"And Edward was born in September."

Tina counted out the months on her gloved fingers aloud. "My heavens, you don't suppose she had a lover in London?" Mary nodded her head. "But if she had and he is the father, why would she marry James?"

"I have no idea. Perhaps her lover was a married man, so she had to trap James into marrying her. I warrant he has no idea that he's not the father. Damn her!"

"Now, Mary, you don't know for certain that is what happened.

Edward could be a premature baby."

"You saw him. He is far too healthy for a seven-month-old baby. Does he look like James's son to you?"

"His complexion is quite dark, but then Gladys did say he resembles her mother's side of the family. Evidently her maternal grandmother is Italian and is alive and living in America, so perhaps we are letting our imaginations run away with us."

"I doubt it. Poor James. Any woman who would stoop low enough to trick a man into a marriage is capable of anything. We had better keep an eye on her for James's sake."

"That doesn't sound like you, Mary. I am sorry to say this, dear, but I think jealousy has a lot to do with your assumptions."

"I won't deny that I thought James might ask me to marry him in time, so naturally I was hurt when he married Gladys, but I had begun to accept it until I saw that baby. I have no idea how she managed to do it, but somehow she has seduced him and led him to believe he was going to be a father. I say again, damn her!"

Mary wasn't the only one who had doubts. Every time Gladys took Edward to town, people made a fuss over him and were very polite to Gladys, but as soon as her back was turned they hurried to find someone they could gossip with. If Gladys had let them see that their gossip bothered her, it would have gone on for much longer, but she knew how to handle gossip. She held her head high and was especially nice to those who were the worst perpetrators.

Tina and Mary didn't voice their doubts in front of Gladys, but James's aunt did. Edward was in his bassinet when Jean first saw him. As she bent over the bassinet, Gladys said, "Edward, this is your Auntie Jean. Can you give her a smile?"

Jean did no more than glance at the baby before looking up at Gladys and, as though she was out of breath, gasped, "You wicked, wicked girl."

Before Gladys could reply, Jean stormed out of the room.

Gladys was shocked. She had begun to really like the woman

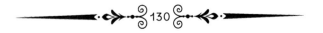

and hoped to become close to her, but her attitude toward Eddy was downright rude. Surprisingly, the thought that the woman was able to tell that James was not Eddy's father never entered her mind. She was so angry she decided to find Jean and confront her.

When she knocked at Jean's door, she had to wait a few seconds before being told to come in. Gladys's anger faded when she saw that the woman had been crying. She sat down on the bed beside her, but Jean pushed her away and got up. "Don't touch me."

"Why, Aunt Jean? What did I do?"

"And do not call me Aunt Jean. How simple do you think I am?"

"I don't understand. What it is that I have done?"

"What have you done? You have fooled my nephew into thinking that child is his. Well, you Jezebel, you shan't get away with it. I shall tell James what a fool you have made of him. And we shall see what the law can do about it. Now get out of my room or I vow I shall scream."

Gladys knew it was no good talking to her, so she left and went to look for James. She found him in the stable. "James, your aunt has guessed that Edward is not your son. She refuses to listen to me, so I think you should tell her everything. I don't know what else we can do."

James ordered a pot of tea sent up to his aunt's room and went up to see her. Gladys was his wife now, and she was there to stay; so he decided to take her advice and tell his aunt the whole story. He had made up his mind that if she refused to accept Gladys as one of the family, then she wouldn't be welcome in their home. Jean listened attentively, and when he was done, she shook her head sadly and said that she thought he had made a terrible mistake.

"Auntie, do you recall what a recluse I was until Gladys came to live here? I had no friends and Four Oaks was a gloomy place. Now it is a different place altogether. And for that matter, Auntie, even you look ten years younger, and I know Gladys had a lot to do with that. She made a terrible mistake, I grant you, but she is a good person and an excellent wife. Will you please give her a chance?"

Jean was too upset to answer, but she nodded her head affirmatively.

Although she was cool with Gladys for a time, she couldn't help but admit that Eddy was an exceptionally pretty child. She only stayed a few more days, but before she left she told Gladys that she wasn't angry with her and would return soon.

Dolly loved her little brother and wanted to help with his care, but she had little opportunity. Gladys insisted on doing everything for the baby herself whenever his nanny wasn't with him. Before long, Dolly gave up trying.

Although James had no desire for an intimate relationship with Gladys, he took a great deal of pride in being married to such a talented and beautiful woman. He also thought that because Gladys's Italian lover was no longer part of her life, he would be able to take to her child as though it was his own. Unfortunately, Gladys made the mistake of telling him how much the baby looked like his father, and after that, every time James looked at the child, he felt a twinge of jealousy and dislike.

Nevertheless, he did make a half-hearted attempt, but the disapproval in his eyes was so obvious that Gladys kept them apart as much as she could. As soon as Edward learned enough words to ask for what he wanted, Gladys catered to his every whim. Before he was even two years old, he was well on his way to becoming a mama's boy.

Gladys continued to accompany James whenever he asked her to, but he could tell she did it out of duty, and he soon began spending most of his time in the company of Percy.

Edward refused to go to bed by himself. Although his nanny, who was an expert on handling such problems, offered to help, Gladys insisted on lying down with him in her bed every evening until he fell asleep. This not only meant she was often late for dinner engagements, but she missed a lot of choir practices as well.

When Lionel questioned her about it, she said that she was very sorry, but poor little Eddy suffered with a nervous condition and needed her at home. A few days later, he met James as he was riding on the moors and happened to mention how sorry he was to hear that Eddy suffered with a nervous condition, a sickness he thought only plagued adults. James refuted Gladys's excuse and informed Lionel that his son was in perfect health, and the only thing he suffered with was a mollycoddling mother.

Lionel confronted Gladys the following Sunday in the choir room, telling her that it disrupted the choir if a member missed more practices than they attended, therefore, he might have to ask her to leave. Gladys wanted to stay, but she knew she couldn't leave home unless Edward was sleeping peacefully. "But, Lionel, I told you why I can't always come," she said.

"Your husband seems to think there's no reason why you can't, Gladys. He said that your boy is a perfectly healthy little fellow and has a capable nanny who can look after him while you are away."

"James has no idea what my son is suffering from, and I am sorry if you think he does," Gladys answered sharply. Then, realizing how rude she sounded, she apologized, "I am sorry, Lionel. I didn't mean that. I really enjoy being in the choir, and as soon as Eddy gets over these attacks, I would like to come back, if that is acceptable."

Lionel said he'd be more than happy to have her.

Gladys waited until she and James were far enough away from the church before she lit into him. "Why did you tell Lionel I needn't stay home with Eddy? You know he will only go to sleep if I am with him," she said accusingly.

"I am sick of the way you treat the boy. We all are."

"Who do you mean by all?" she asked.

"Gladys, it really matters not who I mean. You are spoiling the child, and the sad thing is that it is not making him happy."

"I might spoil him, but that is much better than hating him."

"I do not hate him. I merely want to see him grow up to be a decent young man, but if you don't stop pampering him, there is little chance of that."

Although Gladys disagreed with James, what he said made an impression on her, and she began to notice how much she had alienated Eddy from the rest of the household, especially Dolly. She recalled how Dolly had at first begged to hold him and play with him. But now she hardly looked at him. She also realized that her daughter had grown apart from her as well. She tried to reason that the problem had to do with the amount of time Dolly had to spend on her studies since, shortly after their marriage, James had insisted on hiring a tutor for her—but she knew that was not the problem.

Edward's nanny, Miss Edna Bruin, was a pleasant-natured, middle-aged spinster who had been a nanny most of her life and came with excellent references. Although it sometimes took a month or more to teach her charges proper manners and behaviour, she never failed to achieve excellent results, but Edward's possessive mother seemed about to mar her record.

"I cannot understand why they hired me," she complained to a friend in Sandwich, who she visited every second Sunday on her day off. "The boy's mother does everything for him, and there am I, left with nothing to do." Then she went on to say how sad the little fellow was and how even his father dare not interfere. "I can feel the tension in the house, Bertha. It is most troubling." To add colour to what could be thought of as a dull life, Edna often enjoyed dramatizing every little happening, and now that she had Bertha's attention, she continued, "Now, I do not know if you remember hearing about that poor young governess, Henrietta DeLuzey?" Bertha shook her head.

"Well, about ten years ago, she moved to France after she was hired by the Duc and Duchess de Pralin as their children's governess. I still remember how sad it was. You see, in 1847 the Duchess was brutally killed, and the Duc was charged with her murder! The authorities claimed he and Henrietta were lovers."

"Oh, yes, now I remember," Bertha spoke up. "You actually knew her?"

"Yes, but only for a short time. The family she worked for in England were friends of the family I worked for, and because their little ones enjoyed playing together, we often took them all for outings."

"But according to what was written in the papers, Miss DeLuzey seduced the Duc and poisoned the children's minds against their poor mother," Bertha exclaimed.

"That was what Victor Hugo wrote, but I never did believe one word of it, not one word. That girl was the most honourable girl I have ever known. She would never allow such a thing to happen. Thank heavens they found her not guilty. Mind you, she was practically forced to leave the country."

"I wonder what happened to her."

"I have no idea."

"You don't expect something as bad as that will happen with your family, do you?" Bertha asked, secretly hoping Edna would say yes.

"I should hope not! Because of his friendship with the King, the French peasants wanted to see the Duc hung, but it seems he denied them the pleasure by committing suicide, or, as some believe, he was poisoned! This made it seem as though the King and his friends were above the law. And I heard that may have had something to do with starting the revolution and forcing the King to advocate! I hardly think my lady's handling of her little one would bring about such drastic results, but still, I cannot help feel that things at Four Oaks are not as they should be, and like Henrietta, I fear that no good will come of it."

Chapter Fifteen

One day, James had gone riding with Percy, Eddy was napping, and Gladys was enjoying a quiet time reading in the library. She was unaware of the stranger who had come to the open door and stood watching her. Horace was about to enter, but the picture Gladys made sitting on the widow seat with her back against the wall, her knees pulled up, and the sunlight highlighting the hue of auburn in her hair was so lovely, he found it captivating. He took her to be his stepmother's daughter, Dolly, who his father had written about, although he had imagined she was much younger. She had a lovely profile, and he thought if she resembled her mother, he could easily understand why his father had remarried.

Finally, Gladys sensed his presence and turned her head. Although she knew there was someone there, she was still startled and almost fell off the seat before she managed to stand up.

Horace apologized, "I hope I haven't upset you, but you looked so comfortable that I didn't want to disturb you."

Gladys slipped into her shoes. "Are you looking for James?" she asked.

"Yes, I am, but first let me introduce myself." He held out his hand. "I am the prodigal son, Horace. You must be my stepsister, Dolly."

Gladys, always apprehensive toward strangers, was relieved when he introduced himself, and she returned his smile as she took his hand. He had a mischievous air about him that she found appealing. He didn't resemble his father in the least and looked nothing like she had imagined. In fact, she thought he looked a little like Toughie.

Realizing she had been staring at him, she lowered her eyes and said, "I'm so happy to meet you, Horace, but I am not Dolly. I am Gladys, your stepmother."

Horace was shocked, but before he could reply, she continued, "Your father didn't tell me you were coming. He will be home soon. He and his friend Percy went riding. Did Jenkins take your luggage to your rooms?"

Horace replied that he had taken his bag up himself.

"Oh dear, I am afraid your rooms are not ready, but I shall see to that right away. Would you care for a cup of tea while you are waiting?"

"I suppose so," he answered rather gruffly.

"I shall have one of the girls bring us some," she said as she walked over and pulled the bell cord. "This is such a nice surprise, but I do wish James had told me you were coming so I could have had things ready for you."

"He didn't know, and you needn't worry about my rooms; I can only stay a few days, so it's hardly worth fussing over."

"Nonsense! Rita, our housekeeper, will see that it is ready in no time at all, but I had better tell Freda that you are here. I know she will want to make something special for dinner. I shall be right back. I am so happy you are here at last," she said as she was leaving the room.

Horace had been so stunned when Gladys said she was his stepmother that he welcomed her absence so he could collect his thoughts. He guessed by her appearance that she was about his own age, so he couldn't help but to be suspicious. He wondered why such a beautiful young woman would marry an old man. She was obviously well bred and, according to his father's letters, had been married to one of the richest men in Dover. Therefore, her reason must not have been financial. He also found it difficult to believe that his father would have taken advantage of her. As far as he could recall, his father was not an affectionate man, so he was certain that it would have to be Gladys who had done the seducing.

Horace and his father were never close, and that was one of the reasons he left home shortly after his mother died. At first, his father's letters were short and formal, but gradually they became more and more personal. In time, Horace began to look forward to them, and, for the first time in his life, he experienced feelings of fondness for the father he hardly knew.

Now, as he waited for Gladys to return, he couldn't make up his mind whether he should be angry with her or angry with James for being such an old fool. She had seemed sincere when she said that she was happy to see him, so he decided to be civil until he learned more.

"Molly will bring us tea shortly," Gladys said when she returned. "I thought it would be nice if we have it in the parlour."

When they entered the room, Horace was amazed at how bright and pleasant it was. His grandmother had always insisted on the house being kept in good order, but when she died, his mother, who had no interest in household matters and whose health was declining, had allowed the servants to become errant in their duties. By the time he had left home, the entire house had become very dark and gloomy.

He was still looking around the room when Gladys remarked, "It must be nice to see the place again. Does it look the same?"

"God no! Sorry, Gladys, but I find it rather hard to believe it is the same room. In fact, none of the rooms look the same. It's rather like walking into a different house. Dad wrote and said he had hired a new housekeeper and that she had made an improvement to the place, but I didn't think anyone could make this much difference."

"I couldn't have done it without the housemaids; they are all splendid workers."

"You surely don't mean that you were the housekeeper father wrote about?"

"Did you not know?"

Horace shook his head. He felt disappointed. He didn't know what he had hoped to learn, but it wasn't what now seemed obvious—she had married his father for his money.

Gladys noticed his look of disapproval and was going to say something when Molly entered with the tea. When Gladys introduced her to Horace, she didn't know how to respond so just nodded then gave a small and awkward curtsy and left.

Horace had never been introduced to a kitchen maid before, and he found it embarrassing.

"Do you always introduce your servants to your guests?"

"Oh, no, but then you are not really a guest, are you? You are family, and the girls will be waiting on you from now on, so I think they should know who you are, don't you?"

"I have no idea, but I suppose it does make sense."

"I am afraid your father and I have different ideas on how the servants should be handled, but then, I was one of them for a time, so perhaps that explains why I like to treat them like fellow human beings instead of slaves."

Horace had never met a lady who spoke so candidly before, except for the woman he was planning to marry—one of the reasons he had fallen in love with her. "They must enjoy working for you," he replied.

"I think they do, but don't let your tea get cold, and you must have some of this currant cake; it is one of Freda's specialties."

"I know."

"Oh, that's right! I forgot that she was here before you left."

"Yes, and father wrote that Jenkins is still with us as well. I look forward to seeing them both again, but I am most anxious to meet Edward. It's hard to believe that I actually have a sibling."

"Eddy is sleeping right now, but as soon as he wakes, I shall let you know."

When James returned, he was delighted when Gladys told him Horace was home and insisted Percy stay to meet him. Leaving Percy with Gladys, he practically ran up the stairs and into his son's apartment.

Horace had taken off his coat, washed his hands and face, and had a towel in his hand when James burst through the door.

"Horace, my boy!" he exclaimed giving him a hearty embrace.

Horace was so surprised, he unintentionally backed away. He had no memory of ever being touched by his father, and this show of affection was unexpected. "Hello, Father," he stammered.

Not realizing how atypical his enthusiasm must seem, James ignored Horace's reaction and went on to welcome him. "My God, it is good to have you home at last. I do hope it is for a good long visit."

"Sorry, Father, but I only have a few days. I have bought a home in Antwerp, and I have some carpenters remodelling it, so I should be there to keep an eye on them."

"Well, at least Antwerp is much closer than Africa. I am glad you decided not to settle there after all."

"I really like South Africa, Father, but I found there were more opportunities for my business in Belgium. Besides, my betrothed lives in Antwerp."

"You didn't write to me about this," James complained.

"I just asked for her hand before I left."

"Well, this is great news. Congratulations, son," James said, once more giving Horace a hug.

Horace was ready for it this time and hugged him back.

"Sarah is Jewish, Father."

James frowned, but only for a second; then his face lit up again, and he remarked, "Your grandmother was Jewish too, before your grandfather married her, and she had no trouble becoming a Christian."

"Grandmother never converted to Christianity, Father. Did you know she sent for a Rabbi to circumcise me eight days after I was born?"

The news stunned James, and his answer was brusque, "No, I did not, or I would not have allowed it."

"But you did know that Grandmother insisted that I attend Cohen's Hebrew Academy in Dover for two years before I went to London?"

"Yes, I did, but I thought that was because the man had such a notable reputation as a scholar. As soon as I found out what he was teaching, I put a stop to it. However, that is all in the past. As I wrote you, I am sorry I was not a more attentive father, but now I would like to try to make up for it if you will allow me to. I do care for you, Horace, and I would like us to be close from now on."

"You may not feel that way when you hear what I have to tell you."

"I cannot imagine anything you can say that will change how I feel."

"I hope not, Father. You see, I am considering converting to Judaism."

James couldn't hide his dismay, but all he could think of to say was, "We shall have to talk about this later. Now, hurry and put on your coat. I have a dear friend who is waiting to meet you."

When Horace entered the parlour, they were all waiting for him: James, Gladys, Percy, Dolly, and Edward. James introduced him to Percy, Dolly, and finally Edward, whom Horace was most anxious to meet.

Percy seemed a likable chap, and although Dolly lacked her mother's beauty, Horace thought she had a pleasant personality. When he came to Edward, he smiled and said, "We meet at last, my little brother, and what a handsome lad you are. I shan't be here for long, but I hope your mother will allow me to spend most of my time with you, so we can get to know one another. I quite like the idea of having a brother, don't you?"

Eddy wasn't quite sure what the nice man was talking about, but he politely smiled. Horace reached into his vest pocket and pulled out a little leather pouch before addressing Gladys, "Here is a little keepsake that I would like Edward to have. My grandmother gave me a pouch of gems similar to these when I was a young boy. I found them fascinating then, and still do. If she was alive today, I am sure she would want me to do the same for my brother. I shall give you a list of their names as well, so you can keep it for him."

He untied the cord on the pouch and spilled the contents onto a little table. Everyone gasped as they looked at the assortment of sparkling stones, stones that were obviously very precious. Gladys said it was far too generous a gift, but Horace only laughed and, looking up at James, said, "What do you think, Father?" He caught James off guard, and the look on his father's face brought back unpleasant memories.

James offered a weak smile and tried to sound pleased when he answered, "I think Edward is a very lucky little boy. That is very kind of you, Horace."

After a lovely dinner, which Freda had prepared with Horace's favourite dishes, they retired to the parlour where Gladys impressed her stepson with a medley of songs.

Horace would have enjoyed the evening more if he hadn't had such a perceptive mind. It was obvious to him that James was not fond of Edward. Horace didn't like to think of the child suffering the same neglect he had endured as a young boy. He also noted that the relationship between his father and Gladys lacked affection. In fact, James paid much more attention to his friend, Percy. There was something amiss, and Horace intended to find out what it was before he left Four Oaks.

James was disappointed during the next two days when Horace spent more time with Gladys and Edward than he did with him. Therefore, the day before he was to leave, he confronted him. "Son, I think we should go riding this afternoon. Just the two of us. We have a lot of things to talk about."

"I agree. I am sorry I have neglected you, but I promise that the whole day is yours." After suggesting they do a little fishing, he and James rode out to the lake, stopping to visit with two of their tenants whom Horace remembered. Freda had made them a hearty picnic lunch and said she would expect a dozen trout for dinner.

They set their lines, then sat on a log by the lake before Horace broke the silence. "My God, I had forgotten how beautiful this place is!"

"You have been away far too long, my boy. You will own it all one day so you should visit more often, and if you are set on marrying this girl of yours, you must bring her home, so she can see where she will be living for the rest of her life."

"It will not all be mine, Father. Edward shall have his portion too."

"Of course, I shall see that Gladys and the boy are provided for, but you are the firstborn, and you shall be the sole owner of Four Oaks when I am gone."

Horace decided to be blunt. "Why do you dislike Edward, Father?" James began to protest, but Horace interrupted him. "No, please don't deny it; I am not blind. I do not think we can ever have a close relationship if we are not honest with each other."

James knew Horace was right, so he decided to tell him Gladys's story and why he had married her. At first, Horace couldn't understand how his father could be so stupid, and he said as much, but when James explained what a phenomenal difference her presence had made to both his home and his life, Horace had to agree.

"However, Father, none of this is Edward's fault, and since you have declared him to be your son, I think you should treat him a little more civilly. You have said yourself that you wish you had been a more attentive father to me. You don't want to make the same mistake with Edward."

James promised to try to change his attitude toward the boy. Then he said, "Now what is this about you converting to Judaism? I hope you are not doing it just to impress your future in-laws."

"Not at all. I had made up my mind long before I met Sarah, although talking to her father helped convince me that my decision is the right one. He is a Rabbi and a very learned man. I don't know if you want to leave Four Oaks to a Jew, Father, but whether I inherit this land or not, I am determined to be Jewish."

To have a Jewish son was almost unimaginable for James, and he said, "I find it difficult to accept your decision, Horace, but you shall always be my son and heir no matter if you are Jewish, Buddhist, or any other faith you adopt for yourself. I only ask that you accept me for what I am as well and try to love me as I have learned to love you."

"I will, Father. I promise, and I know that Sarah and her family will feel the same."

Horace left the following day, promising to bring his bride home soon after they were wed, but he didn't invite James and Gladys to the wedding. James, feeling offended, complained until Gladys reminded him that Horace didn't expect to be married for at least a year and was probably waiting until they set the date before inviting any guests.

After he had left, James told Percy and Gladys about Horace's plans to convert to Judaism. Gladys didn't think anything of it, but Percy knew full well how prejudice often showed its ugly face where it was least expected.

James and Percy played on the same cricket team in Sandwich. James, a fairly good batsman, usually took the position as tail-ender while Percy, who was adept at both batting and bowling, was the team's all-rounder. They only played once a month, but they thoroughly enjoyed it.

One Saturday, they won a match against a Scottish team that they had never beaten before and returned to the club in high spirits. More rounds of drinks were bought than usual, and it was dinner time before Percy and James took their leave.

They decided to dine in one of the pubs before James left for home. He had left his horse and buggy at Big John's, a blacksmith shop close to Percy's home, but because it was a clear night, they were in no hurry to end their celebration.

As they ate and drank, they discussed books they had read by the author Alexandre Dumas. James owned copies of *The Three Musketeers*, *Twenty Years After*, *The Vicomte de Bragelonne*, and *Louise de la Valliere*, but he didn't have *The Man in the Iron Mask*. Percy informed him that he had two copies and would be happy to give James one.

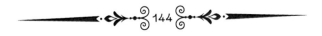

They had a few more drinks after dinner, and by the time they left the pub, they were walking with such drunken leans that they would have toppled over if each one hadn't supported the other.

"That was indeed a fine roast dinner, was it not?" Percy asked James.

"It most certainly was! Now how does that song go?" James asked, but before Percy could answer, he began to sing.

> "When mighty Roast Beef was the Englishman's food,
> It ennobled our brains and enriched our blood.
> Our soldiers were brave and our courtiers were good
> Oh! The Roast Beef of old England,
> And old English Roast Beef!"

Percy joined in.

> "But since we have learnt from all-vapouring France
> To eat their ragouts as well as to dance,
> We're fed up with nothing but vain complaisance
> Oh! The Roast Beef of Old England,
> And old English Roast Beef!"

"You sing like an angel, James, my boy," Percy announced.

"And you, my good man, warble like a bird," was his reply.

"I appreshiate your appreshiation," Percy answered.

"You may not be so appreci—appreciatable when I tell you which bird I am referring to."

"Ha! A nightingale, no doubt."

"Sorry, old chap, I was thinking more of a seagull."

"Well, at least I can sing louder than you." They began once again, trying to outdo each other until a constable came along.

"Here now, what's all this about?" he asked. When they explained how they had just won a game against a Scottish team, the constable laughed and said, "Well now, I should think that's a bonnie good reason for singing." Then, looking around to make sure there were no witnesses, he added, "I think a chorus or two of 'Rule Britannia' is more in order, gentlemen." The constable sang along with them for a few minutes as they made their way to Percy's flat.

James had never been inside Percy's little home before, but he felt at home as soon as he walked through the door. It was obvious there had been major alterations to the place since the décor was quite unconventional. Instead of the usual small rooms found in most houses, a wall between the parlour and the sitting room had been removed, creating a large and airy all-purpose area. One wall was outfitted with bookshelves and served as Percy's library. The other outside wall had two large windows that let enough light in to read by during the day. The wallpaper was patterned with warm tones of tan, brown, and rose-coloured stripes, and the drapes were made with a rich cream-colored damask. Four comfortable-looking armchairs and the two divans were covered in a floral print, adding brightness to the room.

There were only three other rooms on the first floor: a pantry and a large kitchen, which that contained a stove, a sink, and some well-built maple cupboards, and a solarium built off the kitchen, which overlooked the garden. It was that room where he ate his meals.

There was one large bedroom on the second floor and one room that could be used for guests or a servant. However, Percy seldom entertained guests at home, and he didn't hire live-in help. Being such a fastidious person himself, James was impressed by the tidiness of the place and was also surprised that it didn't spoil the warm and welcoming ambience.

"Now that you have seen how humble my little abode is, I do hope you won't write me off your 'best friends' list," Percy said after he showed James through the place.

"I like it. You have done wonders with it. It has everything a man needs in a space that would almost fit into my ballroom. Well done, I say!"

"Your approval means more to me than you shall ever know. Now I think it is time we had another drink before you take your leave."

"We do have a lot to celebrate. But if you don't want me falling out of my buggy on the way home, it had better be a small one."

After they finished their drinks, James rose to leave and then remembered the book. The extra copy was on one of the top shelves, so

Percy pulled out a small ladder and climbed up to get it.

James was standing below him glancing at the titles on some of the book jackets when Percy accidentally knocked a large book off the shelf. He hollered, "Look out," but instead of moving aside, James looked up, and the corner of the book hit him squarely on the forehead, rendering a small wound. Although the cut wasn't very deep or large, it bled profusely. Percy rushed him into the kitchen, sat him down beside the sink, and began applying cold compresses.

Perhaps the generous amount of liquor consumed was responsible for any lack of discomfort James felt because he laid his head back contentedly, closed his eyes, and enjoyed Percy's tender attention. The liquor was having an effect on Percy as well, and after applying a few compresses, his feelings toward his dear friend overtook him; he bent down and, very gently, kissed James on the lips.

As though in a dream, James felt a sensation of deep pleasure such as he had never felt before. Then, as he slowly opened his eyes, the reality of what was happening struck him like a bolt of lightning. Pushing Percy away, he jumped off the chair. "What do you think you are doing?" he shouted.

"My God, James, forgive me. I couldn't help myself," Percy cried.

The wet compress slid off James's forehead and a stream of blood began to run down into one of his eyes. He wiped at it with his arm, staining his shirt sleeve. "I want my coat. Where is my coat?" he hissed.

"At least let me bandage your head, James," Percy said, but when he took a step forward, James jumped back as though he was threatened by the devil himself.

"Keep away from me!" he ordered. Percy held up his arms in a hopeless gesture and went to fetch the coat. James reached out and snatched it from his hands, and without bothering to put it on, he left, running up the street like a madman with blood dripping down his face and onto his clothing. When he arrived at the blacksmith's shop, he lied and told Big John he had fallen and cut his head.

The name, Big John, was a contradictory title for the blacksmith, since he measured no more than five-foot-two in height. However, what he lacked in stature, he made up in strength, with a torso and arms to match those of a six-foot wrestler. Although James protested, Big John insisted on bandaging the wound before he left for home.

Once on the road, James was unable to erase the feeling of Percy's warm lips on his own, and he began to moan. Like the opening of Pandora's Box, all the thoughts he considered sinful and had struggled to suppress throughout his life began to run through his head.

"I am not like him! Oh, dear God, I cannot be like him. Damn him! Damn him! Damn him!" James cried aloud, but it did little to dispel his feelings of fear and guilt.

When he arrived home, he went directly to his apartment and pulled the bell cord. When Jenkins came, James asked him to fetch a basin of hot water. The butler was aghast at the sight of his master's attire and the bloody bandage on his forehead. He attempted to help James undress while inquiring about his injury, but James pushed him aside and ordered him to fetch a hot toddy. The blood had stained every item of James's clothing, and he stripped down to his skin before scrubbing himself thoroughly, as though Percy's lips had touched every inch of his body.

He was in bed by the time Jenkins returned with his drink. "Will that be all, sir?" There was something so enigmatic about the master's behaviour that Jenkins felt it wise to refrain from asking if he should apply a fresh bandage.

"Yes, that shall be all." Then, just as the butler was about to leave, James added, "Wait, there is one thing more. I had a slight accident and cut my head. As you can see, the blood has soiled my clothing, so you may take them with you and tell the housekeeper to have them cleaned. If they cannot be cleaned, she has my permission to discard them."

Jenkins gathered up the soiled garments, and after emptying the pockets and placing the contents on the dresser, along with James's watch, chain, and fob, he left. Through the years, Jenkins had become very fond of James; therefore, he was deeply concerned by the blood, which he noticed had soaked through the bandage on James's forehead. He decided to find Gladys and report what had happened.

Edward was sleeping peacefully, and Gladys had gone to spend a little time with Dolly, hoping to renew the close relationship they had enjoyed before Edward was born.

She found her daughter in her quarters sitting by the fireplace, reading. Although Dolly was surprised and pleased to see her mother, she found they had little to say to each other, and both were relieved when one of the housemaids brought Gladys a message that Jenkins would like a word with her in the kitchen.

She was shocked when she learned of the accident and wasted no time gathering together items to treat James's wound.

Chapter Sixteen

When someone knocked on his door, James, thinking it was Jenkins, called out to enter, but when he saw it was Gladys, he was visibly embarrassed. He had always been overly modest and wasn't happy to receive her while clad only in a nightshirt. Gladys sensed his aversion to her presence but chose to ignore it. She was carrying a jug of hot water and bandages and greeted him with a business-like tone. "Well now, James, let's see what damage you have done to yourself."

Before he could protest, she had the bloody bandage off and had started to bathe the cut. "Well, it doesn't look too deep, but it does need to be cleaned up," she said, smiling.

James had a headache from the moment he left Percy's flat, and the warm cloth on his forehead proved very soothing. He closed his eyes, lay back on the pillow, and relaxed. Once Gladys was satisfied the wound was clean, she dried it, applied a little salve, and put on a clean bandage. Her cool, confident hands brought back memories of his childhood and his beloved mother, who had died suddenly not long after Keith was killed.

"There you go. That should do it. I can tell by the look of you that you are properly knackered, as my da used to say, so I shall leave and come back in the morning." Then she surprised him by bending over and kissing his bandage. "There now, I've kissed it all better, so you can close your eyes and go to sleep." Without another word, she blew out his lamp and left the room. James allowed the serenity she had brought into the room to linger in his thoughts. He was asleep within minutes.

He had been dreaming about his mother when he awakened early in the morning. Although she had passed away years ago, James still missed her. He couldn't recall what the dream was about, but it left him with a pleasant feeling. Gladys's hand had the same soothing effects on his forehead as his mother's, and he stretched out in the bed contentedly and was about to doze off when the memory of Percy's kiss came back to him.

"Damn," he muttered as he got out of bed and into his clothes —clothes that he chose for himself rather than wait for Jenkins to lay them out. Not wanting to talk to anyone, James had breakfast early, hoping to be done before Gladys and Dolly came to the dining room.

When Gladys awoke in the morning, Edward was still asleep, so she decided not to disturb him and left her apartment hoping to take James a cup of tea and change his bandage before she had breakfast. To her surprise, he was already seated at the table when she entered the dining room. She could see he had eaten his breakfast and was drinking a second cup of tea.

"James! You are up early this morning," she said. "You should have stayed in bed. I was going to bring you some tea and toast and change your bandage."

"Thanks to you, it does not need it," he replied quickly. His hand was shaking, and he spilled tea on the tablecloth as he set his cup down. "I am going for a ride this morning, Gladys, and I do not know if I shall be home for lunch."

Gladys, noticing how pale and upset he appeared, was quite con-

cerned and offered to go with him, but he said he preferred to go alone and abruptly left. Shortly afterward, Jenkins came into the dining room, and Gladys related what had happened.

"Oh my," he said, "I did not have his clothes laid out. I was certain he would want to sleep late, and I didn't want to disturb him." Gladys assured him it wasn't his fault, but the idea of his master picking out his own clothing upset Jenkins so terribly that Gladys's assurance did little to help.

James left the yard on his horse at a gallop and sped across the fields, using the whip on the animal, hoping the speed would clear his head. He didn't see the fence until they were almost upon it, and it was only his horse's strength and agility that got them safely over. The realization that he could have crippled the animal brought James to his senses. Stopping beside a small pond, he dismounted and apologized as he rubbed the foam from the animal's neck with his kerchief.

Sitting down on a moss-covered log beside the pond, he tried to set his thoughts in order. He knew he had to get hold of himself and stop acting like a child, or worse, like an idiot.

He also realized how naïve he had been. He should have known that Percy and Helmut were more than just friends. But what puzzled him the most was why Percy would think he was like them.

He shook his head, but it did little to settle his mind. As he looked down into the pond, the iridescence of the water softened his features and reflected his image, bringing back memories of his youth.

James had always been a reticent child. "You will have to excuse James," his parents would say whenever company arrived and James failed to present himself. "He's very shy, you know."

They were exceptional parents, in that they allowed him his own peculiarities. However, as a sixteen-year-old young man entering Cambridge University, those same traits caused him to feel like a misfit. Whenever he was in the company of people his own age, he found he shared nothing in common, unlike the other new students who greeted each other as though they were old friends, instead of complete strangers.

Because there were no accommodations to be had on campus, James was forced to share a room in a boarding house next door to the university. His roommate was a strapping young man by the name of Norris Nottingham, whose temperament was the exact opposite of James, earning him the nickname of "Naughty Nottingham." Naughty's talents were all in sports, and he soon became one of the best players on the school's rowing and cricket teams. Although his features were rugged, he was popular with both sexes and soon had a good many friends.

James wasn't too fond of Norris, but it didn't take long for Norris to realize he had a dedicated scholar for a roommate. As much talent as Norris displayed athletically, he lacked academically. As a result, James spent a great deal of time that first year tutoring.

Norris was a campus hero. He usually accepted the role courteously, but there were occasions, especially if there were ladies present, when he was a braggart. Surprisingly, he also boasted about his intellectually talented roommate, since he considered James a genius. James's dislike for Norris gradually waned, perhaps because no one had ever looked up to him before, especially a person who was as popular as his roommate.

Norris insisted on James coming along whenever he was invited to a party or a social gathering. Before long, James overcame some of his shyness, except when he was in the company of young ladies, at which time he found himself afflicted with vocal paralysis.

When Norris found that James also enjoyed playing sports, he talked him into joining both the school's cricket and rowing teams. James's father was overjoyed when he received the news, having suspected that his son was something of a sissy.

Norris, a year older than James, laid claim to having seduced many young maidens. In truth, there was only one young maiden, and she was in a dream he had when he was twelve years old. James, on the other hand, had never learned to lie and readily admitted to being a virgin.

So Norris and two of his buddies decided it was time James became a man. Besides, Norris was anxious to make his false conquests a reality.

One night, they told James they were going to a gambling house and wanted him to come along.

James, always attempting to prove he was a good sport, said he thought it was a jolly good idea.

They took a cab to a part of town he had never visited before, and as they entered the district, he couldn't help but stare at the people as their carriage went by. Until he went to university, he had never ventured far from Sandwich. Although there were poor people in Sandwich as well, they were nothing like the ones he saw that night. He was appalled by their filthy appearance and felt more disgust than pity, since he could see no reason why a person couldn't keep clean, regardless of their income.

Most of the adults seemed to be dressed in layers of rags, while the children were clad mostly in layers of grime and wore hats or caps pulled down over their faces, as though seeking anonymity. Beggars held out their hands when they saw the carriage approaching. Then, when they received nothing but a look of disgust, they threw stones at the cab and used such profanity that James found himself blushing.

The houses and businesses on the street all looked alike, and when the driver pulled the horses to a stop in front of one of the doors, James wondered how he could tell one place from another. He said as much to Norris, who pointed to a dim red light that could barely be seen through the soot-covered window. A red light held no significance for James, so he thought nothing of it.

After paying the driver and knocking at the door, they were invited into a small vestibule by a very large woman. She was wearing a bright red wig and a black lace gown with what appeared to be nothing underneath but the lady herself. The intricate pattern of the lace against her white flesh made an intriguing, if not attractive, picture.

When she asked each of them for two pounds, James was surprised but didn't object. After she deposited the money in a metal box on a small table, she opened a door and stood in the opening so only one person could squeeze past her at a time. No one knew whether she did this for safety reasons, but as each boy brushed up against her generous body, a smug smile showed on her countenance.

James was the last to enter.

The room was dimly lit and smelled strongly of perfume. Instead of card tables, it contained plush divans and fancy chairs. James couldn't see any gamblers, but about ten scantily clad ladies, who appeared to be between the ages of fifteen and twenty, were lounging about.

Suddenly James realized where he was and why they were there. His face turned a deep crimson as he watched his companions choose which girl they wanted. Although he desperately wanted to leave, he knew his friends would never allow it.

Having no alternative, he was looking around the room trying to decide which of the girls looked the cleanest when one of them took hold of his hand and asked, "You've not been to a place like this before have you, dearie?"

James was speechless, but he managed to shake his head.

"Well, don't you worry, lovey. My name is Goldie, and you and I are going to get along just fine. I think a drink would help, don't you agree?"

James, surprised by the refined tone of her voice, managed a weak smile while nodding his approval. He hadn't noticed a small bar in a corner of the room, or the large and muscular black man behind it, until Goldie motioned for him to bring them two drinks as she led James to one of the settees.

When the bartender delivered the drinks, James was shocked at the cost, but the size of the bartender prevented him from complaining. The drink relaxed him a little, and they sat and talked for a short time. She surprised him by asking intelligent questions about his studies before taking his hand and leading him to one of many rooms off a long hallway, each with a different girl's name on the door.

Goldie's room appeared very small to James, but she said it was much larger than most, because she had seniority. She was also proud to point out that it was one of the only rooms with a window. Although it was sparsely furnished, it smelled clean. The walls were covered with wallpaper patterned with harp-playing angels, and the inappropriateness struck James as humorous, and he couldn't repress a giggle.

His calmness, however, began to wane as Goldie began unbuttoning his trousers. Once she had loosened them, she gently pushed him down on the bed and took off her robe.

He had never seen a nude woman before except in paintings and books, and they weren't nearly as intimidating.

Noticing that he wasn't yet aroused, Goldie lay down on the bed beside him and placed his hand between her legs. He yanked his hand back as though she had put it into a vat of boiling oil.

"Oh my, you are edgy, aren't you?" she said and then jokingly added, "It won't bite, you know." Next, she took hold of both his hands and put one on her breast and the other back between her thighs.

James was shocked motionless for a second, but when Goldie's hips began to gyrate, the bile rose in his throat.

He pulled his hands away, jumped up from the bed, ran to the open window, and heaved. Goldie, taking little umbrage, went over to him, held his head as gentle as a mother, and offered "tsk" after "tsk" sympathetically.

When he finished vomiting, he mumbled an apology as she led him to the bed, sat him down, and began wiping his face with a wet cloth.

"There's no need to apologize, my dear. You will find as you grow older that there are many more like you."

James had no idea what she was talking about, so he just said it must have been the drink that upset him.

Goldie didn't argue. Instead, she said that she wasn't that fond of her work either.

"I have to support my two little ones and my sick mother-in-law. My husband died five years ago, so I have no choice," she said, but James was dreading facing his friends so much that he hardly heard her.

Goldie seemed to understand, and when they returned to the salon and saw that the three boys were waiting for him with silly grins on their faces, she came to his rescue. Putting an arm around his waist, and making sure everyone in the room overheard, she praised his performance and made him promise to choose her the next time he came.

Norris and the others dubbed him "Lord Stallion" and congratulated him all the way home. He accepted the compliments with feigned pleasure but felt like a cheat and a liar, a feeling he had never experienced before and didn't enjoy.

Now, as he looked into the pond, Goldie's words came back to him. "You will find as you grow older that there are many more like you." It was odd that he could recall her words after all those years, and he wondered if she had thought he was like Percy and Helmut. He assured himself that she was mistaken. Unlike him, neither Helmut nor Percy had ever married, and that should be proof enough.

What he refused to admit was how he took little pleasure in consummating his marriage. However, there was something about Percy's kiss that scared him.

By marrying Gladys, he had hoped to prove that he had the same sexual desires as all the other men he knew, should anyone think otherwise. Now he had to prove it to himself.

Chapter Seventeen

James returned home late that afternoon and was told Percy had been there and left a message to say he would return the following day.

James thought it would be better to settle things with his friend at his home rather than at Four Oaks. It was a pleasant evening, so he decided to take his buggy and leave directly after dinner.

He now realized that his lack of sexual interest in the fairer sex may have caused Percy to misjudge him. Once he explained that he could never be more than a good friend, he thought there was no reason they couldn't forget the incident and resume their friendship.

He arrived at Percy's flat in good spirits, but when his friend answered the door, his heart began to pound and he felt faint.

"What's wrong, old boy?" Percy asked, noting James's sudden pallor.

"I'm fine, just fine," James stammered.

"Well, you don't look it. You had better come in and sit down before you fall down." When he went to take James's arm to steady him,

James avoided his touch. Percy became a little perturbed.

"Look here, James, you needn't worry. I have no intention of molesting you. I apologize for what happened last night. What I did was out of order, but I promise it shall never happen again. Now come in and sit down while I put the kettle on."

Neither spoke again until they were seated at the kitchen table drinking tea. Percy began, "I think we need to talk, James."

"You could have told me about you and Helmut," James burst out accusingly.

"I just took it for granted that you knew."

"Why would you do that? Surely you did not think I would approve?"

"Are you saying that had you known, Helmut and I would not have been welcome under your roof?"

"Of course not, but that does not mean I sanction that sort of relationship."

"I never thought I would be accusing you of being a bigot."

"I hardly think objecting to a criminal act has anything to do with bigotry."

"Oh, come now, James. You know perfectly well I am not a criminal."

"What you and Helmut did was against the law. Sodomy is indecent, and anyone who does it is committing a sin."

"Good Lord, you surely do not mean to say that someone as saintly as Helmut should be judged a sinner? Why, that man did more for mankind in one week than you or I shall do during our entire lives. And his sexual preference did not hurt a soul."

"Say what you will," James replied sharply, "but according to the Bible, God intended men to couple with women and not other men."

"God intended us to show unconditional love for one another, but few of us do it. Most men and women are the way you think they should be, but a good percentage of us are not. I have no idea why, but I do know that someday someone will find out, and when that day comes, we shall be able to be together without worrying about being thrown in prisons."

"You do not have to surrender to your passions, Percy. You can fight it."

"I have seen too many who thought that. They ended up jumping off the London Bridge. No, James. I have known true love and happiness, and for a while I thought I might find it again, but I am sorry to say that if you remain in denial, you shall die a very sad old man."

"That may be better than dying a sinner."

"You may call me a sinner if you choose to, James, but would you call all those who are born with some deformity sinners? Like myself, they did not ask to be created that way, but since we were, we should have as much right to happiness as anyone. Now if you cannot understand that, I have nothing more to say to you, so I think you had better leave. I shall be selling my place here and moving back to London. If you want to terminate my employment, you know where to reach me."

Percy handed James his coat and opened the door.

Unable to think of anything pertinent to offer, James silently took his coat and left. Unconscious of his movements, he climbed into his buggy and took the reins. He was well out of town before he fully realized what had happened. It was over. He had lost the best friend he ever had. He shuddered as a feeling of emptiness overtook him. Although he put on his jacket, it did little to warm him.

Gladys was upset when James told her that Percy was selling his house in Sandwich and intended to live in London all year round. When she suggested that they host a farewell party for him, James confessed that they were no longer friends. She knew how fond the two men were of each other, and for days she continued to pester him to do all he could to resolve their differences.

Finally, he confided in her about Percy and Helmut's relationship. He could hardly believe it when she took the news lightly and added that she had assumed as much.

"And you approved?" he asked.

"I saw how happy they were, so how could I not?" Gladys answered.

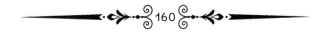

"But it is against the law."

"I had a friend called Millie who was an actress, and she told me that there were many very well-known and respectable men who fancied men rather than women, but they had to keep it a secret. She said there were those who even suspected that Shakespeare might have had a beau or two."

"I care not who they are, they should be ashamed."

They were sitting in the library, and Gladys reached over, put her hand on his, and, in an understanding tone of voice, asked, "James, are you worried that you may share the same sort of feelings toward Percy that Helmut did?"

James yanked his hand away and snapped, "No! Certainly not. But that is what Percy thought. I am not like him and never shall be."

"I never meant to hurt your feelings, James; it is just that if you were, I would not blame you. Percy is a very charming and kind man."

James jumped up and angrily declared, "I do not wish to discuss the subject, and I do not want Percy's name mentioned in this house again." With that, he left the room.

For the next few months, James did his best to appear happy, but memories of the good times that he had shared with Percy kept haunting him, and the only relief he could find came from a bottle of alcohol. For a while, Gladys did her best to involve him in the social life they once had. She invited Bob and Tina Rudyard, Mary, and other friends for evenings of singing or playing games, but James refused to join in. He would, however, make a brief appearance before feigning a headache or some other ailment and excusing himself. Before long, he even refused to do that, and Gladys stopped inviting people.

One evening after she had attended the theatre with Tina and Bob, she returned home late and was surprised to find James had waited up for her. As usual, he had been drinking heavily, and when he rose to welcome her, he had trouble standing.

Gladys hastened to put her arm around him and said, "Here, James, let me help you to bed."

Instead of resisting, James answered, "Yes, my dear, it is about time we went to bed."

As she led him down the hall and went to turn into his apartment, he stopped short and announced, "Oh no, not my bed, my love, your bed."

Gladys was stunned. "What do you mean 'my bed?'"

"Just that. It is high time we made this a true marriage."

"But, James, remember your promise?"

He shook his head side to side and mumbled, "Sorry, Gladys, so sorry. You see, I must do this."

Gladys heard the anguish in his voice, and her heart went out to him. She owed him so very much, how could she refuse? She reasoned that because she would never see Toughie again, she wasn't being unfaithful, and perhaps it would erase the doubts that she knew were driving James to drink. "What about Eddy?" she asked.

"Edward? He is sleeping in the nursery," he answered.

James managed to consummate their marriage that night before he passed out, but he did it without pleasure and was not even fully aware of the act.

Gladys spent the rest of the night on her divan and was up, dressed, and out of the room before he awoke. Without realizing it, James had mumbled Percy's name during the coupling, which confirmed Gladys's suspicions as to his true sentiments.

When James woke in the morning, he had such a pounding headache that he didn't feel he could open his eyes, so he kept them closed as he reached out to his night table to ring the bell for Jenkins.

After waving his hand about wildly, he slowly opened one eye. The other eye opened much quicker when he realized the bed he was in was not his own. For a second, he couldn't understand not only why he was in Gladys's room but stark naked as well. Then some of the events that took place the night before slowly came back to him.

He remembered telling Jenkins to go to bed and that he would wait up for Gladys. He knew he had spent the evening drinking more than usual but had trouble remembering why. There was only one reason he could think of for being in his wife's bed, and the realization of what he had done made him feel sick with guilt.

Sitting up very slowly, he looked around. There was no sign of Gladys, but his clothes were folded over a chair. Hoping he had come to her room and passed out and that she had put him to bed was the only thing he could think of to ease his conscience.

Hurriedly, he put on his clothes, peered out the door, and looked furtively up and down the hall. Seeing no one there, he made a dash to his own apartment.

It was a tremendous relief when he came down to breakfast and Gladys greeted him with her usual smile. He longed to apologize for his behaviour but wasn't quite sure what to apologize for, so he didn't say anything.

Gladys was disappointed in him for breaking his promise, but because she felt indebted to him, she decided not to make an issue of it.

James never requested her company in bed again, and afraid he might make the same mistake, he even cut down on his drinking, and life in the manor improved.

For a time, Gladys dreaded the evenings in fear that James would want to sleep with her again. When a month went by and he made no inappropriate advances, she began to relax, until she discovered that she was once again expecting another baby. Having a baby with someone she didn't love didn't appeal to her, and she was certain James would feel the same.

She waited a few months before she told him, and his only response was a nod and a curt, "Thank you for letting me know."

It was as she had expected; he appeared as disappointed with the news as she had been. Oddly enough, instead of understanding his lack of empathy, she felt offended.

After he left Gladys, James went into the library, poured himself a drink, and sat down to think. If she had just phrased her announcement differently, he might have accepted the news more graciously, but she had said "I am having a child" instead of "we are having a child", and the first thing that came to his mind was that, somehow, she had managed to have another rendezvous with her Italian lover. As considerate as James was, he didn't intend to be saddled with another bastard, and if Gladys had committed adultery, he would insist she and her two children leave Four Oaks.

Luckily, the second drink calmed him down, and he began to

think more rationally. He recalled the night he had spent in Gladys's bed and realized that the timing coincided. He had been ashamed for breaking his word to her, but the relief he felt over knowing that he finally had proof, which he had been quite desperate for, was exhilarating.

He was so relieved to have proof that he overlooked a substantial flaw in his reasoning: he already had Horace. If the existence of his son had not proved his preferences, how could a second child?

He went to Gladys's apartment and knocked on the door but received no answer, so he began looking for her. She was working in her flower garden, kneeling on a small mat. Hearing him approaching she looked up.

"Did you want something?" she asked without smiling.

"I just want to say I am sorry for my abrupt behaviour. It was rather a shock, especially for a man of my age. I also want to say that although I wasn't the best father to Horace, I shall endeavour to do better this time." When she didn't answer, he started to walk away but turned around and came back. "I say, Gladys, should you be down on your knees digging? You must take care of yourself, you know."

Looking down at her, he continued, "How are you feeling?"

"I am quite fine, I assure you," Gladys replied neutrally.

"If you need anything, or if I may do something for you, please let me know."

As he walked back to the house, James was thinking that now that he was going to be a father, Percy would know that their sexual preferences were nothing alike. He was even tempted to get in touch with his old friend to tell him the news, but, although he would never admit it to anyone, not even himself, he was still too unsure of his feelings to risk being in Percy's company again.

Eliza Mary Hornsby was born on the fourth of November, 1857. Dolly fell in love with her little sister as soon as she laid eyes on her, but Edward, who was not yet three, had no intention of allowing the infant to come between him and his doting mother.

Every time Gladys attempted to feed Eliza, he would try to push the baby away. Gladys was relieved when her milk began to dry up and she could hire a wet nurse. She also found Edward's attitude toward his baby sister stressful. Therefore, she allowed Dolly and Nanny to look after Eliza more and more each day until she barely saw the child. Dolly was delighted with the task, and, although only twelve, she displayed a natural talent for the chore.

James was also enchanted with his little daughter, and he and Dolly often took her for long walks in the pram when weather permitted. Although Eliza didn't resemble her mother, she was blessed with beautiful features. To capture her likeness, an artist might use a pleasing mixture of soft watercolours, whereas Gladys's portrait would be more suited to brightly-coloured oils. Eliza was also a happy child and very seldom cried, which made her a favourite among the servants.

James could hardly wait for his Aunt Jean and Horace to see the baby, so he wrote to them both a few days after Eliza was born, inviting them to come for a visit.

Jean arrived a week later and was so taken with the child, she stayed for two weeks. During that time, she treated Gladys with more respect than she had previously, and she was even kind to Eddy.

There was something about Jean that caused Gladys to feel they shared a common bond, and, although she had no idea why, she no longer felt intimidated by the woman.

After Eliza was born, Jean's visits were more frequent, and she always came with some little gifts for all three children, a gesture that Gladys remarked was unnecessary but very much appreciated.

Horace had married his Jewish sweetheart but hadn't brought her to Four Oaks until he received James's letter with the birth announcement. He and Sarah arrived two months later, after he had written to explain that he and his wife would be unable to eat non-kosher food now that he had converted to Judaism. He suggested that Freda should get in touch with the Heildelkoff's cook, who was also Jewish and could give her instructions on how to prepare kosher food.

It seemed that Horace wanted very much to please his new bride, but Freda wasn't happy about it. "I love that boy, mum," she complained to Gladys. "But I don't hold with having to make special dishes just because he went an' married a foreigner."

"The reason she has to eat different foods is not because she is foreign, Freda. You see, according to the rules of their church, they are forbidden to eat certain foods. I am sure it will not be difficult to oblige them. Since I have met Mrs Heildelkoff at one of Mary's teas, I shall go with you when you go to talk to her cook," Gladys promised.

That seemed to satisfy Freda. In fact, she looked forward to a trip to town with her mistress, and it would give her a chance to wear the lovely coat Gladys had made her.

James and Gladys's first impression of Horace's wife, Sarah, was not as favourable as they had anticipated. Her appearance was that of a mousy little woman dressed appropriately in a plain, dark-grey ensemble that, when she stepped away from the lamplight, tended to render her invisible.

However, it only took a few days before she had James wrapped around her proverbial little finger. Never had he met a woman who could give such highly intelligent and interesting opinions on a vast variety of subjects. They enjoyed each other's company and spent hours discussing history and authors, leaving Horace and Gladys free to entertain each other and the children.

The newlyweds stayed at Four Oaks for one month. Sarah may not have been a striking beauty, but she had other attributes that made up for it. In spite of her plain features, she showed no signs of an inferiority complex. She was brighter than most men she knew and proud of it. Although Gladys wasn't as learned as Sarah, they had the same ideas about women's rights.

Gladys could see why Horace was in love with Sarah. Her eyes were like a door that welcomed you into her heart. Gladys thought she was wonderful.

As for Horace, Gladys felt as though she had known him all her life. He was like the brother she had never had, and he must have felt the same because they both found it easy to confide in each other. Horace had invested in diamonds when they were in demand and was clever enough to foresee a drop in the market and had begun purchasing other types of stones that were rapidly becoming popular. Gladys was intrigued with his stories of the exotic countries he had visited in order to find the gems, and the obvious interest she displayed encouraged him to go on for hours.

He also told her about his feelings toward James and how happy he was to convert to Judaism. "I only wish my grandmother could have witnessed it. She would be so happy. Until I converted, I felt as though I had no true identity. It was as though I was an empty shell, but now I feel whole. It is truly amazing!"

Gladys said she knew exactly how he felt, and since James had told him all about her past, she tried to explain how she felt going through all the different changes in her life.

"I would die if I had to go back to Old Nichol, but even so, I don't feel I belong here either."

"Are you and father not happy together?"

"We are not miserable, but we both have lost the only person in our lives that could make us truly happy."

"I suppose you mean Eddy's father, but who has Father lost? Not mother—I don't think they were all that happy."

"You remember James's friend, Percy? Well, Percy and your father had such good times together before they had a falling out that James hasn't been the same since. Percy has tried to contact him to no avail. If you get a chance, Horace, I wish you would try to persuade him to visit Percy again."

Horace had sensed that there was something more than just a friendship between the two men the first time he had seen them together, but the thought was not a pleasant one, and he had ignored it. Now that he was Jewish, Horace had experienced bigotry for the first time, and it had taught him the value of tolerance.

"Of course I will, but what about you? What can we do about your unhappy situation?"

"There is nothing you can do. My love lives in another world with a family of his own, and I shall never see him again. That is the way it must be. But I have three wonderful children, and your father has given us everything a family could wish for, so you mustn't feel sorry for me. My goodness, Horace, this is heaven compared to some places I have lived."

"Well, Father is lucky to have you, and if you ever need someone to talk to, you just write to me, yes?"

Gladys promised she would, but, oddly enough, it was Sarah who she eventually came to regularly corresponded with. Perhaps because Sarah had written to her announcing the news of her pregnancy, saying she hoped she would be as perfect a parent as Gladys.

After Horace and Sarah left, James asked Gladys if she had noticed any difference in Horace since he converted to Judaism, and when she said he was still as nice as ever, James replied, "I pray all our neighbours and friends will feel that way when they learn he is no longer a Christian."

Chapter Eighteen

For over a year, Eddy continued to resent Eliza's presence. Things changed one morning. When Edna, the nanny, wasn't looking, he dropped a spoonful of porridge on the floor for the cat. Eliza giggled with delight and did the same thing. When Nanny saw what was happening, she scolded them both, and, for the first time, Eddy felt a sense of kinship with his little sister. From that time on, Eliza adored Eddy, and to his delight, all he had to do was make a funny face, execute a somersault, or just jump up and down on one leg, and she would clap her hands and beg for more.

Eddy's personality changed for the better now that he had an admiring audience, but James's dislike for the boy continued, and, without realizing it, he often referred to him as "that boy" or just "him," and seldom by his proper name. Like Dolly, Eddy referred to James as "sir," whereas James insisted Eliza call him "Papa." It was only natural that the boy began to have strong feelings of antipathy toward the man who he thought was his father.

Nevertheless, the family did enjoy many outings together as well as celebrations of different holidays and birthdays. Aunt Jean was always invited to these celebrations, and she seldom turned one down. Gladys returned to the choir, and she and James attended church on a regular basis. By all appearances, they were an idyllic family and were well thought of in the town. But in truth, Gladys still longed for Toughie and James for his dear friend, Percy.

James and Gladys received many invitations to balls, dinner parties, and other social events. Neither was fond of socializing, but they attended quite a few events for appearance's sake, and sometimes they reciprocated. This meant many previously unused rooms at Four Oaks would have to be reopened. Because these rooms hadn't been used for many years, Gladys thought they should be redecorated and James agreed.

She was delighted when he left the matter in her hands with no limit or budget. Having decided to choose the furniture first, then drapery to match, she began her shopping in Sandwich but wasn't happy with the selection there. She was tempted to visit Dover, where there were stores that carried the styles she preferred, but the fear of running into Peter was too great, so she decided to go to London.

At first James thought he would accompany her, but his cricket team had been challenged to a match he didn't want to miss. Gladys was happy to be travelling alone and she enjoyed the train ride.

After she arrived and was settled in, she took a cab to a furniture store nearest to James's flat. As soon as she entered the building, a short elderly gentleman rushed to greet her. Smiling, he said, "Why, hello, Mrs Pickwick. How very nice to see you again. And what may I help you with today? If I remember correctly, your preference was Tudor, was it not?"

Gladys was so surprised when he called her Mrs Pickwick that she didn't answer for a second. Then, when she looked around at her surroundings, it was as though she had stepped back in time. This was the same store she had bought many of the furnishings for

Oaken Arms. The same little man, the same arrangements of settees and chairs, and the same smell of polished oak.

She must have paled, because the clerk reached for her arm. "Oh my, Mrs Pickwick. I pray you are not going to faint. Here, let me help you over to a chair."

She allowed him to seat her, then she took two deep breaths and the colour returned to her cheeks.

"I am sorry, Mr Samson." Gladys remembered his name because Andrew had thought it so unsuitable that, as soon as they left the shop, he laughed and remarked about it. "I am quite recovered now," she assured him, but she didn't know whether to leave or stay. It had brought back so many memories that for a minute she couldn't think clearly.

"I am pleased to hear that, Mrs Pickwick."

"I am not Mrs Pickwick anymore, Mr Samson. I have remarried and my name is Mrs Hornsby now."

"Please accept my apology and my congratulations, Mrs Hornsby," he said, adding a slight bow.

When Gladys remained silent, he seemed to have trouble thinking what to say next. Gladys guessed that he was trying to decide whether to ask about her father-in-law or not, and she didn't want to have to explain what happened to Andrew so she pointed to a settee.

"I am pleased to see that you still carry the same line."

"Yes indeed, Mrs Hornsby. But if you will come this way, I have something special I would like to show you."

She followed him up the stairs to the second floor where he pointed to a row of armchairs. "I just bought these last week, and I was hoping that someone like you, who I know appreciates fine craftsmanship, would come in."

Gladys had never seen such exquisite chairs. The grain of the wood they were made of had different shades that swirled and curled in delicate patterns and shone like treacle. "What kind of wood is it?" she asked.

"Walnut, mum. They are handcrafted out of walnut by one man. They took him two years to make, and they are the only ones like it. They have an extra thick layer of horsehair to make them even more comfortable. Please sit on one."

Gladys sat down. "This is the most comfortable chair that I've ever sat in, except for one of those big leather chairs you have downstairs. Is there a matching settee or two?"

"I agreed to take these twelve chairs on assignment for the chap, and he said that was all he had made, but perhaps if you were to meet him and tell him you intend to purchase all twelve, he might agree to make a settee to match. I can give you his name and address if you like."

"You don't mind doing that?"

"Mrs Hornsby, you and your father-in-law were good customers back when I was just starting out, and you have no idea what that meant to me."

The cost of the twelve chairs was as much as Gladys intended to spend on redecorating the dining room and the ball room, but if the craftsman would make her two settees, she could buy material and make the drapery herself. She had promised to meet Percy for lunch, so she thanked Mr Samson, took the address, and left.

Percy was waiting for her at a little tea shop near James's flat. After they ordered their lunch, Gladys told him about the chairs. Percy was very interested and suggested they take a cab and visit the craftsman as soon as they finished their meal.

"Where does he live?" he asked.

Gladys hadn't looked at the piece of paper the salesman had given her, so she took it out of her purse and read it. "Let's see. His name is Richard Ellison and he lives on West Bethal Green Road," she gasped.

Seeing the look of concern on Percy's face, she explained, "He lives very near Warehouse Corner." Percy still didn't understand why that should bother her.

"Remember I told you and James how Ma and Da had a junk-yard in Old Nichol? Well, Warehouse Corner is what the junk men called the place where they came to pick up whatever the wealthy threw away. And when I was old enough, I helped push the cart with Da."

"Gladys, if it is going to upset you, I can go alone to see him for you."

"Thank you, Percy, but there is no one there I know anymore. The last time I was there was when Laura Watt sent me to bring Pinky Davis and Ellie O'Brian back to the inn in Dover. Things were, and likely still are, so dire that, rather than see their girls die of starvation, many families sold them or gave them to people like the Watts so they could work for their room and board. I must say though, that the Watts were one of the few who gave their girls a small wage, even though it wasn't mandatory.

"No, I think I can handle it now, Percy, but having you with me makes it much easier."

Richard Ellison lived right on the border of Old Nichol. Although his house was not much better than some of the shacks in the slums, he did have more room, and there wasn't an open sewer running past his back door. There was a large shed at the back of his house, and since smoke was coming from its chimney, Percy said that must be where he did his work.

After asking the cab driver to wait, they approached the house and knocked at the door. Someone with a very sweet-sounding voice called out, "I'm comin'." Then they heard the same voice say, "Lizzy, luv, come stir this 'ere pot while I gets the door."

It would be impossible to describe the woman who opened the door without using the word sweet. Not only did she have a sweet voice, but her delicate features and her blonde ringlets could be best described using the same adjective.

She offered a dimpled smile and said, "Hello."

She was so childlike that Gladys was about to ask if her father was home when one of the four children sitting around a table asked, "Who is it, Momma?"

"Hit's a proper lady and a gentleman," was her reply.

"Are you Mrs Ellison?" Gladys asked.

When the woman confirmed that she was, Percy spoke up and inquired if her husband was at home.

The woman said she would send one of the children out to the shop to fetch him, then insisted they come in and wait for him.

After seating them, she said, "I'll jist go an' check on the stew, if you don't mind. Won't be a minute." She left Gladys and Percy with three children staring at them like they were creatures from another world. Gladys saw they had all been working on their slates, and she thought they might have been practicing their sums.

Smiling at the girl, who appeared to be the eldest, she asked, "Do you like school?"

The girl blushed and mumbled something Gladys couldn't hear. Realizing the girl was shy, she gave up trying to have a conversation when the smallest child surprised her and spoke up, "We don't go to no school, ma'am."

"We don't go to *any* school, Nicky," a young lady corrected the boy as she entered the room.

"Hello. I am Liz Ellison." She gave them both such a firm handshake that Gladys liked her immediately. "I am the oldest of these ragamuffins, and after hearing Nicky, I am rather ashamed to admit that I am responsible for their education."

When Gladys and Percy looked surprised, she explained, "You see, I had a cousin who was fortunate enough to have a tutor, and I was allowed to visit her whenever she had her lessons. I learned enough to teach my siblings. Because my mother died when I was born, I am the only one of us that is related to my wealthy aunt. Unfortunately, she refuses to acknowledge the rest of the family."

Mrs Ellison came back just as Liz finished talking, and she jokingly scolded, "Liz, I'm sure these folks didn't come all the way out 'ere jist ta hear about your aunt, bless her soul. Maybe you'd best go an' see what's keepin' your da."

Liz left and Mrs Ellison said, "Hopes you'll scuse the smell. I 'as a pot o' rabbit stew cookin'."

"It smells delicious, Mrs Ellison," Gladys replied. She meant it, too. It reminded her of the smell of stew she and Dolly had been given when they visited the Romani camp back in Dover.

"You can calls me Nell. Oh, I hears them comin' in now," She announced as her husband entered the room.

Richard Ellison was tall and dark complexioned. He wore his hair in a single long braid that hung down his back. His countenance portrayed intelligence, solemnity, and a hint of obduracy, but there was enough kindness in his eyes to make him likable.

"You wanted to see me?" he asked.

Percy stepped forward and held out his hand. "Yes, Mr Ellison. My name is Percy Hudson, and this is Mrs Gladys Hornsby. Gladys, would you like to tell Mr Ellison why we have come?"

"My husband and I are redecorating our home, Mr Ellison, and I came to London to purchase some new furniture. Mr Samson was kind enough to show me the chairs you made, and I would like to purchase them all."

Nell couldn't control her excitement and she jumped up and down, clapping her hands. "Oh, Ricky, luv, isn't this wonderful?"

Richard put his hand on her head and smiled down at her before answering, "I am pleased to hear that, Mrs Hornsby, but I fail to see why you had to come and see me. Mr Samson will be the one you will be dealing with."

"Yes, of course. But, you see, I wondered if I could also commission you to make one, or perhaps two, settees to match the chairs? Mr Samson agreed to let me deal directly with you so you wouldn't have to pay his commission."

"I am sorry, Mrs Hornsby, but I promised Nell and the children that as soon as the chairs sold, we could move out of this neighbourhood. I don't know where I will find a place, but I hope it is somewhere that has good water and smells a lot sweeter."

Gladys thought about all the families she had talked Lord Sorenson and his benevolent friends into bringing out of Old Nichol and she had an idea. "Mr Ellison, Richard, if I may, what if I could find you a place in the country where the water and the air are fresher than any you have dreamt of? Would you be interested in moving there?"

"And how would I make a living? The money I will make on the chairs will not last forever. Right now, I work on the docks now and again, and that keeps food on the table."

"My husband has a large estate, and he is need of good carpenter to keep things repaired. He has a few cottages on his property, and I'm sure you would find one of them to suit you. There are also some large sheds that I'm sure a man of your talents could convert into a shop. You could work on pieces like my settees when you weren't busy mending. You could make a lot of money with your work, Richard. Have you any idea how envious our friends will be when they see my chairs?"

She paused and gazed at Mr Ellison thoughtfully. "What do you say?"

"Well, we shall have to think about it, Mrs Hornsby. I don't have any more of that walnut wood I used for the chairs, but I think if I made the settees in the same style as the chairs and used oak instead, the contrast would be striking. Nell, where are your manners? Liz luv, help your ma get the tea."

Percy hadn't said a word, but he was shocked at Gladys's offer. She was hiring a man and offering him a house for his family without discussing it with James. James wasn't going like it and he couldn't blame him. He decided to intercept on James's behalf. "Excuse me, but I wonder if I could have a word, Gladys? In private."

Richard didn't look pleased, but he took the children into the kitchen.

"Gladys, what on earth do you think you are doing?"

"I know it seems a bit crazy, Percy, but it's not just that I want the settees. If you saw that man's work, you would understand that he should be famous. I can't see him living in such a place when he has so much talent. James will agree, I'm sure. I shall wait until the chairs are home before I tell him."

"You are not being fair to this family unless you talk to James first. You have no right to promise them anything." Gladys realized that she hadn't thought about what James would say, and she had to admit that Percy was right.

"What will I do?" she asked.

"Leave it up to me. After all, I am a lawyer and I'm sure I can settle this to everyone's satisfaction."

As they were having their tea, Percy explained that Gladys was obliged to have James's approval before they settled the matter. He suggested that Gladys would return home and if James agreed, Gladys would send word to him and he would come and tell Richard.

"We'll keep our fingers crossed, mum," Nell said as they were saying goodbye.

Gladys only stayed in London long enough to have the chairs shipped and to buy some drapery material. When she arrived home, she told James that she had bought twelve chairs but waited until they were delivered before she told him of her plan.

"When I lived in Dover," she explained, "I talked my father-in-law, Andrew, and some of his wealthy friends, who were raising money for the poor people in Ireland, into doing something for England's poor as well. They brought many families out of the slums and found them jobs and homes. Lord Sorenson even hired a few families. Although the Ellisons do not live in Old Nichol, they live right beside it, and I think they should have a better home. Besides, James, Richard Ellison is an excellent carpenter and craftsman, and I'm sure he would be more of a help than a burden."

James was also taken with the chairs, and he knew that his lone handyman was finding it difficult to keep up with the repairs needed on the estate and could use some help, so he agreed.

Richard Ellison and his family arrived before the month was out and were overjoyed with their new surroundings. Liz Ellison soon made friends with Dolly and Blossom, and they convinced her to join them in the church choir.

Gladys was very pleased with herself. She experienced the same satisfying feeling of accomplishment that she had felt years ago when she talked her father-in-law into bringing other poor families from Old Nichol and finding them jobs and places to live.

Among the social invitations Gladys and James received was one inviting them to a ball hosted by Lord and Lady Nichols. The Nichols estate was halfway between Dover and Sandwich, so Gladys and James were invited to stay for the weekend.

They arrived in time for tea then retired to their rooms to dress for the ball. Gladys wore her best gown, and when James took her arm and they came down the stairs, she received many admiring glances from the male guests, except for one: Lord Cedric Sorenson.

Cedric still blamed Gladys for his dear friend, Andrew Pick-wick's, sinful behaviour. Andrew had confessed to his Lordship that he had persuaded Richard Ledingham, the Duc de Artois, to seduce Andrew's estranged wife, Rose, in order to obtain a divorce and marry his daughter-in-law, Gladys. Lord Cedric thought the act despicable and had suggested that Gladys had taken advantage of her beauty and seduced him. He continued to blame her even though Andrew swore Gladys knew nothing of his plans.

"I say, what is she doing here?" he asked Lady Sorenson as soon as he saw her.

"She is married to James Hornsby now, Cedric. As mistress of Four Oaks, she has just as much right to be here as you or I. Now please do your best to be polite, or I shall insist we leave." She took his arm and pulled him toward Gladys and James. "Gladys, my dear. It is so good to see you, and how are you, James?"

James replied that he was fine and shook hands with Cedric.

"Hello, Madeline, and how are you, Cedric?" Gladys asked. She didn't know why, but she deliberately omitted the titles of Lady and Lord.

Cedric didn't answer but Lady Madeline smiled. They talked about the children and Gladys invited Lady Madeline to bring the children to Four Oaks for a visit. Finally, she took Lady Madeline aside and said, "He still doesn't believe that I knew nothing about Andrew's devious plans, does he?"

"No, my dear, but now that we are all staying here it would be a good idea if you had a talk with him. I shall see if I can arrange it." The following day all the guests were invited to take part in a fox hunt. Gladys never liked the idea of so many dogs chasing one poor little fox, so she declined. She was taking tea in the garden when Cedric came in and sat down beside her.

"Would you like some tea, Your Lordship?" she asked.

"That would be nice, thank you." He answered brusquely. Gladys poured the tea, then she waited for him to speak. He took his time.

"This, as you probably know, was not my idea. I see no reason why we should be cordial to each other, but, for some reason, Madeline is fond of you and she thinks we can be friends."

Gladys's answer surprised him. "That's ridiculous!"

Shocked, Cedric sat straight in his chair, turned to look at her, and said, "I beg your pardon?"

"I said that is ridiculous! How can we be friends? You, Sir Cedric, seem to think I am a wanton woman, and I cannot help but think you are a stubborn ass!"

In spite of himself, Cedric had to laugh. "I say, Gladys, that is going a little too far, wouldn't you say?"

"No, Cedric. Not really. I had nothing to do with Andrew's actions before he was murdered, or I certainly would have put a stop to his plans. I loved him, but only as a father-in-law. Now I've told you this before and yet you still choose not to believe me, so how can we be friends?"

Cedric didn't answer for a while and Gladys could tell he was thinking, so she sat back, drank her tea, and waited. Finally, he must have made up his mind.

"Well, Gladys, first I would like you to tell me something."

"Yes, Your Lordship?"

"Is there any more tea in that pot?"

Gladys laughed and poured him another cup.

"Now, my dear, will you still think me a stubborn ass if I say I am sorry?"

In spite of their newly-formed friendship, Gladys didn't see the Sorensons often. She and James soon tired of social events and both agreed that they enjoyed a more casual life at home.

Chapter Nineteen

James had a weekly London newspaper delivered to Four Oaks, and one day while he was away, Gladys decided she would read the entertainment section. When she saw the name "Othello" in large print, her heart missed a beat. Then, when she read that a group of Italian players had returned from America and would be playing their last performance of *Othello* in London, she knew it had to be the troupe belonging to Toughie's uncle.

She spent the next two days on edge, waiting for James to return. When he did come home, she wasted no time in showing him the notice. When he had finished reading it, she said, "James, what do you think I should do?"

"I certainly fail to see what good it would do for you to see him again. You are a respectable married woman now, and an affair would not only jeopardize your reputation but mine as well," he replied.

"I have no intention of having an affair. I made that mistake once, and I shall not do it again. But, James, he has the right to know he has a son. I feel I cannot deny him that."

"Well, only you can decide, Gladys. I shan't stop you from going, but if you do, I think I should accompany you. You shall have to make up your mind soon though. The performance is in a week's time."

"Thank you, James. I will let you know tomorrow."

"Well, I think I shall have one of my employees in London reserve two tickets anyway; then we shall have them if we do decide to go, and if not, I am quite sure there are people in my office who would be happy to use them."

Gladys had a difficult time coming to a decision. She knew it was useless to hope for a reunion with Toughie; he would never betray his wife again, especially since they now had one, or perhaps more, children to consider. Finally, she decided to go and take Eddy with her, but she wouldn't go to the theatre. Instead, she would leave Toughie a letter and allow him to decide if he wanted to see her again.

When she told James her plans and said that she would rather he didn't go with them, he forbade her to go alone. It took another day to convince him otherwise, and he only agreed after she promised that she would not tell Eddy that Toughie was his real father.

James began to worry immediately after he gave Gladys permission to take Edward to London. He felt that if he was with her when she met the young Italian, it would prevent her from doing something irresponsible, something that would threaten the tranquil, if not happy, life he and Gladys had built together.

A few days later, Gladys and Eddy, dressed in their Sunday best, were ready to leave. Even James had to admit that Eddy was a very handsome little lad in his new sailor suit.

When Eddy learned that he was going to London on a train, he was pleased, but when he found out that Eliza wasn't going with them, he stamped his feet and declared he wouldn't go without her. Gladys managed to calm him down with the promise that they would go shopping in London and buy Eliza a special present.

Once on the train, Eddy kept his mother so busy answering questions as they rode past different towns and farms that she didn't have time to think about what she would say to Toughie if she saw him.

They were both tired and hungry by the time they arrived, so they went directly to the flat to freshen up before going out to dine. Eddy was too tired to fully enjoy the sights of the city and the fish that was served with deep-fried potato wedges. He was asleep minutes after being put to bed. Gladys joined him after writing a letter to drop off at the theatre the following day.

Eddy woke up full of life, and it was all Gladys could do to persuade him to eat a little breakfast before going shopping for Eliza's present.

On the way back to the flat, she asked the driver to stop at the theatre for a minute. Leaving Eddy in the cab, she went to the front door. Luckily, it was open, but the only person she could find was a woman cleaning the theatre. Gladys wasn't sure whether she should leave the letter with a cleaning woman, so she called out, "Hello, is there someone here who might be able to deliver an important letter to one of the actors?"

"Oh no, missus, there ain't no one important what comes 'ere until 'bout six or seven. But I'll still be 'ere if you wants to leave it with me. I'll give it to the bloke what takes the tickets if you wants me to."

"Are you sure you will be here when he comes to work? It's most important that this letter be given to the man whose name is on the envelope."

"I'll be 'ere, missus. We cleaners ain't 'lowed to leave until the rest of the workers gets 'ere."

Gladys took a pound note out of her purse and handed it to the woman who thanked her profusely and added, "You can count on me to see it gets to the right bloke, missus."

Gladys, on the verge of giving up hope of ever seeing Toughie again, doubted the cleaning woman could be relied upon to deliver the letter.

That evening, she was in her dressing gown and about to retire when she heard someone knocking on her door. She knew better than to open the door without knowing who it was, so she called out, "Who is it?"

"It's me, Angelo—Toughie."

Her hand was shaking so badly that she could hardly turn the door knob.

"Oh, my darling!" Toughie exclaimed after kissing her lips, face, ears, and neck. "I thought I'd never see you again."

He picked her up, carried her into the sitting room, and swirled her around before throwing his head back and exclaiming, "It's a miracle, a bloody miracle."

"Shush, Toughie, shush!"

Frowning, he set her down. "Is there someone with you?"

Gladys laughed and answered, "Yes there is, and he's someone special whom I want you to meet."

"Well, I can't say I'm looking forward to sharing your company with anyone else tonight, but it seems I have no choice in the matter," he answered rather sullenly.

Gladys couldn't wait another minute. She grabbed him by the arm and pulled him toward the stairs. "Come on, darling, but be quiet; he's sleeping."

Reluctantly, Toughie followed her as she took the lamp and made her way up the stairs and into the bedroom. She held the lamp close enough so he could see that the person in the bed was a young boy.

Glancing quickly at the child, he mumbled a polite compliment to do with his appearance and was about to take his leave when something made him turn for a second look. The resemblance was unmistakable. He looked up at Gladys beseechingly. There were tears in her eyes as she nodded.

He knelt down and gently touched the boy's head. "My boy, my son," he whispered.

Gladys allowed him a minute more before touching his shoulder and motioning toward the door. Once in the living room, Toughie caught her in another embrace and cried excitingly, "I have a son—we have a son."

Then he let her go and danced around the room swinging his arms in the air, "Oh my God, I've never been so happy! I have a son. I have a wonderful, beautiful little boy."

Suddenly, he stopped and said, "But I don't even know his name. What name did you give him, Gladdy?"

"Edward."

"Edward. Edward. Ah yes, yes, that's a good name. Eduardo! Eduardo Matthews Rossini. You see, my love, I've added my mother's maiden name." Smiling, he added, "I like the name. Eduardo. Eduardo. My son Eduardo. It sounds amazing, don't you think?"

"I call him Eddy."

"I suppose you could call him that, but everyone else must call him Eduardo. Eduardo Matthews Rossini."

Gladys started to say something, but Angelo put a finger over her mouth and added, "And you, my sweet, will have to learn to call me Angelo. Toughie was just a name people called me when they didn't know my real name."

Gladys resented his dominant attitude. She was relieved he was happy Eddy was his son, but she had no intention of letting him tell her what the boy's name should be. She decided to put things straight before it was too late.

"Angelo," she said, pronouncing his name with more emphasis than necessary. "You talk as though you have the right to decide what's best for Eddy. You've never even asked what happened to me—to us—during all the time you were away. How do you think we managed? Or do you even care?"

"Of course I care, and I do want to hear all about it, so please tell me."

"When I found out that I was having a child, I was devastated. As I told you when I last saw you, I held a good position as a housekeeper for a wealthy gentleman, well, I knew I would be discharged as soon as he found out I was in the family way. I know what happens to unmarried women in that situation, and I was so afraid that my daughter Dolly and I would end up in the poor house. I couldn't imagine any worse place for our child to be born."

"Oh, Glad, I'm so sorry. Forgive me for being so thoughtless. My God, what did you do?"

"I confessed to James Hornsby, my employer, and begged him to keep me on until I could find a place in town to rent where I hoped to earn enough money sewing to support the three of us. Luckily, James is a very caring man. In fact, he's the kindest man I've ever known. He offered to marry me. It was a way to ensure Dolly and our child would have a respectable upbringing, and because I thought you were married and had a family and I would never see you again, I accepted his offer. Now everyone thinks Eddy is his son. James provides us with everything we need. We live in a grand manor and even have servants to wait on us."

"I'm happy to hear you've been looked after, Gladys, but you are mistaken; I have no family."

Gladys's mouth fell open. She shook her head and said, "I don't believe you, unless . . . unless you were lying to me six years ago when you said you had a wife and were expecting a child."

"It wasn't a lie. I did have a wife. Her name was Rosa, but she died in childbirth aboard the ship. The baby, a boy, was born dead."

Stunned, Gladys replied, "Oh, I'm so sorry, Toughie, er, I mean, Angelo."

"It was an ill-fated crossing from the start. The weather was against us all the way. For two weeks, there wasn't so much as a soft breeze, and it seemed as though we would spend the rest of our lives floating in the same spot in the middle of the ocean. Then, when the wind finally came, it brought the rain. Oh, Glad, I've never seen it rain like it did out there on the sea. It was as though we had sailed under a giant waterfall, and no matter how fast the wind blew, we couldn't get out from under it. There were two inches of water in all the cabins. With nothing waterproof to wear, we walked about barefoot.

"It was during this time that I lost Rosa and my son. Then, a few days later, when the weather finally cleared, we suffered an outbreak of mumps. There were three families aboard—two without a man, and amongst them they had fifteen children. All but three were stricken with the disease. To keep my mind off my troubles, I volunteered to help with their care, and by the time they had all recovered, I came down with the disease. I don't know if you've heard what can happen to a man with the mumps, but the ship's doctor told me that I would probably never be able to father a child again. I'm sorry, Gladdy, but Eduardo will be our only child."

Gladys pulled his head down, held it tight to her breast, and said,

"You poor, poor darling. What a time you've had."

"Yes, I have, but that's all in the past. Now that I have you and Eduardo, I will never be alone again."

Realizing that he thought she and Eddy were going to stay with him, Gladys knew she had to tell him the truth.

"Angelo, please sit down. There's something you should know." When he was seated, she continued, "I only brought Eddy here to meet you because I wanted you to see how wonderful he is. But you have to understand that the only father he has ever known is James Hornsby."

Toughie felt fear building up inside his chest. He was afraid of what her answer would be to his question, but he had to know, "I hope you are not trying to tell me that this James Hornsby will try to keep me from taking what is rightly mine?"

"I am sure he will allow you to visit with Eddy now and again, but he only allowed me to come see you if I promised never to tell Eddy that you are his father. If it were to become known that we had been living a life of lies, it would ruin his reputation in Sandwich. I could never do that to James. You can understand that, can't you?"

"No! No, I can't. This won't do. I have to return to America in two weeks' time, and I intend to take you and Eduardo with me."

"I wish that were possible, Tough . . . er . . . Angelo, but you must remember that I have two daughters. Dolly is fifteen now, and Eliza, James's and my daughter, is three."

"I don't care. In fact, I'm delighted that Eduardo has sisters. It's better than being an only child. We will take them all to America."

"James would never allow it."

"I can't believe you allow him to tell you what to do. You don't love him, do you?"

"Yes, yes, in a way I do. But I don't love him like I do you. He's much older than me, and we don't sleep together, but he has been good to me, and we are very fond of each other. And, more importantly, I respect him."

"You'll never belong to anyone but me, and you know it. If you come with me, he can probably get a divorce on the grounds of desertion. The troupe is breaking up now, and Uncle and I have invested our money in a restaurant in New York City. We have to go back in two weeks to open it, and I do not intend to leave without my son."

"First, Angelo, I do not belong to you or to James. And second, I shall never let anyone take Eddy away from me."

"I don't want to take him from you, Gladys, but if you won't come with us, I'll have to. He is my son. You only have to look at him to see that."

"Because he looks like you does not prove anything, and if I deny having slept with you, there's nothing you can do. Please, Angelo, you must listen to me. I have my other two children to think of, and I could never part with Eddy."

"What do you expect me to do? Forget I have a son?"

Before she could answer, Eddy called out, "Mother? Mother, where are you?"

Gladys ran up the stairs, and, after a while, she brought the boy down.

"Eddy darling, this is an old friend of mine. His name is Angelo Mathews Rossini," she said.

"Hello, Eduardo, I'm very pleased to meet you." Angelo reached out his hand while he fought the urge to take the boy into his arms and say, "I am your father."

Eddy didn't seem to notice that the stranger had called him Eduardo. He rubbed his eyes and mumbled a greeting before asking, "Mother, why didn't you come to bed? I woke up, and you weren't there."

"I know, dear, we'll go to bed in a minute, but first we will have a little visit with my friend," she replied in such a stern voice that he didn't argue. Besides, there was something about the man's appearance, especially his smile, that Eddy liked.

"How old are you, my boy? I would guess by the size of you, you must be about seven," Toughie said.

The flattery wasn't wasted. Eddy stuck out his chest and answered, "Oh no, sir, I am only five, but I can read very well. I often read stories to my sister."

"I think she must be a very lucky little girl to have a big brother like you."

"Yes, sir, she is! Sometimes I put her in front of me on my pony, Chestnut, and take her for rides around the corral. She is going to have a pony of her own soon, and then we can ride together. She could not come to London on the train with me, so do you know what we did?"

"No, I can't imagine."

"We bought her one. Of course, it is just a toy train, but it even has a whistle. Would you like to see it? Can I show it to him, Mother? Please?"

"You certainly can, dear, but why not show him the one you have? Then you won't have to undo all the pretty wrappings."

When Eddy left to get the train, Toughie remarked, "My God, Glad, he's wonderful. He loves his little sister, doesn't he?"

Gladys nodded, and, for the first time, Toughie began to realize that it would be years before he could give the boy what his stepfather provided him with. It didn't help when Gladys started to tell him about the wonderful estate they lived on before Eddy returned with his train and interrupted her.

For over an hour, Angelo and his son sat on the floor playing with the train and talking. Eddy, having ridden on one, felt he knew enough about trains to explain all about them and was very pleased to find such an attentive audience. Toughie listened intently while doing his best to memorize Eddy's every word and expression.

Seeing the two of them playing with their heads together wrenched Gladys's heart. She was ashamed of herself for not thinking of Dolly and Eliza, but she wished time would stand still and the three of them could remain where they were forever.

"Come now, dear, you must get some sleep," she said as she reached for Eddy's hand.

"But, Mother, we are having such fun!"

Toughie knew he had to agree with Gladys, so he added, "I suppose your mother is right, son. I had a wonderful time. You certainly taught me a lot about trains. I'll never forget it."

"If you come home with us, you could even ride on one."

"I am afraid that's impossible. You see, I have to leave London before long and sail to America."

"Is that where you live?" When Toughie said it was, Eddy then asked if he had any children.

Toughie had to swallow a lump in his throat before he could answer. "I have a boy the same age as you."

"Where does he live?"

Gladys interrupted, "Now, Eddy, that's enough. I'm sure Angelo is tired of answering questions, and it is really not polite to ask such personal things. Come on, off to bed now."

"Are you coming too, Mother?"

"I'll tuck you in, then I'll come down and say goodnight to Angelo before I come to bed."

When Eddy went over to say goodnight, Toughie could no longer hold back. He embraced the boy and held him tightly. Eddy didn't appreciate the gesture and pulled away. Then he noticed the moisture on the man's cheeks, and he could sense his sadness.

"Why was the man crying, Mother?" he asked Gladys when they were in the bedroom.

"I think he misses his little boy, my darling."

After a pensive moment, Eddy replied, "I wish I had hugged him back."

Chapter Twenty

A wave of depression came over Toughie as he sat waiting for Gladys to put Eddy to bed. Just two hours earlier he had been light-headed with joy when Gladys told him they had a son. After having the mumps, Toughie had given up hope of ever having a family.

At first, he thought that Gladys brought Eddy to London so they could be together for the rest of their lives, but when she said she intended to return to her husband and take Eddy with her, he could hardly believe it. He did his utmost to persuade her to change her mind, but when she told him of all the advantages Eduardo would have if they stayed in Sandwich, he realized how little he could offer in comparison, and his hopes were shattered.

"When are you leaving?" he asked as soon as Gladys returned.

"We were going back tomorrow, but I think we could stay for another day, if you want us to."

"Of course I do."

She could tell by the subdued tone of his answer that he was beginning to see she was doing the right thing. Feeling more guilt than pity as she watched him slump down on the divan with a look of defeat, she began to think she and Eddy should not have come to London. It would have been far easier for him if he had never known about Eddy.

Sitting down on the floor by his feet, she laid her head on his knee and said, "My poor dear. I wish it were different, but there is nothing I can do."

Annoyed by what he felt to be a tone of insincerity, he pushed her aside and stood up. "That's not true! If you truly loved me, nothing could stop you from coming with me."

After thinking he was beginning to understand why she couldn't leave, Gladys was losing patience. "I have already explained why I can't! Please, Angelo. I, oh fiddle! I really cannot talk to you if I am forced to call you by that new name. I have spent years dreaming of someone named 'Toughie,' not 'Angelo,'" she cried as she got up and started to pace back and forth. "Now you say that I mustn't call you that anymore. Very well, Mr Angelo Rossini, if you don't like what I call you, perhaps you had better leave."

Her outburst not only surprised him, but aroused him. She looked so beautiful when she was angry.

"Not on your life! You're not getting rid of me that easily." He got up and put his arms around her. "You can call me anything you like, but don't ever stop loving me."

At first, their lovemaking was more passionate than tender, but after their lust was sated, they took time to enjoy the closeness of their naked bodies. "Do you know what I wish, my darling?" Gladys asked.

"I hope it's the same thing that I wish."

"What's that?"

"I wish we could be together forever."

"Of course I wish that too, but since it can't be, I wish we were made out of butter, so we could just melt into one another."

Toughie laughed. "I think for a while, we came close to making your wish come true."

"Oh, Toughie, I love you so much," she said as she snuggled against him and put her face under his chin. "Do you know that when I'm not with you, I close my eyes and feel my face right here against your neck? I love your neck. I don't know why, but it makes me feel so safe and warm. Which part of my body will you miss the most?"

His answer surprised her. "Your tummy."

"My tummy?"

"I love lying with my head there while you scratch my back."

She laughed and said, "That doesn't seem very romantic. Why can't you be like all other men and dream about breasts?"

"And how would you know what other men dream about?"

"You'd be surprised what I know."

They were enjoying a few minutes of light-heartedness, but the thought of their forthcoming separation soon sobered their mood, and they spent the rest of the night holding each other and dreading the moment when they would have to say goodbye.

Eddy was glad to find the man was still there in the morning and pleased that he no longer seemed so sad. When he asked Gladys why she called the man Toughie, she explained that it had been his nickname when they were children.

"I think it's a jolly good name, Mother. I should like a nickname like that," he remarked. Then he asked, "Toughie, could you give me a nickname?"

Gladys spoke up. "You must not call him Toughie, Eddy; it isn't proper. And you do not need a nickname. Eddy is your nickname, and it's a lovely one."

"Eddy is a sissy name! And why shan't I call him Toughie? You do," Eddy said crossly.

"Now, darling, you know it is not polite for someone your age to address an adult by his first name," Gladys replied, hoping to calm him down.

Eddy was all set to demand his way when Toughie intervened, "Your mother is right, but, perhaps, since we are only going to be together a short time, she will forget the rules and allow you to call me anything you like. Perhaps she will even allow you to have another nickname if we promise to keep it just between us. What do you say, Gladys?"

"Well, I suppose it cannot do any harm," she replied.

Eddy beamed. "Good show! I should like one much like yours, Mr Toughie."

"I think we can do better than that. Let's think about it for a while." Then he suggested they spend the day visiting the Zoological Gardens in Regent Park.

They spent all that day at the gardens. Gladys gave Eddy a pencil and a piece of paper and helped him print the names of all the animals, so he would be able to tell Eliza about them. In the afternoon, they found a pleasant place in the garden where they could buy refreshments and some nuts to feed the animals.

When Eddy became too tired to walk, he rode on Toughie's shoulders. It was the first shoulder ride he had ever had, and he felt like a giant looking down on all the people as they passed by. James often gave Eliza rides on his shoulders but never him.

They were enjoying a delicious dinner at a little inn on the way home when Eddy announced that he had decided on a nickname. "I should like to be called 'Tiger,'" he said. Then he laughed and clapped his hands with delight when both his mother and Toughie agreed that it was a fitting name for such a brave boy.

By the time they arrived back at the flat, Eddy was sound asleep. Toughie carried him upstairs and was undressing him when he woke up. "Well, Tiger, let's get you into your nightshirt, so you can go back to sleep," Toughie said, hoping the boy wouldn't object.

Hearing Toughie call him Tiger gave Eddy a warm tingling feeling, and he grinned. When he had his nightshirt on, he remarked, "You had better call Mother now; she always likes to hear my prayers. You know what mothers are like." Toughie stifled a laugh and nodded his head seriously.

After they listened to his prayers, Toughie agreed to tell Eddy what it was like to go to sea. The lad was fascinated to hear about the schools of inquisitive dolphins, the huge whales that blew water from their spouts, and the seagulls that sometimes rode high up on the yardarms and dove down to catch the pieces of stale bread the cook threw to them. Before Toughie had finished talking, Eddy fell asleep. It was all Toughie could do not to wake him up, so they could spend more time together.

The two lovers spent their last night making love and holding each other. Gladys didn't tell Toughie, but she was pleased he couldn't have any more children. She even thought that it was a shame there hadn't been an epidemic of mumps in England instead of cholera. She knew that if she went with Toughie, they could make love every night without having to worry about having babies they might not be able to afford.

Gladys had become resigned to the chaste life she led during the last decade, but now that she and Toughie had spent two nights together, it was going to be extremely difficult to live without him. She certainly couldn't look for love in James's bed, and she knew that he felt the same way. How badly she longed to say yes to Toughie's proposal and sail off to America, but she was compelled to think of her children and their future.

Nevertheless, she was so curious that she begged him to tell her all about New York. Much of what he told her was what she had dreamt it to be, but when he said that there were areas in the city where people lived in conditions as bad as they were in Old Nichol, she was disappointed. She thought America would be free from all the poverty that prevailed in England and Ireland.

In the morning, Toughie was up and dressed before dawn. "I'm going to leave now before Eduardo wakes up. I can't bear to say goodbye to him."

Gladys knew it was for the best, so she didn't object, but when he went to go out the door, she started to cry.

"Don't cry, my darling. Someday I'll be back, I promise. Maybe then, when our son is older, we can tell him the truth."

"Will you write to me?"

"I will. And I'll give you my address, so you can write and tell me everything Eduardo does. Maybe if you were to remind him, from time to time, about our trip to the park, he won't forget me."

"I shall ask him to write to you himself. I know he would like

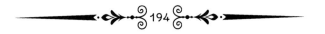

that. You've made quite a favourable impression on him," she said as she wrote down his American address and the address of where he was staying in London.

"Hearing from you both, from time to time, will make our separation a lot less painful," Toughie said with a weak smile.

"I don't want to you to leave," she cried as he was going out the door.

"I know, my love, but just remember, if you change your mind and decide to come with me, let me know in a week's time. And I don't mind if you bring along the girls as well. I know of someone who can forge identification papers, and you can come as my wife and family."

Gladys knew he would spend the week waiting for her to change her mind, but she also knew it wasn't likely. She tried to smile as he hugged her one last time before he left. Her heart was breaking as she stood and watched him walk down the street.

Toughie could feel her eyes on his back and turned a few times to blow her a kiss. Then he turned the corner and went out of sight.

"I love you, Toughie. I love you too, Angelo Rossini," she cried out to the empty street.

Eddy was disappointed that Toughie had left before he could say goodbye, but when Gladys told him they were going to visit an old friend, then stop on the way to the station to buy some marzipan mice for James, Eliza, and Dolly, he couldn't wait to leave.

"Do hurry, Mother," he said. Noticing her red eyes, he added, "Are you sad, Mother?"

"No, dear, just tired. A little powder and I shall look as good as ever."

Luckily, Percy was at home when they arrived at his apartment. He was overjoyed to see her and made a fuss over Eddy. Although he appeared to have aged since she last saw him, he still had that wonderful twinkle in his eyes when he smiled. His smile always lifted her spirits no matter how depressed she was feeling. She hadn't realized

how very much she had missed his company, and she hugged him for a long time. Fortunately, Percy had some puzzles he kept for his little nephew, and he brought them out for Eddy to play with on the kitchen table while he and Gladys visited in his parlour.

He could tell she was troubled, so wasn't surprised when she told him why they had come to London. She also told him how difficult it was for Toughie to say goodbye to the only child he would ever have.

After they had talked for a while, Gladys could tell Percy wanted to ask about James, so she told him that they had a daughter named Eliza, who was now three. He congratulated her but couldn't hide his true feelings, so she decided to speak boldly. Gladys confessed that James had told her why he and Percy were no longer friends.

"Now that you know my secret, Gladys, do you still want to be my friend?"

"Of course. Why on earth would I not?"

"James thinks I'm a sinner and a criminal, and I was afraid you might feel the same."

"Well, you needn't worry; I think you are wonderful, and I love you. I know how much you cared for Helmut, and James should consider himself lucky you feel the same about him."

"I wish he did, but he wants nothing to do with me, even though I promised to never make that mistake again."

"Percy, James loves you, but he is far too afraid to admit it, and I don't know if he ever will. I do know that he will never be truly happy until he does. He misses you so very much."

Before Gladys and Eddy took their leave, Percy gave her a letter. "Will you give this to James, Gladys? I wrote it over a year ago and have never had the nerve to mail it."

When he handed her the letter, Gladys realized that she had left Toughie's addresses in the flat and would have to go back for them. Luckily, the two apartments were only a block apart so they would still be able to buy some candy and arrive at the station in time to catch the train.

After retrieving the addresses and buying the candy, Gladys and Eddy were standing on the side of the street waiting for a cab when they saw Toughie running toward them.

"I'm so glad I got here before you left," he said as soon as he caught his breath. "I've some great news!"

Before he had a chance to tell her his news, an empty cab stopped to pick them up. Gladys didn't want to leave without hearing the news, but she knew they had to go or they would miss the train.

"I'll ride to the station with you and tell you all about it as we go," he said.

As soon as the coach was on the road, Gladys asked, "What is it, Toughie? I hope it's that you are not going to America after all."

"I'm sorry, but no, it's not that," he replied, and then he told her that his grandmother, who was in her late seventies, had decided to go to America with them.

Victor had left Carlotta and their twins in America and was anxious to return, but it would take about two months to pack up the old lady's belongings and settle her affairs. "We'll be sailing from here to Italy and return in a month's time," Toughie said. "And the good news is that we will still have to wait here for a fortnight before our ship sails for America."

Without waiting for Gladys to comment, he addressed Eddy, "So, Tiger, what do you think of another trip to the park in a month's time?"

"Oh, I should say so!" Eddy said, clapping his hands. "And Sidder could come too! You would like her. She is a jolly good sort, for a girl."

Gladys promised they would be in London before Toughie sailed. Their farewell at the station was awkward and unsatisfying. With Eddy looking on, they were obliged to be discreet and had to contend with nothing more than a handshake.

Chapter Twenty One

When Gladys and Eddy arrived in Sandwich, there was no one at the station to meet them because James didn't know what day they would return. Luckily, cabs were plentiful at the train station, and they were quickly on their way home.

The warm reception they received from Dolly, Eliza, and the rest of the household managed to lift Gladys's spirits a little.

James had feared Edward's father would insist on returning with them. The man stood no chance of taking Edward away from Gladys, but if he were to publicly state the reason he wanted the boy, it would be sure to cause a scandal that would tarnish James's reputation. He was so relieved when they returned alone that he surprised everyone by suggesting they all spend the evening in the parlour so Eddy could tell them what he thought of his journey to London.

His unexpected show of affection helped Gladys feel that her decision not to go with Toughie was the right one. She had returned home determined to speak to James about his aloofness toward Eddy, and now she was beginning to think that it might be unnecessary.

Eliza was thrilled with the toy train and listened intently to her brother's account of the wonderful place he called a zoo. James managed to hide his displeasure as Eddy described all the animals, but he couldn't help but wince every time Eddy mentioned the nice man called Toughie, who had given him a ride on his shoulders. Although he wasn't fond of the boy, he was overcome with an unexpected feeling of jealousy.

When it came time for the children to retire, Eddy, feeling very grown up, said he would be sleeping in his own bed from now on and would say his prayers with Sidder. Instead of being pleased, Gladys was saddened. She would miss having his warm little body next to her at night.

Anxious to hear what had taken place between Gladys and the Italian, James asked if she would join him in the library for a drink before she retired. Gladys settled down into one of the large wingback chairs in front of the fireplace while James poured them each a generous glass of sherry. "Ah, this is nice," she said as she sipped on the sweet-tasting liquid.

"I imagine you are tired after the long trip home," James said, then added, "but, as you can imagine, I am most anxious to know how your friend reacted when he learned that he had a son."

"He was thrilled, James! You see, he lost his wife and child when they were on their way to America. Then he became very ill as well. When he recovered, the ship's doctor told him that he would never be able to have any more children, so you can imagine his delight when he found out about Eddy," Gladys replied.

James had secretly hoped that the fellow would want nothing to do with Edward, which would simplify matters. "I can understand his sentiments, my dear, but I hope you explained that his relationship to Edward must be kept a secret. Of course, I shall allow him to visit with the boy now and then, but the visits must be in London or wherever he lives, and never in Sandwich. And I shall have to insist that Edward continue to believe I am his father."

"I explained all that to Tou . . . er, I mean, Angelo."

Gladys suddenly understood what Toughie had meant when he said that Toughie was nothing but a childish nickname. The name

Angelo had a far greater ring of sophistication. She made up her mind to try to think of him by his proper name from then on.

"I pray he took it well?"

"Not at first, but when he realized that it may be several years before he would be able to provide his son with all that you can give him, he changed his mind. It was a heart-breaking decision for him."

"Is he still going to be travelling with the troupe?"

"Oh no, the troupe has disbanded. Angelo's going back to America in six weeks' time. He and his uncle are opening a restaurant there. I hope you won't mind, James, but I said I would take Eddy back to London in a month's time so he could spend another day or two with his father before he leaves."

James was slow to answer, but he agreed. "I am sorry for him. I know how I would feel if I should ever have to leave Eliza. I hope he will be successful in his endeavours. Now, I want to know about you. How do you feel? Knowing what the fellow means to you, I can imagine how difficult it must have been to know that you can never be together."

"Yes it was, but we both felt better when we decided to write to each other. I promised that Eddy would write to him too."

"Do you think that was wise?"

"I couldn't say no to him, James. He wanted Eddy and me to go with him, and I had to tell him we couldn't. The least I could do was to allow him to keep in touch by correspondence. If his business goes well, he hopes to visit Eddy again someday."

James was relieved to hear that Angelo was leaving the country but sorry to hear that he planned on returning. Although he had told Gladys that he wished the man success, he wasn't being totally honest. James wasn't in love with Gladys, but he didn't want to lose her. He was afraid that if Toughie became a success, he might persuade her to leave. He knew he was behaving like the proverbial dog in the manger, but he couldn't help it.

He was also anxious to know if Gladys had visited with Percy while in London, but his pride kept him from asking. After a few seconds of silence, he rose and said, "It's good to have you back—both of you. Now you had better get some sleep."

Gladys was on her way out the door when she remembered the letter. "Oh yes, I almost forgot; I hope you don't mind, but I went to visit Percy before we left London, and he gave me this to give to you." She took the letter out of her skirt pocket and handed it to him. She left the room before he could reply.

James sat down and looked at the envelope. He didn't know whether to open it or throw it in the fire. The feel of it in his hands caused him sensations of both pleasure and dread. For years, he had strived to overcome his desire for Percy's company and was almost convinced he had succeeded. Now he was afraid that if he read the letter, his efforts would be in vain. On the other hand, now that he and Gladys had a child, what harm would it do to renew their friendship?

After all, he reasoned, Percy had apologized for his rash behaviour and even stated that he would like to continue being nothing more than just good friends. Thinking about all the good times they had together, James began to wonder if he had any right to judge the man. Leaning his head back in the chair, he closed his eyes and allowed his thoughts to drift reminiscently. The memories warmed his soul, and without realizing it, he held the letter close to his heart as he recalled those good times. He could picture Percy as clearly as though he were in the room, standing as he so often did, with an arm resting on the mantle, a drink in his other hand, and telling amusing stories about his eccentric relatives.

He could even picture his features: his thick crop of salt-and-pepper hair; his large but well-shaped nose; his hazel eyes, which lit up whenever he smiled; and his generous mouth. Then the memory of that sensuous mouth on his interposed and put an abrupt end to his musings.

He quickly jumped up and threw the letter into the fire. There were only a few embers left among the coals, and, for what seemed like eons to James, the letter lay un-scorched on top of them, as though deliberately allowing him time to change his mind. His whole being ached with the urge to reach down and grab it, but he stood firm. Then, as the envelope began to smoulder, his resistance gave way, but it was too late. Just as he reached for it, the envelope burst into flames. He watched until there was nothing left but ashes. Then, brushing the tears from his cheek, he left the room.

Even though the thought of losing Angelo once again was foremost on her mind, Gladys did her best to be cheerful. During the weeks following the London trip, she tried to concentrate on the good life that James was providing for her and her children. They spent most of their free time together riding their horses or playing games. In the evenings, she played the piano and sang, but only the gayest of songs. Both Eddy and Dolly had inherited her love of music, and even Eliza was beginning to enjoy their musical evenings.

Eddy liked to sing, and he would make up his own words if he didn't know the lyrics to a song. It wasn't long before he and Eliza began performing for the family. Eddy would play the piano with one finger and sing while Eliza danced. He didn't know how to play, and she didn't know how to dance, but they put on good show.

James seemed just as determined as Gladys to create a happy atmosphere in the home. However, there were times when Gladys thought their simulated actions might be so obvious that even a child could tell they weren't sincere. She needn't have worried. The children were enjoying the harmonious atmosphere so much that they wouldn't have acknowledged any imperfections if they had noticed them.

The groom's daughter, Blossom, and Dolly had remained close friends, and they were both helpful in keeping Eddy and Eliza entertained. Two swings hung from a branch of a large oak tree in the back yard, and one of the yardmen, who was very handy with tools, had fashioned a chair out of a wooden box and tied it to one of the swings for Eliza, so the girls could push her as high in the air as they did Eddy.

Blossom was now old enough to go to work. Normally she would have had to seek employment as a housemaid, but, because she had acquired proper mannerisms by spending so much time in the company of Dolly, James had hired her as Dolly's maid.

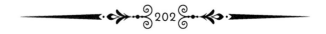

Although she was a servant, Dolly treated Blossom more like a companion, and their close friendship often caused Gladys to be envious. When Gladys was Dolly's age, she was scrubbing floors and working from morning until night and had no time for girlfriends, so she didn't know that it was typical for a fifteen-year-old to form a closer relationship with another girl than with her mother.

Not knowing that it was just a phase Dolly was going through and that it would soon pass, Gladys blamed herself, thinking she had neglected her and spent too much time looking after Eddy. She prayed it wasn't too late to make amends.

She recalled her friendship with Millie and how they had shared all their secrets. Millie was the only close friend she had had since leaving the ghetto. After Millie died, Gladys confided in Dolly. Now she felt that she had no one. Aunt Jean was easy to talk to, but she was beginning to be so forgetful that she might repeat anything without realizing it. It would have been nice if Horace and Sarah lived with them, since they were both easy to talk to, but they lived in another country.

She had thought that Mary and Tina would be her close friends, but, ever since Eddy had been born, they seemed distant toward her, especially Mary. She had a feeling they suspected that James wasn't Eddy's father, but they hadn't come out and accused her. She couldn't help but grin when she pictured how shocked they would be if they found out where she had grown up.

Gladys was so lucky to have met Millie when she did. It was a time when they had both needed a friend. Whenever Gladys reminisced about the good times they spent together, the memory of the night Millie died came back to haunt her. Although it had waned over the years, there were still times when she could still feel that pillow under her hands and she would feel sick.

One afternoon, James sent John, the footman, into town on an errand, and he returned with a pamphlet announcing a Romani fair being held in the town square. Remembering the wonderful time that they had enjoyed the last time they had attended such a fair, both Dolly and Gladys were anxious to attend.

Thinking it would make for a fun family outing if they all went,

Gladys suggested it to James while they were sitting in the garden having a drink of lemonade.

James was quick to reply that he would prefer that no one from Four Oaks attend the fair. Surprised, Dolly wanted to know why.

"They are not only a lazy bunch of vagabonds, my dear, but thieves as well. A fitting simile would be to say that they are like weeds in a bed of roses."

"And I suppose you consider yourself one of the roses?" Gladys retorted.

"I was merely using a garden as an example with the honest, respectable people as roses and them as weeds. It is rather fitting, don't you agree?"

"Certainly not, but if I were to think of them as weeds, they'd be daisies. Did you ever see anything more beautiful than a field of wild daisies?"

Dolly spoke up, "Oh, Mother, remember the daisies at Oaken Arms? I used to pick a huge bouquet of them for Gamby every time we were there." Their eyes connected, and they hugged each other as thoughts of those wonderful days picnicking with Andrew under the old oak tree returned. Both suffered with a bout of melancholy for the rest of the day.

James was very fond of Dolly, and he had noticed her disappointment when he said they shouldn't go to the fair. It weighed on his mind for a day or two until he finally relented and even agreed to accompany them.

He wouldn't let on to anyone, but he recalled the frightening stories he had been told when he was a child about Romani coming into town and stealing little children. Common sense made him realize how silly those stories were; nevertheless, he still held Eliza firmly by the hand the entire time they were there.

Eddy, Eliza, and Blossom enjoyed the event, but Gladys and Dolly were disappointed to find that the Romani were a different group than those they had met years before. With James along, Gladys began to perceive the band with a more critical eye. The costumes, although bright and pretty, were very worn, and the children were too persistent in begging for money. Even she became annoyed when they pulled on her skirt while begging for coins.

Even so, when James remarked about their shortcomings on the way home, she defended them by snapping back, "Just because they asked you for a few pence to buy food with, you condemn them."

He surprised her by confessing, "I suppose I did, didn't I? I should probably adopt more of a Christian attitude to the poor souls. I do believe that our government has treated them rather shabbily. And they do cook excellent food. Did you have one of their currant cakes?"

His light-heartedness put them all in a good mood, especially when he began singing a lively tune. They all joined in and sang all the way home.

It was one of the warmest Julys they had had in years, so James decided to take them all to Brighton for a weekend. The children loved playing on the beach, picking up seashells, and wading in the water. Meanwhile, Gladys and James spent their time sitting in the latest model of canopied chairs and discussing books and authors. When the weekend ended, they both agreed to return soon, as the entire family had loved the beach.

The warm feelings toward each other continued after they returned home and gave off a pleasant ambiance that was felt throughout the manor. Then, two weeks before Gladys and Eddy were to meet Angelo, a heart-breaking incident occurred that would have a profound effect on every member of the family.

Chapter Twenty Two

The day began with a heavy rainfall, so Dolly spent the morning in the nursery listening to Eddy read and showing Eliza how to arrange furniture in her dollhouse. Dolly had read Eddy all her books until he had learned to read them himself, so when she asked him what book he wanted to read that morning, he said, "I am rather bored with these books, Dolly. Could you ask sir if we could borrow some of his?"

"Why don't you ask him?" Dolly replied.

"I do not think sir likes me, not like he likes Sidder."

Dolly knew James wasn't fond of Eddy. She hadn't been fond of him at first either, but, after watching him play with Eliza, she'd begun to appreciate his kind nature. He was exceptionally thoughtful for such a young boy, but she thought he was a little too forthright to suit James. Hoping to convince him otherwise, she said, "I am certain that is not true, Eddy. He treats you differently because you are a boy, but if you would rather I ask him, I shall."

When the sun came out in the afternoon, the children, tired of being indoors, begged to go outside and play on the swings. Eliza was wearing a white eyelet pinafore over a pretty pink frock, and Eddy was dressed in a pair of navy corded knickers, a blue vest, and a white shirt. Since they only had time for a quick swing before dinner, Dolly didn't think it necessary for them to change into their coveralls.

Years ago, Gladys and Dolly had visited the Sorenson family, and their children had been playing quite happily in coveralls that kept them neat and tidy, preserving their good clothing from becoming soiled and worn while they played. Gladys had been so impressed with the coveralls that she had made both Eddy and Eliza a pair to wear whenever they went outdoors to play.

The grass directly under the swings had been worn away by the children's feet and left a small area that became very muddy whenever it rained. Careful not to stand in it, Dolly lifted Eliza into her swing, neglecting to tie her in before she turned to give Eddy a few pushes. Eliza was wiggling back and forth in the swing, trying to see how high Eddy went, when she suddenly wiggled too far and fell off into the mud.

Before Dolly could reach her, she jumped up, looked at the mud on her hands and dress, and said, "I falled off!"

"You certainly did, you poor darling! Are you hurt?" Dolly asked.

"Uh, uh, I just muddy." Eddy got to Eliza first, and he tried to brush the mud off her dress.

"Thank you, Eddy, but it will be easier to get off if we just leave it alone." Then she patted Eliza on the head and said, "Thank goodness you are not hurt. Now, I think you had better run in and ask Nanny to clean your hands and change your clothes before dinner. Go in the kitchen door, dear, and ask Cook to call Nanny, and she will take care of you. Eddy and I shall be along in a minute or two."

Eliza ran off, but on the way to the back door, she saw a beautiful big butterfly and followed it as it flew around the house. When it flew up in the air and disappeared, she was closer to the front door than the kitchen door, so she went in that way. She was walking past the library when she noticed the door was ajar, and remembering what Eddy had said about wanting more books, she forgot about her dirty hands and went in hoping to find a nice one for him.

Spotting a small book lying on a table beside her father's chair, she picked it up to examine it closer. It was covered in soft leather and smelled like her father's gloves. A green ribbon with a tassel on the end was hanging from inside the book, so she was sure it would have pretty pictures too. She smiled, thinking how proud Eddy was going to be when she showed him what she had found as she opened the cover and began turning the pages.

A few minutes after Eliza had left, Dolly spotted James over by the stables. Wanting to talk to him about borrowing some books for the children, she told Eddy to go in and make sure that Eliza had found Nanny.

Eddy also went in through the front entrance and, like Eliza, noticed the open library door. He was almost past it when he saw Eliza holding one of James's books. Knowing how possessive his father was of all his books, Eddy was afraid his sister would be scolded if she were caught, so he rushed in and snatched it out of her hands. He was about to put it back on the table when he saw the muddy smudges on the pages. Speaking sharply, he said, "Naughty, Sidder."

"I looking for pictures, Eddy," she answered. Then her face puckered up, and she started to cry.

Seeing he had frightened her, Eddy said, "Don't cry, Sidder. I shall take care of it. You leave now and go and wash your hands. And, Eliza," she knew when he called her "Eliza" it must be important, so she listened intently, "never, ever, tell anyone what you did, understand?"

She wiped her nose on her sleeve and nodded.

"Go on now," he ordered, gently pushing her out of the room.

After she had gone, he pulled his shirttail out of his britches and tried to rub off the muddy fingerprints, but it just made a worse mess. Although James had never punished either of them, Eddy was afraid he would be so angry over the soiled book that Eliza was sure to receive a spanking, so he decided to tear out just the muddy pages, hoping they wouldn't be missed. Unfortunately, he was tearing out the last dirty page when, without warning, James, followed by Dolly, entered the room.

"What the devil are you doing?" James cried out. Without waiting for an answer, he snatched the book out of Eddy's hands. "My God, you've ruined it!" He threw the book down, grabbed Eddy by the collar, and shook him until the boy almost choked. Then he slapped him twice across the face and shouted, "You spoiled little bastard!"

Gladys was just coming down from upstairs and overheard him. Appalled, she hurried into the room to find Eddy with his arms over his face, sobbing. Putting her arms around him, she held him close, looking up at James with a confused expression. She was unable to believe he could be so cruel. She asked, "How could you say such a thing?"

James was shaking as he bent down and picked up the book. He held it out for her to see. "This book was given to my grandfather by Cowper himself, and it is irreplaceable."

Ignoring his words, Gladys asked, "Did you strike him?"

Shaking the book at her, he replied, "Look at this. He has torn out pages, can't you see?"

"Did you strike my son?" she demanded.

"Yes, I struck him, and he damn well deserved it," James cried.

Gladys said nothing, but the abhorrent look she gave him before she and Eddy left the room expressed how she felt far more than words could have.

Dolly had been so shocked by the confrontation that she watched it all dumbly, as though it were nothing more than a staged performance. Now she looked at James, who was slumped in a chair with the book in his hand, teardrops falling on the open pages. She couldn't help but feel sorry for him. He had told her how much he treasured that particular book, but, nevertheless, as much as she sympathized with him, she couldn't condone his actions.

What had just happened was slowly replaying itself in her mind, and the cruel manner in which James had handled Eddy, along with the horrid word he had called him, upset her deeply. She knew what the word "bastard" implied, and now, the thought that Eddy might actually be a bastard entered her head and wouldn't leave. She began to wonder if it could be true as she walked slowly out of the library.

James, engrossed in his own troubles, had been unaware of her presence as well as her departure.

In 1782, James's grandfather had met the famous poet William Cowper in Olney at the home of Mary Unwin, where the poet was recovering from a bout of insanity. James was never told what circumstances brought the two men together, but since his grandfather had been a lawyer, it may have been a legal matter. Four years later, Cowper sent his grandfather the leather-bound book containing a selection of what he considered his best poems. The inscription he wrote in the book said, "To James Hornsby; Your kindness will never be forgotten. William Cowper."

The monetary, as well as sentimental, value of the book had increased as it was handed down from one generation to the next, and James had planned to leave it to Horace, so he could likewise hand it down to his son when he had one. Now it would be meaningless, since the page with the inscription was one of the pages Eddy had torn out. James was a pacifist by nature, and the only other time he had ever lost his temper to such a degree was after Percy had kissed him.

He was still shaking as he got up and poured himself a glass of whiskey. As the drink began to take an effect, he calmed down and realized how badly he had behaved, not for disciplining Eddy—he fully believed the boy deserved a thrashing for what he had done—but for what he had called him.

He was afraid that if any of the staff had heard him, they would be sure to know that the boy was not his. Although James had always been a recluse until Gladys came to live at Four Oaks, he was a proud man and valued a spotless reputation. He had allowed everyone he knew to believe Edward was his son. If they were to find out he wasn't, they would consider him both a fool and a liar. James had a dual purpose in marrying Gladys: he sincerely wanted to help her, but he also wanted to erase any doubts that he may not be a normal man with honourable ethics, a debauched soul like Percy. He refused to admit that the doubts he hoped to silence were mainly his own.

"I do not like him, Mother. He is thoroughly wicked," Eddy said between sobs when they reached Gladys's apartment.

"Don't you cry, my darling. I promise he will never hurt you again."

When he quieted down, she ordered dinner sent to her sitting room, but when it arrived, neither she nor Eddy could eat more than a few bites.

Shortly after, Dolly knocked on the door. Not only did she want to have a serious talk with her mother, but she was anxious to see Eddy. During the last few years, she had become almost as fond of him as she was of Eliza.

Now that Eddy had finally dropped off to sleep, Gladys didn't want to disturb him, but she knew that Dolly had been present when James attacked Eddy and could give her a first-hand account of the incident.

"We will have to be quiet. The poor darling just dropped off," she said as she led Dolly into her sitting room.

Dolly tried to explain what had happened, "James just lost control when he saw what Eddy did to his book—I doubt he was aware of his actions. I know that is no excuse for slapping Eddy, Mother, but I am certain he is sorry for what he has done."

"No, Dolly. I don't think he is sorry, but don't you worry, he soon shall be."

Dolly, hearing the threatening tone of Gladys's words, attempted to soften her anger by saying, "I do hope you won't be too angry with him. That book meant so much to him."

"Not nearly as much as Eddy means to me. Eddy told me it was Eliza who made the smudges on the book, and he was just trying to save her from a scolding. He made me promise not to tell anyone, but I am going to tell James, you can bet on that."

Dolly could see it was no good trying to convince her mother that Eddy wasn't telling the truth; Eliza was not even in the room when they caught Eddy tearing out pages, so she changed the subject and said, "There is something else I think we need to discuss, Mother. You know, I am no longer a child."

"No, my darling, I realize that. You have grown into a lovely, strong, and sensible young lady, and I am very proud of you. I only wish your father could see you now."

"Did you love my father, Mother?"

"Of course I did! You have his eyes, you know. I see him every time I look at you."

"And do you love James, too?"

Gladys didn't know what to say. She rose from her chair, went over to the window, leaned her forehead against it, and stayed that way for a few seconds before she replied, "Dolly, I know I should have talked to you before. There are things that I hoped you would never have to know, but now I have no choice. I suppose you have every right to know what sort of mother you have. Only I'm sorry, but it will have to wait until tomorrow. I really must have a talk with James now. Do you mind?"

Dolly did mind. She knew she wouldn't be able to rest until she had some answers, but she also hoped her mother would settle things with James as soon as possible, so she kissed her and left. When Gladys learned that James had gone riding, she waited in the library for his return.

Although he was still angry at the boy for what he had done, the ride allowed him time to reflect on his actions. He knew he had allowed his resentment toward the boy to augment his temper. He recalled when Edward was a baby and how he had done his best to treat him as his own, but he had begun to dislike the lad when Gladys insisted on mollycoddling him.

Unfortunately, he had just started to think that the boy wasn't such a bad sort when the book incident occurred. Now he wondered what was to be done. By the time he arrived at the stables, he was certain he had the answer. Handing his mount over to Ruby, he was on his way to change his attire when Jenkins told him that Gladys was waiting in the library.

"Ah, Gladys, my dear," he said as he entered the room smiling. Gladys was standing by one of the windows when he entered, and his light-hearted greeting was more than she could bear. She ran over to him and slapped him hard across the face.

"That's for Eddy!"

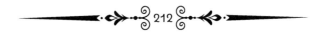

James rubbed his stinging cheek. His reaction was subdued since he understood her anger. "I suppose I deserved that, Gladys. I do apologize for my childish behaviour. The only excuse I am able to give you is that the book was one of my most treasured possessions. I lost my temper when I saw Edward tearing out pages."

"And did you bother to ask him why he was doing it?"

"I fail to see what he could have said to excuse such behaviour."

"Well, for your information, James, it was Eliza who soiled your book. Eddy was just trying to remove the evidence so she wouldn't get into trouble."

James walked over to the table, picked up a decanter of brandy, and as he poured himself a drink said, "Come now, Gladys, you surely don't believe that?"

"Of course I believe it. Eddy would not lie."

"My God, woman, don't be so naïve. Can you not see, the boy not only committed the crime but now he is attempting to place the blame on his little sister? We must do something to help him before it is too late, and I think I have the answer."

"What on earth are you talking about?"

"I have decided to send him to St Joseph's School for Boys in Glasgow. It is quite expensive, but I have heard they have good results with boys of his nature."

Gladys could hardly believe her ears. "You must be out of your mind if you think I will allow you to send my son to Scotland."

"I am afraid you have no say in the matter. I am the boy's lawful father you know, and it is up to me to shape his character."

Taking Gladys's silence as a sign of compliance, James felt rather pleased with himself and poured her a glass of sherry. "Now, my dear, I think we should forget what happened today. I understand that you only wanted to protect the boy," he said, handing her the drink. "Here you are. I am sure this will make you feel much better."

Gladys accepted the drink, only to throw it in his face. "Oh, I'm going to protect him, you may be sure of that. I am taking him so far away from here that you will never be able to hurt him again."

James was both shocked and shaken, but he did his best to remain composed as he slowly took out his handkerchief and wiped the sticky liquid off his face, determined to control his temper before addressing her. "Now, Gladys, you are being very childish. I must admit I was a little hard on the boy, but let us not become carried away. In spite of the details of our marriage, we have managed to build a happy home for the children."

"How do you think we can ever be happy again after you've called Eddy a bastard? I know Dolly heard you, and I would not be surprised if most of the help heard you, too. Edward will be thought of as a bastard for the rest of his days if he remains here."

"You are making a mountain out of a molehill."

"I hardly think so, but even if I am, I am taking Eddy and the girls, and we are going to America. You can sit in this room with your treasures, all safe and sound, for the rest of your life, and you will never have to worry about Eddy touching them; he will be miles away living with a father who loves him. And if you try to stop me, I shall see that your reputation in this town is ruined. You can wager money on that."

James had had enough. This time she had gone too far, and he didn't bother to curb his ire when he replied, "Oh no, you won't! You may take your son and Dolly, if she wishes to leave, but there is no way you can take my daughter from me. And I warn you, Gladys, if you attempt such a thing, I shall have the law on you. Damn my reputation."

"You know it would break Eliza's heart if Eddy and Dolly were to leave her. It would be cruel to separate them."

"If you leave, you leave without her. And I doubt very much whether Dolly will agree to go with you either."

"We shall see!" was all she could think of to say.

It was a sleepless night for both of them. James didn't want Gladys to leave; her companionship had helped fill a little of the loneliness he felt after Percy left. During the past year, he had thought they were content, if not happy, and that she felt the same. He knew his feelings toward Edward were not as fond as they were toward Eliza, but she was his daughter and Edward was not his son.

Besides, Gladys had spoiled the boy right from the start by her possessiveness, and now the damage was done and Edward avoided him whenever he could. James recalled how the same thing had happened with his son, Horace. His mother had been as possessive of him, and it was only when Horace had moved away that they had gotten to know each other through correspondence. He wondered if the same thing would ever happen with Edward.

But then his thoughts returned to the matter at hand, and after some thought, he convinced himself there was no need to worry. Gladys would never give up all the luxuries she had become accustomed to. Her threats were made in a fit of anger, and after a good night's sleep, she was sure to change her mind.

Gladys kept her hand on Eddy as she lay in bed, patting his back every time he shook with a sob in his sleep. She was sure she would never be able to feel the same toward James again. She also told herself that the exhilaration she had felt when she told James that she was leaving was not just because she now had an excuse to be with Angelo. Although James had attacked Eddy, Gladys knew he was still a compassionate person in many ways and would never separate her from any of her children. Picturing what it would be like for the four of them aboard ship on their way to a new world, she smiled and kissed the back of Eddy's head before drifting off to sleep.

To look at James and Gladys the following morning at the breakfast table, one would never guess what a row they had the evening before. They weren't as cheery as usual, but they were civil to one another. Gladys asked James if she could have a word with him in private, and, thinking she regretted what she had said the night before, he readily agreed. However, once they were alone in the library, he was disappointed when, in a calm and controlled tone of voice, she told him that she was still planning on leaving.

"Before you make up your mind, Gladys, will you listen to a suggestion I have?" He kept his tone calm in accordance with hers, and when she agreed to listen, he continued, "I have never in my life hit anyone before, and I shall never do it again: this I promise. I will admit that I have not made enough of an effort to become close to Edward, but I shall endeavour to rectify that from now on. I only suggested sending him to Scotland to ensure that he receives the best education. You do understand that most boys whose parents can afford it are sent away to private schools, do you not?"

"James, I do not want to argue with you, and I sincerely hope we can continue to be friends, for the children's sake as well as our own, but you and I both know that you will never care for Eddy as a father should. Angelo loves him, and no school in Scotland can give him the love of a father. We have to leave."

"Don't you even care about our daughter? What sort of mother are you to even think of running away and leaving her behind?"

"I love Eliza with all my heart. I really do, but if I have to leave her, I know how much you care for her and that she will be well looked after until I return."

"By law, I may be able to prevent you from going."

"Even if you could, it wouldn't solve anything, James. We would both be miserable and that sort of atmosphere would not be good for anyone. I shall never be able to repay you for all you have done for Dolly and me, but it's over between us, James. I am truly sorry."

"Do you really think you shall be content to live over there in near poverty after living as you have the last six years?"

"America is not like England, James, and we won't be living in poverty."

"So you say, but I wager you shan't have servants waiting on you."

"I know it is hard for you to believe, but although I thought I wanted to become a society lady more than anything else in the world, I was mistaken. I know I wear fancy clothes and have servants waiting on me, but I have never felt truly free. I may have changed on the outside, James, but not on the inside."

"You mean once a sow's ear, always a sow's ear?"

"Someone else said that to me once, and I guess she was right."

"So you are determined to leave Eliza and run away with a man you are not even married to? What if Eliza becomes sick?"

"She will have Nanny to look after her, and, now that there are ships that take only a little more than a week to cross the ocean, you can send for me."

"It is all very well to leave your daughter without a mother, but your son cannot live without a father?" he said with a clear note of sarcasm. "If you leave, she shall never forgive you, and mark my word,

Gladys, you will never forgive yourself."

"I pray you are wrong, James. I do intend to return in a less than a year, so she doesn't forget me."

"And what if I forbid you to see her when you return?"

"I do not believe you would do that. I know you too well."

"Will you be coming home to stay then?"

"I really don't know. I may feel I can leave Eddy with his father by then, but we shall just have to wait and see. Right now, I have no idea what the future holds. I know we have a lot to discuss before I leave, but it will have to wait. Now I must have a talk with Dolly."

"Do not forget to tell her that you care nothing for her or her sister. I am certain she will be happy to hear that."

"Please don't talk that way, James."

"I shall talk any way I damn well please! You do not deserve your children, Gladys, and I just may stop you from taking any of them, so do not think you have won, not by a long shot."

"I am leaving with at least two of my children, James, and you cannot stop me."

Chapter Twenty Three

Dolly decided to allow her mother and James a little privacy to settle their differences, so she and Blossom left right after breakfast to take the children for a picnic. When they returned, she sensed an unusual and foreboding quietness in the house that reminded her of the time her grandfather died.

As loyal as all the members of the household staff were, they weren't above eavesdropping, and hearing that Gladys was leaving was even more upsetting than the news that Eddy was a bastard, since they had suspected as much. Fearful of what was to come, they went about performing their duties in such a quiet and serious manner that a stranger might have thought there had been a death in the family.

After lunch, Dolly and Gladys left the children with their nanny and went for a walk. Dolly had looked forward to hearing about her mother's secret, but now the sombre expression on Gladys's face caused her to feel apprehensive, and she almost wished she hadn't insisted on finding out the truth.

When they came to the orchard, Gladys sat down on a bench that James's first wife had had built under a huge cherry tree. Dolly sat on the grass at her mother's feet and waited patiently for her to begin.

Laying her hand gently on Dolly's head, Gladys said, "You do know that I love you and Eliza just as much as I love Eddy, don't you, darling?"

"I suppose so, Mother, but there are times when you fail to show it."

"I know, and I am sorry. I promise it shan't be like that anymore. One of the reasons I spoil Eddy is because of James's lack of interest in him. I know it hurts Eddy's feelings, and I suppose I try to compensate by giving him too much attention. Do you understand?"

"Perhaps, but I cannot understand why James does not like Eddy. Until he destroyed that book, he has always been a good boy."

"I wish you would believe that Eddy did what he did for Eliza's sake, but never mind that now. After I tell you my story, I think you will understand why James feels the way he does and not blame him for his neglect. I just pray you will still love me when I'm finished."

It took a long time before Gladys finished talking. She omitted nothing but the circumstances of Millie's death. She tried her best to explain what it felt like to escape from the slums and live in fear of being found out and sent to prison, but she didn't know words poignant enough. Nor was it possible to fully explain the love she and Angelo shared because Dolly had yet to experience such feelings. Nevertheless, Dolly did have an active imagination, and, at times during the explanation, she showed signs of empathy.

When her mother had finished, Dolly sat without saying anything for a time. She was an avid reader and had read many books, but she had never come across a more intriguing and romantic story. Unfortunately, it was almost impossible for her to associate any of it with the person she had always known as her mother. She had grown up believing her grandmother was a respectable governess and her grandfather a brave captain. Now she learned that they were nothing but drunkards and that her mother had actually killed a person. Surely that woman could not be the same beautiful, gentle woman she had always adored?

She was appalled to learn of her maternal grandparents' real identity, but it was anger she felt toward Gladys, not pity. She might have felt sympathy for her, and even admiration for the amazing accomplishments she had managed to achieve, if Gladys hadn't lied to her. Ever since Dolly could remember, she had thought her mother was the quintessence of what a lady should be. Now she didn't know what to think, but feelings of betrayal overshadowed all other sentiments.

Gladys waited patiently for Dolly to say something, knowing it was a lot for her to digest, but when she did speak, it wasn't what Gladys had hoped to hear.

"Are you really my mother?"

"Of course I am, sweetheart. Everything I've told you is the truth. You have to believe that."

"I do not know if I can believe anything you say anymore! I really do not know you, do I?" Gladys didn't know how to answer so she just shook her head as Dolly continued, "I heard rumours about Eddy, but I chose to ignore them, thinking you would never do such a thing. You committed adultery and then lied about that too. Now it seems all you care about is a man you hardly know."

"Oh God no, that's not true, Dolly. Please, darling, don't say that. I love you and Eliza so much. I know all this comes as a terrible shock, and I had hoped you would never have to hear it, but please don't hate me. I couldn't bear that. I have told you all this so that you would understand why we have to go to America. If we stay here, Eddy will grow up as a bastard. That is a stigma that he will always suffer. You know that is true."

"It shall be the same for him in America, shall it not?"

"No. I intend to tell him who his father is and then see to it that he has his father's name."

Although Dolly was more of a pragmatist than a romantic, she had never forgotten the wonderful exhibits the Americans brought to the first World Fair in London and the thought of visiting such a place whet her imagination. Besides, what her mother said about Eddy being better off with a father who loved him was beginning to make sense—she would have given anything to have known her own father. She didn't know if she could ever forgive her mother, but she began to feel a twinge of excitement over the idea of going to America.

"What will happen to James if we go with you, Mother? He would miss Eliza terribly!"

This was the first time she had referred to James by his first name, and she was surprised by how grown up it made her feel.

At first, Gladys was distraught by Dolly's accusing attitude, but now hearing her say that she would be coming to America too, she gave a sigh of relief. Giving Dolly's shoulders a loving squeeze, she said, "I'm afraid that Eliza won't be coming with us, dear. James refuses to let her go."

Dolly was shocked and jumped up, saying, "We cannot go to America and leave Eliza here!"

"There is nothing I can do about it, Dolly. James will never give her up."

"Well, I shan't leave if Eliza is not coming, and I do not see how you can either."

"It will break my heart, dear, but I have to for Eddy's sake. Can't you see that?"

"No, I cannot! Perhaps I could understand it if you were to leave me behind. I am old enough to look after myself, but Eliza? She is only three years old."

"Nanny will take good care of her, and we shall be back before too long. I promise."

"Not we, Mother. You may go, but I shall remain here. I shall ask James for a maid's job, if I have to. And you need not worry about Nanny looking after Eliza, I intend to see to that," she said angrily. Then, without giving her mother time to respond, she walked away.

Gladys cried out, "Dolly, darling, please come back, please!" Dolly didn't answer. The girl had inherited her father's stubborn streak, and Gladys knew she would never change her mind. She wondered if she would be able to go to America without her. The girl had an assuredness to her that Gladys had always envied, and as close as they had been through the years, there were times when Gladys felt as though

Dolly was the mother and she the child.

Even though it had shocked Dolly to learn that she had been lied to for years about her lineage, Gladys was glad she had kept it a secret for all that time because Dolly was as at ease among the wealthy as any other highborn young lady: a trait Gladys knew she could never acquire herself.

Getting up slowly, Gladys experienced her first sense of aging, an unfamiliar feeling of weariness and fragility. For the first time since telling James she was leaving, she wondered if she would be able to do it. She had planned on taking all three of her children, and now she would have to leave two behind.

She looked around at the splendour of her surroundings. The trees were in bloom, and the scent was so lovely that it brought back memories of the first time she found that air could actually smell sweet. Eighteen years had gone by since then, and so much had happened. Her entire life had been a seesaw of ups and downs. There were almost as many happy memories as sad ones. She had worked hard for what she had accomplished, and her rewards were plenty. She breathed the fragrant air deep into her lungs, as though storing it there until she returned. Straightening her back, she held her head high and walked toward the house with the same determined strength that had once saved her life.

Dolly went to find James as soon as she returned to the manor. He was in the dining room having a cup of hot chocolate. Oddly, addressing James by his proper name instead of sir gave her a feeling of maturity, and she came right to the point, stating that if her mother left, she would not be going with her but would remain in England to look after Eliza, if he would allow it.

"Although you are not legally my stepdaughter, Dolly, I have always considered you so, which means you have every right to live here for the rest of your life. If your mother is determined to run away, she shall have to give you and Eliza up. How she can do that, I do not know. I certainly could never do such a thing."

Dolly managed to hold back her tears. "Thank you, James. I would rather stay here than go to America anyway."

Eddy hadn't been the same since James struck him. Although he still played with Eliza, he was much quieter and was often seen wearing a sad expression. Eliza was too young to understand why, but she instinctively knew something was very wrong and hugged him whenever she had the chance. As much as Eddy loved his sister, her embraces did little to cheer him up, nor did James's attempts to be nice to him.

James, hoping to prove he felt no animosity toward the boy, tried to seek him out as often as he could to impress Gladys, thinking it might convince her it would be in Eddy's best interest if she were to stay. However, Eddy was just as determined and managed to avoid him whenever possible. This wasn't always easy, so when Gladys told him they were soon going on a very long trip to a new country called America, he could hardly wait to leave.

However, when she told him that Dolly and Eliza were not going with them, he cried and demanded to know why. Gladys told him that Eliza was too young to travel and that Dolly said she would stay home and look after her. "We shall have to bring them both something very special if we are going to be gone a long time, Mother," he said.

James knew that Horace and Sarah, who now had a little boy and were expecting another child, could not come in time to change Gladys's mind, so he sent for his Aunt Jean. He knew she and Gladys had become very fond of one another and thought that if anyone could help, Jean would be the one to do it. She arrived about ten days before Gladys planned to leave.

James decided it would be a good idea if both he and Gladys were to talk to her together, but Gladys didn't like the idea. She was

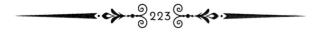

convinced the meeting would end in an argument and upset the elderly lady, so she insisted James talk to her first.

When James told Jean that Gladys was going to America with Eddy's father, she mumbled, "If the boy resembles his father, I can believe it."

Shocked, James asked, "What did you say?"

"Forgive me, my dear. That was a thoughtless thing to say. I was not thinking. You mean to say that she is actually planning on leaving you?"

"Not only me, Auntie. She is going to leave Eliza and Dolly too."

"Oh my, this is serious. What on earth happened to bring this about?"

"Nothing. Oh, she blames me for an incident that happened a while ago. I caught the boy ripping pages out of father's book of poetry and I struck him, but I am certain she is merely using that as an excuse to be with her lover. I thought perhaps you could have a talk with her. She is fond of you, you know."

"And I of her, but I must say I was afraid something like this would happen when you married her." She used her cane to get up before saying, "Well, James, I shall do what I can, but Gladys has always had a mind of her own."

Gladys was afraid that Jean wouldn't want to speak to her after her talk with James, but, surprisingly, she was as friendly as ever. Then, when Jean said she would like to have a private talk where they wouldn't be disturbed, Gladys knew she was not getting off so easily. Jean suggested they use James's library because he had gone riding. They even helped themselves to some of his sherry.

When they each had a drink, Jean came right to the point. "Now, Gladys, my dear, I should like to hear your side of the story—all of it, if you don't mind."

When Gladys was finished, she said, "I expect James asked you to try and persuade me to stay, Jean, but I'm afraid I have made up my mind."

"Yes, he did, but now I am not sure staying here would be the wisest thing to do."

"You mean you actually agree with me?"

"That is not what I said. However, I would appreciate it if both you and James were to join me here tonight. Perhaps what I have to suggest shan't be what either of you want to hear, but I intend to have my say. There is one thing I should like you to answer for me before James is with us, Gladys. Have you thought what this will do to him?"

"Of course I have, but he hasn't been happy for a long time, and it has nothing to do with me."

"You must have been happy together for a time. You had a beautiful daughter together."

Gladys took Jean's statement as an accusation and thoughtlessly defended herself. "The night that Eliza was conceived was the only time we were intimate. James had been drinking heavily and insisted on coming into my bed, despite my unwillingness. It was not a pleasant act for either of us. I don't know if you can understand this, Jean, but James has no desire to be intimate with any woman. He only slept with me because he thought it was his duty as a man. You might say he is a man's man. He was happy when he was friends with Percy, but since they've had a disagreement, he hasn't been the same."

Gladys stood up and walked over to the window as she tried to think of a subtle way to explain the different reasons why James had married her. Not able to come up with anything, she decided to tell the truth.

"Although James married me out of pity, he also wanted a family without a romantic relationship, and because I was in love with another man, he knew it would suit me too. That way, life at Four Oaks could go on as it had. So while I might hurt James's pride when I leave, you may be assured that I shall not break his heart."

Gladys suddenly realized how cold and cruel her words were, and, before Jean could respond, she added, "Your nephew is one of the kindest and dearest men I have ever known, and if you want to help him, Jean, you should try to convince him to regain Percy's friendship. They have so much in common and enjoy each other's company more than anyone else's."

If Jean had understood exactly what Gladys was implying when she called James a man's man, she certainly didn't respond accordingly, but said, "I have known a few men who prefer the company of men to that of women. I suppose they enjoy the more rugged things in life. I never thought James was that way though—in fact, there were some in the family who thought him quite fragile."

That evening, after the children were in bed, James, Gladys, and Jean retired to the library. With the door closed, it was the most soundproof room in the house. For the sake of the children, James and Gladys had been pleasant at the dinner table, but now neither said a word, so it was up to Jean to begin.

"Now, then, you have both confided in me, and I must say I am flattered that you think enough of me to do so. You, James, are like a son to me, and, Gladys, I have begun to think of you as one of my family as well, so please be assured that whatever I have to offer in the way of advice comes from my heart. I think by relating an experience I had as a young woman, you might understand my sentiments a little more clearly.

"Looking at me now, you might find it difficult to imagine that I was once young, pretty, and in love. Oh yes, very, very much in love! The young man was an artist. I always enjoyed painting and even dreamt of becoming a recognized painter myself. I had seen a painting in a window one day and was so impressed with it that I was determined to meet the artist and beg him to teach me his technique. I learned he was a Spaniard and his name was Juan Sanchez. I later learned that he lived in the basement of a house in a rundown part of town. Nevertheless, I was so taken with his work that I ignored the squalor and visited him once every week.

"During the good weather, we sometimes took our easels down to the shore or into the forest to paint. Juan was a handsome fellow with a carefree nature. He was also a popular man, and my lessons were often interrupted by friends dropping in with food and bottles of wine. Then they would stay, eating and drinking until dawn.

"I am afraid I have become carried away with my story. I have never talked about Juan to anyone before, and I find it quite liberating. Yes, that is exactly what it is, liberating.

"Before long, Juan and I had fallen in love and could hardly wait to be married. Realizing how poor he was, I asked Father to set him up in a lucrative business, so we could afford a home and at least a few servants. I suppose because I was in my late twenties and Father was anxious to see me married, he agreed. Juan was invited to spend a weekend at our estate so Father could get to know him before telling him of his generous offer. Mother also invited some of their other friends so they could meet him.

"The weekend was a complete disaster. Juan felt ill at ease the entire time. I had thought his accent romantic, but it soon became obvious that, while our other guests thought it amusing, they also considered it common, and their attitude toward him was noticeably condescending. After the other guests departed, Father kept his word and offered to set Juan up in business. Instead of being pleased, Juan was humiliated. However, he thanked Father before refusing to accept what he considered charity. When Father asked him how he intended to keep me in the manner that I was accustomed to, he answered that he didn't—at least not until he sold a lot more of his paintings.

"Juan had a glimpse of our life that weekend and, unfortunately, did not like it. So a short time later, and much against my Father's wishes, he convinced me to move in with him, intending to marry me as soon as we could afford it. I really had no idea what sort of life he lived, but I thought that I would love it as long as I could be with him. I wish I could say I had enough perseverance to stay, but I was every bit as out of place in his world as he was in mine, and after a week, I knew it would never work. I returned home heartbroken and did not see Juan again until six years later."

Jean stopped talking for a few seconds, and Gladys, anxious to hear what happened when the two lovers met again, couldn't wait and asked, "What happened then, Jean?"

Before she could answer, James, who was becoming irritable and anxious for his aunt to try to dissuade Gladys from leaving, demanded to know what Jean's affairs had to do with his and Gladys's problem. Jean, taking her time, informed him he would just have to wait until she finished her story. She requested a cup of tea before she continued.

Gladys rang for a maid, and once they had their tea, Jean continued with her story.

"As I said, I did not see Juan again for six years after I returned home. Then one day I went shopping and my footman was just helping me down from my carriage when a little girl ran into me, almost tipping me over. A man rushed over to apologize, and I almost fainted when I saw his face. It was Juan, and he was even handsomer than I remembered. He was with a woman who was obviously in the family way. He called her over to me and introduced her as his wife.

She was not a pretty woman, but she did have a pleasant countenance and a friendly smile. Besides the little girl who had bumped into me, there were two more little ones, and Juan insisted I meet them all. We talked for a while and I learned that although he was still painting, he was also working as a clerk in order to pay the bills. One of his little ones then began pulling on his britches, urging him to leave, so we said goodbye, and I never saw him again. I still love the man, but I shall never forgive him."

"Because he married someone else?" Gladys asked.

"Goodness no! I hardly expected him to stay single—a man needs a family. The reason I shan't forgive him is because he looked so bloody happy."

James and Gladys gasped. They had never heard Jean use such vulgar language before. Jean apologized, saying, "Forgive me, but that is how I felt."

"Oh, Jean, I am so sorry. Do you wish you had married him?" Gladys asked.

"No, Gladys. Even though I never met anyone else I could love, I know Juan and I could never have been happy together. Our backgrounds were so very different."

"I think your story was more for my benefit than Gladys's, is that not right, Auntie?" James said sharply.

"James, when I saw how happy Gladys was with the servants at your wedding party, I knew she would never feel completely at home with our kind," Jean said sympathetically.

Addressing Gladys, Jean continued, "You may have fooled some people, Gladys, but I was reminded of Juan every time I looked at you. I am sorry, James. I know that is not what you wanted to hear."

"But surely you cannot condone her leaving her three-year-old daughter? Could you do such a thing?"

"I do not know, James. I think not, but truthfully, I do not know. You did say you intend to return before long, did you not, Gladys?"

"Of course, and now with the new steamships, the voyage only takes about a week."

"And while you are gone, I shall be only too happy to come and help look after the girls," Jean announced.

James stood up, and throwing his hands in the air, said, "Well then, it sounds like you two have it all planned. It matters not to either of you that I shall be the laughingstock of the town." He didn't stay to hear a reply.

Although Jean was very fond of Gladys and would miss her, she felt rather pleased when she heard she was leaving. Ever since Gladys had made such wonderful improvements to James's home, Jean had hoped to be invited to stay permanently. Now all she had to do was convince James that she could take Gladys's place as mistress of Four Oaks. The next day, before leaving, she mentioned it to James. Knowing how fond she was of Eliza and Dolly, he said he would think about it. When Jean said goodbye to Gladys, she hugged her, wished her good luck, and then gave her fifty pounds. Gladys didn't refuse the money, not knowing how healthy Angelo's finances were.

Chapter Twenty Four

Gladys only had a week to prepare for the journey. She decided on one trunk for their clothes and one for their personal belongings.

Dolly had convinced James that even if his aunt were to move in, she was far too elderly to take Gladys's place. She then convinced him that she could easily replace her mother as mistress of the manor, at least until Gladys returned. Having gained his approval, she put her feelings aside and asked her mother to write out a list of her duties and explain how best to do them. Gladys was pleased because it would give them more time together before she left.

"I can't take my sewing machine, Dolly, so I'll show you how to operate it before I leave. Everything else that I can't take with me, you may have, and that includes my dear Tig. Your grandfather gave him to me just after your father and I were married. He's a bit stubborn at times but a joy to ride." Then, when she only received a nod, she added, "Please don't be too angry with me, darling. I love you so very much, and I promise that I shall write often, and I hope you will answer my letters. I shall be back before long, Dolly. I promise."

Dolly didn't really believe her but managed to smile as she answered, "That will be nice."

They were busy going over all the duties Dolly would have to perform, but whenever they stopped to have tea or eat, they would talk, and it hurt Gladys to hear the bitterness in her daughter's voice when she said she was thankful she had never known her grandparents. It was then that Gladys began defending them.

"They were not as fortunate as your Gamby, Dolly. He was born into aristocracy, as were you, but my parents were born in poverty. There was no money for education, but Mama could sing more songs than anyone I ever knew. You would have loved to see her dance, Dolly. She looked like a fairy princess with her beautiful, shiny red hair—hair much like yours. And your grandpa was the most handsome man in the neighbourhood. He was taller than Gamby and stronger than Ruby. His eyes twinkled, and he had the jolliest laugh."

Time had softened Gladys's memories, and the parents she described were the ones she knew when she was little more than an infant. Her words had a profound effect, and Dolly began to think about her grandparents in a kinder light.

As the time for her mother's departure came nearer, Dolly became aware of how very much she would miss her. Nevertheless, because she could hardly wait to take over the grown-up position of mistress of Four Oaks, she didn't attempt to dissuade her from leaving.

The week went by far too quickly, and Gladys was kept so busy that she didn't have time to visit with the staff, but she did manage to take her horse out for one last ride. She was about to ride past the Ellison's cottage when Richard came out and flagged her down. He hadn't heard that she was leaving and smiling broadly he said, "Can you spare a moment, Mrs Hornsby?"

Gladys had wanted to say goodbye to the family so she got off her horse. "What is it, Richard?" she asked.

"I've something to show you—it's in the shop here," he said as he led her to the shop he had made out of an old feed shed behind his house.

"I don't have much time."

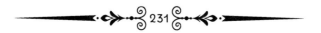

"Oh, it won't take a minute."

"Is Nell home?" she asked as they were walking toward the shop.

"She's over to Mrs Palmers. Taking her some of her rabbit stew. Mrs Palmer's not feeling too sprightly these days." They had reached the shed and Richard had opened the big door before Gladys could reply. She couldn't help but squeal when she saw the beautiful settee he had built to go with the chairs. Then she couldn't stop the tears.

Richard thought she was disappointed, and he felt like crying too. "You don't like it, missus?" he asked.

"Oh, Richard, it is the most beautiful piece of furniture I have ever seen. I love it!" Then she told him that she was leaving Four Oaks. "But I shall be back someday, and I know that James will treasure it as much as I would." She hugged him and said goodbye.

The first thing she did when she arrived home was to tell James about the settee and ask him to make sure that Richard received a very generous payment for it. It was another thing she was going to regret leaving behind.

Once James realized that Gladys wasn't going to change her mind, he tried to avoid her as much as possible. The day before she was to depart, she asked him if they could have a talk. Knowing it would be foolish to refuse, he suggested they meet in the dining room after the children retired. He did not want to tarnish his memories of the library, where they had shared so many enjoyable evenings.

He was waiting for her when she arrived. She was pleasantly surprised to see that he had poured them both a glass of sherry, which helped ease the tension.

James cleared his throat and broke the silence, "Have you arranged for Ruby to take your luggage to the train station?"

"Yes. Jenkins has offered to take us down to the station in the buggy as well."

"What time tomorrow do you plan on leaving?" he asked.

"I'd like to be at the station early so that I can see to our luggage and secure a compartment on the train. I think we should leave here around six."

"Then I shall say my goodbye tonight. I am certain Dolly and the others will be up to see you off."

"I had a long talk with Eliza this afternoon. She was so sweet! She said that she would write to us as soon as she learned her letters. I do love her, James, although I know you find that hard to believe. I shall miss her and Dolly so very much." With a grin, she added, "I'll even miss you. In spite of our differences, we've had some good times together, haven't we?"

"I shall never forgive or condone what you are doing, Gladys, but yes, we did have some enjoyable times."

"And, James, don't be upset with me, but I wish you would please go and see Percy. He misses his friendship with you so much."

Instead of resenting her suggestion, James surprised her by saying, "I just might do that. I should like to ask his advice about getting a divorce."

"A divorce?" Gladys exclaimed.

"As far as I am concerned, our marriage is over. I know you love this Angelo and want to be his wife, and besides, contrary to what you may think, I do feel responsible for Edward's future. It would save him a good deal of embarrassment if his parents were married."

Gladys couldn't stop the tears of joy. "Thank you, James. That's so very kind of you, but divorced or not, I do intend to return to Four Oaks inside of a year."

Not letting on that he had heard, James said, "And I shall consent to Edward's adoption after your marriage. It is only right that he has his father's name."

Gladys was very relieved to know they were parting on speaking terms, if not as friends.

All the residents of Four Oaks except James were on hand to say goodbye early the next morning. Cook had made some sandwiches and a bottle of lemonade for them to have on the train.

Eliza had wrapped a string of beads, which Dolly had given her, up in a piece of pretty paper for Eddy. He would have laughed if he weren't so sad. When she handed it to him, she said in a serious tone,

"These are for you to remember me."

Although Dolly loved her mother dearly, she didn't agree with what she was doing. She had made up her mind not to give her mother the satisfaction of seeing her cry, but when the time came to say goodbye, tears ran down her cheeks. She wasn't alone—there wasn't a dry eye amongst the assembled crowd.

Dolly watched until the buggy was out of sight. As everyone walked toward the manor, the last verses of the song, "The Gypsy Laddie," ran through her head.

> "It's I can leave my house and land,
> And I can leave my baby,
> I'm a-goin' to roam this world around,
> And be a gypsy's lady.
> Oh, soon this lady changed her mind,
> Her clothes grew old and faded,
> Her hose and shoes came off her feet,
> And left them bare and naked.
> Just what befell this lady now,
> I think is worth relating,
> Her gypsy found another lass,
> And left her heart-a-breaking."

She picked up Eliza, kissed her, and promised, "I shall never leave you, my little princess."

Later that afternoon, James asked Eliza if she would like him to read her a story, but when he picked her up and carried her toward the library, she started to cry.

"Whatever is the matter?" he asked.

"I do not want to go there," she said.

"Why not?"

"Eddy said I am not supposed to."

"Well, Eddy was mistaken," he answered as he carried her into the room. "I have some nice books in here that I had when I was a child."

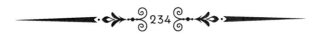

"Papa?"

"Yes?"

"Did Eddy go away because I smudged your book?"

James could hardly believe what he heard. "You mean to say it was you who soiled the book?" he asked.

"Eddy told me not to tell, Papa, but I don't want him to go away."

"Oh, Eliza, how I wish you had told me this before. It was not your fault he left, my darling, it was mine. And for that, I shall never forgive myself. Eddy is a good boy, and I am certain he will write to you with all the news of his adventures in America. It shall be something to look forward to. And I shall even help you write to him."

Chapter Twenty Five

Eddy said very little on the train going to London.

When Angelo met them at the station, he noticed the change in the boy's personality. He did his best to cheer the lad up during the two weeks they spent waiting for their ship to sail, but it was Angelo's grandmother, Isabella Rossini (Nonna), who brought back Eddy's beautiful smile. The old lady had been as cheerless as Eddy until they met each other, but as is often the case among children and the elderly, they seemed to have a language of their own.

Angelo had found a man who would sell them forged identification papers stating that Gladys was his wife and Eddy their son, but Gladys didn't want to use them. She didn't want to begin a new life in America built on lies, but she was unable to purchase a cabin in her own name, so she had no choice.

The day they were allowed on the ship, Gladys had been waiting on the dock for Angelo to find out if they could go aboard when a wagon loaded with baskets of vegetables, fruit, and cages of live chickens came onto the wharf and stopped beside their ship. A heavy-set man came running down the gang plank, calling out in a deep and commanding voice, "Hold up there! I'll have a look at those before you unload them, and they had best be fresh or you can bloody well take them back and bring me some that are."

Gladys could scarcely believe her eyes: the man was her old friend, Sandy, the cook from The Whale's Tail restaurant in Dover. She was so pleased to see him that she rushed over to greet him.

Sandy threw his arms around her and began asking questions without waiting for answers. "Gladys Pickwick! Is it really you? How many years has it been? Why in heavens name did you run off without saying goodbye? Was it because of Andrew's useless stepson? That scoundrel did his best to tarnish your name, but I don't know of a soul who believed him. How are you, my girl? What are you doing down here on the docks?"

He finally wound down and let Gladys answer. "I'm very well, Sandy. Don't tell me you are now a ship's cook. What about The Whale's Tail?"

"I left there a week ago. My friend, Rob Rawlins—he's the captain of this here ship—well, he's been trying to get me aboard for a long time, and I finally decided I should give it a try before I get too old to enjoy it. This will be my first voyage, and if I like it, I may never return to The Whale's Tail. Besides, it's never been the same there without your father-in-law sitting at his old table every day. I still miss the old boy and his lad, your dear man, Tom, as well. I don't suppose you are going aboard are you?"

Just then, Eddy ran up and took her hand. "Do come, Mother, we are going on the ship right now!"

"Of course, dear, but this is a dear old friend of mine, and he will be cooking some of our meals on the ship. I'm married again, Sandy, and this is my son, Edward. Maybe we shall get a chance to talk on the ship." Sandy gave her another hug and promised to spend as much time with her as he could.

Instead of being afraid to have someone from her past nearby, Gladys welcomed it. It was wonderful to be able to talk to someone who remembered Tom, her first husband and Dolly's father, and all the people she had known while living in Dover.

That day some of Eddy's enthusiasm returned. He had almost outgrown his sailor suit, but he insisted on wearing it. As he set foot on the deck, he honoured the captain, who was standing on the bridge, with a military salute. When the captain returned the gesture, Eddy's grin spread from one ear to the other.

Although Angelo had purchased first-class cabins, the rooms weren't made to accommodate the latest style in ladies apparel. With only one foot of space between the bunks, Gladys and Angelo's grandmother found it far more convenient to navigate without their cumbersome hoops. Fortunately, there was ample space at one end of the room for luggage, a wardrobe, a small table, and two chairs. Although it wasn't as roomy as a hotel room, both of the women thought it adequate.

Gladys would have been thrilled with it if only Dolly and Eliza were with her. There had been no satisfactory solution to her predicament, so she had done what she thought was right, but the promise she made to return in a year or less did little to ease her conscience. Now she wondered if Isabella would still like her if she knew that not only was she married to another man, and not her beloved grandson, but she had deserted two daughters as well. She needed Angelo to reassure her, but he and Eddy had to share the adjoining cabin with his Uncle Victor.

Angelo was having similar thoughts. He had looked forward to sharing a cabin with Gladys as well. They had only been alone once since she had arrived in London, and that was when his uncle was kind enough to take his grandmother and Eddy for a short walk to have a dish of ice cream. Now they wouldn't be together until thy landed in New York. "I'll be damned if they keep us apart after that!" He had vowed to Gladys.

The ship left London on June 15, 1860, and they all went out on deck to wave goodbye to the crowd of people standing on the pier. It was quite chilly. After a short time, Angelo's uncle suggested that they return to their cabins, as he was afraid Nonna might catch a chill. Gladys wanted to remain on deck, but Eddy was so eager to explore the rest of the vessel that Angelo offered to be his guide and left her on her own.

While she could still see England, her sorrow over leaving the girls wasn't coupled with remorse, but as the last speck of land disappeared from her sight, she reached out, as though to grab it back, and cried out, "God, forgive me!"

Part Two

Chapter Twenty Six

On the second day at sea, the weather was more favourable, and they all went for a stroll along the small promenade. Isabella took note of the admiring glances she and Gladys received from some of the other passengers, and she felt a sense of pride for the first time in years. For decades, she had worn nothing but black, until Gladys had taken her shopping in London. Gladys had insisted that she buy three new outfits. She had dressed as though in mourning ever since she had disowned Angelo's mother, Maria. Maria had left home to marry an Englishman who was not only a protestant but a commoner as well.

Victor and Angelo, Isabella's remaining family, had travelled from Italy to England and America before deciding to leave the theatre and begin a business in America. Isabella, afraid she would never see them again, insisted on going with them.

They were all waiting in London for their departure when Gladys and Edward arrived, and Angelo introduced them as his wife and son. Isabella could tell by the likeness that Edward and Angelo were indeed father and son, but she instinctively knew that Gladys was not his wife. Nevertheless, she realized they were deeply in love. It brought back memories of her dear Maria and the Englishman, and she thought that her daughter might still be alive if only she had accepted their relationship.

Isabella adored five-year-old Edward right from the start, and it only took a week before she began to like and respect Gladys as well. Now, when she saw the admiring looks they received as they strolled up and down the deck, she began to look forward to her new life in America with enthusiasm and not with regret.

Gladys was so busy seeing to Isabella and Eddy's needs that it helped to keep her mind off Dolly and Eliza. She missed them both terribly, but Dolly the most. Dolly was now fifteen, and they had been through so much together. She was such a level-headed girl, but now Gladys couldn't forget the look on her face the day Gladys said that she intended to leave Eliza and go to America without her.

At first Dolly looked like she didn't believe it, then she had given Gladys a look of utter disdain before declaring that she intended to remain in England with Eliza. Gladys had almost changed her mind then, but she knew Dolly would watch over Eliza while she was in America. Instead of making her feel better, the thought just made her feel sick with guilt.

Even though Dolly had been present when James had struck Eddy and called him a bastard in a fit of anger, she didn't think it was reason enough to leave Eliza when James refused to allow her to go with them.

Now, aboard ship, Gladys kept going over it all in her mind. She kept wondering if there was anything she could have said or done to make Dolly understand why she had to take Eddy to be with his father, but there seemed to be no answer.

On the third day at sea, they were all in the dining room having tea when one of the crew came running in with the announcement, "Captain said everyone on deck what wants to see the Great Eastern go by."

"What on earth is the Great Eastern?" Isabella asked Victor.

"She's the biggest steamship ever built, Momma. Shall we all go and have a look?"

They all ventured up on deck to see the marvel, and what a sight it was! Although the ship was about half a mile away, it made their ship feel like a rowboat in comparison.

"It's like an island," Gladys said.

"From what I've heard, the inside is like the inside of a palace," Angelo replied. "Look at the size of her paddles, Uncle Vic. And I think I can count six masts, but I can't make out if there are four or five funnels."

"For all her power, she doesn't seem to be moving a great deal faster than we are," Victor commented.

They watched the giant ship off and on all that day, but the next morning she was out of sight.

Gladys wrote to both girls every day, telling them everything about the voyage. Seeing the Great Eastern steamship sail past on her first visit to America was an exciting happening to report.

She was sitting at the table writing about it when Eddy came bursting through the door, and, jumping up and down, he excitedly announced, "Mother, Sandy asked me if I wanted to meet the Captain. Please, may I?"

"Shh! Your Nonna is trying to rest. And, Eddy, didn't I tell you not to call Mr Sandlund Sandy?"

"But, Mother, he said that he would like me a damn sight more if I was to call him Sandy."

"And what did I tell you about using profanity?"

"But that is precisely what he said, Mother."

Gladys raised an eyebrow and suggested in a friendlier tone, "You don't need to quote him word for word."

"I know, Mother. I am sorry, but please may I go with him to see the Captain steer the ship?"

"As long as he is with you at all times. And make sure you behave and don't touch things unless you are told to."

"Yes, Mother." As Eddy went by his great-grandmother, who was lying down in one of the bunks and had been enjoying listening to the conversation, he stopped, patted her arm, and whispered, "Sorry, Nonna."

Eddy had been unusually quiet since leaving Four Oaks, and Gladys was worried about him. Although he had seemed happy to learn that Angelo was his real father and had even begun calling him that, having never addressed James as anything but sir, he still missed his sisters and his pony. But when he returned from visiting the Captain, there was no doubt that he had enjoyed himself.

"Momma, you should have seen me. Captain Bob even let me steer the ship with the big wheel. And you know what he said?"

"No, dear, I have no idea. What did he say?"

"Well, when I told him I was going to be a captain someday, he said that he thought I should be a very good one, but that first I would have to do well in school and then I could work my way up to captain."

"I imagine he is right, Eddy. Do you think you can do that?"

"Oh yes, Mother, because Captain Bob also told me that when I am old enough, he will take me on as a cabin boy and start training me. Isn't that wonderful?"

Gladys wasn't sure she agreed, but she didn't want to spoil his dream so she nodded.

"Where is Father? I want to tell him. Do you think he shall be proud of me, Mother?"

"I'm sure he will, Eddy. You had better write to Dolly and Eliza and tell them all about it too."

The weather was lovely for four days, but on the fifth, a wind blew up that developed into a storm lasting for two days, delaying them severely. Gladys and the rest of her party didn't suffer with sea sickness, but many others weren't as fortunate. Sandy was one of those stricken. For the first four days, his wonderful meals were the talk of the ship, and he even spent time getting acquainted with Angelo, his uncle, and his grandmother.

When they had time alone, Gladys explained to Sandy what had happened to her after she left Dover. They also talked about the wonderful wedding feast he had prepared for Tom and her at the Watt's inn and how sad it was when Tom had been killed in India before he was commissioned and had a chance to return to England to meet his infant daughter.

Sandy wanted to know why she and Dolly never moved into the lovely big mansion that Tom's father, Andrew, had built for them and why she didn't even attend his funeral.

"His stepson, Peter—actually, Andrew adopted him, so I suppose he was his son—inherited it all, and Dolly and I were forced to move to Sandwich where I found work as a housekeeper. We did return to Dover once though, and we had a little service of our own along with a few more of Andrew's old friends," she said. She didn't say that she had married her employer and was, in fact, still married to him.

When they were out of the storm and the sea was much calmer, Sandy did his best to return to the galley, but he only managed to stay there long enough to direct the other cooks on how to prepare the food. Thus, the meals were still better than the Captain had ever had at sea, although nowhere near as good as the first four days. When they arrived at New York, the Captain did his best to convince Sandy to remain on board as head cook.

"Sorry, Bobby, but I know now that I'll always be a land-lubber, and I don't intend to get back on a ship until I'm so homesick that I've no choice. Then, you can bet that I'll not be setting foot in any galley!" Sandy replied.

When Angelo and Victor heard this, they talked him into staying with them until he had time to decide what he was going to do in America.

"We should be ready to start up our restaurant in at least a fortnight, and we could use a good cook to get us going. You seem to make dishes to suit any nationality, and there's people coming here every day from all over the world. What do you say?" Victor asked.

Sandy was happy to accept. He intended to travel across this new world, but he needed a place to stay until he got his bearings, and he liked Gladys's family.

On the ninth day of the voyage, they finally got their first look at New York. Everyone was on deck and standing at the railings, even the crew who had seen it more than a few times.

Angelo came up behind Gladys and put his arms around her. "Well, Gladdy, say hello to your new home."

Gladys didn't say anything. She knew that England would always be her true home.

Chapter Twenty Seven

Victor's wife, Carlotta, and their twelve-year-old twin sons, Paulo and Louis, had remained in New York when Victor and Angelo returned to London to put on their last performance of *Othello* before their Shakespearean troupe disbanded. They were anxiously waiting for Victor to return.

When she was a young woman, Carlotta's aunt, Theresa, had been a governess for a wealthy Dutch family. When they immigrated to America, they took her with them. One year after arriving in America, Theresa married Peter Rutten, a young, wealthy Dutch businessman who, among his other possessions, owned a few buildings close to the docks in New York.

One of his buildings had a restaurant on the ground floor and four apartments on each of the other two floors. Although the restaurant was near the pier, an ideal location, the tenants who rented it were not very successful and seldom paid their rent. They also allowed the place to become run down to such a degree that the New York Health Board had threatened to close them down, so Peter had decided it was time to evict them.

Realizing that all the apartments in the building needed remodelling, he decided to hire some carpenters and began with those on the second floor, along with the restaurant. The repairs were almost complete when Peter suffered a stroke that left him partially paralyzed. Not wanting him to be bothered with renters, Theresa convinced him to sell the building.

At that time, Victor and Angelo were still involved with the theatre and had plans to return to England, but Carlotta liked living in New York near her wealthy relatives. She didn't want to return to England or Italy, so when she heard that her uncle was selling the building, she persuaded him to sell it to Victor and Angelo. Peter wasn't in need of money so he offered it to them at an attractive price. The opportunity was too good to reject, so Victor and Angelo pooled their savings as a down payment, feeling certain they could make enough income to pay off the rest in a few years.

Victor had written to inform Carlotta of their travel arrangements, including the detail that he would be joined by his mother, but he neglected to say how long she intended to stay. Carlotta found the woman's company depressing and prayed it would be a short visit. However, the boys seemed pleased, so she pretended that she was too.

She knew the day they were scheduled to arrive, but she had no idea what time they would be allowed to disembark. Because their house was only a few blocks from the pier, she sent the boys to see if they could find out what time the ship would disembark. It wasn't long before Louis was back with the news that the harbinger said the ship had just docked and it wouldn't be long until the passengers would be allowed ashore.

Carlotta had dressed with care that morning, and she looked in the mirror to make sure her head of generous curly black hair was tidily pinned up before she donned her cape and bonnet. She didn't bother getting a cab since she had a good stride and knew she could walk there almost as quickly as she could arrive in a carriage.

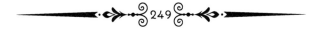

Until a week ago, Carlotta and the twins had been staying with her Aunt Theresa and Uncle Peter Rutten. The Ruttens only had one boy, Mitch, a successful architect who was seldom home, and, since they owned a big house, they had insisted that Carlotta and the boys stay with them while Victor was away. They had also offered to house Victor and Angelo when they returned, but, because they had already been so kind, Carlotta didn't want to take advantage of them. A week before the boat was due, she had rented a house near the restaurant, knowing that they would be able to accomplish more if they were close by. The boat was later than expected, but Carlotta checked regularly until it finally arrived.

She was standing on the pier, anxiously waiting, when the passengers began to come down the gangplank. Her heart gave a happy little twinge as soon as she saw Victor. They had been married for sixteen years, but the sight of him among the crowd still excited her as much as the first time she laid eyes on him. They waved at each other as he made his way up the gangplank. Then she realized he didn't have his mother with him.

She could also see Angelo amid the crowd, and there was an elderly lady hanging onto his arm, but this lady was dressed in a beautiful purple suit and wore a very chic and saucy chapeau on her head. She didn't look like the mother-in-law Carlotta remembered, but when one of the twins waved and called out, "Here we are, Nonna! Over here, Nonna, over here!" she knew it had to be Isabella. Then Victor was through the gate and had her in his arms.

"Hello, Lottie, love," he said in between kisses. Then he grabbed the boys and hugged them. By that time, Angelo and Isabella had joined them.

Isabella hugged her two grandsons before she spoke to Carlotta. "Hello, Carlotta. How nice you look, my dear."

Carlotta just stared at her for a second, then, she surprised Isabella and herself by holding out her arms for a hug. She was looking over Isabella's shoulder when she noticed Gladys and Edward. At first she thought they would just walk past, but they stopped and stood beside Angelo as though they were with him. She thought the woman beautiful. She took her to be a woman of quality due to the fineness of her attire. Then Gladys bent her head to address Eddy, and Carlotta looked down at the boy. She almost fainted. He looked so much like Angelo that he had to be related.

She was trying to figure out how that could be when Angelo saved her the trouble by introducing Gladys as his wife and Eddy as their son. The news was so shocking that Carlotta couldn't hide a look of disapproval when she shook Gladys's hand.

Victor had noticed the look of dismay on his wife's face, but he thought she was worried about where she would put two extra people, so he apologized, "I am sorry Lottie, we didn't have time to let you know that Gladys and Edward were coming with us, but you did get my letter saying Mother would be here, didn't you?" he asked. Not waiting for an answer, he added, "I hope you rented a house big enough to accommodate us all."

Gladys could tell Carlotta didn't approve of her, so she could have kissed Angelo when he interrupted his uncle and said, "I'm certain we can find lodgings close to the building, Uncle. We don't expect Lottie to look after us all, and don't forget, Sandy has to have a place stay as well."

"Oh, I had forgotten Sandy. Where is he?"

"He's down by the boat, guarding the cooking utensils he brought with him from Dover," Gladys replied. "He won't let them out of his sight."

"And we shall have to collect his gear as well," Angelo suggested. "Lottie, are there any rooms ready in the building?"

Lottie didn't look at him when she answered, "I think all they need is some furnishings. Uncle had them just about ready to rent when he had his stroke, but I remember him saying there were some beds stored in one of the rooms that just needed to be put together." Then she asked Victor, "Who is Sandy?"

"He is going to be our cook as soon as the restaurant is ready," he replied.

"Uncle Vic, it shouldn't take long to put a few of those beds together, and that would be a great place for us and Sandy to stay. We would be right there to work on things every day. What do you think?" Angelo asked.

Victor agreed, but he insisted his mother stay with Lottie and him, and then he asked Lottie if she would go home to make a hot meal for them all while he helped Angelo and Sandy prepare the rooms in the apartments. Gladys offered to go along and help, but Lottie said that her aunt had asked her cook to prepare a meal for them all, so she should go and tell her there would be three more. She started to leave then looked around for the twins. They were over by the railing looking down at the boats with Eddy.

"Boys, come along now! I can use your help," she said rather sharply.

"Can Eddy come with us, Mom?" Peter called out.

"No!" she snapped. Then, realizing how abrupt her answer sounded, she spoke a little more softly. "I imagine his mother will want to get him settled in his own place. You will see him later at Aunt Theresa's. You had better come with me too, Isabella. Auntie will make you a nice cup of tea."

Isabella didn't want to leave Gladys. She had never cared much for Carlotta, but not wanting to cause a fuss, she complied.

The boys left reluctantly. They had taken a liking to their little cousin and he to them. Although they had sailed to England and back once, they had never been invited to visit the captain or touch the ship's wheel, so when Eddy said, "I'm going to be a captain when I grow up!" they didn't doubt him. Instead, they wanted to know if his friend Sandy could take them on the ship to meet the captain.

Carlotta was usually a very warm and loving person. She did, however, like to be in complete control of all her family, and Angelo was a member of that family. Now here he was with a wife and a son, and he and Victor had only been gone for four months. That she had nothing to do with it was not what angered her the most; it was that the boy looked to be about five years old, which meant he had to have been conceived while Angelo was married to Carlotta's sister, Rosa. It was all she could do to remain composed as she sat beside the twins on her way to her aunt's. What she really wanted to do was go back and tell Angelo and Gladys to catch the next boat back to England and stay there.

The building Victor and Angelo bought was on Maiden Lane,

only a few blocks from Peck Slip, where they had disembarked from the ship, so they all walked to their building after Victor hired a carriage to transport their luggage. Maiden Lane was one of the busiest streets in the neighbourhood, and there were so many people on the street that they had to walk single file to get to their apartment.

New York wasn't at all what Gladys thought it would be. There were no open spaces dotted with log cabins and Indian tepees, and most of the buildings, like those in England, were made with bricks. Even the streets were paved and equipped with streetlights.

When she first saw their building, Gladys was a little disappointed. She had envisioned it with its own uniqueness, like the Scots Inn in Dover, but this building was sandwiched between a row of buildings that all looked alike. However, it was only a block from the pier, which reminded her a little of the quay where her father-in-law had had his office in Dover.

She recalled how she had enjoyed visiting Andrew on stormy days and having a cup of tea while sitting in one of his big leather chairs in front of the big window overlooking the water. She had loved watching the ships sway back and forth like graceful dancers.

Some ships tied up at the pier had their bowsprits hanging over the dock so far that people walking by could look above them and see the sailors at work tying down the jibs. The scene brightened Gladys's spirits. She took hold of Eddy's hand and gave it a little squeeze, which caused him to look up at her. They grinned at each other as though they were sharing a secret.

There was a different entrance leading to the apartments than the one to the restaurant, so they went directly up to the first floor. As soon as they entered the hallway they were welcomed with a pleasant smell of fresh paint and plaster. This floor had a one-bedroom and a two-bedroom apartment at the front of the building and another pair at the back. Victor said the top floor was the same. He explained that, since Carlotta's uncle hadn't begun renovating that floor, the tenants were still there.

Gladys and Angelo chose the two-bedroom flat at the front, and Sandy took the one-bedroom one at the back, thinking it would be quieter for him when he began working.

Gladys was delighted to find that, besides the two bedrooms, they had a kitchen/living room and a pantry. The beds Carlotta mentioned were soon found and set up, but there was no bedding or other furnishings. The kitchen cupboards and the pantry were empty as well, but when Victor went upstairs to talk to one of the tenants, they told him that Mr Rutten had a lot of boxes delivered to the restaurant before he took ill, and there might be furnishings they could use in them.

Fortunately, two of the boxes contained bedding and an assortment of other linens. There were also boxes of china and cooking utensils. When Gladys saw the kitchenware, she said, "Mr Rutten must have sold all the old items and bought new ones. By the look of the china and the linen, it appears as though Carlotta's aunt must have advised him. Everything is just lovely."

The kitchen had a sink with cold running water and a two-burner gas stove. Gladys heated enough water so they could all have a quick wash, but they didn't have time to change their clothes before they had to leave. She hated to go. It would have been wonderful if she, Eddy, and Angelo could buy some food and spend their first night in New York in their own home, even if it meant using her trunk for a table and sitting on the floor. She envied Sandy, who refused to go with them, insisting that he had intruded on the family enough.

Chapter Twenty Eight

After receiving such a cold reception from Carlotta, Gladys didn't know what she could expect from the Ruttens. When she saw what a grand home they lived in, she wished she had had the time to dress more appropriately.

Although the building was constructed mostly of brick, it had a warm and happy look. The bricks were such a light colour that they were more dark pink than red. The blue shutters on all of the rectangular floor-to-ceiling windows gave the mansion a warm cottage look, even though it had three stories above ground. The third floor had three attractive dormer windows, and, although Gladys didn't get a very good look at the side of the house as they drove up, she did notice that it had a large glass solarium. The yard was encased by a black cast-iron fence, not high enough to discourage visitors but high enough to add neatness.

"Oh, Eddy, isn't this a lovely home?" Gladys asked, but all Eddy could think of was how hungry he was and how nice it would be to see his cousins again, so he just nodded his head.

Having heard that slavery had been abolished in New York, Gladys was surprised when a black butler answered the door and ushered them into a nice little sitting room where Carlotta and her aunt and uncle were waiting.

Aunt Theresa rose and held out her hand to Victor. "Ah, it is good to see you again, Victor."

"It's good to be back, Aunt Theresa," he replied. He took her hand but added a hug before speaking to her husband who had remained seated, "And how are you, Uncle Peter?"

Peter's stroke had left him partially paralyzed on his right side, and he was still having a little trouble with his speech, so he used as few words as possible. "Can't complain," he replied before pointing to Angelo with his cane and adding, "Know this one. Angelo, right?"

"That's right. You have an excellent memory, Mister Rutten," Angelo replied.

Peter just nodded then used his cane again, pointing to Gladys and Eddy. "Who are they?"

"This is my wife, Gladys, and my son, Edward."

Peter beckoned Victor to help him up. Once standing, he said, "Come closer, my dear. You too, young man."

Gladys went over to him, smiled, and shook his hand. "It is pleasure to meet you, Mr Rutten." She was surprised by how tall he was. Although the stroke had left him with a permanent slump, she was able to look directly into his bright blue eyes as she greeted him.

"Not Mister! Name's Peter. Now, I want a hug."

Gladys hugged him before she introduced Eddy, who Peter insisted should call him uncle.

Theresa also insisted on a hug. She laughed and nodded toward her husband, informing Gladys, "He really is harmless you know, but he does enjoy flirting with pretty women!" She brought his wheelchair from the corner of the room, lined it up behind him, and jokingly said, "Well, Don Quixote, now that you are up, we may as well have our dinner. Carlotta, will you please tell Bess that we are ready?"

Carlotta didn't appreciate the warm welcome Gladys had received, and she left the room without answering.

Once she tasted the meal, Gladys was glad she had come. The

meat for the main course was chicken, and it was prepared differently than she had ever had. The skin on the individual pieces was brown and crispy, and the inside was juicy and tender. Along with the colourful assortment of vegetables, there was a large bowl of cooked corn, and each cob was skewered at each end with a little China handle.

She had never seen anyone eat corn before. In England, it was only used for silage. However, this corn had been lathered with butter and sprinkled with salt and looked most tempting. After watching his cousins, Eddy didn't hesitate, and it didn't take him any time to chew the kernels off a cob and accept another. Gladys couldn't wait to tell Sandy about the meal, and after complimenting Theresa, she said she would love to have her friend, Sandy, who was going to cook when they had the restaurant ready, meet her cook and exchange recipes.

"I'm sure Bess would appreciate that, Gladys, and goodness knows I would too. Bess and her family come from the south, and although she is an excellent cook, it would be nice to have a little more variety with our meals," Theresa replied.

Gladys felt at home with the Ruttens. They reminded her of the Watts, the proprietors of the inn in Dover, England, where she had worked when she was a young girl, but she couldn't think why. The two couples were nothing alike. The Watts weren't nearly as affable, and they certainly didn't look alike. Both Laura and Neil Watt were short and stout, while the Ruttens were both tall and stately. That was it! Both couples resembled each other as though they were a set of book ends, or two matching chairs. For a second, her thoughts drifted and she wondered if that would happen to her and Angelo after they had been together for a long time.

We are about the same height, she thought, *and although Angelo's hair is much darker than mine, it probably won't be long before we are both grey.* Then she couldn't help thinking how nice it was that she had chosen such a handsome man. The thought filled her with desire and she longed to return to their flat, but when they finished their meal Peter insisted they join him in the sitting room for brandy and go over a list he had had Theresa draft of all the things that still had to be done to the building. It seemed he had already bought furnishings for the apartments, so all they needed to do was to have them delivered.

Peter explained that they were lucky to have a restaurant so close to the pier, now that the big steamships were coming to New York. That was also one of the reasons he had decided to redecorate the building. "You can raise the rent on apartments twenty-five percent," he said. "Heard a lot of Italians coming this year; Lottie, you'll be busy cooking."

"Oh, I doubt I will be needed, Uncle. Gladys has brought a cook of her own to do the cooking now," Lottie said, her sarcasm shocking them all.

"Gladys had nothing to do with it," Victor snapped back while sending his wife a warning look. "Angelo and I were the ones who asked him, and you shall be glad we did when you taste his food. Anyway, if we are as successful as we hope to be, we shall need both of you in the kitchen." Lottie didn't reply, nor did she apologize. Victor changed the subject.

The sitting room was decorated with plenty of expensive furniture and window dressings without being too ostentatious. What really took Gladys's eye was an accordion sitting on a table beside a piano. She mentioned how lovely both instruments were, then she wished she hadn't. Peter asked if she played, and when she said she did, he insisted she play for him.

"I had friends who were from Scotland, and this one by Robby Burns was their favourite. I hope you like it too," she said.

"I'm sure he will, Gladys," Theresa replied. "Especially if you sing it. You know, Lottie has a fine voice as well. Sing along with her, Lottie, dear."

"I won't know the song, Auntie. Besides, I am certain Gladys is used to entertaining by herself," Lottie replied, meaning it more as an affront than a compliment.

Gladys, not letting on she noticed, sat down at the piano and said, "If you know the song, I would appreciate it if you join in, Carlotta." Then she began playing and singing.

"Flow gently, sweet Afton, among thy green braes,

Flow gently, I'll sing thee a song in thy praise
My Mary's asleep by thy murmuring stream
Flow gently, sweet Afton, disturb not her dream

Thou stock-dove whose echo resounds thro' the
glen
Ye wild whistling blackbirds in yon thorny den
Thou green-crested lapwing thy screaming forbear
I charge you disturb not my slumbering fair"

After the first two verses, she stopped playing and asked, "Do any of you know it?"

Peter, almost shouting, answered, "No, but please don't stop!"

Even Carlotta was impressed with Gladys's voice, but she didn't say anything.

After Gladys finished the song, Peter wanted more. The only way she could refuse was to promise to return soon for another musical evening.

It was a nice warm evening, and Peter had his coachman hitch up a wagon so that everyone could ride home together. Just as they were about to leave, Bess, the cook, came out with two baskets of food for Gladys to take home. When Gladys saw that Bess was also black, she was sure the Ruttens were still keeping slaves, and, as thankful as she was for their kindness, she didn't intend to be their friend.

Eddy had enjoyed playing a game of checkers with his cousins while they were visiting the Ruttens, and now he was having a good time with them on the way home. As Gladys watched him, he turned and asked, "Mother, why don't we sing some songs?"

Gladys asked the twins if they had a song they liked to sing, and they said, "Row, Row, Row Your Boat." Because Gladys and Eddy hadn't heard it, the twins asked Carlotta to sing it with them. When she refused, Victor volunteered.

Eddy couldn't stop laughing when he heard the lyrics and begged them to sing it again, so he could join in, especially the first verse.

"Row, row, row your boat,
Gently down the stream.
If you see a crocodile,

Don't forget to scream.
Row, row, row your boat,
Gently down the stream.
Throw your teacher overboard
And listen to her scream."

When it was time for Eddy to pick a song, he chose "Froggie Would A-Wooing Go." The twins listened attentively to the song, but it wasn't finished when they arrived at Victor and Carlotta's house, and since they didn't want to miss any of it, they asked if they could stay in the wagon until it was over. Carlotta said it was too late, but Victor came to their rescue again.

"I want to hear the rest of it too, Lottie, so please keep on singing you two, or we shall never get any sleep tonight wondering what happened to Mr Froggie!" Isabella agreed and when the song was finished, everyone but Carlotta offered a hearty farewell.

They hadn't gone more than a few blocks before they arrived at their building, and the coachman helped Gladys and Eddy down off the wagon then drove off.

"Well, here we are: our first home!" Angelo said proudly as he opened the door to the apartment. "What do you think, Tiger? Do you suppose you will like it here?"

"I should say so," Eddy said as he ran to the window. "Look Mother, if I open the window and look out, I can see the ships. It shall be great fun spending time down on the docks with all the sailors."

"Oh no, you shan't!" Gladys said emphatically. "You are not to go down there by yourself. Do you understand?"

Eddy shrugged his shoulders. "Well, may I go with Paulo and Louie?"

"We shall see. Now let's see if there's anything in Bess's baskets that we can have before we go to bed." Bess had put in almost everything they needed, including meat and eggs for breakfast, fresh milk, chocolate, and cookies.

"It's like Christmas, isn't it Mother?" Eddy said, grinning from ear-to-ear as they unpacked each item. But as excited as he was, he could barely stay awake long enough to drink a cup of hot chocolate and eat a cookie.

"It's been a long day for him but such a happy one," Gladys said after Eddy had gone to bed. "That was so thoughtful of Mrs Rutten to have Bess put up those baskets. I only wish I could be friends with her."

"Why on earth can't you? Is it because she's too rich?" Angelo asked.

"Of course not! Why would that that bother me? You must have noticed that they keep slaves."

"If you're talking about their butler, their cook, and the man who drove the wagon, well, they certainly are not slaves. They all work for wages, and they're lucky to have a job. Most people in New York refuse to hire them. There are a good many who are so poor they're practically starving to death."

"Why won't they hire them?"

"I'm not too sure, but I have heard it's because they are taking jobs that the local people need, and there are some people here who still believe in slavery. But whatever the reason, the Ruttens support that fellow, Lincoln, and they haven't owned slaves for many years."

"Thank heavens! I hope we can visit with them often."

"Well, you promised to play for Peter again. My God, Gladdy, I never knew you could play and sing like that! It makes me realize that there is a great deal we have to learn about each other after all."

"We weren't much more than children when we last saw each other, so in some respects, we are strangers."

"But our love for each other is just as strong as it was back then," Angelo said as he came up behind her and wrapped his arms around her. "At least it is for me. And now I have everything I've ever dreamt of."

Whether it was because she was tired or because of the sound of smugness to Angelo's voice, Gladys couldn't help but feel resentful. She slipped out of his arms and snapped, "Well, good for you! It's too bad we can't all have everything we want."

Her change of mood shocked Angelo, and he threw up his hands. "Now what have I done?"

"You have no idea, do you?"

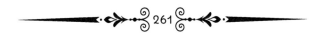

"No. So suppose you tell me."

"You stand there and say that now you have everything you've ever wanted and expect me to feel the same. Don't you realize what your happiness has cost me? I've left my daughters to come here with you, and my heart is breaking. But as long as you have everything you want, I should be dancing with joy." She didn't wait for a reply but ran into the bedroom crying.

Angelo waited for five minutes then he went in. She was lying on the bed and he lay down beside her but didn't touch her. "I am so sorry, Glad. It was thoughtless of me, I know that now, but I just felt so happy. I will never forget what you have done for me, and I'll do everything I can to see you are with them soon."

Gladys turned over and put her face on his neck. "I do love you. I guess I am just tired and feeling sorry for myself. I'm sorry, Toughie, oops, I mean Angelo. Oh, fiddle! I've been so good about calling you Angelo, but sometimes I feel like we are still those two kids back in Old Nichol."

"Actually, I don't mind if you call me that sometimes, and Eddy really gets such a kick out of it."

When they were getting ready for bed, Gladys remembered to ask Angelo if he had noticed how cold Carlotta was toward her.

"I think she is jealous, and I can't say I blame her," he replied.

"No, that's not what it is. I'm sure it has to do with her sister: your wife, Rosa."

"You may be right, but she's really not a bad person. I'm sure she will get over it when she gets to know you."

"I doubt it, but I hope so. If she doesn't like me now, she will like me even less when she finds out about Dolly and Eliza. You know, I think under different circumstances we could have become good friends. I like the way she says what she thinks. She's actually quite beautiful, isn't she?"

"Lottie? I never noticed."

"Well, I shall just have to hope I can win her over. Did you give my letters to the postman that we saw at the dock?"

"Yes, and he said they would be going with the mail ship tomorrow. Now get in here, woman. I've waited long enough!"

Chapter Twenty Nine

As soon as they finished making love, Victor would have liked very much to fall asleep with his arm over Lottie and his hand on her bosom, but she wasn't about to allow that to happen until she gave him a piece of her mind. Pushing his arm off her, she rolled over to face him.

"Now I want to hear what in Hades went on while you were over there!"

"Let's talk about it tomorrow, luv. I'm properly knackered," Victor replied, hoping his use of slang would put her in a better mood.

"I don't give a damn if you're knackered, knockered or, or, whatever. You owe me an explanation, and you are not getting any sleep until I get one."

Knowing she meant what she said, Victor got out of bed and put on his dressing gown. "We may as well have a cup of tea then." Lottie was going to tell him to stay in bed while she made it, but she knew he would fall asleep if she did. She followed him into the kitchen and got out the cups, cream, and sugar while he put the kettle on.

Victor was the first to begin. "Before you start, I want you to know that I only found out about Gladys two weeks before we left England, when she and Eddy arrived at the inn where we were staying."

"Then when were they married?"

"I never asked, but, to tell the truth, I don't think they are married. I think they intend to marry, but I suspect she is already married to someone else and is waiting for a divorce. Now that's only a guess, so don't repeat it."

Lottie stared at him with her mouth hanging open for a second before she could answer. "And you went along with their charade, knowing she might be committing adultery?"

"I can see that they are in love, Lottie, and that's what really matters, isn't it?"

"No, that's not what matters! They are living in sin, and they even lied to your mother. Surely you can't condone that."

"Lottie, we were no angels before we were married, if you remember."

"That's not the same. That boy, Edward, must have been conceived at the same time we were in London waiting to come to America and the same time that Rosa was with child. I've thought about it, and I remember Angelo saying he was spending his last nights in England with his friends. He must have been with her the whole time while Rosa was waiting with us. I wonder if that's why she became so sick on the boat. Maybe she knew he had a lover, and she didn't want to survive. They killed her, Victor!"

"They did not kill her! Rosa was never well, and Angelo never left her side on the ship until she passed. You remember how genuinely sad he was. If he had an affair with Gladys, I'm sure he didn't intend to continue with it. Angelo and Gladys went through so much together when they were young, and then, when she recognized him at the theatre and left a note for him, I guess he felt he had to see her for the last time. They hadn't seen each other since they left that horrible place called Old Nichol, and they were very fond of each other."

"So you knew about their rendezvous. How could you allow it knowing how frail Rosa's condition was?"

"Listen, Lottie. I didn't know he spent that night with her. I thought he really was spending it with friends. Anyway, whatever the situation, I want you to keep out of it. And I wish you would be a little more civil to her from now on. Angelo and I are not only family, we are partners. We shall have to forget our differences if we are going to work together."

"Hah! I can't see her ladyship getting her hands dirty. She's probably never done a day's work in her life. I just hope for her sake that she stays out of my way. I'll never forgive either of them for what they did, and I'm sure when I tell your mother and Aunt Theresa what sort of a woman she is, they won't be so fond of her either."

"Don't you say one word to them, you hear? Things are running smoothly now, and that's the way it has to be. We need all the help we can get from your aunt and uncle, and as for Mother, well, she has never been this happy in years. Darling, I know how this has hurt you, and I do understand, but we must think of our future and the twins. Please try to carry on, and remember none of it is Eddy's fault. We mustn't take it out on him. Come on, luv, I'm home now and I am staying, so let's go back to bed and forget everything but that, at least for tonight."

Lottie knew it wouldn't be easy, but it was so wonderful to have Victor home for good, she said no more.

Isabella had woken and heard voices. Thinking one of the boys might be ill she had risen and was just opening her door when she realized Victor and Lottie were having an argument. Although she knew she shouldn't eavesdrop, she remained where she was with her hand on the door knob. What she heard was not surprising. It seemed Victor, like her, had suspected that Gladys and Angelo were not legally married.

After she heard Victor order Lottie not to tell her aunt about Angelo and Gladys's affair, she went back to bed. As she lay there, she went over everything she had overheard, and she couldn't help but feel sorry for Lottie, since she knew how much her sister had meant to her. Lottie had been twelve when her mother, a widow, died and left her to look after her little sister, Rosa. To make matters worse, Rosa was a victim of cerebral palsy and didn't have full use of her left arm and leg.

Lottie had married Victor when she was just sixteen and he was twenty-five. She was a good Italian wife and Isabella could find no fault with her. That was, until Victor brought Angelo home and Lottie began scheming to have him marry Rosa. Whenever Lottie made up her mind to do something, nothing short of death would stop her, and before they knew what was happening, poor Angelo and Rosa were married.

Isabella recalled hearing about that trip to America and how Lottie had to stand by and witness her sister suffer an agonizing death, taking her unborn child with her. That she died in Angelo's arms had eased Lottie's sorrow at the time, but Isabella knew what a horrible shock it must have been to learn that, while Rosa was still alive and with child, Angelo and Gladys were making love not far from where she was waiting for him. She now understood that every time Lottie looked at Gladys she would be reminded of that time. Isabella vowed that she would try to be as nice to Lottie as she was to Gladys.

Victor and Angelo had decided they would take the next day off. Victor wanted to spend time with his boys and Angelo and Gladys wanted to be alone with Eddy for a time.

Gladys and Angelo were lying in bed enjoying a cuddle while waiting for Eddy to wake up. They intended to call Eddy into their room so he could see them sharing a bed and know this was the way things would be from then on. Angelo wasn't worried, but Gladys was afraid he might not approve. As soon as Eddy woke, he jumped out of his bed, came skipping into their room, jumped into their bed, and said, "Move over, another monkey's coming in," before he wiggled down under the blankets between them.

They were still in bed when they heard a loud knock on the downstairs door. Angelo opened the window, looked down, and saw a delivery wagon with the name "White's Furniture" printed on the side. He realized it must be the furniture that Peter had ordered, so

he called out that he would be down directly. He dressed quickly and went to knock on Sandy's door, but the cook didn't answer.

Luckily, the delivery man had a helper with him. Between the three of them, they managed to store all the furniture in the empty rooms until Gladys could help sort it out. Later, two more wagons arrived with the rest of the pieces. Sandy was back from having his breakfast by then, but Gladys wouldn't allow them to put the furniture anywhere but the empty apartment until she had scrubbed the floors in her apartment and Sandy's.

The thing that pleased Gladys the most was that there were three wardrobes for each of the two-bedroom apartments, and two wardrobes for the one-bedroom apartments. She could hardly wait to unpack her clothes and hang them up.

Besides the six chairs and matching dining table, there were two comfortable easy-chairs and a divan for the living room. For each bedroom, there was a velvet-covered chair and a dresser. The furniture was very plain compared to the furniture Gladys was accustomed to, but, once she had everything properly placed, the apartment felt like a palace to her.

Gladys had lived at Four Oaks for the past eight years, where she had enjoyed the peace and quiet of the countryside. When the three of them stepped outside the building that morning, they were surrounded with noisy shoppers, merchants selling their wares, and horses and wagons lined up waiting to deliver or collect goods, which made Gladys suddenly realize how much she had missed city life.

When Theresa Rutten heard that Gladys was going to be living in one of their apartments, she had been shocked. She said it was far too near the docks and warned that there were all sorts of unsavory characters loitering about that would rather commit robbery than do an honest day's work. Gladys almost blurted out that she had been brought up in a far worse place and knew how to look after herself. But she realized that it might be best if Theresa didn't have any idea of her past, so she just promised to be extremely careful. Eddy hadn't been brought up in the slums, so Gladys was a bit worried about him, and she made him promise to stay inside the apartment or the restaurant unless he was with someone.

It was a lovely day, and, as they walked up and down the streets, Gladys felt more light-hearted than she had since leaving England. There were so many interesting shops that she soon had a collection of little gifts to send to Eliza and Dolly. She also bought all the staples she needed for baking and a large supply of other groceries. On their way back to the apartment, they happened to walk by a Singer's Sewing Machine factory. The machines had become so popular during the last few years that Mr Singer had recently expanded his business by adding a few more New York factories.

"Oh, Angelo, I must go in and see if the same man is here that I met at the fair in England. Do you mind?" Gladys asked. Angelo said he and Eddy would wait in the ice cream parlour across the street. There was a small office directly inside the building, but since no one was behind the desk, Gladys was on the verge of leaving when a very portly gentleman came out of what she thought must be the factory. In fact, the gentleman was so portly that he had to squeeze through the door.

He looked nothing like the man she had met in England, but he was just as friendly. When she inquired if she could purchase a machine, he said she could indeed and that he would even have it delivered free of charge. Gladys intended to sell the silver toothbrush and tongue scraper set that James had given her as a wedding present to pay for the machine, so she kept her fingers crossed when she asked the gentleman how expensive the sewing machine would be. She was pleasantly surprised when he said ten dollars. It was still expensive enough to be beyond the average buyer, but Gladys was lucky to have received money from Aunt Jean.

The next morning, Victor, Carlotta, and the twins arrived early in the morning. Victor and the twins went upstairs to knock on Angelo's door, but Lottie, not wanting to see Gladys, said she would go directly into the restaurant and start to work. The door was open, which surprised Lottie. When she entered, she noticed that all the tables were pushed to one side of the room with the chairs stacked on top of them while a cleaning lady was down on her knees scrubbing the rest of the floor. She didn't stop but walked right through into the kitchen.

The door to the alley was open, and a heavyset fellow was sitting on a chair drinking a cup of coffee and looking out at a heap of waste piled up under the roof over the alley door. He heard her coming, turned, and held out his hand, saying, "Hello, you must be Victor's wife, Carlotta. A pretty name for a pretty woman."

Carlotta hated false flattery, but his smile portrayed such honesty that she returned his smile. "And you must be Sandy. I have been told that you are an excellent cook."

"Well, I've been at it for a time, but your man tells me you make the best Italian dishes he's ever tasted. I'd be very grateful if you would be kind enough to share some of your recipes with me."

"I can do that. Well, I came here to work this morning, but it looks as though you have most of it done already. And by the shine on this floor, that cleaning lady has finished in here and has almost done the big one out there. How on earth did you find such a worker so fast?"

"Cleaning lady? We don't have a—oh! You must mean Gladdy. She was at it when I came downstairs this morning. I tried to get her to stop for a cup of tea, but she said she'd rather wait until she was finished. Nobody can work like that girl. Laura Watt used to say she did more in one day than three of her other housemaids."

"Housemaids? Gladys, a housemaid?"

"Not a housemaid, Sandy." Gladys had finished the floor and was coming into the kitchen and heard them talking. "I was a mere chambermaid when I first worked for the Watts." She then addressed Carlotta. "I was also a barmaid in the same establishment in Dover. You were correct, Carlotta, when you said I probably was used to entertaining by myself. I often sang for the customers." She went to the stove and drew a measure of hot water from a pot with a dipper. She took the dipper to the sink where she washed her hands before she said, "Now, Sandy, I would love that cup of tea."

Carlotta had been so sure Gladys was a woman of high quality that she didn't know what to say. Before she could think of something, Victor and the twins came in the through the front door and Angelo came in the back.

"Ah, there you are," Victor said to Angelo. "What have you been up to?"

"Well, it took a little time to find the fellow who is supposed to pick up our garbage, but I finally found him and arranged for him to come by this afternoon and haul that trash away from the back. I signed a contract for him to come twice a week from now on. It took a bit of talking though, since most of his customers only want him once a week."

Sandy didn't wait for Victor to complain but confessed, "Sorry, Victor, that's my doing. I can't tolerate rats, and if you don't keep the garbage away, you soon have more of the vermin than you can handle, even with the help of cats, dogs, or traps."

"Whatever you think best, Sandy. The running of the kitchen will be up to you for as long as you wish to work here. Is that agreeable to you, Lottie?"

Lottie, still trying to take in the sight of Gladys dressed in working clothes with her beautiful hair hidden in a dust cap, just nodded her head.

"Well then, I think it's time you showed Sandy how to make a good cup of American coffee, then we should have a meeting to decide where we go from here. You should join us, Sandy. You may have some ideas we can use," Victor suggested.

The meeting lasted for three hours. Gladys was careful not to pick fault with any of Lottie's ideas. Whenever she had an idea herself, she always asked Lottie her opinion, which took a lot of restraint on her part. Everyone, even Lottie, was pleased and excited with the end results. Sandy suggested that they name the restaurant "The International Café because they intended to cater to a variety of different nationalities. Everyone thought it was a good idea, and Gladys said they could try having different menus for different nights.

They also agreed that, although the walls of the restaurant were freshly painted, they were far too bare and stark. It was Paulo, one of the twins, who came up with the solution. He was quite an artistic lad, and Lottie had been sending him to art school. "My teacher could paint pictures of different countries on the walls," he had suggested. At first no one took him seriously, but the more Gladys thought about it, the better it sounded. Finally, Gladys said she thought it was a brilliant idea, and Lottie agreed because she was proud of her son.

Teachers didn't make a great deal of money, so when he was approached, Paulo's teacher, a handsome young Italian named Bruno, was thrilled to accept the challenge. It took him many weeks to complete the task. Although the restaurant had opened before he was finished, he continued painting early in the morning and late at night, so it didn't bother the customers. He painted a scene from each country, along with a likeness of their flag. These were done on both side walls and on the wall at the end of the room where, except for the door to the kitchen, he painted scenes of America and a very large flag with stripes and thirty-three stars. The murals were almost as popular with the customers as Sandy and Lottie's cooking.

Isabella soon tired of staying alone while Lottie was at the café, and she persuaded Victor to allow her to move into the one-bedroom apartment next door to Gladys. Gladys, knowing how lonely life could be for the elderly woman, invited her to help with the shopping. It wasn't long before she became acquainted with some other elderly Italian ladies, who, although not from as high a station as herself, were seasoned gossips and made interesting company.

Although Lottie still found it difficult to be civil to Gladys, she had to admit that she did more than her share of the work around the restaurant, so she kept her temper. Things went well for the first three months, then something happened that caused her pent-up anger and resentment to burst forth like water from a broken dam.

A letter from Dolly had fallen out of Gladys's handbag, and Lottie found it on the restaurant floor and read it. When Gladys and Isabella returned from shopping, Lottie was waiting. She grabbed Gladys by the arm and said, "You cold-hearted witch."

Isabella tried to clam her down, but Lottie shouted, "No,

Nonna, it's time you knew what sort of woman she is. She's a cruel, cold-hearted adulteress, who is not only a home breaker, but a terrible mother as well. To think I was blaming Angelo for Rosa's death as much as I blamed her. Now I can see that she had seduced him, hoping he would take her out of the country." Then she addressed Gladys, "But that time he came to his senses and left you, didn't he?"

Not waiting for an answer, she directed her words to Isabella once more. "So then she had to find another poor man who would marry her and look after her and her bastard son. When she found out that Angelo was back in England, she arranged a meeting where she talked him into saying they were married so she could come to America with him. I don't know what she is running away from, but it must be something serious because she has left her two daughters in England."

Isabella couldn't help but look shocked, so Lottie continued, "Yes, Nonna. Your sweet little Gladys has two daughters and one is practically a baby. What kind of mother leaves her baby and runs off with a man?"

Isabella looked at Gladys pleadingly, "Gladys, is this true?"

Gladys couldn't deny it. "Yes, Nonna, it is true, but they are in excellent hands, and I promised I would go back inside of a year. You see, Eddy needed his real father and I didn't know what else to do. Perhaps if you knew the whole story you would agree."

Gladys turned to Lottie, and, in a low voice that had a timbre of strength and admonition to it, said, "Lottie, I don't blame you for hating me, but if you ever, ever, refer to Edward by that name again, I shall not be responsible for my actions. Do you understand me?"

"You don't frighten me, Gladys, but I will admit that I shouldn't have used that name. I think we all have a right to hear what sort of woman Angelo has brought into our family. I'm sure Auntie and Uncle will want to hear it too."

This time Nonna agreed with her. Gladys said she would be happy to tell everything and would arrange a meeting with everyone.

Chapter Thirty

Sandwich, England

It had been two weeks since Gladys and Edward left Four Oaks, but their absence still cast an ambiance of gloom over the entire household. Dolly had taken over her mother's duties as mistress of the manor. Although she had tried her best to run the household as efficiently and as seemingly effortlessly as Gladys had, the staff took little interest in their work and did no more than necessary, causing her to think they resented her.

Actually, they all liked and respected Dolly, but Gladys's cheery disposition had a way of making their chores enjoyable. Since she had left, there didn't seem to be any joy left in the house.

Even James began to fear that Four Oaks would soon revert back to the dismal state it was in before she became his housekeeper. She had not only brought new life and vitality to the manor but to his life as well. Up until then, except for his business dealings in London, he'd lived the life of an introvert without friends. And it was because of Gladys that he had met Percy.

During the two weeks since Gladys had left Four Oaks, James had done a lot of thinking, and came to the conclusion that she had had no other alternative and was right to leave. Edward deserved a father who loved him, and James had shown him nothing but mistrust and dislike since he was born. He also thought a lot about his own future and past, and he finally admitted to himself that he would never be happy without Percy.

When he first discovered that Percy was a homosexual, he was shocked. But what frightened him the most were his own feelings. Believing that such thoughts were as sinful as taking action, he immediately broke up their friendship. He hadn't talked to or seen Percy for four years, but the last thing Gladys had said to him before she left was, "James, please go and see Percy." Now he had finally decided to take her advice.

The following morning, he and Dolly were sitting in the conservatory and had just finished breakfast when Dolly excused herself and got up to leave. James stopped her saying, "Please sit down for a minute, Dolly. I want to talk to you."

Dolly, afraid he hadn't been pleased with her work, waited for him to say as much as she held her breath and clenched her fist under the table.

"I have decided to go to London and I am not certain if I will be there for a day or a week. I pray this won't leave you with too much responsibility to handle, my dear. Auntie has offered to help, and I know she means well, but she is becoming exceedingly forgetful. I dare not trust her with important jobs. I am sorry, Dolly, but I haven't told you what a splendid job you are doing. Your mother would be very proud of you. In fact, I shall write and tell her how splendidly you have done."

Although she was relieved, Dolly still harboured a lot of anger toward her mother, so she merely mumbled, "I doubt she cares."

James surprised her when he replied, "She does, Dolly. I can assure you, she does. You know, your mother has been through some very difficult times, but she loves both you and Eliza; you must believe that. Now, do you think you can manage while I am away?"

"Yes, James, I think I can, but I wish I had Mother's talent for cheering everyone up."

"It will come, don't you worry. Now I shall run up and say good-bye to Eliza. I hope Auntie doesn't give you any trouble."

"I think I can find her something to do that will satisfy her," Dolly replied, smiling.

James shook his head, thinking that Dolly had a lot more of her mother's talents than she knew.

James felt four years of Percy's absence keenly, and he slept very little the night before he left for London. He was worried that Percy wouldn't want to see him, and he could hardly blame him. Percy had tried to be friends, and had even written to James, but James had thrown the unopened letter into the fireplace.

The train ride seemed to take forever, but after the cab driver let him off in front Percy's flat, he wished it had taken even longer. He probably should have gone directly to his own flat, but he had only brought a small valise with him, and he could easily walk from Percy's. His heart was pounding as he took hold of the knocker. When no one came, he didn't know if he was relieved or sorry, but he started to leave. He had taken a few steps when the door opened and Percy was there.

My God, he thought, *he hasn't changed a bit.* The same full head of salt-and-pepper hair. The same beautiful eyes. And that mouth; he could never forget that mouth.

Percy was just as surprised to see James, and it was a second before he managed to say, "James, what a pleasant surprise!"

"I know I don't deserve it, Percy, but may I come in?"

"Of course you can. It's good to see you, James. Come in. Come in." Not daring to touch him, remembering how James had behaved the last time they saw each other, he stepped back and let James find his own way into the parlour. Just seeing his dear friend again had caused James's knees to weaken, and he felt he would have collapsed if Percy hadn't offered him a chair. Noticing his valise, Percy inquired, "Did you just arrive in London?"

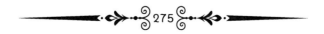

"Yes, I came directly here from the station. You look well, Percy."

"So do you, but you must be ready for a good cup of tea. I shall have it ready in a moment. Make yourself at home. Here's today's paper, you can glance at that while I get the tea. Two sugars and a little cream, if I recall?"

"If it's not too much trouble."

"Nonsense." Percy left the room, but instead of reading the paper, James laid his head back in the chair, closed his eyes, and tried to relax.

"Oh, I say! I didn't know we had company!" Except for a towel around his waist, the tall, handsome young man standing in front of James was naked.

James's heart sank. He immediately assumed that Percy and the young man were more than roommates.

"Name's Mike," the young man said before holding out his hand, but it happened to be the hand that was holding the towel together, and it fell to the floor. "Oops," was the only apology offered.

James's face had turned beet red, but he managed to reach out and shake the fellow's hand while keeping his eyes focused on the lad's face. Mike noticed James's embarrassment and couldn't hide a cheeky grin as he picked up the towel, excused himself, and was on his way to the kitchen just as Percy was coming out with a tea tray.

"How many times have I asked you to use one of my dressing gowns before you come out of your room undressed?"

"Oh, mercy, Percy," the young man joked. "Sorry about that, but I just came down to ask if I may borrow some of your drawers. Mine all seem to be at the launderers."

"They are in the bottom of my dresser. Thank heavens my trousers don't fit you. Now, for God's sake, go and put some clothes on."

The boy took the stairs two at a time while laughing.

"Sorry about that, James. The young fellows these days have no modesty. Do you remember Mike, my nephew? He is my sister's boy. I think you met him when he came to Sandwich to stay with me for a week one summer, several years ago now. He's been staying here for a few days. He has a girlfriend in London. Her folks have invited him to stay there for the rest of the week. I hope his underwear comes back before he leaves tonight."

Neither man said anything while Percy poured the tea. They sipped and sat in silence for a time, savouring each other's company as though they had never parted.

Percy was the first to speak. "Now, tell me old man, are you here on business?"

"I think I might be. It really depends on you."

"Me?"

"I have no right to ask, but I wonder if you would consider being my lawyer again."

"I never resigned, dear boy! Of course I shall be your lawyer. I imagine this has something to do with Gladys, right?" James nodded, and Percy continued, "She visited me quite a bit while she was in town. Do you want to get in touch with her?"

"I have her address, but what she needs, Percy, and I am in favour of it too, is a divorce. I thought we may be able to obtain one on the grounds of desertion. What do you think?"

"I think you are being a jolly good sport in all this."

"Well, I have thought a lot about it, and I owe Gladys more than anyone will ever know. You know, the last thing she said to me was to come and see you." James reached over and took hold of Percy's hand as he added, "She often told me I would never be happy unless we were friends once more. Now that I am here, I know she was right."

This time it was Percy who withdrew his hand. He was afraid to guess what James meant by the gesture, and it caused him discomfort. Picking up the teapot, he asked, "More tea?"

Now James felt he had behaved foolishly. Although his reply was a simple, "No, thank you," it lacked warmth.

Percy could have kicked himself. All he could think of to say was, "And what about the boy, Edward? A splendid little chap, isn't he?"

"Yes, I know that now, but it is too late." James admitted how he had wrongly accused the boy and had treated him poorly. "I don't know if it is possible, but it would be very helpful to the lad if he could have his real father's name instead of mine."

"I agree, James. Just leave it all to me and I shall see what I can do. I haven't worked for a time, but I still have some very influential friends in this town."

"Thank you, Percy. Now I had better get along," James said as he rose from his chair.

Percy had made up his mind that he wasn't going to let his friend leave this time without a clear understanding, so he said, "Sit down, James. We haven't seen each other for ages, and I am not letting you leave my house until you and I have straightened a few things out. Can we be honest with each other?"

"Yes, I think it's time we were. I was a complete ass, Percy, and I am so sorry. I have missed you more than you will ever know."

"I'm glad to hear that, James, but I am still the man I was, and I shall never change. I won't lie about it; when I saw you standing there on the doorstep, I wanted to grab you and hug you to death. Now, that doesn't mean we cannot be the sort of friends we were, but I do not want to have to worry that you will run for your life if I happen to accidentally bump up against you, or give you a slap you on the back every so often."

"Percy, I have been miserable most of my life and, as Gladys has often told me, I have denied my true feelings long enough. When you answered that door, not only could I have hugged you to death, but I could have kissed you to death as well!"

A different James arrived home the following week than the one who left. His cheerfulness was just what was needed to change the atmosphere in the house. Before long, there were smiles and laughter once more.

James informed Dolly that his old friend, the man she used to call Uncle Percy, would be coming to Four Oaks for a visit in a fortnight, and when he was there, James intended to invite some old friends for an evening or two. This time, Dolly was thankful to have Aunt Jean around to give her advice.

For many weeks after Gladys and Eddy left, Eliza kept asking when they were coming home, but she eventually accepted their absence and seemed content. Dolly and James made sure she didn't lack affection. Although they spoiled her, she remained a good-natured little girl.

The first three letters arrived one month after Gladys and Eddy's departure.

Dolly's hands shook as she opened the one addressed to her. There was also one for Aunt Jean and one for James, but Dolly's was in a bigger envelope and contained a letter for her, one for Eliza, and one for Eliza and her from Eddy.

Dolly read Eliza's letters to her first, and she loved them so much that she begged to have them read again. She made Dolly promise to read them once more before she went to bed.

Dolly waited until she was alone in her bedroom before she read the letter from her mother. As soon as she saw the beautiful handwriting on the envelope, she knew it was her mother's. *One might even presume the writer to be of a kind and honest nature,* Dolly thought as she studied the handwriting, but she knew otherwise. As far as she could see, her mother's penmanship was just another of her clever pretences. She almost threw the letter in the fireplace, but her curiosity was too great.

Thinking it would be full of false apologies and pleas for forgiveness or, even worse, confessions of how lonely she was and how much she missed her daughters, Dolly was surprised. Gladys must have surmised how Dolly would feel and she wrote about meeting Sandy and how he was such a good friend of Dolly's father and her grandfather. She wrote about what the cabin on the ship was like and how she was sharing it with Eddy's grandmother, a dear elderly Italian lady whom Eddy adored. She mentioned how Sandy had taken Eddy to meet the Captain, and now all he could talk about was becoming a captain when he grew up. She did say she missed her and Eliza and loved them, but it was just one sentence at the end of the letter.

In spite of how she felt, Dolly found the letter very interesting. It brought back memories of the good times she had spent with her mother and her dear Gamby when she was a child. She thought about how often she had longed to know her father, and she was suddenly pleased that Eddy was going to know his real father and that he had a grandparent to love. Gladys's letter had done more to rebuild the tight bond that she and Dolly had previously had than all the pleading Gladys had done before she left.

Gladys and Eddy had written their letters on the boat and

mailed them as soon as they arrived in New York, so there was no news of America, and now Dolly waited for the next letter with as much eagerness as Eliza.

Gladys's letter to James wasn't very long because she wasn't sure he would even read it. She just mentioned that the wait in London had been difficult, and there were times when she almost changed her mind about leaving, but every time she looked at Eddy with Angelo she knew she had made the right decision. She also mentioned that she had told Eddy that Angelo was his real father and he had taken it very well. She asked James to try to forgive her and thanked him for all he had done for her and the children. Lastly, she pleaded with him not to turn Eliza against her. When he read that, James smiled as he imagined how relieved she would be when she received the letter he had written to her.

Chapter Thirty One

New York

Gladys could understand Lottie's reason for telling Isabella and the Ruttens what sort of a woman she was, but she had hoped to confess to everyone in her own words and in her own time. Now it was too late.

Lottie hadn't waited for a meeting but had already told her Aunt and Uncle that Gladys had abandoned her two daughters. They were both notably shocked. It was the reaction Lottie had hoped for, but strangely, she didn't enjoy it as much as she thought she would.

Angelo didn't think Gladys owed anyone an explanation, but she was determined to rid herself of a life of lies. When the evening of the meeting arrived, the restaurant was closed and they were all waiting for the Ruttens to arrive and for Isabella to come downstairs. Eddy and the twins were up in Gladys and Angelo's flat playing checkers, and Sandy was helping Gladys prepare tea and snacks in the kitchen.

"I want you to hear what I have to say too, Sandy," she said.

"No, Gladdy, love. I don't need any explanation. I've known you far too long to judge you."

"I know, Sandy, but I really would like it if you would stay."

Sandy agreed and everyone arrived shortly afterward.

Gladys, guessing that the Ruttens were disappointed in her, expected a cold reception, so it wasn't surprising when neither offered a hug or even a handshake. Isabella was far kinder and greeted her with more pity than anger.

Once everyone had a cup of tea, Gladys began, "If you are going to understand why I lied to you, I think I had better start at the beginning of my story. You see, Toughie—that is what Angelo was called then—and I were born in unbelievable squalor. Both of us were parentless from about the age of five. I did have parents, but they suffered with alcoholism to such an extent that they could not look after me. If not for Toughie, I would have never survived."

Gladys went on to tell them how she cut her hand one day while stealing food, and Toughie had taken her to see Sally Tweedhope, a lady who acted as midwife and nurse in the neighbourhood, to have it bandaged.

"Sally and Bob had lost their twins with cholera and they were both very good to us. Sally taught us to read and write, and when they moved away, Bob gave Toughie his junkyard."

Toughie spoke up and said, "By that time, Gladys and I were planning on getting married, although Gladys was only twelve and I was just sixteen. You see, you grow up very fast in places like Old Nichol. At the time, I was living in O'Brian's barn and trying to build a place in the junkyard for not only the two of us, but for Gladys's ma and pa too, but it was taking me a long time to gather enough lumber."

Gladys looked up at Angelo to give her the courage to go on with her story. She told them how her mother had taken money from the landlord, allowing him to have his way with her. She explained that she was forced to murder him and run away to save herself. Shaken from her confession, she paused for a minute.

Her rapt audience was silent for a few moments, then Lottie asked, "Why couldn't you call the police and explain what happened or go and find Angelo to help you?"

"Constables rarely came to Old Nichol, but if one had come, I knew that he would have seen the dead landlord, and I would have been taken and hung, no matter what the circumstances. That always happens in Old Nichol. And although I wanted to find Toughie and ask him to run away with me, I knew that if we were caught, he would be hung too. So I went alone."

They were all anxious to know what happened next, so she told them about her trip to Dover and how she found work in Neil and Laura Watt's establishment the day after she arrived.

"I was used to working hard pulling the junk cart, but I never worked as hard as I had to work there. I don't think I could have taken it if it wasn't for Millie McIver, a dear seamstress who took me under her wing. Millie taught me a lot about etiquette and diction.

"After a few years, I was promoted to the job of barmaid and entertainer. That is where I sang, Carlotta. It was while I worked there that I met my first husband, Tom Pickwick. He and his friend, Keith, were both stationed at Dover Castle taking officer training. Tom's father was one of the wealthiest men in Dover, so when Tom asked me to marry him, I was both flattered and intimidated. I never thought I would be able to pass as a proper lady, but with Millie's help and advice, I managed."

Then Gladys told them about Tom's father, Andrew, and how he had been duped into marrying a scheming woman named, Rose, who then talked him into adopting her two children. "It only took a short time for Andrew to realize what a mistake he had made. Rose didn't like living in the country, so Andrew allowed her and her children to move into his home in town while he and Tom stayed on his estate."

When she told them how Tom and Keith were killed after being sent to India to fight in the first Sheik wars, they were all visibly sympathetic.

"Tom never received my letter telling him that he had a daughter, so he died not knowing he was a father. I named the baby Dorothy, after Tom's mother, but she's mostly called Dolly. That was fifteen years ago. This is the first time Dolly and I have been apart for more than a few days." She said it with such obvious sadness that even

Lottie could tell how much she missed the girl.

Gladys continued her story, relating how kind her father-in-law was and how he had looked after her and Dolly in the aftermath of Tom's death. "He had a big, beautiful mansion built on the outskirts of Dover for the three of us, and we were all ready to move in when Andrew went to Ireland to rescue another family. While he was there, he was brutally murdered. Although he had his lawyer draw up a new will that left the estate and mansion in Dolly and my names, he had neglected to sign it before his departure.

"One day, Dolly and I were getting ready to move into our beautiful new home. Dolly was upstairs packing her toys, and I was in the living room wrapping some ornaments when Andrew's adopted son, Peter, knocked on our door. I had never seen him before so he introduced himself. He recognized me by the scar I bear from stealing pickles with Tou—Angelo. He explained that he had hired a detective in London to look into my past. The man had found out my real name was Gladys Tunner, not Gladys Tweedhope. You see, I had taken Sally and Bob's last name when I ran away. Then, without a trace of emotion or consideration for my feelings, he informed me that Andrew had been murdered.

"I didn't know what else the detective had found out, so when he ordered Dolly and me to leave Dover, I dared not argue. Peter inherited all of Andrew's property, and Dolly and I were left homeless. Luckily, Lady Sorenson, an old friend of Andrew's, had heard that James Hornsby, a widower who lived on the outskirts of Sandwich, was looking for a housekeeper. Mr Hornsby did not want to hire anyone with children and I would have not have been hired had we not discovered that he was Keith's halfbrother."

As Gladys continued, she tried to explain how she and Angelo had felt when they found each other again in London. She expressed how sorry they were for allowing their passions to get the best of them.

"Angelo made it clear that he would not abandon Rosa, and when we said goodbye, we expected never to see each other again. When I found out later that our interlude had left me carrying his child, I confessed everything to James Hornsby, my employer, who offered to marry me. At first, I refused. I could never love anyone but Angelo. Then, when James promised that our marriage would be merely a marriage of convenience—he wanted company, and I needed a home for my children—I said yes. My only alternative was the workhouse."

She continued explaining that the only time they were intimate was when James drank too much and insisted he share her bed. "Eliza, our darling little girl, was the result of that night.

"When I read the notice about a Shakespearian troupe's final appearance, I knew immediately that it must be Angelo, and I made up my mind to introduce him to his son. When we met, Angelo told me about the tragic deaths of Rosa and their baby. Then he asked if Eddy and I would to return to New York with him. I said I couldn't.

"I don't think I would have ever left James and the girls if it wasn't for an incident that happened a month later. You see, James never took to Eddy, but he wasn't cruel to him either. Then, one day, he accused Eddy of something he did not do, and in a fit of anger, he struck him and called him a bastard loud enough for the staff to hear. I knew Eddy would be tarnished with that title for the rest of his life if we remained in Sandwich. I also knew how much Angelo loved Eddy. I decided that it would better for Eddy to have a warm father who loved him than a cold, distant man who thought of him as a bastard every time he looked at him. That's when I made up my mind to come to New York with Angelo.

"I intended to take all my children with me, but James refused to let Eliza go, and Dolly would not leave without her. It was the hardest decision I have ever had to make. My only consolation was that James is a very wealthy man who cared deeply for both my girls, despite his dislike for my son. Eliza has a wonderful nanny. Both James and Dolly dote on her, and I promised I would return in a year's time. I intend to keep that promise."

"Do you intend to stay there?" Nonna asked.

"I am not sure what I am going to do, Nonna. I have made rather a mess of things, haven't I? But I will tell you this: I love all my children equally, and I pray we can all be together in America someday.

"That is my story. I know that Angelo and I did not tell the truth when we said we were married, but I have heard from James and he said that his lawyer is working very hard to obtain our divorce, so it shan't be long until Angelo and I can marry. James is also seeing to it that Eddy can have his proper last name.

"Now, your friendship means a great deal to me, and I promise I shall be perfectly honest with you from now on. Goodness knows, I've been running away from the truth ever since I left Old Nichol. I do not want to run anymore. When Angelo and I are legally married and Eddy has his proper name, it will be the beginning of a new life for us, and, for the first time since leaving Old Nichol, I shall be proud of who I am.

"In spite of the poverty we lived in, there were good memories. I've had years to think about it, and I know now that Ma and Da would have been good parents if it wasn't for their dependence on alcohol. At one time, Da was about the strongest man in Old Nichol, and yet he was also the gentlest. And Ma kept her house cleaner than most ladies.

"She wasn't very big, but she could work all day, then sing and dance all evening. I can still hear her and see her too. She had curly red hair, and when she danced, twirling around and around, it seemed as though she wore a halo of flames. And Angelo, everyone who remembered your father considered him a hero. He saved a little girl from the third floor of a burning building then returned to try to save her sister. He suffered so terribly from the smoke that day that he couldn't work and did not live very long. Then your dear mother worked hard looking after you until she passed away."

Gladys glanced at Isabella. When she saw the pain on the woman's face, she suddenly realized how difficult it must be for her to hear of her daughter's tragic life. She embraced her and said, "Oh, Nonna, I am so sorry. How dreadfully thoughtless of me!"

Isabella shook head. She looked up at Gladys and said, "Victor told me that Maria had died in the slums, but I had no idea it was such a horrible place. I blamed her husband for her death, and I was very upset when Angelo used his father's name instead of changing it to Rossini. Now that I know Hugh Matthews was a very brave man, it helps me to understand why Maria fell in love with him. Don't feel bad, Gladys, dear. If anything, your story has caused me to see everything more clearly. You have a great deal of spunk, my girl, and you shall not receive any criticism from me. In fact, I think you deserve to be congratulated for what you have accomplished. Don't you agree?" she addressed the rest of the group.

Sandy was the first to clap, and everyone else joined in, including Lottie. When they finished, Sandy said he would make a fresh pot of tea and Gladys asked if anyone wanted to ask her any questions.

Lottie was the first. "What happened to that awful landlord's body? Did your parents get arrested?"

"No one except Ma and Da knows what happened to him. I don't think they ever told anyone," Gladys answered.

"I remember that a constable came looking for him a few times, but even if anyone had known what happened, they wouldn't have said anything," Toughie said.

There were many more questions, and by the time everyone left, they all felt as though they had been a part of Gladys's life and that she was now part of theirs. Lottie and Victor were the last to go and Gladys could tell that Lottie was still a little hesitant about their relationship, so she put her hands on her shoulders, looked into her eyes, and said, "Carlotta, I know I have no right to ask you to be my friend, but the minute I saw you, I admired you. I think we are very much alike, and, if you will allow me, I shall do everything I can to earn your trust. Do you think you can do that?"

Lottie bit her lip and looked down at the floor. Gladys felt she had failed to change the woman's mind, but then Lottie looked up, held out one hand, and started counting on her fingers as she spoke, "I might forgive you if you do some things for me. Number one: teach me some of those lovely songs my uncle is so fond of. Two: teach me how to sew on that strange machine you have. Three: promise to take me shopping for material. Four: promise to look untidy sometimes. Five: and this is the most important one, you must promise never to call me Carlotta again. The name is Lottie. Now come here so I can hug you."

The International Café soon became one of the most popular dining facilities in New York. The wall murals and the variety of ethnic foods that Sandy served, with the help of Gladys and Lottie, were so popular that they had to take reservations and look for more waiters within four months.

Chapter Thirty Two

A month before Christmas, Angelo was working at the restaurant desk when the evening customers started to arrive. A well dressed, middle-aged man he had never seen before came in, so Angelo asked him if he had a reservation.

"No, I don't, but I do have a dear friend who I would guess happens to be your wife," the man said.

"My wife?"

"You are Angelo, are you not?"

"Yes. And you are?"

"Percy."

"Oh my goodness! Gladdy is going to be so happy to see you." Angelo sat him down at one of the tables. "Just pretend you are a customer, Percy. I want to surprise her," he said before going into the kitchen.

Gladys was about to ladle out two bowls of soup when Angelo came in and said, "Gladdy, there is a customer out there who refuses to allow anyone but you to wait on him. Sorry, but he is most insistent."

"Oh fiddle, not one of those again! All right, but I hope he doesn't want to do anything but eat." They all laughed and she took off her apron and went out.

The man had his back to her when she approached him. "Yes, sir, may I help you?"

Percy turned around.

"Percy!" she squealed before throwing her arms around his neck.

After the restaurant closed, Gladys and Angelo took Percy up to their flat. After Eddy went to bed, Angelo poured them each a glass of wine, raised his glass, and said "This is indeed a pleasant surprise, Percy. I've heard so much about you, and now here you are." They clicked their glasses then Gladys began asking questions about Dolly and Eliza. She didn't want to stop, but finally, Percy said that he had told her all he could.

"Don't you want to know why I am here?" he asked.

"Of course. I am sorry, Percy. It's just that I miss them so much. Why are you here?"

"I've come to bring you an early Christmas present." He got up, opened his briefcase, and handed her an official-looking envelope. "Can you guess what that is?"

Gladys had a good idea. She looked at Angelo then back at Percy. "Is it really?" was all she could say.

Percy nodded. "Yes, my dear, it's your divorce. We have to see an old friend of mine tomorrow. He's a lawyer who studied in England, and he has some papers for you to sign, then you will be free to marry this good man."

Gladys hugged him and then she offered to make up a bed for him in the adjoining flat, but Percy said he had already checked in and left his bag at the Fifth Avenue Hotel.

"I had wanted to stay at the Metropolitan, but a delegation of Japanese is there and there were no rooms available."

"I heard that the Fifth Avenue is grander anyway. I went there for tea once with Lottie's aunt, and the dining room is quite elegant," Gladys said.

Percy said he would come for Gladys in the morning, and they would go to his friend's office to get things signed. Before he left, Gladys asked him how long he intended to stay in America. She was happily surprised when he answered, "Just long enough to see you two wed. That is, if you think you can arrange it sometime in the next two weeks."

"What do you think, Angelo?" Gladys asked.

"It sounds too good to be true."

"Would you give me away, Percy?" Gladys asked.

"If you hadn't asked, I would have been very disappointed," he replied.

They wanted to be married quietly with little fuss. Angelo asked his uncle Victor to be a witness, and Gladys said she would like Lottie there as well. Gladys had finally found someone almost as dear to her as her old friend Millie had been—someone she could confide in—and Lottie felt the same toward Gladys.

Gladys and Angelo were married on the fifth of December, 1860, in the front room of Reverend Reginald Field's home in Manhattan. Victor, Lottie, their twin boys, the Ruttens, and Sandy celebrated their wedding in a private reception room at the Fifth Avenue Hotel, courtesy of James Hornsby and Percy Hudson.

Gladys had been right. For the first time since leaving Old Nichol, she knew exactly who she was, and she even felt confident that her girls would soon be with her again.

Gladys knew Percy was anxious to get back and spend Christmas in England, but bidding him goodbye was more difficult than she had anticipated. It had begun snowing as they stood on the pier, and Percy was worried she would catch cold so he suggested that she not wait for the ship to sail.

"I shall find my cabin and get settled, my dear. That is if there is any room in it for me among all those Christmas presents you have given me for the girls. I don't want you to stand here and catch a cold."

"I'm fine. I really don't want you to go, Percy. Tell the girls that I said it is going to be a sad Christmas for me without them. And please tell them I shall be thinking of them every minute, and it won't be long until I am with them again. I don't know if James shall insist we meet in London, but it doesn't matter as long as I can be with them."

"I wouldn't be surprised if he invites you to Four Oaks. You would like the new James, Gladys. I'm certain he is going to be happy when I report that you are keeping well and that Edward has had no trouble adapting to his new surroundings. I am sorry, Gladys, but I never had time to discuss this with you before, because I only met with the man a few minutes before I left the hotel this morning. You see, James still feels guilty for misjudging Edward, and he's determined to make up for it. He wants to ensure that the boy has a good education, so, according to his instructions, I have arranged for a tutor.

"But he doesn't have to do that. He is going to see that Eddy will have Angelo's name, so please tell him that is more than we could hope for. He doesn't need to feel he owes us anything else."

"It is something he wants to do, Gladys, so I've taken the liberty of hiring a teacher. His name is Arthur Van Dyke, and he's well qualified. He has agreed to be at your flat every morning from eight until noon. I am certain the boy will gain more knowledge during that time than he would at a public school in a full day, and when he is old enough, James wants to pay for his higher education as well. The choice of wherever that may be is, of course, up to you and Edward."

"It is far too generous an offer, Percy, but I can hardly refuse seeing as it is Eddy's future we are talking about. Tell James I will see to it that his generosity is not in vain, and thank him for me, please."

"I shall. Now we must say goodbye." Percy hugged her then boarded the ship and entered his cabin so she wouldn't stay on the pier. Wiping the tears away, Gladys walked back to the flat.

There was a large stove in the restaurant and Angelo had gone to fetch a load of wood that day, and since Eddy had begged to go with him, they had said goodbye to Percy the night before. When Angelo came home for dinner that night, he asked if Percy had sailed. When Gladys said he had, Angelo remarked, "I sure hope he has good weather. When it's snowing, the sea is often the calmest so that's a good thing, but it's not the best time of the year to be on the ocean."

"Thank heavens we have steamships now, and it doesn't take

weeks to get there," Gladys replied. She knew she would have to tell Angelo about the tutor coming for Eddy, but she had a feeling he wasn't going to like it. She waited until they were getting ready for bed before approaching the subject.

Trying to be as diplomatic as she could, she began, "Percy said James is a different man now, Angelo. I think he meant that he was much more understanding and tolerant than he used to be. Percy even said that he wouldn't be surprised if James invited us to stay at Four Oaks when we go back to England."

"That would be nice, but I wager I shan't be included in that offer."

"You never can tell. And Percy said that James still feels guilty for misjudging Eddy. He wants to make it up to him and has offered to pay for his education."

"I hope you told him to tell James that I am Eddy's father now and I intend to pay for everything he needs."

"He knows you are his father, Angelo. That is why he is having Percy see that Eddy has your name. He just wants to do something to make up for his mistake. He asked Percy to hire a tutor for Eddy, and he has offered to pay for his higher education too, when it's time."

"You can write and tell him thank you, but I will be taking care of all that."

"Percy has already hired a man. He is coming after Christmas every weekday morning for four hours."

"He is not going to tutor my son, so you had better put a stop to it right now!"

"The twins had a tutor and I hear the public schools here are not that good."

"They are good enough for my boy and I don't want to hear any more about it!"

"Well, your boy can go to public school. My boy is going to have a tutor."

"We shall see about that."

Gladys and Angelo had promised each other they would never go to sleep without saying "I love you," and they were determined to keep that promise, but the "I love you" they each said that night sounded more obligatory than loving.

This would be Angelo's first Christmas with his son, and, although he knew Gladys's enthusiasm was tempered by the absence of her daughters, he couldn't contain himself. It was still two weeks away, but he wanted to put up a Christmas tree and decorate the apartment. Gladys told him the needles would all fall off before Christmas morning, so he reluctantly agreed to wait. He and Victor had bought a horse and wagon for the business and one week before Christmas they loaded it down with hay and blankets and both families went out to the woods behind the Ruttens' farm to find their trees.

There was a small amount of snow on the ground and a sprinkle of it on the trees causing them to look as though they were already decorated. They sang carols all the way there, but when they left the wagon alongside the road and began looking for the trees, Victor looked up at the sky and warned the boys, "You will have to choose your trees in a hurry, boys. It looks like we could have more snow and Prince could have trouble getting us home."

"We will need a big one for Auntie's parlour too," Lottie reminded him.

"Can't we get one for the restaurant too?" Gladys asked.

Victor said they would get one if they had time, otherwise they would have to settle for boughs as greenery. The boys ran ahead of the adults and when they found one they liked, they would call out "Over here. I found a dandy," or "Here's the perfect one, hurry, bring the axe!" Most times the trees they found were far too tall, but they finally selected ones the right size. Eddy insisted on trying to carry his out by himself, but when Gladys said he would spoil it by dragging it in the dirt, he allowed Angelo to help him. Victor chopped a large one down for the Ruttens, and Angelo chopped down a medium one for the restaurant.

Rosy-cheeked and boisterous, the three boys knocked at the Rut-

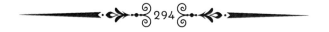

tens' back door then hid behind the tree they were holding up and called out, "Merry Christmas, Merry Christmas!"

Bess opened the door and, having a good sense of humour, she threw her hands in the air and exclaimed, "Land's sakes! It a talking tree! Now you stay right there, mister tree, ah'm going ta fetch Mrs Rutten. Ah wager she's never laid eyes on a talkin' tree before." The boys couldn't stifle their giggles and snickers, but Bess didn't let on she heard them. She hurried away and came back with Theresa Rutten. "Look, missus, it's a talkin' tree, jist like I told you. Now what was it you all said, mister talkin' tree?"

The boys called out, "Merry Christmas, Merry Christmas!" Then they stuck their heads out so Theresa could see them, and Paulo said, "It's your Christmas tree, Auntie. Do you like it?"

Theresa was delighted and invited them all in for hot chocolate and cookies, but Victor insisted they leave, so the cookies were put in a bag for them to have on their way home.

The next few evenings were dedicated to making decorations for all the Christmas trees. They all gathered after the restaurant was closed, sang carols, made paper chains, and strung pretty beads. The three boys were so busy chasing each other around the restaurant and wrestling that they weren't really accomplishing anything, and Lottie had to settle them down with threats of no Santa if they didn't behave. They laughed.

Louis went up to Victor, who was sitting at a table cutting out strips of paper for the chains, and put his hands together as though he was about to pray and said, "Please, please, dear Santa, do not forget us. We have been such good boys, Santa dear."

Eddy and Paulo laughed so hard the tears were rolling down their cheeks. Gladys was shocked. She had no idea that Eddy didn't believe in Santa anymore. She had been so busy working in the restaurant that she hadn't been aware of what Eddy was thinking or doing. Now when she looked at him, she realized how American he had become. His speech had become less articulate, and although he was still polite, he treated everyone with the same amount of respect whether they were young, old, rich, or poor. Gladys thought he was wonderful.

After the decorations were made, Angelo bought some candles and clip-on candle holders, and Gladys finally allowed him to put the tree up on Christmas Eve. Then they put on the decorations and lit the candles. Gladys was thinking of Dolly and all the decorations they had made and taken with them to Four Oaks, and she wondered if Dolly thought of her when she put them on James's tree this year.

In spite of missing the girls, she and Eddy did have a jolly Christmas. They had their Christmas dinner at the Ruttens'. They had sung carols after dinner, and everyone joined in.

Angelo had spent far too much money on Eddy's presents. Gladys didn't argue with him, but she warned him that this year was to be an exception. Many of their customers had never seen a Christmas tree, so having one in the restaurant added gaiety to the season.

Chapter Thirty Three

Gladys had come to New York in March and she was determined to return to England in a year's time so she began making plans. Although the restaurant was doing well, Victor was determined to make large monthly payments to Peter Rutten in order to pay off the mortgage as soon as possible. Ike Murphy, the owner of the building attached to theirs, came in to dine often, and he and Victor had become good friends. Victor told Angelo that Ike only rented the building out as a warehouse and he had hinted that if the right man came along, he might sell and move out west.

"I think he would make us a better deal than anyone else, Angelo. We could expand the restaurant and put in some apartments upstairs like we have now. We have to keep growing if we are going to get anywhere in this town. It is the time of opportunities, and we have to grab them while we can. The sooner we get this place paid for, the sooner we can buy another, don't you agree?"

Angelo agreed, but such a generous payment left very little by the time he gave Gladys money for food and other necessities. He worried that she was going to be extremely upset when he told her that he hadn't been able to put aside any money for their trip to England.

The next few weeks, were so busy at the restaurant that Angelo didn't have time to worry about money. A colourful variety of customers came to dine regularly and they were all treated equally. At first this bothered the upper classes, but they kept coming back and bringing friends. Surprisingly, they had very little trouble with drunkards. Perhaps they stayed away because the policemen that worked in their area often came in for a free bowl of chowder or a cup of coffee.

A good number of captains and sailors frequented the restaurant, which probably had a lot to do with the recommendation of Captain Bob, Sandy's friend. With such an interesting array of customers, Gladys had some amusing stories to tell the girls in her letters, but not all the happenings proved to be amusing.

During the next two months, Gladys began purchasing little gifts for everyone at Four Oaks. She wrote and told Dolly she was planning on being in England around the end of March. When James heard about it, he was kind enough to write and say that she, Edward, and Angelo would all be welcome to stay at Four Oaks. She was happy that neither he nor Dolly had asked how long they would be staying in England, because she hadn't discussed it with Angelo.

At the beginning of March, Angelo knew he couldn't wait any longer. He had to tell Gladys that he hadn't been able to put aside any money for their trip to England. Besides, he couldn't possibly leave Victor to run the restaurant and the apartments alone, not for more than a week or two.

He hadn't objected when Eddy's tutor showed up. The man was a most likable sort, and Angelo could tell Eddy would benefit from his teaching, so he hoped that would be something in his favour.

One weekend, Angelo asked Victor to invite Eddy to stay at their house overnight, then he suggested Gladys and he go out to a pub. Gladys thought he was being very sweet and romantic. They hadn't had much chance to enjoy time together since arriving in New York, and she hadn't worn her best dresses since then either. They both dressed up in their finest and went to one of the most respected pubs in town.

"You look beautiful, Gladdy," he said once they had been seated. "I wager every man here is wishing he was in my shoes right now."

"I think the women are far more envious of me." She took a drink of her wine before she smiled and added, "Sometimes it seems too good to be true, doesn't it?"

"What's that, Gladdy?"

"That we are really married and are going to be together for the rest of our lives."

"I know. It seems like yesterday we were in Old Nichol talking about how happy we would be if we could get married, and now here we are. There was never anyone but you for me, Gladdy, and there never will be."

"I know, darling." A three-piece band started to play. Gladys asked, "Will you dance with me, Toughie?"

The use of his old name suited their mood and he said he would try. If he made mistakes, Gladys didn't notice because they were looking in each other's eyes with such love, they weren't even aware they were dancing. The music had stopped for a minute before they realized it. They were both feeling a little tipsy when they caught a cab and returned to the flat.

It was such a nice evening that Gladys suggested they go for a short walk before going in. Angelo hadn't wanted to spoil the evening by telling Gladys the bad news, so he thought perhaps a walk might be the best place to do it.

They walked down to the wharf and sat on a bench to look at the ships. Watching, Gladys said, "It won't be long before we are on one of those ships, Angelo. I guess we had better book our passage soon."

He couldn't wait any longer. "Gladdy, I have something to tell you. Something you are not going to want to hear."

Gladys knew by the sound of his voice it was going to be bad news. She looked at him and waited.

"Gladdy, I don't have the money for our passage."

"Oh, Angelo! I should have been keeping the money. You are not that good at finances, you know. Luckily, I still have some money left in my savings. How much are you short?"

Angelo hung his head and didn't look at her when he answered, "All of it."

"All of it? I do not believe you, Angelo. You cannot mean that you haven't saved a penny." She got up and put her hands on his shoulders. "We need it. You have to have it, Angelo. You have to."

"I am so sorry, Gladdy. Victor was determined to pay off our mortgage in a hurry. I've just been able to give you only enough to run the house with. I haven't been able to save anything."

"And what are we supposed to do about going to England?"

"We will have to wait until next year, I suppose," he said, getting up and going over to the railing.

She followed him and grabbed his arm. "Why didn't you tell me a long time ago? I could have saved money. Instead, I bought a sewing machine and presents, and you spent so much money on Eddy this Christmas. We could have been saving the whole year."

"I kept thinking I would save the next month, and, before long, the months had gone and I had nothing. I can't borrow from Uncle Victor because he doesn't have any savings either."

"Damn him! What right had he to decide our finances by demanding we pay off that stupid mortgage?"

"Glad, I am so sorry."

"What angers me the most is that you could have told me right from the start. I only hope I still have enough left of my own money to pay for the three of us."

"How long do you want to stay in England?"

"That depends on how long they will want me there and if James will allow me to bring Eliza back here with me. At least two months."

"Two months! I can't possibly leave Uncle Victor with all the work for that long. I thought we would only be staying for a fortnight."

"I have been away from my daughters for a whole year, and you expect me to just spend a fortnight with them? No, Angelo, I am going to spend a lot more time than that with them, so if your uncle means more to you than I do . . . Well, Eddy and I shall just have to go without you."

"What about Eddy's schooling? You insisted he have a tutor, and now you are going to take him away?"

"He will be able to study with Eliza's tutor, and his tutor will still be here when we return."

"Maybe you should ask *James* to hire someone to work with Uncle Victor while I take a few months off. It seems he gives you everything you ask for."

"Now you are being petty. You know very well that James has been more than fair to both of us, Angelo."

Angelo was about to answer when three drunken and noisy sailors came out of a building. They were unsteady on their feet, supporting each other as they walked by. Gladys and Angelo heard one say In a slurred voice, "She runs the best goddamned whorehouse in the whole country. That girl I had tonight, she was the sweetest gal. If she wasn't a whore, I'da got down on my knees and proposed." Putting his head back, he hollered, "Whooey!" then threw his empty bottle into the water.

The tide was out and it seemed to take forever before Gladys heard it splash. She watched the three sailors disappear down a gangplank as though they were descending into the sea. Angelo took off his overcoat and put it over her shoulders.

"You are cold, Gladdy," he said tenderly. "Come on, my dear, let's go home and have a cup of tea."

After they undressed, they sat in their nightwear drinking tea. Gladys broke the silence. "What are we going to do, Angelo?"

"I don't know, but as much as I'll miss you, I think you and Eddy will have to go alone. This building is our future, Gladdy. I want to be able to give you and Eddy a decent home and everything else a family deserves. Uncle thinks that as soon as we have this place paid for, we shall be able to buy the building next door. Then we can expand the restaurant and rent out more apartments.

"In time, we should be able to have a nice home. When we get old, we'll be able to sit back and enjoy life. But if you don't want me to stay here, I won't. I cannot expect Victor to buy me out, because he hasn't the money, but I can probably find work down on the docks. We could manage somehow. It's up to you, Gladdy. I know I can't live without you, so whatever you say is what we shall do."

"I'm sorry, darling. I was just so disappointed when you said you hadn't saved any money. I understand how you can't leave Victor with all the work. I feel guilty for leaving Lottie, but I must go. You can see that, can't you?"

"Of course I can. And I don't expect you to come home in a fortnight either, but I will miss you and Eddy so much. You know, I am afraid he might want to stay there."

"He would never do that. He worships you, and I think he is going to miss the twins as much as he missed Dolly and Eliza when we left Sandwich."

The next day, Gladys told Eddy that his father would not be going to England with them.

"If Dad isn't going then neither am I," he declared.

"But don't you want to see Dolly and Eliza and your pony?"

"You can take them a present for me, but I will stay here with my dad," he insisted. Gladys had heard him call Angelo "Dad," and it made her realize just how close the two had become.

Eddy was determined to stay in New York until Gladys told him that the more times he sailed across the ocean, the better sailor he would be. If he intended to be a captain someday, he would have to sail a great deal. Then she promised him he could wear long trousers.

Before she booked their passage, Sandy's friend, Captain Bob Nicholson of the ship they had sailed to New York on, came to the restaurant to enjoy some of Sandy's excellent cuisine. When he learned that Gladys and Eddy were going to England, he said he was sailing in three days' time and had a cabin that they might be able to have free of charge.

A gentleman from out west had paid for it and told Captain Bob to assume he had struck it rich and would not be leaving America if he didn't show up two days before the ship was to sail.

"I think he must have been one of the lucky ones, because he would have been here otherwise, Gladys. If he does not show up tomorrow, the cabin is yours. Can you be ready in three days?" Bob asked.

"I have been packing for weeks now, Captain. My girls do not expect me to be there until the end of the month, but your offer is so kind that I don't think I can refuse. What do you think, Angelo?"

Angelo agreed that it was too good an opportunity to pass up. He told Gladys that the sooner she went, the sooner she would return. Overall, he thought it was a good idea.

The next day, when the gentleman failed to appear, Lottie helped Gladys finish packing. She and Eddy were ready to leave two days later. Everyone came to see them off. Angelo just about broke one of Gladys's ribs hugging her goodbye. Tears were beginning to run down Eddy's cheeks, so he mumbled a goodbye and quickly ran aboard the ship where no one could pick them out of the crowd.

Angelo stayed on the pier and waved until they were out of sight. He had never prayed before, but, as they disappeared from view, he looked up at the sky and said, "Go with them, God, and please bring them back to me."

For the first few days, Gladys enjoyed the voyage. Captain Bob invited Gladys and Eddy to join him on the bridge, which heightened the boy's desire to be a captain when he grew up. Bob insisted Gladys call him by his first name instead of Captain.

Bob was a Norwegian man who had grown up on the sea. His father had been a captain, and Bob's oldest son was a second mate on another ship; he was slated to become a captain as well. Bob was a handsome man. His complexion had darkened with the bright skies and salty air. His tanned skin contrasted nicely with his head of generous blonde hair and blue eyes. He also had a charming personality and was very popular with his female passengers.

Bob had been attracted to Gladys the first time he saw her, but Angelo was with her at the time. Now that she was traveling without her husband, he took advantage of the situation and invited her and Eddy to dine with him at his table frequently. He also spent most of his off-duty time with her, discussing books and sitting out on the deck enjoying the fresh air while Eddy played games with two other young boys.

Although he enjoyed innocent flirtations, Bob had always been a loyal husband. However, there was something about Gladys that made him want more. When she was near him, he would foolishly picture himself in the role of one of his Viking ancestors. Sometimes he had a ridiculous urge to emit a manly howl, pick, throw her over his shoulder, and take her to his cabin. Fortunately, he was a gentleman and kept a firm control over his fantasies.

Gladys was thoroughly enjoying Bob's company—she hadn't been so pampered since her father-in-law had died. She didn't think anything of his attentive behaviour toward her until she was sitting in the ship's salon with two other women one afternoon. As soon as Bob entered the room, both of the women got up to leave and one of them winked at her and said, "We had better leave now. Here comes *your* captain, Mrs Matthews."

Gladys felt both guilty and embarrassed.

Bob put his hand on her shoulder and said, "Ah, here you are, my dear. It's a lovely day and I am off-duty for an hour. Would you care to take a stroll?"

Suddenly, the feel of his hand on her shoulder didn't feel as innocent as it should, and she knew it was time she put a stop to their close friendship. She had been so flattered by his admiration that she hadn't realized how much time they were spending together.

Rising from her chair, she said, "Thank you, Bob, but I want to write a letter to Angelo. I like to write to him every day so I can mail it as soon as we land. I have been telling him how kind you have been to Eddy and I, but I'm afraid we have taken advantage of you and monopolized too much of your time. You mustn't neglect the other passengers. I also promised Eddy I would have a game of checkers with him this afternoon. He is in the cabin reading and waiting for me now."

Bob was visibly upset and would have argued with her, but she didn't give him a chance and quickly took her leave.

The next few days were awkward for Gladys. She appreciated Bob's kindness in giving them free passage. If he hadn't given the cabin to her and Eddy, he may have been able to find someone else to pay for it and made a little profit for himself. When he no longer asked her to join him, she was both relieved and sad.

A day before they were due to land, she knocked on his cabin door and asked if he could spare a few minutes. This time it was he who was embarrassed. After Gladys had made it clear that she didn't think they should see each other so often, he realized that he had behaved badly. He also realized that he was becoming too fond of her. Before she could say anything, he apologized for encroaching on her privacy.

Gladys thanked him but said that she enjoyed his company as much as he enjoyed hers. "It was lovely of you to spend so much of your time with me, Bob, but I think we both know it is better this way. We are both happily married, and I am certain neither of us would want to jeopardize that. I am fond of you, Bob, and I hope we shall continue to be friends."

"I will be your friend for as long as you want, Gladys. If I can ever be of help to you, all you have to do is ask. When you and Eddy are ready to return to New York, simply contact me, and your cabin will be waiting for you."

They arrived in London on the fifteenth of March. By the time they disembarked, it was too late for them to catch a train to Sandwich. They took a cab to Percy's flat but found he wasn't at home. They checked into a hotel instead.

Eddy's demeanour changed as soon as they arrived in London. Although he wanted to see Dolly and Eliza, he dreaded seeing James again. Gladys tried to convince him that James was sorry for the way he had behaved and would be happy to see him, but the only image Eddy could bring to mind was James's angry and contorted face as he shook him and slapped his face.

They boarded the train to Sandwich in the morning, and it arrived in the afternoon. Gladys hired a cab to take them out to Four Oaks and made arrangements for their other luggage to be delivered by wagon. When the gateman came to let the cab in, he recognized Gladys and Eddy. He reached up to touch Gladys's hand. "My heavens, it's yourself, mum! And there's Master Edward too. I must say, mum, 'tis good to have you back. I 'spect you remember where to go!"

"Yes, Andy, I remember."

The driver took them to the front entrance, and he left after Gladys paid him. Gladys tried the door and found it open, so they went in instead of waiting for Jenkins to announce them. Everything looked just as it had when she left, only now it seemed twice as grand. She took off her gloves and ran a hand over the smoothness of the big curved banister as she walked past. She could sense Eddy tensing up as they went past James's library. No one was about, but they could hear Freda moving pots and dishes as they neared the kitchen. When they entered the room, Freda had her head bent over the sink and didn't see them.

"Is there any chance one could have a cup of tea and one of your Eccles cakes, Freda?" Gladys asked.

Freda stopped what she doing and, without turning around, she answered, "I'll praise the Lord myself if that's really you, missus." Then she turned and saw them. Holding out her arms, she cried, "Come here, you two. You come and give old Freda a big hug." After they hugged, Freda said, "The good Lord himself must have told you how much you are needed this very day, missus."

Gladys was almost too afraid to ask the meaning behind the cook's ominous words, but she had to know. "What is it, Freda? Where is everybody?"

"It's Miss Dolly, missus. She's very sick. Blossom's taken Eliza for a walk, and Sir and Mister Percy, they are up there with the doctor now."

Gladys wanted to run upstairs immediately, but she managed to keep calm and said, "Eddy, I want you to stay with Freda or go out and see your pony while I go up to be with Dolly." Then she took off her coat and bonnet and hurried up the stairs.

When she entered Dolly's suite, Percy was in the sitting room and he jumped up, gave her a quick hug before whispering, "Thank God you are here."

She entered the room quietly. James was standing with his back to the wall, and Doctor Macdonald was bending over, examining Dolly. The doctor turned when Gladys came up beside him and put a hand on her arm and spoke in low, hushed tones: "The poor lass has pneumonia. It's the fever that we have to fight, Gladys. Bathing her with cloths dipped in tepid water is all you can do. If the fever breaks in the next twenty-four hours, I think she may recover." He patted her arm and left.

Gladys told James to have one of the maids bring her a bucket of tepid water and towels, then she knelt down beside the bed and kissed Dolly's hot forehead. She told James he could leave once she had the water, then she stripped the covers off her daughter and began bathing her.

Dolly was delirious most of that day and part of the night. At one point, Gladys felt a hand on her shoulder, and when she looked up to see who was there, James's aunt Jean smiled down at her. Jean motioned that she would take over, but Gladys shook her head. Before she left the room, Jean kissed the top of Gladys's head and whispered that both Eddy and Eliza were sleeping peacefully.

Molly was the maid James had ordered to keep Gladys supplied with water and towels; when she first saw Gladys, tears ran down her cheeks and she couldn't resist kissing her on the cheek. Molly stayed with Gladys and Dolly all night, fetching water and towels whenever Gladys needed them. When she wasn't fetching, she sat in the rocking chair and somehow managed to stay awake.

About five in the morning, Dolly's fever broke. Gladys had blankets warming in front of the fireplace and wrapped them around her as soon as her temperature went down. It must have felt wonderful because Dolly opened her eyes at last. When she saw her mother, she gave her a weak smile and, in an almost inaudible voice, managed to say, "Momma, you came home."

Gladys finally allowed her emotions to surface and tears ran down her cheeks as she answered, "Yes, my darling, I came home. Now you must sleep. I shall stay right here until you wake up."

By midday, Gladys was persuaded to leave Dolly and go down to the conservatory to have something to drink and to eat. Before she went to the conservatory, she paid a visit to the nursery to see Eliza. At first Eliza was shy. Although she let Gladys hug her, she didn't reciprocate. Instead, she said she wanted to see "her Dolly."

Gladys sat down in a rocking chair and took hold of the little girl's hand. She explained that although her Dolly had been very sick, she would soon be well again and would need to rest quietly until then.

"I think by tomorrow we shall be able to pick a bouquet of snowdrops for you to take to her. Would you let me help you pick them, darling?" Eliza smiled shyly and nodded just as Eddy came in.

"How is Dolly, mother?" He asked as he went to Gladys and kissed her.

Before Gladys could answer, Eliza climbed up on her knees and said, "My Dolly is much better, Eddy, and my mother and me are going out and pick her some snowdrops tomorrow. You can come too if you like."

Gladys and Eddy looked at each other and grinned. Neither of them bothered to correct Eliza's poor grammar. Eliza clung to Gladys's hand as they made their way to the conservatory.

Freda insisted on waiting on Gladys herself, and she brought enough food to the conservatory to satisfy ten people. As soon as it was known that Gladys was home, all the staff came to say hello and to ask about Miss Dolly. A soon as they left, James, Percy, Aunt Jean, Jenkins, and Blossom arrived. Gladys and Eddy were kept so busy answering questions that they scarcely had a chance to eat any of Freda's excellent cooking.

Chapter Thirty Four

Eddy was still apprehensive in James's company. James addressed him, saying, "My heaven's, Eddy,"—he had never called him Eddy before and the familiarity of the name surprised Eddy—"what on earth have they been feeding you in America? I think you've grown at least a foot taller. I rather think that you are ready for a much bigger horse while you are here rather than that little pony, Chestnut. Perhaps we can go out this afternoon and see if Ruby has a horse more suited to a young man of your stature. What do you say?"

Not sure what to say, Eddy looked at Gladys. She smiled but didn't offer an opinion, so he stood tall, looked James in the eye, and said, "I might like that, sir." After they had their tea, James checked to see if Dolly's health was still improving. He also made sure that Jenkins had one of the footmen set up a cot beside her bed so Gladys could sleep beside her until she was breathing normally again. Then he and Percy took Eddy out to the stable to look at the horses. "Ah," he said when they came to one of the stalls. "This young gelding looks to be about the right size. What do you think?"

Eddy was so excited he could hardly keep from jumping on the horse's back, but he still didn't trust James and didn't want to appear too friendly. Looking at Percy, he replied, "He looks like he's got a good nature, doesn't he, Uncle Percy?"

Percy laughed and said he thought James could not have chosen a more suitable steed. Eddy knew his mother would have told him to say thank you to James, but he couldn't make himself say the words. Instead, he said, "What's his name, sir?"

"His name is Ali Baba, but we just call him Ali. Do you know the story of Ali Baba and the Forty Thieves?"

"Yes, sir, I do. I think it's a pretty good name." When Percy suggested they go for a short ride to see how Ali behaved, Eddy said he didn't have any riding clothing. "But now that I wear long pants, I really don't need them. When we go to visit Auntie Theresa and Uncle Peter, sometimes we ride on Auntie's old mare, and we don't even use a saddle." Eddy directed his words to Percy, and now that he had begun talking, he had so much to say that James had to interrupt him.

"I want to hear all about your cousins in America, Eddy, but if we are going riding today, we had better do it soon or it will be too late. I took the liberty of purchasing some riding clothes for you, but I did not think you would have grown so tall. I hope they fit. Shall we go and get dressed?"

Eddy was having trouble keeping from smiling, "Yes, sir."

The suit fit well enough, and Eddy was ready and waiting in the stable when James arrived. "Where's Uncle Percy?" he asked while looking around nervously.

"He remembered that he had to take care of some business in town so it will be just you and me, I'm afraid." Eddy wasn't happy to hear that, but he wanted to ride Ali so badly that he didn't object. Once Ruby helped him mount, James suggested he ride around in the corral until he felt comfortable on the horse. It had been a year since Eddy had sat in a saddle, but it didn't take long for him to feel at home. The horse was well trained and easy to handle, so they left the corral and went down the trail toward the open fields.

At first, they walked the horses. Then they trotted them for a few minutes before James asked, "Would you like to try a gallop?"

This time Eddy could not keep his eagerness from showing and answered with an enthusiastic sounding, "Yes, sir!"

"Very well, but only to the end of this field. We do not want you having an accident the very first day you are here." They galloped to the end of the field and then James motioned for Eddy to slow to a trot. As they were riding back to the stable, James said, "Eddy, I hope you will find it in your heart to forgive me. When Eliza told me what you had done for her, I felt so ashamed. I admire you very much, Eddy, and I only hope Eliza turns out to be as honest and kind as you. I would like very much to have you as a friend. What do you say?"

Eddy could still remember that day in James's library, and although James had shown him nothing but kindness since he arrived back at Four Oaks, he couldn't erase the memory from his mind. Not knowing what to do and feeling embarrassed, he just nodded his head.

Later, after they had dismounted and were brushing the horses, Eddy felt more at ease. It was almost as though he was brushing away the bad memories with each stroke. Because he didn't have to look at him, he felt comfortable enough to speak to James directly. "Sir?"

"Yes?"

"I'd like to be your friend. And, sir?"

"Yes, Eddy?"

"Thanks for letting me ride Ali and for the clothes."

James grinned. Although he noticed that Eddy's diction had regressed, he found the boy's directness refreshing. "You are very welcome, Eddy, and you may call me Uncle James if you like. I know it is difficult to change what you call a person, but I am rather envious of Percy when you call him uncle."

There was no response, and James, suddenly realizing that he had been so anxious for the boy to forgive him that he had probably overplayed his hand, regretted his words. He waited a few minutes more than he thought, *To hell with it*, and called out, "Come on, it is time we went to see if Freda has any of that chocolate cake left." As he passed by Eddy, he didn't look at him, but he added, "If I were not so old and crotchety, I'd race you."

James hadn't left the stable when Eddy came running past laughing, and James heard him say, "Poor old uncle!"

James grinned and shouted back at him, "I take back all those nice things I said about you. You are truly a rascal."

Gladys slept beside Dolly for three nights before she thought Dolly was well enough to be on her own. In between hugs, Gladys and Dolly talked about their life in Dover and the people that they had loved and lost. Gladys was surprised when Dolly wanted to know more about Gladys's life in Old Nichol. This time, she was ready to understand what a difficult time it had been for both Gladys and Toughie, and why they loved each other as they did.

"I wish I could have met him, Momma. I think I would have liked him."

"I am certain you would, darling. I hope he will be able to come with us next time. I hope that James will allow me to take you both back to America for a visit one of these times as well."

"You mean you are going back to New York?"

"I cannot stay here, Dolly. I am married to Angelo now, and that is where we live. I'm so sorry, my dear. Did you really think I could come back and live here?"

"I guess I did. How long are you going to spend with us then?"

"I don't know, but let us not think about it now. I have only just arrived. I do not want to think about leaving."

"I don't want you to ever leave. When do you think James will allow Eliza to go to New York?"

"I don't know, but we may have to wait until she no longer needs a nanny. Perhaps in two years. She will be six then, and if she is anything like you and Eddy, she will be quite independent. I know he won't allow her to live in America forever, but if you both can come for half a year at a time, it would be wonderful."

Evidently, no one had told the staff why Gladys had left. Now

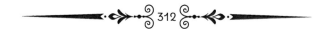

that she had returned, they all thought she and James had settled their differences and she would be home for good. Gladys knew she would have to tell them the truth sooner or later. Since she had bought them all small gifts, she used that as an excuse to call them all together.

She gave Jenkins, John, and Abdul watch fobs made of soft, braided deerskin. Freda received a lovely beaded, leather purse. The other girls received soft beaded, leather necklaces. Everyone was delighted with their gifts, as they had never seen any Native American crafts before. They thanked Gladys profusely.

Earlier, Gladys had consulted with Dolly and James about the staff. They had decided that the staff deserved to know the truth since she and Eddy planned to visit quite often. With that in mind, Gladys told them she had something to say after she had passed out the gifts. She informed them that James and she had divorced and that she was now married to another man. They didn't take the news well. There were some expressions of disapproval as she went on to explain what led to her marriage to James and their separation.

It was difficult for the servants to believe that a woman they had believed to be a member of aristocracy—a woman they had looked up to and revered for years—was just as common as they were. They didn't dare voice their thoughts, but she could tell they were in disbelief as they offered another thank you and took their leave.

Gladys took over the housekeeper's duties until Dolly was up and about. Although the girls did as they were told, they did it in a begrudging manner. After one week of putting up with their denunciating behaviour, Gladys called them all together again, except Freda, who had remained as fond of Gladys as she always was.

"I know you are all disappointed in me, but I shan't apologize. I have worked as hard, and probably harder, during my life as you have. When I was fortunate enough to earn the position of housekeeper, and even after I married Mr Hornsby, I continued to treat you with kindness and empathy. Is that not right?" she asked them.

Molly was the first to talk. "I'm sorry, mum. I remember how you saved me from going to prison and from that other thing too."

Little Ines was the next to speak. "You are right, mum. You gave us new uniforms and time off to bathe and do our washin'. I guess you could say you even gave us our respect, mum. And you must have been thinking of us, because you brought us presents all the way from America." They all had something nice to say before they left, and there were no problems. However, it didn't stop the gossip that went on in the privacy of their quarters.

Once Dolly was well and returned to her duties, Gladys had a chance to go riding with James, Percy, and Eddy. It was wonderful to ride Tig once more. She hadn't realized how much she missed the countryside. It now appeared to be twice as green and lush as she remembered. She was also relieved to see how well Eddy and James got along.

Eddy was very kind to Eliza and spent a lot of time playing and reading to her. As a result, she soon worshipped him as much as she had before they had left. She loved the stories he told about his twin cousins and the games they played on the streets of New York.

Gladys overheard him one day as he was telling her about his cousins teaching him how to stop a bully like the one who lived near his apartment. "If you run, they know you're afraid, and then they're sure to pound you. But if you stay and look 'em in the eye, they don't know what to do. That's when you kick 'em in the tallywags. That makes them cry like a baby, and they don't usually bother you after that," he said.

Gladys interrupted just in time to keep him from answering when Eliza asked, "What are tallywags, Eddy?" She decided that as soon as she arrived home she would have to talk to Lottie and Angelo. It was time they found out where the twins and Eddy went to play.

Percy only stayed a few days at a time when he visited Four Oaks. He told Gladys that he and James had to be very careful when he visited Four Oaks, but since he had no servants looking after his flat in London, they could relax there and be themselves. "I think things are a little safer in France, so we may purchase a summer cottage with a sea view there soon," he said.

"Perhaps when you have that, James will allow me to have Eliza."

"I shall talk to him about it," Percy promised. Gladys gave him a hug.

When Gladys mentioned to James that she would like to go into Sandwich and browse some of the shops, James said that it might be too embarrassing for them both. He explained that it had taken awhile for the gossip to die down after Gladys and Eddy had left him. Only when he let it be known that he and Gladys were permanently separated, did the residents offer their sympathies and welcome him back into the church and his cricket team.

"Although I invited you and Eddy to stay here, Gladys, I think it would be better for all concerned if we limited your visit to the confines of Four Oaks."

"Eddy and I are just happy that we can be here with the girls, James. We don't need to go to town, but surely the servants will have let everyone know we are here."

"Yes, I am certain they will, but I still think it is best if we don't flaunt your presence."

Gladys hardly thought going to a few shops could be considered flaunting, but she didn't want to cause James any more embarrassment than she had to, so she didn't argue.

Gladys had given Eliza a pretty pair of Native American moccasins. They had fringe around the sides and were decorated with beaded flowers. Eliza didn't want to take them off, even at bedtime. Dolly was given the same, but she was afraid to wear hers in case they would get soiled. Gladys's gifts to Percy and James were beaded, leather headbands which they put on display like the artwork they were. She brought Jean a pretty beaded broach.

At first Jean thanked her, but there were days when she didn't recognize Gladys. On those days, she would show her the broach and say, "Look at this lovely broach my fiancé has given me." Those days were outweighed by her coherent days, but it was troubling nonetheless. Even on Jean's bad days, she would recognize Gladys as soon as she began to sing or play the piano.

Gladys loved Eliza dearly, but when she saw how much she enjoyed letting others wait on her, and even think for her, she worried that she lacked spirit and determination. She had a very different personality than Dolly or Eddy. She wasn't the least adventurous or inquisitive, but she was a happy child. Gladys thought that she would probably only absorb as much education as required to be accepted in society. Although she wasn't a vain child, she insisted on wearing dainty frocks instead of pinafores, and her hair had to be kept curled and bowed. Nevertheless, she had expressed a desire to go to America along with Dolly and that made Gladys feel better.

Chapter Thirty Five

After Gladys had left for America and James and Percy had renewed their friendship, Bob and Tina Rudyard and Mary Baker often came to visit. Mary was a very perceptive woman and she had known as soon as she saw Eddy that he was not James's child. Now she was beginning to see that James and Percy's relationship was not what one would consider normal.

Surprisingly, it didn't disgust her, and she intended to keep it to herself. She could now understand why neither man had been attracted to her, and she thought she might be more understanding toward Gladys as well if she hadn't moved away, but she never expected to see her again. Then, one rainy evening, the Rudyards and she paid an unexpected visit to Four Oaks and were surprised to find Gladys had returned.

They naturally assumed that she had come back to stay. The Rudyards were pleased, but Mary thought Gladys had once again come back to take advantage of James and she greeted her coolly. Then Eddy came running into the parlour. James felt obliged to say, "Eddy, do you remember, Mr and Mrs Rudyard and Mary Baker?"

After saying, "I think so, Uncle," Eddy shook their hands.

Gladys noticed the look on their faces and she sent Eddy up to play with Eliza. Then she said, "James, do you mind if I explain?" He shrugged his shoulders, so she continued, "I think we owe the three of you an explanation. Obviously, James hasn't told you, but he and I are divorced. I am now married to Eddy's father, Angelo Matthews. I know that is difficult to comprehend, so if you can be patient with me, I shall tell you how it all began."

When Gladys finished her story, she mentioned that James was kind enough to allow her to come and have a visit with her girls, and she hoped she could do it often. "I also am hoping to have the girls visit me when Eliza is a bit older and Angelo and I have a house of our own. Right now, we live in a small flat above the restaurant we are buying."

Mary was relieved and she wanted to know all about the restaurant and New York. Gladys answered questions for over an hour. The rest of the evening Gladys played the piano and they sang. It was like old times, only more relaxed.

Angelo's letters were short, but he wrote often. He had never written a letter before, so Gladys was amazed at the number she received, and he always added a separate one for Eddy. He wrote that he was working late every night, because he didn't like being in the flat without them.

He mentioned that they were so busy they were probably going to have to hire another cook and serve meals all day long. He said Victor's friend Ike was trying to talk Victor and him into joining the Union League, so they would be ready to help support the war effort if a war did happen. He went on to write, "Victor, Lottie, the twins, and I went to the Ruttens for a short visit last Sunday and I learned a lot about the underhanded methods of our city's politicians. Unfortunately, the Democrats run almost everything, and they do not want to see the end of slavery. It makes me think I should join the Union

army and be ready to fight those southerners. What do you think, Gladdy?"

His letters always ended saying that he hoped they were having a good time and how much he loved them both. Gladys knew he wanted to ask when they would be coming home, but he had promised she could stay as long as she liked, so he was leaving it up to her to set the date.

Gladys and Eddy had only been in England for just over a month when the American Civil War began on the twelfth of April. Gladys knew she should book her passage home in case the government began limiting the number of passenger ships allowed in the harbour, but she couldn't bear to leave the girls so soon. Besides that, she was enjoying herself. Although she didn't regret leaving England and going to America with Angelo, she had been too busy to realize what a luxurious life she had given up until she came back to it. The thought of returning to her work as a waitress, dishwasher, and housewife was not as appealing as it had been.

When James announced that he was going to London for a few days and inquired whether Gladys would like to come, she asked if she might take Eddy, Dolly, and Eliza with her and stay in James's flat. James agreed that it would be a good idea.

At first Eddy wanted to stay and play with one of Richard Ellison's boys, who was about the same age as Eddy, but when Gladys mentioned they were going to visit the Crystal Palace to see the dinosaurs, he changed his mind. There were a number of life-sized replicas of dinosaurs to see, and even James and Percy went along. It proved to be the highlight of Eddy's vacation, and he bought dinosaur figurines for both the twins and Angelo.

Because James didn't believe in importing non-indigenous animals into the country, James and Percy didn't go with them when they visited the Zoological Gardens. Eddy remembered where all the animals were housed and played the role of guide. He had a great time pointing out the cages to Eliza.

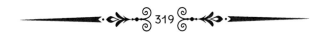

Gladys hadn't received a letter from Angelo for two weeks, and she was beginning to worry. Then, on the last day of April, a letter finally arrived. It wasn't written in his usual tidy handwriting, which worried Gladys greatly. He had written it in a hurry, and Gladys had to read it several times before she could completely understand it. Although Angelo hadn't planned on asking her to come home, he wrote that he had no alternative.

He said that the war had already brought an astounding amount of change to life in New York. There were already many garrisons of Union troops stationed in the city, and most were housed in the forts that were constructed along the waterfront. This meant that the restaurant was kept so busy that everyone had to work twice as hard, which was making them become irritable. They had hired two more cooks but they were not good enough to suit Sandy and Lottie, so they had to train them in the evenings.

They also needed more waiters, but, because there were more jobs than workers, good help was becoming difficult to find, and they were terribly short-handed. They had knocked down part of a wall—the wall with the American paintings on it—and had put more tables in what was once the storeroom. Ike Murphy was letting them use a room on the bottom floor of his building for their storeroom, but there hadn't been time to decorate the old storeroom. They were afraid that the board of health would be around to shut them down.

Gladys knew this could happen whether it met sanitary standards or not, because the restaurant was a favourite with the unionists. But what disturbed Gladys the most was that Angelo had mentioned how much he admired Ike Murphy for joining the 79th New York Volunteer Infantry. He wrote: "There's times when I think it's time we should all follow his example and stand up for what we believe in."

Gladys was so upset that she showed James the letter. After he finished reading it, he could understand why she was so disturbed. He remembered her telling him about her first husband, Tom, and

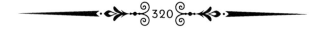

how he had lost his life while fighting a war in India without seeing his daughter, Dolly. Now Angelo had written and hinted that he might be thinking of going off to war. No wonder Gladys was distraught.

"I think you had better leave soon, Gladys. It seems you are needed on that side of the ocean as much as you were needed on this side two months ago. The girls shall miss you more than ever, but they are well looked after so you needn't worry. This war may not last long, and you can come back. You know, I've been talking to Percy about it, and I think I am ready to share our daughter. Soon she shall be able to stay with you for as long as you like, but I rather think I would feel a good deal less anxious if we were to wait until that blessed war is over. What do you say?"

"You have no idea how wonderful that makes me feel, and I confess that right at the present I don't have room for Dolly and Eliza, but we are working hard to save for a house so they will have a place to come to."

"I'd like to help with that if you would allow me to. How much money would you need for a down payment on a home over there?"

Gladys laughed and answered, "Oh, James!"

"What is so funny about that?"

"It's just something Angelo said one night when we were having a little argument. Thank you, James, you are far too generous. We shall manage, but it will just take more time."

"Well the offer is there any time you want it. I shall miss you and Eddy. I like Eddy, Gladys. He is intelligent, thoughtful, and has a good deal of determination, but I cannot say I admire his diction. Please, tell me, is the expression, 'okay,' an acceptable substitute for 'yes, sir', in America?"

"I am afraid so, James, but I will admit, I haven't been paying enough attention to his grammar lately, but I intend to from now on."

James looked in the paper to see which ships were sailing in a week's time and found that Bob's ship was leaving in ten days. Gladys sent a message to him, asking him to reserve a cabin for her and Eddy. Once things were arranged, she explained to Dolly why they had leave. When Gladys told her that James planned to allow Eliza to travel to New York soon, Dolly was pleased. It gave her something to look forward to.

In the ten days before their departure, Dolly and Eliza scarcely left Gladys's side. Eddy was excited about returning home to his father and his cousins, but he was sad about leaving Four Oaks. James did what he could to show the boy a good time and even took him fishing on the lake.

The night before she and Eddy were to leave, Freda made a big suet pudding with lots of raisins—Gladys's favourite dessert. Gladys played the piano while everyone sang some of their old favourite songs, then Freda brought in some currant cakes and hot chocolate. Eliza was allowed to stay up late, but she fell asleep on Gladys's knee soon after they had their refreshments. Gladys, looking around at the cosy scene, thought how much she would miss evenings like this with all three of her children by her side. For a time, there was only a very fine line that separated her regrets and her passion.

After their company left and Gladys had put Eliza and Eddy to bed, James asked her if she would join him for a drink in his library. The fire was going and they sat in the same high wing-backed leather chairs she had always found so comfortable. They had had some good conversations in that room. Gladys would have said it was her favourite room in the mansion until that ominous day when James had lost his temper and struck Eddy then called him a bastard.

James could tell she was uneasy, so he said, "It took me a while before I could come in here without feeling guilty, so I know how difficult it must be for you. I hope, in time, both you and Eddy will be able to look at me and not see the brute you saw that day."

"I don't see you in that way anymore, James, and I am quite sure Eddy doesn't either."

"I think he is even beginning to like me. I thought about inviting him in here to show him some books I have about famous ships, but I thought I had better wait until next time he comes for a visit. However, I would like him to have one. Will you take it and give it to him after you leave London? It shall be something for him to read on the voyage."

"That is so kind of you, James. But I think it would mean

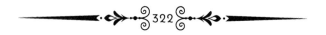

a lot more if you were to write a little something inside it." James agreed, and while Gladys sipped her brandy, he found the book then thoughtfully inscribed what he thought Eddy would like.

Because Gladys and Eddy were told to be onboard the morning of their departure, they made arrangements to stay with Percy overnight, and they left Four Oaks the day before they sailed. Gladys was hurt and disappointed when Dolly and Eliza didn't offer to come to the train station to see them off. In fact, their farewells were less emotional than the rest of the household. Gladys had expected a sad but loving parting, and now she had to leave with the same feeling of defeat as she had a year ago. It was all she could do to keep from crying.

She felt even more depressed the next morning when Percy didn't offer to accompany them to their ship. She could tell Eddy was upset as well when he kept turning around to look at the pier as they made their way up the gangplank. Except for two fishermen sitting with their lines in the water and their legs dangling over the edge of the pier, hoping to snag some bottom fish, there was no one in sight. Even Captain Bob wasn't around to greet him.

One of the crew was kind enough to show them to their cabin which was the same one they had on the way over. He smiled and said that they would not be leaving port until five in the afternoon.

The dining salon wasn't open, but Percy had made them some sandwiches which they ate while sitting out on the deck in the afternoon. It was a nice day and Gladys was talking to some of the other passengers when Eddy jumped off his chair and cried out, "Holy Mackerel! Look, Mother, it's everyone. They came! They came!"

Gladys could hardly believe it. James, Percy, Dolly, Eliza, and even Aunt Jean were getting out of a cab and waving. Then Bob came out on deck and waved them onboard. They were all crying, hugging, and laughing at the same time.

"We fooled you, didn't we, Mommy?" Eliza said after they all calmed down.

"You certainly did, my darling. I thought you were all tired of us and were glad to see us go."

"We had quite a time keeping it a secret. You looked so sad when you left, we almost decided to tell you." Dolly said. "We would never allow you to sail off without being here to wave goodbye."

"But we don't sail until five."

"Then we don't leave until then," James announced.

Gladys had forgotten about Bob until she heard him say that he would have the cook put out a pot of coffee and some biscuits in the dining salon. She was about to introduce him to everyone, but Eddy got to him first. After he had introduced him to the family, Eddy asked him if he would mind showing James and Percy the big wheel that steers the boat. Bob was surprised that both men were as excited with the idea as Eddy had been.

The hours passed far too quickly, and it was time to bid a final farewell. Although the parting was sad, this time they were left with fond memories and no regrets. They knew that they would all be together again in the future, and that was all that mattered.

The voyage was uneventful but not uncomfortable. Gladys and Bob did not spend as much time together as they had on the way over, but they still had some enjoyable conversations. The three of them even dined together in the captain's quarters a few times.

Eddy was thrilled with the book James had given him, and he read the inscription aloud to Gladys: "To Edward Matthews, May 10, 1861. I believe you shall be a fine and commendable captain one day. I look forward to sailing with you on your ship. Sincerely yours, James Hornsby (Uncle James)." Eddy looked thoughtful for a second then said, "I like him, Mother."

The book kept Eddy happy for most of voyage, but he became a little restless during the last two days. Then, as soon as New York came into view, he looked up at Gladys and asked, "Are we there, Mother?"

A warm feeling spread around Gladys's heart. She smiled down at him and answered, "Yes, dear, that is America. We are home."

Acknowledgements

To all the personnel at Amberjack Publishing, for your expertise, patience, and kindness. Thank you for publishing my novels.

About the Author

Born in Vancouver, B.C. in 1927, Betty Annand has resided in the Comox Valley on Vancouver Island since the age of ten. Widowed since 2002, she has enjoyed doing volunteer work at her church, the local hospital and a local theatre, where she writes and directs plays for the seniors group. She resides in the house that she and her husband built sixty years ago and enjoys spending time with her family, who still live on the island. She is the author of three non-fiction books, *Growing up in the White House*, *Voices from Bevan*, and *Voices from Courtenay Past*.

The Woman from Dover continues the story of Gladys, as begun in Betty's first novel, *The Girl from Old Nichol*.

CPSIA information can be obtained
at www.ICGtesting.com
Printed in the USA
LVOW11s0556191017

552951LV00003BA/3/P